A Week of Warm Weather

A Week of

Warm

Weather

A NOVEL

LEE BUKOWSKI

Published by SparkPress, a BookSparks imprint,
A division of SparkPoint Studio, LLC
Phoenix, Arizona, USA, 85007
www.gosparkpress.com

Published 2022
Printed in the United States of America
Print ISBN: 978-1-68463-137-7
E-ISBN: 978-1-68463-138-4 (e-bk)

Library of Congress Control Number: 2021922949

Interior design by Tabitha Lahr

To Rach and Jac,
with much love

For we are always what our situations hand us.
It's either sadness or euphoria.

—BILLY JOEL, "Summer, Highland Falls"

Prologue

It's a strange burden, owning a secret. Even more strange when the secret belongs to someone else. Isn't she now just as guilty? Doesn't the secret belong to her too? It feels that way. It fills the deepest part of her stomach, pushing everything else out of the way to make room for its mass.

At one time she could fool everyone. She'd apply lip gloss and go about her day, her cheery expression belying the inner voice threatening to rise up and scream the truth. "How are you?" people would ask. "I'm fine," she'd answer. She used to be able to fool everyone. Even herself.

The lies were difficult at first. They'd stick on her tongue, spreading redness across her cheeks. When she was a child, she was afraid to lie about even the smallest things, certain that grownups had a magic window into children's minds. They always knew who broke the lamp or stole the quarters from the jar on the kitchen counter. When her adult lies began, they felt as unconvincing as the silly lies of her childhood. But the more lies she told, the more naturally they rolled off her tongue.

She rests her cheek against the window, and the coolness eases the dull ache in her head. Catching her reflection in the window, she imagines a character in a movie whose final scene has long been evident to everyone but her. Two hours pass, and she is stiff from sitting on the floor in the same position. It's after midnight, and the only illumination outside comes from the streetlights in the distance beyond the long S-shaped driveway. She's not tired, but she stands, moaning as she stretches her sore muscles, and makes her way to her bedroom.

She barely disturbs the meticulously made bed as she climbs in with her clothes on. Lying on her back, wide awake, she marvels at her calmness now that the day is here. When she daydreams about it, she's often crying or pounding her clenched fists on the kitchen table. She's so serene that she wonders if she'll go through with it. But then it stirs again, the smoldering in her stomach. She reaches beside her, runs her hand along the vacant space, and she knows the answer.

Chapter One

JUNE 1996

Tessa groaned in the stillness of the dark room. "Let's flip a coin. Best of three."

She reached for her husband, but her hand met only the cool sheet. Tessa sat up and struggled to piece together the scene. On the nightstand, the red digital numbers on the clock blinked impatiently: 3:22 a.m. She rolled over, the remnants of a dream chased away by her baby daughter's high-pitched cries from the next room. Frowning at the undisturbed sheets on Ken's side, Tessa crawled out of bed.

He must have fallen asleep on the sofa again.

She crossed the bedroom into the small corridor separating their room from Veronica's nursery. Inside, a nightlight helped her eyes adjust as she took in Ronnie's tiny form in her crib. Tessa smiled as she gazed down at her daughter. She'd sworn not to cave to nicknames, but her siblings had instantly dubbed their new niece "Ronnie." Ronnie's face was scrunched up and red from crying, and her black hair stood up in feathery shocks. The maternity ward nurses had joked that they tried to slick it down with baby oil, but it seemed to have a mind of its own. Tessa wondered if it was an omen about her daughter's personality.

"Okay, okay, my hungry little girl." She picked up the angry infant and made her way to the changing table. Ronnie squirmed as Tessa applied a fresh diaper and snapped up her daughter's sleeper, and together they padded to the kitchen for a bottle. The few night lights in the little house provided enough visibility to prevent Tessa having to turn on any additional lamps. Val, her father's second wife and the only mother Tessa had ever really known, suggested Tessa keep the rooms dark and quiet for middle-of-the-night feedings. "It will help Veronica to eventually differentiate between night and day," she told her daughter. Tessa thought this made perfect sense. Besides, what did she know about raising children? She welcomed all the advice she could get.

A month earlier, Tessa had restlessly paced the floors when her labor started at about ten o'clock on a balmy Saturday night. At first, she wasn't even sure it was labor; she'd never had a baby before, so she didn't know what it felt like. She had read enough books on the subject, furiously highlighting passages and folding down page corners, but they only confused her. One described contractions as a belt tightening and releasing around the stomach, while another claimed that many first-time moms couldn't distinguish early labor from indigestion. The more she read, the more anxious she became, so eventually she stopped reading. Weeks in advance, she'd packed her overnight bag, and she checked its contents daily, as if someone might have snuck in during the night and pilfered her toothbrush.

Tessa was sure of one fact about childbirth: She wanted the drugs. She'd instructed Ken that no matter how much the nurses tried to talk her into doing this the natural way, he was to hunt down an anesthesiologist and bring him to her, dragging him by his hair if necessary. She'd given Ken notes specifying this just in case she passed out and couldn't speak for herself. Shuffling down the brightly lit hospital corridor, she had grabbed Ken's elbow and squeezed hard. "Easy, Tiger," he'd whispered. "I know. Drugs."

Hours later, as sunlight flooded the maternity ward, and several women bonded with their newborns, Tessa was still pregnant and very aware of what contractions felt like. Her dark brown shoulder-length hair, usually styled in soft waves, was matted against her sweaty forehead and neck. Pain stabbed her back, and she groaned and swore this would be her only baby and Ken better not even think of coming near her again. Ken and Val were with her, helpless as Tessa gripped the edges of the sheet, contorting her body against the searing agony of each contraction. Val whispered to her son-in-law, "Sometimes I can't believe she's not my biological daughter . . . we have the same temperament." Ken smiled but said nothing. They tried to distract Tessa with TV shows and ice chips, but her agitation grew louder.

"*WHERE* ARE MY DRUGS?"

Somewhere around two in the morning, as Tessa yelled obscenities at a contestant on *The Price Is Right* for idiotically overshooting the price of a bottle of shampoo, an anesthesiologist arrived to administer an epidural. Tessa wanted to kiss him. The medicine spread warmth and then heavenly numbness below her waist.

Finally, it was time, and an army of nurses charged into the room, dropped the railings, and propped up Tessa's feet. With the gusto of a cheerleading squad, they yelled, "Push!" "Bear down!" "That's it!" The doctor coaxed, "One more!" and eventually Veronica arrived, coated in blood and vernix, her tiny red tongue fluttering as she howled. Tessa was always skeptical when she heard mothers say she'd forget the pain of childbirth, but they were right. One look at Veronica was all it took.

Now she grabbed a bottle from the fridge and ran it under hot water. Some of her friends heated bottles in the microwave, but

Tessa never did for fear that it might produce hot spots in the formula that would burn Veronica's tiny pink mouth. There was enough that could go wrong; she wasn't taking any chances on things she *could* control. She and her best friend, Mariel, called each other constantly with baby safety questions. Mariel's son, Alex, was six months older than Ronnie, and he'd survived so far with his rookie mom, so Tessa confidently followed her lead. "When did you give Alex cereal before bed?" Tessa asked her during one of their Q & A sessions. "I have one book that says four months, one that says wait until six months, and one that passive-aggressively suggests parents who give babies cereal at night are too weak and spineless to have kids. You believe that?"

"Obviously written by someone who's had a full night's sleep in the past year," Mariel had scoffed. After reading the countless warnings on every baby product and food, Tessa and Mariel marveled that any kid made it to age three.

Tessa yawned and adjusted Ronnie on her arm. An oppressive heat wave had gripped the northeast, so she reveled in the coolness of the tiles beneath her feet and the hum of the air conditioner that ran all day and night. She walked lightly into the living room, careful not to wake her husband, and her eyes adjusted to the dim light.

Ken was not there.

Uneasiness washed over Tessa. This was the third time in two weeks her husband hadn't come home all night. She took a deep breath. *Remember, he's under a lot of stress right now.*

She sat down on the couch and wedged a pink bib under Ronnie's chin. She offered the bottle, and the baby drank hungrily.

While Ken's dental practice was new and he didn't have many patients yet, he claimed to be swamped with paperwork that he needed to deal with after hours. *But it's 3:30 in the morning. He's at the office doing paperwork?*

She thought back to the day Ronnie was born. Tessa had been cradling Veronica, trying to remember what the baby books said about whether it was safe for parents to have a newborn in bed with them, when the door to her hospital room swung open. "How are my girls?" Ken paused in the doorway before entering. He was tall and solid and had thick dark hair that he had a habit of running his hand through from front to back. "Mmm," he wrinkled his nose at the dried-up roast beef on Tessa's tray. "That looks delicious."

"Very funny," laughed Tessa. "You don't happen to have a piping-hot pepperoni pizza in that bag, do you?"

"Even better." Ken fished around in a shopping bag and produced a hoagie from his father-in-law's restaurant. "Sal said no daughter of his will eat hospital food while he has breath in his body. And I quote."

Tessa grinned at her dad's sentiment. "That's a thing of beauty. Here, let's trade." Tessa handed Ronnie to her father and unwrapped the sandwich. "Hey, I called the house last night just after midnight, but you didn't answer."

Ken stilled momentarily, avoiding his wife's gaze. "Really? Huh." He concentrated on the ceiling as if the explanation were written there. "I was beat. I guess I fell asleep and didn't hear the phone."

Tessa furrowed her brow. "Oh, well, I was calling to entertain you with the fact that the nurses kept waking me up to ask if I was sleeping okay."

Her smile turned to concern when she got a closer look at Ken. "Babe, your eyes look really weird. Do you feel okay?"

Ken carefully placed Ronnie back in her bassinet, and Tessa thought she saw his hands shake slightly as he steadied himself before attempting a casual smile. Tess listened as her husband rambled through an uncharacteristically long-winded explanation. "Yeah, I'm just tired. So much work to do at the office. The contractors are finished, but now it's carpet installation, painting, that kind of stuff. And the chairs you helped me pick out for the waiting room? The company sent the wrong ones, so they all have to go back. Hopefully the right ones will be delivered by next week when I open. I'm sure patients will flock in when they find out they have to sit on the floor to wait for their cleaning."

Tessa sank back against the hospital's starched pillowcases and willed herself to believe Ken's explanation as the source of his pallor and irritation. She knew even the most careful preparation veered off course sometimes. An office in a coveted medical building had become available three months prior, and Ken decided he had to jump on it. No one would plan to open a new dental practice the same month his first child was born, but even Tessa, who needed order and routine like she needed oxygen, believed everything would be fine.

Now she chewed her lip, the recollection bouncing off the mysteriousness of Ken's absence tonight. Tessa looked around the living room and tried to calm herself. She and Ken built the house a few months after Ken finished dental school. It was definitely a starter home, but Tessa loved it. Only about a thousand square feet of living space, it was a two-bedroom, one-bathroom ranch. An eat-in kitchen made up most of the front of the house and was connected to the great room in the back by a vaulted ceiling. A tiny hallway led to the master bedroom, a bathroom, and a second bedroom that was now Ronnie's nursery. Off the great room was a small den that had quickly become Ronnie's; her baby carrier, swing, Pack-n-Play, and countless other baby accoutrement now dominated the room that had once been used as an office. At just over a month old, she had acquired almost as much as Ken and Tessa had in five years of marriage. They would probably outgrow the house in a few years, but they thought it best to start small and affordable. No sense adding more stress to their lives by living above their means as so many of their friends did.

Tessa chose soft pastel colors for the sofa and chair fabrics in the great room and complemented them with dark cherry end and coffee tables. French doors led out to the backyard, and she hung sheer window treatments at them so as not to detract from the beauty of the heavy wood doors. In the master bedroom, bright floral bedding offset the lighter oak dressers. Blue, puffy balloon shades adorned the windows. On the walls hung a combination of family photos and prints that Tessa and Ken had found on various trips.

Unlike some men, Ken was fairly fussy about their home's décor and often weighed in on decorating decisions. Val thought this was hilarious; she joked that she could renovate her whole house and Sal would say nothing more than, "Whatever you want, hon. Just make sure there's a comfortable napping sofa. You know I need my beauty rest!"

Tessa gently placed the baby over her left shoulder to burp her. Patting her daughter's tiny back, she thought about her family's sense of humor. As teenagers, her older brothers, Sal Jr. and Joey, had driven Val crazy with their gags, crank calling her from another extension in the house when she was cooking, or hiding her car keys when she was late for an appointment. At only ten years old, her youngest brother, Tony, was following in their prankster footsteps. And six-year-old Gina loved to pretend to be a sassy server during family dinners, her dark ponytail swinging as she charged her family exorbitant prices for a cheeseburger and reminded them not to forget the tip. "I'd go out of business if she worked for me!" Sal would quip when Gina handed him a plastic burger from her play kitchen. Tessa believed her large Italian family's closeness and good humor had helped her as a young girl trying to make sense of an impossible situation.

Ken's family, though nice enough, was not as closely knit as Tessa's. His mother had passed away from cancer shortly after Ken and Tessa's engagement. Sometimes Tessa tried to get him to talk about it, but Ken waved her off. He had a stepfather, two brothers, and one sister, and while they got along fine, they were far-flung, spread out all over the state, and didn't share the day-to-day closeness that Tessa's family enjoyed. When Ken asked Sal's permission to give Tessa an engagement ring, the older man subjected him to a line of questioning that would have made the district attorney proud. Ken fell easily into the fold of his in-laws and felt just like one of the gang, not that he'd had much choice. After Ken passed the inquisition, Sal warned, "Marry the clown, marry the circus."

Ronnie burped loudly and joggled Tessa out of her daydream. With the baby already falling back to sleep, Tessa stood up and walked into the kitchen. She picked up the phone and dialed the number to Ken's office. Thirty rings. No answer. Tessa hung up.

She placed Ronnie carefully back in her crib, confident that she'd sleep soundly until morning. She couldn't say the same for herself.

Chapter Two

1996 was a rough year for the Philadelphia Phillies.
Discouraged, Tessa switched off the TV. With September a few short weeks away, the postseason was quickly getting out of reach. Tessa and her family were lifelong Phillies fans, and her father and brothers yelled at the TV as though they were on the coaching staff. Some of Tessa's favorite memories as a child were of Sunday afternoon jaunts to Veteran's Stadium to see Mike Schmidt, Larry Bowa, and Steve Carlton play. Joey even named his first dog "Lefty" after Carlton. Sporting their T-shirts bearing the names of their favorite players on the back, they'd feast on hot dogs and devour ice cream in little red plastic helmets. It had been a long drought since the world championship in 1980. Sal said it was how he learned to deal with heartache.

Tessa tossed the remote control aside and checked on Ronnie, sleeping peacefully in her crib. "Poor kid," she thought. "One day you'll be screaming at the TV while these clowns give up a walk-off home run."

She glanced at the clock. 10:24 p.m. Ken still wasn't home. His practice had been open for about two months, and he said the long nights were because he was trying out a filing system he'd learned as a resident. He complained that it was complicated and he needed to work on it after hours instead of during the day when there were other fires to put out. Something didn't add up, but Tessa vowed to be supportive. She decided to give him a call just to say hello.

Absentmindedly chewing her lip, she dialed the number to Ken's office and listened to the house's nighttime sounds. *Is the ticking of the mantel clock always this loud?* After several unanswered rings, she hung up. She tried again. Still no answer. Wide awake, she made her way out into the kitchen and looked out at the dark street. She shivered in the air conditioning.

If he's just doing paperwork, why doesn't he answer the phone?

Maybe Ken was on his way home. It was only a five-minute drive, so Tessa sat down at the kitchen table to wait. The salt and pepper shakers stood next to each other in the middle of the table, positioned perfectly in front of the napkin holder where Tessa placed them every night after dinner. She peeked through the blinds, but the street and driveway were deserted. Wiping her sweaty palms on her pajama bottoms, she waited fifteen minutes and dialed the office number again. No answer. She told herself there were a million reasonable explanations and went back to the bedroom.

She crawled into the empty bed and flipped through a magazine. Models with pouty lips taunted her from the shiny pages, their unmarred slender frames showing none of the postpartum signs so evident on her own body. She felt the flesh on her soft abdomen as she scrutinized a bikini-clad woman in a perfume ad, her flat belly, firm breasts, and long blonde hair blowing behind her as she kneeled on a sandy beach. *I bet her husband comes home at night.* Her imagination ran wild and made her head ache. *Is he out with a woman whose life is more interesting than diaper changes and feeding times?* Frustrated, she tossed the magazine onto the floor and eventually drifted off to a fitful sleep.

A noise in the foyer awakened Tessa at 5:45 a.m. After a minute, Ken entered the bedroom, sank onto the bed, and kicked off his shoes.

"You're just coming in?" she murmured, startling him. She hesitated, then added, "I tried to call you a few times at the office last night, but you didn't answer."

He didn't answer right away. After a moment, he sighed. "I guess I fell asleep. I was doing paperwork, and I guess I fell asleep."

Tessa said nothing. A myriad of thoughts buzzed around her head, pounded in her ears. She wanted to scream. She wanted to shake him and ask what kind of man with a wife and new baby stays out all night. She wanted to pound his chest with her fists and accuse him of seeing another woman, one who didn't smell like baby spit-up. But when she opened her mouth, nothing came out.

"I'm going to catch another hour of sleep before I have to shower and go back in." Tessa listened until she heard steady breathing from the other side of the bed. She flung the sheet aside, went into the bathroom, and turned on the shower.

Under the stream of hot water, she gathered her thoughts. She could picture Ken taking a break from his work, stretching out in the waiting room for what he intended to be a few minutes, and falling into a dead sleep. A light sleeper herself, she couldn't imagine sleeping through the ringing of a telephone, but Ken slept more soundly. *Of course that was it.* His exhaustion was getting the better of him. As soon as the word was out and Ken had a decent patient base, he could start working regular hours and establish a more sensible routine. Tessa turned off the water and reached for her towel.

She decided to enjoy the peace and quiet before Ronnie woke up. While the coffee brewed, she retrieved the newspaper from the front porch. She skimmed the front page but had difficulty concentrating. After reading an article three times without comprehending it, she gave up. The coffee maker coughed and sputtered the end of its brew cycle. Sighing, she poured a steaming mug and walked into the living room. She turned on a local morning news show where the anchor announced that today was going to be another scorcher. Great.

Spending so much time in the house was starting to make Tessa edgy. She felt like a caged animal. She'd offer to work at the restaurant this weekend. And she'd call Mariel and arrange to meet for lunch. Maybe she'd take Ronnie out for more walks, in the mornings when it was cool.

She was in the living room feeding Veronica when Ken emerged from the bedroom. He looked rough; his eyes were bloodshot and he seemed disoriented. He poked his head into the living room and mumbled that he was going to shower before heading back to the office.

"Okay," responded Tessa with a cheerfulness she didn't feel. "I made coffee." She watched him disappear into the bathroom and silently promised to be more understanding about Ken's erratic hours. After all, his dental career allowed her to stop working outside the home for as long as she chose. The least she could do was support him as he built his practice. If only she could fight the nagging feeling in her gut.

When Tessa first met Ken, she was home from college for the weekend and out at a local club where the bouncer apparently thought numbers were arbitrary when he checked IDs. Tessa was with Amy, a high school friend also home visiting family. Amy spotted a guy at the bar she thought was cute. She knew he went to Penn State with her and had seen him around campus, but Amy had never met him. He was with another guy whom neither of the girls had ever seen before. Amy gushed on and on about how she would like Cute Guy to ask her out. "Actually," opined Tess, "I'd go for his friend; he's much better looking." Amy ignored Tessa and went on trying to make eye contact with Cute Guy. Finally, Tessa had enough. With courage that came from a few cosmos, she marched over to the two guys as Amy tried to make herself invisible. *Wow, Cute Guy's friend is really good-looking.* He had dark hair and a warm smile. The guys looked expectantly at Tessa from beneath raised eyebrows.

"Hi," she said to Cute Guy. "You see that girl over there pretending she doesn't know me? I believe you two go to Penn State together. Well, she thinks you're hot and would love for you to ask her out. I'm sick of hearing about it, so I thought I'd come over here and speed things along." Cute Guy seemed amused. Tess was aware of how close she stood to his friend and willed herself to push on. Smiling sweetly at his blue eyes, she again summoned the God of Cosmo Courage and asked, "While we're at it, why don't we make it a double date?"

That broke the ice. Amy's face returned to its natural color, and she joined Tessa and the two guys, whose names turned out to be Don and Ken. The four spent the rest of the night drinking and dancing together. They went on a double date a few weeks later. They all had a great time, but Ken and Tessa really hit it off and continued dating. Forever after, Amy credited herself with introducing Tess and Ken and made sure to announce it at the wedding. She was so proud of herself.

By the time Ken showered and dressed, Ronnie was cooing away in her swing. Tessa was pouring a bowl of cereal when he entered the kitchen. She nearly gasped out loud when she saw his face. The shower did nothing to improve his appearance; he was ghostly white and his pupils were dilated. His gaze was distracted and unfocused. *Don't start . . . he had hardly any sleep.* She collected herself before she spoke. "Um . . . would you like something to eat?"

"No, thanks. I think I'll stop at your dad's for a quick omelet."

He kissed Ronnie on the top of her head and said, "I'd better get going. Busy day today. See you later." He gave Tessa a peck on the cheek and was gone.

Frowning, Tessa watched out the window as Ken drove away. She sat for a long moment listening to the whir of the air conditioner. The phone rang and interrupted her thoughts.

"Hello?"

"Hi, hon. How'd she do last night?" Val's familiar voice settled Tessa's nerves. Val called every morning for the update on how many consecutive hours Ronnie slept each night.

"Oh, hi, Mom. Um, she only got up once. I think she's getting the hang of it." Tessa leaned against the wall and pinched the bridge of her nose.

"What's wrong?" asked Val.

Wow, am I that transparent? "Nothing. I'm trying to decide what to do today. I wish this heat wave would break. I'm going a little stir-crazy in this house. Hey, does Dad need any help this weekend?"

"You must be psychic. The new girl called off already, so Dad asked if you could pinch hit."

Tessa laughed. "You know you're restless when running around a diner pouring steaming coffee and sweating your ass off during a heat wave sounds appealing."

"True," Val agreed. "It's not fit for man or beast out there. Let Ronnie sleep here tomorrow night. You and Ken go out for dinner, and then you don't have to worry about waking the baby early Saturday morning before you go into work. Does that sound good?"

"Better than good. Thanks, Mom." Tessa hung up and chastised herself. Even her mom could tell something was bothering her.

Surely, hormones caused all new moms to feel conflicting emotions. Last week in a card store she saw a sympathy card that read *As You Mourn the Loss of Your Cat* on the front. There was a picture of a family sitting next to a large tree in a meadow. The family cat was nowhere to be seen, presumably, Tessa thought, because it had been killed by a speeding car or had succumbed to some horrific cat disease. She'd stood in the card store and wept openly—and she didn't even like cats. *I'm fine. I just need to get used to this new routine.* She busied herself with household chores and put Ronnie down for her morning nap. Mariel wasn't available to get together, but they chatted on the phone while the babies napped, and it helped Tessa's mood. Secretly, she was almost glad she didn't have to face her friend today. Mariel was Tessa's college roommate and knew her well. Tessa wasn't sure she'd be able to hide her concerns about Ken, and she wasn't ready to voice them. She imagined telling Mariel that Ken sometimes stayed out all night, nonchalantly waving it off, sure it was nothing to worry about. She could picture Mariel's blank look, wanting to believe Tessa's stoic assurance but furrowing her brow. *No, don't say anything.*

Instead, Mariel had entertained Tessa on the phone with a story about a music therapy class she and Alex attended last week. A dad Mariel had never seen before brought his fifteen-month-old and was the only man in the class. He'd been laid off and was giving his wife "a break." Tessa laughed as she visualized Mariel making air quotes as she said it. "I'm not sure what he was laid off from," Mariel said, "but judging from his long greasy hair, stained T-shirt, and beard stubble—and I mean 'laying on the sofa eating Doritos for a week' stubble not 'sexy, rugged star of a cologne commercial' stubble—I don't think he's going to a lot of interviews. He came in high-fiving the moms and saying, 'Okay, let's do the good parent thing! Is this what you girls do all day? Cool!' His wife was probably at home trying to figure out how to mix antifreeze into his coffee and make his death look like an accident." Mariel ended the hilarious story by saying that they were both lucky in the husband department, despite Ken and Rob's minor faults. Tessa was grateful that Mariel couldn't see her reaction.

Lucky. Tessa heard that all the time. *You're lucky, your husband changes diapers. You're so lucky you can take time off from work. You're so lucky you have a successful husband.*

Later, Tessa ventured out in the heat for a Wal-Mart excursion where Ronnie was cranky the entire time. She screamed down every aisle, scrunching up her face like a mean old man and batting away the bottle Tessa offered her as if it was an annoying mosquito. The other shoppers put on their best *Oh, someone's having a bad day* faces when what they really meant was *Shut that damn kid up.*

Back at home and a bit cranky herself, Tessa prepared dinner. She wondered idly whether Ken would make it home for dinner or if she would have to eat alone. Just as she removed the flounder from under the broiler, she heard Ken's key in the front door.

He was in a much better mood. "How are my girls?" he asked, kissing first Tess and then Ronnie.

"We're good," Tessa answered. "Dinner's almost ready."

Ken scooped up Ronnie and walked into the living room. "Saw some pretty nasty choppers today, kiddo. You're lucky your old man is a dentist." Ronnie flashed her gummy smile, and Ken laughed. "Not that you need to worry about that yet!"

As Tessa mixed the salad dressing, relief flooded her body. Ken's appearance this morning was the result of long hours and hard work. After all, didn't she wake up bleary-eyed and unfocused when the baby didn't sleep well?

Ken gently put Ronnie into her infant chair. He poured a glass of water for Tessa and himself. "Smells delicious, doll. I'm starving."

As they ate, Ken apprised Tessa of the day's events. He was getting busier by the day. Word of mouth seemed to be his greatest asset. Their families and friends were his first patients, and they quickly spread the word of Ken's new practice. Ken entertained Tessa with comical anecdotes. She always looked forward to this part of the day, his vivid descriptions allowing her to visualize the patients. "Remember the Oswalds? They said you graduated with their daughter. They came in today. Nice people."

Tessa thought as she cut her fish. "Yes. Mr. Oswald is a painter, right? He's been in business for years."

"Yeah, that's him. I'm glad he has a successful business. He needs some work on his teeth." Ken expounded on the declining state of poor Mr. Oswald's incisors until Tessa put up her hands.

"Stop! I'm trying to eat here!" she laughed.

"Sorry. I guess funky mouths are becoming commonplace to me. I'm not sure if that's good or bad! Anyway, stop in the office with Ronnie soon," said Ken. "I want to show off my beautiful girls to the staff."

Tessa stood to clear the table and gazed at Ronnie. "You mean beautiful *girl*. Singular."

"Ah, you're nuts, Tess. Where do you think Ronnie gets her good looks?" Ken winked at his wife. Tessa laughed out loud at this. At eight weeks old, Ronnie already showed a striking resemblance to her father.

"Oh, I almost forgot," Tessa said. "I'm helping my dad at the diner Saturday morning."

"Good idea. I can tell you have a bad case of cabin fever."

"I really do. It'll be good for me. Oh, and Ronnie is going to sleep at my parents' house tomorrow night, so you and I can go out to dinner."

"Great," Ken replied, thinking. "Where do you want to go?"

"I don't know, but I'm going to wear something with no spit-up stains on it for a change." Tessa laughed as Ronnie protested being confined to her seat. "Why don't you hold her while I clean up? Maybe after she goes to bed, you and I can watch a movie and have a glass of wine."

"I'll hold her while you clean up, but then I need to go back to the office." Tessa's shoulders stiffened, and her expression soured. "Come on, babe," Ken reassured her. "It won't be like this much longer."

"I know. I just get lonely here every night. It's just, I'm starting to wonder . . ."

Ken's eyes darkened. "Don't overreact. It's not every night. You have no idea what goes into starting a dental practice." Irritated, Ken carried Ronnie into the nursery. Tessa washed and dried the dishes. She hated when Ken played the "you don't know what it's like" card. She'd made numerous sacrifices along their journey. She postponed pursuing a post-graduate degree and worked seven days a week to support them while Ken was in dental school. She thought she had a pretty good idea "what it's like."

When Ken emerged from the nursery, Tessa was more conciliatory. "Why don't you get going? Maybe if you go back now, you won't have to stay so late."

"Okay." He put an arm around his wife and played with a lock of her hair. His breath was cool on her cheek. "Listen, Tess, I know you feel lonely right now, but you know I'm doing all this for you and Ronnie."

Tessa looked at her husband. She opened her mouth to ask why he never answered the phone at the office late at night, but decided against it. She didn't want to put Ken on the defensive before he left.

Ken kissed his wife and daughter and headed out the front door. Tessa bounced the baby in her arms as she listened to her husband's car back out of the driveway.

"Well, kid, looks like you and me again. What should we do tonight? Take a bath? Have a bottle? That's something different!" Tessa nuzzled her nose in Ronnie's neck. *Oh hell. I'll put her to bed and have that glass of wine myself. Lord knows I'll need it if the Phillies are on.*

Chapter Three

How is a person supposed to eat pancakes as big as the plate? There is no room for error. One wrong move and the melted butter and gooey syrup cascade off the stack and onto the table. This quandary was the source of endless debate among customers at the Sunrise Diner.

"Simple. Just dig a hole in the middle and pour the syrup in there like you're filling a swimming pool," offered Sam, a mechanic and old friend of Sal's. He'd been a regular customer for over twenty-five years. He carefully carved out an opening precisely in the center of the giant fluffy creation.

"I disagree." Randy shook his head. "No good. See, then you can't control the syrup distribution. The sections near the hole get too soggy. It's better to cut the stack in half, pile one on top of the other, and drizzle syrup over the whole top surface. That gives you room on the plate for runoff." Randy's analytical mind no doubt worked to his advantage when he managed people's financial portfolios, but did not impress Sam when it came to managing Sal's three-cake stack.

"Nah." Sam waved his hand in exasperation. "Then the stack is too tall. You don't want it to topple over onto that fancy suit of yours, do you? How do you expect people to invest their hard-earned dough on your mutual funds when you're sitting there with a sticky glob of syrup on your Pierre Cardin tie?" He grabbed the syrup from the counter and began filling the pool. "Hey, Sal," he asked before taking a large bite. "Why don't you just make these beauties a little smaller?"

Sal wiped his hands on his apron. "What, and miss listening to you two chuckleheads? Not a chance." He laughed and turned back to his next order. At the Sunrise Diner, the cooking space was in plain view of the customers, not hidden in the kitchen like most diners. This allowed Sal to banter with the customers, and people loved it. It was one reason many of them sat at the counter instead of at one of the ten yellow booths, which did not have such easy access to Sal. He did all the cooking, but his jovial personality attracted as many, if not more, customers than the food.

Randy and Sam were just a sampling of Sal's customers. Doctors, lawyers, local politicians, mechanics, plumbers, store clerks, students . . . Sal could hold a conversation with anyone on any topic. Kids and adults alike loved him and considered him both a member of their families and a local celebrity.

"Poor Tess. She came in today to get some adult interaction. Honey, you'd get more intellect out of Veronica." Sal grinned and shook his short dark hair. His hairline had begun to recede, which showed off more of the glint in his eyes. He perfectly flipped a pair of over-medium eggs in a small pan and slid them onto a plate. Then he used an aluminum spatula to add a heaping serving of golden-brown home fries and carefully arranged three slices of crispy bacon on top. "Here you go, Tess. This is for Mrs. White in booth five. Toast her rye twice; she likes it dark."

Tessa was glad for the distraction of the busy diner. Life with Ken was becoming an exhausting balancing act of trying to talk rationally about his troubling behavior when he was in a good mood and fighting with him about it when he was not. She'd broached the subject at dinner the night before, but he quickly shut her down. She'd almost persisted since she had his undivided attention, but they rarely went out for dinner, and she didn't want to ruin it. If there was something besides work keeping Ken out all night, Tessa wanted to approach the subject calmly. Most likely the pressure of having a baby and opening a dental practice at the same time was getting to him. She fought her mind's occasional wandering into the dark cavern of infidelity. Whatever it was, she didn't want to drive him further away.

She carried the plate in one hand and a pot of steaming coffee in the other. She set the plate down in front of Mrs. White. "Your toast will be right up. More coffee?"

"Yes, thanks, Tessa. It's good to see you again. How is the baby?"

"She's great! She looks different to me every day. She's starting to have a personality." Tessa left the table momentarily and returned with the dark toast. She remembered that Mrs. White preferred strawberry jelly and put a packet next to the toast.

"Oh good. The new girl isn't doing very well. Last week she gave me mixed fruit jelly. Can you imagine?"

Tessa saw her dad shoot the lady a look and tried to hide her amusement. Val often said Sal spoiled fussy customers too much. "Well, Mrs. White, she's only been here a week. Maybe we can cut her some slack? It takes some time to learn every customer's preferences," Tessa offered gently.

"I guess. But mixed fruit! Of all things! Anyway, what did you name the baby?" She opened the strawberry jelly packet and stuck in her knife. Tessa chuckled inwardly. It was notoriously tough for a teacher to choose a baby's name. During the last half of Tessa's pregnancy, Ken lobbed names at her daily, only to have his wife reject them. Every name he suggested reminded Tessa of a student who picked her nose or threw up before a unit test.

"We named her Veronica, but we call her Ronnie. Somehow she just *looks* like a Ronnie."

"She's a cutie. Her proud Pop Pop has been showing us her pictures. He claims she gets her beauty from him." The elderly lady smiled and dunked a slice of toast into her eggs.

Tessa laughed. "Well, luckily she doesn't have his moustache." She moved from table to table, filling coffee cups and clearing empty plates.

Sal had overheard this exchange. "Not yet, anyway. But she's young. There's time!" He turned back to Randy at the counter. "Going into the office on a Saturday, huh? That's unusual, isn't it? Lots of people with money to throw at the stock market?" He moved some potatoes around on the grill so they wouldn't stick and stirred a large stainless-steel pot of creamed chipped beef in the steam table.

"No, unfortunately I'm dressed up for a funeral today. Karen's aunt on her mother's side. The rest of the family is getting ready, so I thought I'd pop in for some pancakes and sausage. It's going to be a long day. A lot of family coming in from out of town." Randy reached into his wallet and took out a ten-dollar bill. He drained his coffee mug and wiped his mouth on his napkin. "Here you go, Tess. Keep the change."

Sal's look softened. "Sorry to hear that. Give your wife our regards. Tess, pack up a few pastries for Randy to take home. On the house." Tessa grabbed a white cardboard box from a shelf and filled it with half a dozen donuts, bear claws, and sticky buns. She closed the lid, taped the top of the box, and handed it to Randy.

Sam also stood up. He shrugged into his jacket, which read *Sam's Auto Repair* on the back. "Well, I have to get to work, gentlemen, so I don't have any more time today to debate the giant pancake dilemma. Sal, I still think you should cut down the size. Think about it; you could keep the price the same and make a few more dollars' profit."

"I have an idea." Sal ladled more buttery batter onto the sizzling grill. "You don't tell me how to cook, and I won't tell you how to fix a transmission." He put down the bowl of pan-cake batter and looked up at the order slips dangling from the metal strip above the electric burners. He whistled softly as he cracked two eggs into a bowl and scrambled them with a fork.

Sam laughed. "Fair enough. See ya, buddy. Bye, Tess." Tessa cleared Sam and Randy's coffee cups, empty creamers, and napkins. As she walked away, Tessa heard Sam add in a low voice, "Geez, Sal, Tess looks just like her, doesn't she?" Sal nodded, and the look in his eyes spanned decades.

"Yeah, and more so as Tess has gotten older."

"Does she ever mention her? I know she took it harder than the boys."

"Not anymore. She used to ask questions here and there, but she hasn't in years." Sal returned to the present and turned back to the grill to roll a few sausage links around with a pair of metal tongs. "Just as well. Good riddance."

Tessa rang up Randy's bill and put the change in her apron pocket. Then she leaned over the counter, wiped the area with a wet cloth, and put the condiments and napkin holders back in their place. She cleared another area further down the counter and handed the tip to Linda, the other waitress.

"Here, you waited on that guy. Your order is up for booth four, so go ahead and deliver the food and I'll clean this up." She nodded toward her father. "You know what a bear he can be if we let hot food sit for longer than twenty seconds." Tess got along well with Sal's employees, but she suspected the other employees thought she received special treatment because she was the boss's daughter. Actually, Tessa thought it was just the opposite. Sal was much more likely to point out her mistakes because he didn't have to worry about her quitting. She joked that she had lifelong job security, whether she wanted it or not.

Linda nodded knowingly. "Thanks, Tess. Don't you miss this?" She chuckled and stashed the bills in her apron pocket before heading to pick up her order.

Tessa took the dirty dishes back to the kitchen and dumped them into a big gray tub. The weekend dishwasher, a high school senior, plucked them out and rinsed them under a sprayer in a square metal sink before loading them into an industrial dishwashing machine. Tessa returned out front and turned to Sal. "Thanks for giving me the nod today, Dad. I needed to get out." She blew a wisp of hair that had escaped her ponytail out of her eyes and wiped her brow with the back of her arm. "It is hot, though. I wish this heat wave would break."

"Tell me about it. Standing over this grill all morning is no picnic. Is that what's on your mind, hon? Cabin fever and the heat wave? You don't seem like yourself." He put his arm around his oldest daughter and drew her close to him. "You're not your cheery self."

Tessa fought the urge to cry. Her dad's concern brought on a tidal wave of emotion, and she felt like when she was a little girl and didn't get a solo in the school concert. Sal always made her feel better, and she almost blurted out what was really bothering her.

Just then, she heard a commotion. "Tess, Olivia spilled her orange juice! Can you bring some paper towels?" The family in booth seven frantically mopped up the puddle spreading across the table. The offender, four-year-old Olivia, held her plate above her head to save her cinnamon toast from drowning in the sea of orange. Tessa rushed over to the table with paper towels. Some of the juice flowed off the table, so Linda brought out a mop from the kitchen. Tessa stifled a laugh at the *Why don't people watch their kids better?* look on her face as she swirled the mop around on the tile floor.

"I'm sorry." Olivia hung her head.

"Oh, don't worry about it, sweetie. Just an accident." Tess cleaned up the mess and resituated the family's plates and cups on the table. Then she brought them dry napkins and silverware. "I've got to get used to cleaning up messes now that I have a little one at home. She'll be destroying the house in no time!"

Sal walked over to the table with a fresh glass of orange juice. Near tears, Olivia hugged her stuffed rabbit. "I'm sorry, Mr. Sal."

He ruffled her hair. "That juice was no good anyway. This one is better. I poured it myself." Olivia's face brightened, and Sal winked at her parents.

The door chimed, and a couple Tessa did not know entered. After a minute, Linda approached them with silverware and empty coffee mugs. "Would you like coffee while you decide? The special today is two eggs, home fries, corned beef hash, toast, and coffee for $4.95.

"Uh, sure," they answered, looking around. "Can we see a menu?" Linda tried to hide her annoyance while the regulars all stopped talking for a moment and raised their eyebrows at each other. The small diner suddenly sounded like a record album whose needle had skidded across the surface and come to an unexpected halt. It was a longstanding joke with the regulars that the worst faux pas a first-time customer could commit at Sunrise was to ask for a menu.

"The menus are posted on the walls. All you have to do is look around. But, honestly, whatever you want, Sal will make." Linda filled their cups, put the pot down on the table, and took out her order pad. "What are you hungry for today? The Belgian waffles are to die for."

"Oh, that sounds like heaven. But are they a million calories?" the young woman asked.

"Two million." Linda licked her thumb and flipped through the pages of the pad. "And worth every one."

"Does he know how to make omelets?"

Tom, a regular now seated at the end of the counter near Sal, leaned in and whispered to him, "They must've just gotten out of prison." He speared a sausage link with his fork. Tom and Sal chuckled as Linda approached and hung up their order.

She shook her head at them but couldn't help grinning. "Knock it off, you two."

Two hours later, Tessa waited on the Andersons, a couple who'd known her parents for years. As she poured their coffee, she noticed Mr. Anderson rubbing red indentations on the sides of his nose. "Ooh, that looks sore. What happened?"

"It's my new glasses," Mr. Anderson said. "They're too tight on the bridge of my nose. I need to get them adjusted, but my eye doctor is on vacation this week. I'm only wearing them when I have to because they make these sore indentations on my nose." He poured some sugar on his spoon and dumped it in his coffee.

"Hmm." Tessa stared at him a moment longer. A memory flashed through her mind but was gone in an instant. *Why is this bothering me?*

Mrs. Anderson chimed in. "I told you that you should have just kept your contact lenses. You never listen to me. And that's enough sugar!"

Mr. Anderson saluted his wife. "Yes, ma'am." He turned to Tessa. "You see what I go through? I hope you don't badger that nice husband of yours like this!" Mrs. Anderson stopped stirring her tea and threw her napkin at him.

"You're lucky you have me to look out for you. You'd be lost without me."

"True enough, old girl. True enough." They were expressing their concern to a township supervisor at the next booth about an empty store lot that attracted teenagers after dark when Tessa returned to the table with their breakfast.

"Okay, one tomato-and-cheese omelet with home fries and dry toast, and one order of French toast with bacon. Enjoy." She set the plates on the table. Mr. Anderson tried to snatch a piece of bacon from his wife's plate, but she playfully slapped his hand.

He looked up in the air like a thought just occurred to him. "Hey, Tessa," he said. "You should tell Ken to have his glasses adjusted also. I was in his office the week before last for a cleaning, and he had marks on the sides of his nose too. He must have the same problem." Mr. Anderson sprinkled salt and pepper onto his home fries. Tessa stopped and turned to face him. He pointed to the sides of his nose. "It's really bothersome when I wear my glasses all day. I'm sure he knows what I mean."

"Right." Tessa felt inexplicably dizzy. "I'll tell him."

Uneasiness seized her stomach like a tight belt.

"Linda, I'm going to the restroom. All my people have their food." She pulled off her apron as she hurried to the restroom.

Inside, Tessa leaned against the door with her eyes closed.

He had marks on the sides of his nose too.

But Ken didn't wear glasses.

He must have the same problem.

Ken had twenty-twenty vision.

A knock on the door jolted her. Her face and hands were clammy. She quickly splashed cold water on her face and opened the door. "All yours."

She went back to the floor of the diner and glanced at the clock. Sixty minutes until they stopped serving breakfast. Tessa inhaled deeply. She picked up the coffee pot and a handful of creamers. As she refilled mugs, she made small talk and picked up empty plates. When she got to the Andersons' table, she tried to act casual. "Everything okay? More coffee? Um, Mr. Anderson, what day did you say you were in Ken's office?"

"Well, let's see now. It had to be Tuesday a week ago because that's the day I meet the guys for lunch over in Shelbourne Square. The second Tuesday of every month. I left Ken's office and went straight to lunch. I remember because I was ten minutes late and the boys didn't let me hear the end of it. Those old coots! They have nowhere to go and all day to get there and you'd think . . ."

Tessa was no longer listening to him. She was thinking about the Tuesday Mr. Anderson was describing. She was sure she had the right day.

Ken never came home for dinner that night. She'd called his office repeatedly, but he didn't answer. Finally, after she'd put the baby to bed, she'd eaten her cold dinner alone staring into the dark kitchen, the light over the stove the only illumination in the room. She'd pushed her pasta around on her plate before giving up and scraping it into the garbage disposal. She'd fixed a plate for Ken, knowing it wouldn't get eaten. As she'd stretched plastic wrap over the food, bitterness spread through her stomach, up into her rib cage.

She was sure it was last Tuesday.

She was sure because that was the night she decided she would confront Ken.

That was the night she was going to demand answers.

She'd somehow fallen asleep sometime after midnight and awoken at 4 a.m. to hear Ken vomiting in the bathroom. She'd sat straight up in bed. Hearing more vomiting, she had jumped up, run to the bathroom, and flicked on the light. Ken still had his dress shirt and tie on. He was leaning over the toilet.

"Ken." Tessa had touched his shoulder, but he batted her hand away.

"Leave me alone. I'm sick." His voice had been dull, lifeless.

"I can see that. Can I help . . ."

"No! Turn off the light. Go back to bed." He hadn't sounded like the husband she knew. He'd sounded angry, almost vicious.

She'd backed away slowly and turned off the light, but not before she saw that his face was swollen and his pupils were eerily dilated.

And he'd had red indentations on the sides of his nose.

He must have the same problem.

She'd forgotten that detail until Mr. Anderson mentioned it now. Ken had stayed in bed until almost noon the next day. Tessa had felt sorry for him. She'd told his receptionist to cancel Ken's patients all day because he had the flu. When he eventually woke up, the marks on his nose must have faded, because Tessa didn't recall seeing them.

Until now.

"Tessa? Are you all right?" Mrs. Anderson interrupted her thoughts.

No, she thought. "Yes," she said.

"Can we get our check? We have to babysit the grandchildren, so we better get going."

"Um, yes, okay," Tessa stammered as she fished in her apron pocket for the Andersons' check. They handed her some money, and she headed toward the cash register. Her head was spinning with unanswered questions. Ken did not wear glasses, so what could cause red indentations on the sides of his nose? She felt like she'd just snapped a few key pieces into a jigsaw puzzle but had no idea what the finished picture was supposed to look like.

He must have the same problem.

As she counted out the Andersons' change, she overheard a mother and her young son at the counter debating how to pour syrup on their pancakes without having it run off the plate. For a long moment, she studied them with envy. She wished that were her biggest problem.

Chapter Four

K en hated himself.

He was lying to everyone he knew.

He could live with lying to his staff. They didn't need to know everything about him. His receptionist, Tracy, was no problem; this was her first job in a dental office, so she wasn't sure what was standard operating procedure and what wasn't. Brenda, the hygienist, was a different story. She came to Ken with ten years of experience. She knew the ropes. He'd have to watch her.

It pained him to lie to his in-laws, but it was getting easier. Lately, he even amazed himself. At first the lies were clumsy, but he was getting better at it. Today he'd made up a story about not being able to pick up Ronnie from their house because of an emergency patient. He could always fill in the phony details later—how the poor guy was plagued with tooth decay because his parents never took him to the dentist as a child, or how he was drunk and had fallen and chipped a tooth on the kitchen counter. He'd worry about that later. The lies did not give him any pleasure. Tessa's parents were good to them. One of the things he loved most about Tess was her close relationship with her family.

He loved it and he hated it. It made him miss his mother even more.

Several years ago, when Ken and Tessa began dating seriously, he had taken his mother into Sal's diner for breakfast to meet Tessa. Tessa was home from college for the weekend and working as a server. She'd ignored Mary's outstretched hand and instead given her a big hug. She brought Sal over to the table to introduce her, and he also embraced her. "Italians don't shake hands, we hug!" he'd offered unapologetically. While Tessa refilled their coffee mugs, she'd leaned comfortably against their booth and listened as Mary talked about Ken, throwing her head back and laughing at stories that embarrassed him. If Ken wasn't convinced before, seeing Tess interact so easily with his mother clinched it in his mind. When they'd left the diner, Ken had held open the car door for his mother. Before she got in, she looked her son squarely in the eye. "You're crazy" was all she had said.

Ken was stunned. It had gone so well. "Mom, what do you . . ."

Smiling deviously, Mary had cut him off. "You're crazy if you let her get away."

Now, as Ken rode the elevator to his office, he felt a pang of shame. It was hardest to lie to Tessa. She was his staunchest supporter. A year after she graduated from college, Ken had proposed. Tessa willingly put aside her plans to go to graduate school when he was accepted to dental school. They couldn't support themselves if they were both students, so Tessa was the breadwinner while Ken pursued his dental degree. She'd worked as an English teacher, and when her salary didn't pay the bills, she worked weekends and even holidays at her dad's diner. She'd often dragged herself home exhausted after working two jobs, but she rarely complained. They had a plan, and she was doing her part.

Her support made Ken fall even more in love with her. He thought back to his dental school graduation. Tessa's proud smile had beamed brighter than any graduate's at the ceremony. He'd done it. *They'd* done it.

And now here they were, just where they dreamed they'd be all those nights in their cramped apartment near the dental school. They'd drink cheap wine and look out at their view of the trash dumpsters in the alley and know one day it would all be worth it. And it was. They had a beautiful healthy baby, and Ken had his own practice. Tessa could stay home and raise her children, go back to school, work, or some combination of the three. He knew she loved Ken and their life together.

Sometimes he wished she didn't love him so much. If she were judgmental and critical, if she screamed at him and threw things when he stayed at the office all night, if she threatened to take the baby and leave, it would be easier to do this to her.

Ken exited the elevator and crossed the hall to his office door. Making his way into the exam room, he cleared his head. He didn't think of Tessa's face, her blue eyes, the soft curve of her neck, the slender body he made love to. He didn't think about her sense of humor or her funny habit of twirling her hair without realizing it. He gave no thought to her compassion, her love of family, or the easy way she fell into motherhood.

He readied everything he needed and lay down in the dental chair. A frowning image of his mother fleetingly crossed his mind. He pushed it away.

He didn't want to do this.

He needed to do this.

It was as simple as that.

Chapter Five

Tessa flipped the sign on the door of the Sunrise Diner from "Open" to "Closed." Together, she and Linda finished cleaning up the dining room. They wiped all the tables, refilled napkin dispensers and sugar containers, and swept the floor. In the kitchen, the dishwasher scoured the stainless-steel sinks and threw all the day's soiled linens into the laundry bag. Tessa untied her apron and said good-bye to the other employees as they gathered their keys and headed for the door. Before she left, she picked up the phone on the old desk in Sal's office and dialed the number to her house. Her thoughts raced, setting her nerves on edge. As she listened to the phone ring, her conversation with the Andersons tormented her.

He must have the same problem.

She waited impatiently for Ken to answer. She would tell him to put Veronica down for her nap because she was on her way home and she needed to talk to him. She wanted answers.

She tapped her pen rapidly on the desk and organized her thoughts. The answering machine picked up after several rings.

Frustrated, Tessa hung up and dialed the number to her parents' house. Val answered on the second ring.

"Hi, Mom." She rushed to the point. "When Ken picked up the baby, did he say where they were going? I just tried calling the house, and they aren't there." Tessa forced herself to speak casually so as not to trip her mother's innate "something's wrong" alarm.

"Hon, Ken never picked up Ronnie. She's still here. As we speak, your little sister is putting a paper Burger King crown on her and proclaiming her as the reigning queen of the household." Val turned her attention to her granddaughter and younger daughter. "Gina! Don't let it slide down over her eyes." She laughed and continued, "Wait till you see her. She looks so cute and—"

Tessa cut her off. "Ken didn't pick her up? Why?" A knot formed in her stomach.

"Didn't he fill you in? He called me around ten o'clock and said he had an emergency at the office. A patient with excruciating tooth pain. He said he might have to do an extraction. I told him to take his time. Ronnie is fine. She's giggling away at Gina."

Tessa closed her eyes and rubbed her forehead. "I guess he didn't want to bother me while I was here working." A plan formulated in her head that made her slightly dizzy. "Okay. I'm done here, but I need a few things at the grocery store. Do you mind if I stop there before I pick up Ronnie?"

"That's fine. If you can make it into the house. Now Gina is filling cups of water to line the front walk. She says it's a moat to keep the enemy from attacking Queen Veronica's castle!"

They hung up, and Tessa stood rooted in place for a moment, thinking. Finally, she hugged her dad good-bye and headed out the back door.

Tessa felt foolish. She turned off her ignition in the parking lot of Ken's office next to his car.

See? He's here. Why was I making myself crazy?

Since she was already here, she decided to pop in and say hello. As she crossed the steamy parking lot, her nerves settled. There had to be a reasonable explanation for all the recent changes in Ken's mood and behavior. She was being paranoid, and it was not doing anyone any good.

The building, a satellite of a local hospital, housed about twelve doctors' offices. Ken's office was on the second of three floors, and Tessa pressed the button on the elevator. It was Saturday, so the noises in the building were limited to routine cleaning and repairs made by the maintenance staff.

On the second floor, her footsteps echoed as she turned right down the corridor. She nodded to a custodian dusting window blinds at the end of the hall. She reached Ken's office and looked proudly at the sign next to the door: Kenneth P. Cordelia, D.M.D. He had worked so hard to get to this point, and Tessa felt a twinge of guilt at her mistrust of him. *I'm turning into one of those nagging wives whose husbands make any excuse to get away from them.* She turned the doorknob, vowing to make it up to him.

The door was locked.

Tessa figured Ken locked the door because technically his office was closed today, and he didn't want anyone who happened to be in the building to inadvertently venture into his waiting room. She reached into her purse and found the spare key amid baby wipes and teething toys. After inserting the key in the lock, she stepped into the reception room.

One of the three exam room doors was closed, so Tessa surmised that was where Ken was treating his emergency patient. Not wanting to startle them, she called out softly, "Hello?"

Only silence answered her.

She decided to wait a few minutes for Ken and the patient to emerge from the exam room. She looked around the reception area at the furniture, paint colors, and artwork she and Ken had picked out together. Since people were often nervous about having dental work, they'd chosen soothing colors: a soft gray shade on the walls and a warm mauve fabric on the chairs. Picking up a magazine, she dropped her purse on a chair and sat down. After a few moments, the all too familiar unease crept into Tessa's gut.

No sounds of any activity came from the exam room. No talking, no instruments clanging on the metal chairside tray, no shrill whir of a suction hose or drill.

Nothing.

Tessa stood and crossed the room. Straining to hear, she leaned against the Formica counter top of the reception desk.

Still nothing.

She walked down the short hallway to the closed exam room door. She put her hand on the doorknob and suddenly became conscious of a sound emanating from the room. Barely audible, it made a low, continuous humming noise. Tessa turned the knob quietly.

It, too, was locked.

Alarmed, Tessa clumsily stepped back from the door and struggled to make sense of the situation. *Why would Ken be in a locked exam room with a patient?*

She did not wait to find out. She approached the door again and knocked. "Ken? Open the door."

No answer.

She knocked again, louder this time, and raised her voice. "Ken! It's me. Open the door!"

Nothing.

Panicked, she jiggled the door handle and continued knocking. "Ken, what's going on? Open the door." She remembered the key she used to enter the outer office and wondered if the same key opened the exam rooms. Not at all sure she wanted to see what was going on inside, she reached in her pocket for the key. She inserted it into the lock and heard the lock disengage with a *pop*. Feeling like Alice tumbling down the rabbit hole, she pushed open the door.

Her breath caught in her chest, and her hand flew to her mouth. "What . . . ? Ken!"

He was alone in the room, reclined on the exam chair. His resting hands folded on his chest, he looked like a patient waiting for a checkup.

Except for one thing.

A mask covered his nose and mouth.

A hose from the mask was attached to a cylindrical tank of nitrous oxide, the source of the humming, which sat in a cart on wheels next to the chair. Ken appeared to be sleeping. There was no indication he heard Tessa enter the room.

Tessa comprehended the scene bit by bit, taking in the room by inches, all her senses heightened. Her fingers reached forward but found only air; her feet felt like weights as they guided her toward her husband. Sunlight streamed in through the window, its brightness belying the garish scene in the room.

When she reached Ken, she placed her hand on his shoulder. He didn't move. She shook his shoulder, gently at first, then harder when he didn't respond. Panicked, she was afraid he wasn't breathing, but the rise and fall of his chest quelled that fear.

Finally, the floodgate of Tessa's emotions gave way. Her heartache washed over her husband from his disheveled hair, down his face where the tight mask explained the mysterious marks on his nose, into his folded hands that had clasped hers when they looked at their daughter together the first time.

The fear that plagued her, gnawed at her insides for more than twenty years, filled her heart and mind. She'd kept it at bay most of her life, but now it reared its ugly head, coming to claim her. Like a sink whose stopper was stuck, it rose upward and threatened to overflow.

No. Not again.

Tessa had had a lifetime filled with bad things, everything from ordinary little bad things that all kids and teenagers experience to one great big bad thing, the one that haunted her, the one she didn't talk about, the one that had left a permanent scar on her heart even though Val came along and was a loving mother to her. This bad thing before her felt akin to that one, so bad that she couldn't comprehend it all at once but rather would need to dissect it over and over again to somehow situate it on the canvas of her life.

Suddenly, she vigorously shook Ken's shoulder. "Ken! What are you doing? Please! Wake up!" She lifted the mask off his face.

Or tried to.

Ken sprang up so suddenly Tessa fell backward. He grabbed her arm with such detached brutality Tessa had difficulty reconciling that he was the same man she'd seen when she left the house this morning. He looked nothing like the gentle man she'd exchanged wedding vows with, who rushed to her parents' house in the middle of the night when a water pipe burst, who held Ronnie tenderly as she curled her tiny fingers around his.

"Get . . . get the hell away from me . . ." Still disoriented, Ken slurred his words as he fumbled with the mask, trying to replace it over his nose and mouth. He looked around blankly, and Tessa wasn't sure if he even knew who she was.

She was shaking. "Ken, you have to stop this. Come on. Let's talk. I want you to leave here with me. Now." She approached him tenuously and once again reached for the mask.

Ken slapped her arm away. "Get out! Just get out!" He was already repositioning himself on the chair. "Just . . . get . . ."

Stunned, Tessa backed away from Ken as though he were a dangerous animal. Moving faster now, she grabbed her purse from the reception room chair and fled the office. Hands trembling, she pressed the elevator button. After what seemed like an eternity, the door opened. She staggered into the elevator and rode to the first floor. She ran to her car and flung open the door.

Safely inside her car, she burst into tears.

Chapter Six

Tessa imagined this was what it must feel like to drown. To try to swim to the surface, to think you see daylight, only to be dragged under again by the force of crashing waves.

Her mind felt like a jigsaw puzzle someone had abruptly knocked from a table with a brush of an arm. Here was a red piece. Was it part of a sweater sleeve or a piece of a heart shattered into bits? And a pink piece. Was it a petal of a silky petunia or a lip turned downward in anguish?

She curled up in a ball on the sofa. A bathing suit she'd bought Ronnie—a bright orange one-piece with a duck on the front and a ruffle around the bottom—was still in a bag on the floor. Tessa felt a strange nostalgia for the person she was before today, the person who bought cute bathing suits for her baby daughter. The person so upset when she spilled wine on the sofa cushion that she'd gone to three stores to find the right spray cleaner. The person who felt guilty pretending the grocery store didn't have the cut of steak he wanted because she didn't feel like cooking. Before today, those were the problems she thought worthy of fretting about.

The image of Ken in that exam chair was engraved in her mind's eye.

No. This can't happen again.

It's not your fault, Tess. She's sick.

She had somehow managed to pull herself together long enough to pick up Ronnie from her parents' house. She'd avoided eye contact with Val in case her outburst left telltale signs on her face. Haphazardly, Tessa gathered up Ronnie's bag and hurried from the house. She had driven home with her daughter smiling and cooing in her car seat, her innocence breaking Tessa's heart even more.

Once at home, operating on autopilot to keep her composure, she'd fed and changed the baby and put her down for her afternoon nap.

Now she covered her face and wept again. She had no idea what to do. She knew only that she could not talk to anyone about it. It would be easier to make it go away if only the two of them knew about it. She had to keep it contained, nice and neat. To let it out would ensure its growth into something so monstrous it could never be reeled back in.

She had to fix this. She would get through to Ken. She would make him see that this was not the answer to whatever stress he was feeling, that he was only making it worse. He was on the edge of a cliff, but she could pull him back.

It was all a puzzle to her. She'd thought she and Ken had made it, their past struggles behind them, their future holding so much promise. She'd survived, if not completely dealt with, what her biological mother had done. Together, they'd coped with Ken's mother's death. They'd weathered the storm of balancing Ken's education with endless bills and hurdles.

Tessa hadn't felt this despondent since the last time she saw Ken's mother alive, but at least then, she'd known on some molecular level—where facts and logic take over the brain to keep emotions from breaking the heart—that people get sick. They even die. As agonizing as it was, death was a natural part of life.

But this? Tessa couldn't think of a less natural situation.

When Tessa first met Ken that night at the bar, she learned that he was a student at a local liberal arts college. He was a biology major who planned to go to dental school. Tessa was drawn to him instantly. She loved college, but she was growing tired of loud parties in crammed apartments and immature guys with only one thing on their mind. Drinking beer out of a red plastic cup was getting old, and she longed to be a "grown-up" and be wined and dined by a *real* man.

Ken was different. He was soft-spoken and polite, not a loud, obnoxious attention-seeker like many guys his age. When he and Tess went out, they talked. *Really* talked. He took her to nice restaurants and sent her flowers for no reason. When they shopped at the King of Prussia Mall, he'd look in the windows of Bloomingdale's and Neiman Marcus and remark how beautiful she would look in the silk dresses and cashmere coats. With Ken, Tessa *felt* beautiful. The center of his universe. Like he would rather be with her than anywhere else on earth.

Ken had a plan. He was focused and motivated. The more time she spent with him, the more Tessa thought they might have a future together. They both wanted to travel and have a family. They'd drink wine for hours, talking about their aspirations.

But the thing that endeared Ken most to Tessa was the way he treated his mother. Ken loved Mary dearly, and Tessa loved him for that. Val always said you could tell a lot about a man by the way he treated his mother. "If he's a jerk to his own mother," she'd warn, "run for the hills. He won't respect you." If Ken's treatment of Mary was any indication, Tessa had nothing to worry about. Ken doted on his mother and often invited her to dinner when Tessa was home from school and they went out for Italian or seafood. Sometimes, Ken and Tessa would pick up pork lo mein and won ton soup, Mary's favorites, and eat with her in front of the TV.

Mary was diagnosed with breast cancer shortly before Ken and Tessa met. She had felt a lump about a year prior and gone to the doctor immediately, but her doctor was an old cranky sort who should have hung up his stethoscope years before and told her to wait six months to see if there were any changes before getting the lump biopsied. Mary was relieved and trusted her doctor. By the time she went back, the tests showed the lump was indeed cancerous. Thus began the chemotherapy and radiation treatments, but the cancer had spread to her lymph nodes, and Mary's health declined rapidly.

Ken did not accept this and told her every day that she would be all right. Ken's father seemed more interested in hunting and riding his motorcycle than caring for his ailing wife. He sometimes disappeared for days at a time, not even calling to check on Mary. Ken despised his father for this and vowed that if he was ever fortunate enough to have a wife like Mary, he would love and care for her above all else.

Tessa and Mary got along well from the moment Ken introduced them at her dad's diner. As her cancer limited Mary's activity outside the house, they'd trade books and watch *Jeopardy!* together. Ken's older sister quit her job in public relations to care for her mother full-time. She was wonderful and patient with Mary, but periodically she needed to get out of the house for an hour to avoid going stir-crazy. If she could, Tessa would offer to take shifts when Ken and his brothers were at school or work. If Mary was feeling up to it, Ken and Tessa would take her to Sal's diner for eggs and scrapple or over to Sal and Val's house for a short visit. Sal had always been a softie; every time Mary left, he'd shake his head tearfully at her hair loss and ghostly complexion. "That poor woman; it's a damn shame."

Sometimes when Tessa kept Mary company, Mary begged her to convince Ken to accept she was dying so she could go in peace. Tessa would cry with her and promise she would talk to Ken, but she could never bring herself to do it. Near the end of Mary's illness, she was in so much pain from the radiation treatments she needed to be sedated around the clock. Sickness hung in the air of her bedroom like heavy wet snow on fragile tree limbs. It reached the point where they couldn't bear to be near her, and when they weren't there, they couldn't wait to get back to her. As often is the way with cancer patients, she seemed slightly better for a day or two near the end. During that time, Ken and his siblings had pleasant talks with Mary. They laughed at childhood stories and talked about the future, no one mentioning the torturous truth that it wouldn't include her, at least not in body.

One night when Tessa was home from college on spring break, she'd stood in the doorway of Mary's bedroom for a long moment. She listened to Mary's shallow breathing and sensed it was the last time she would ever see her. When she went to work the next morning, the sky was clear, and the air was crisp and cool as though the previous day's pain and suffering had moved away like a band of dreadful storms. When Ken called her at the diner to tell her it was over, she heard a visceral pain in his voice that she hoped she would never have to hear again from someone she loved.

Tessa thought about Mary now. Her mind alternated between racing with thoughts of what she had witnessed earlier and slowly recollecting events in their lives that may have led them here.

Ken and Tessa married eight months after Mary died. They had chosen the date when Mary, while diagnosed, was still in fairly good health. Everyone tried to remain hopeful, but in the year leading up to the wedding date, Mary's health deteriorated quickly. Tessa's parents had offered to cancel the wedding and give them the money instead if Ken felt it was too soon, but he said Mary had made him promise not to alter their plan. She said she'd be there, even if only in spirit.

Ken was in his second year of dental school in Philadelphia when they got married. They found a one-bedroom apartment in King of Prussia, halfway between Reading and Philly, since Tessa worked as a teacher during the week and at Sal's diner on weekends. Tess didn't mind working seven days a week to put Ken through dental school. She knew the sacrifice was worth it. Ken worked hard in school, and Tessa knew one day he'd have a successful dental practice.

Tessa loved those early years when the marriage was new. She and Ken had coffee together in the morning before she headed to work and he began the hour commute to school. No matter how late Ken was stuck at school, they always had dinner together. If Tessa was too tired to cook, he'd pick up pizza or Chinese on his way home. Ken would tell her about the new periodontal instruments he'd experimented with, and Tess would tell him about the ever-changing state standards in public education. In the evening, they'd sit on their tiny balcony holding hands. They'd talk about the house and family they both wanted one day and what they might name their future children. At night, they would lie in each other's arms and fall asleep smiling. Although they didn't have much money, Tessa had felt like she had the riches of a queen.

When did things change?

Recently, when she pressed Ken about why he was so sullen, he initially refused to talk about it but finally reluctantly admitted he missed his mother. He was becoming obsessed with the idea. He told Tessa that he couldn't bear that his mother would miss all the big moments in his life: getting married, graduating from dental school, having children. On their wedding day, he'd stood outside gazing up at the sky, weeping openly. Graduation day, though well-attended by various members of both Ken's and Tessa's proud families, was shrouded in melancholy for the one person who wasn't there. Most recently, it broke Ken's heart that Mary could not be a grandmother to Ronnie. Tessa often heard Ken telling his tiny daughter how much her Baba would have loved her.

Tessa rose from the sofa on shaky legs. She couldn't clear her mind of the scene at Ken's office. She went into the bedroom and stared at her reflection in the bureau mirror, and it came to her.

Ken was depressed.

And worse, she was partly to blame. She'd not paid enough attention to the signs. She'd been so caught up in her new role as Ronnie's mother that she'd neglected her husband. She'd fix that. She'd help Ken find a healthy outlet for his feelings. She'd find him a good counselor, even go with him if he wanted. Ken shouldered most of the burden in their marriage. Now it was her turn.

She would not let this happen to someone she loved again.

She looked at the clock. According to Val's claim that Ken went to the office at ten o'clock this morning, he had been there for almost five hours.

How long will Ken stay there on that gas? She had to do something. She paced the floor. She needed to get back to the office. She needed to tell her husband it was all going to be okay now.

Chapter Seven

Tessa sat at the rectangular kitchen table and stared at the clock on the microwave. She racked her brain, chin resting on folded hands, fingers interlocked.

She had to get back to Ken's office without anyone knowing why. She couldn't take Ronnie back to her parents'. She'd just left there, so they'd ask too many questions she wasn't prepared to answer. She also couldn't take the baby to the office with her. Ken was disoriented and confrontational when she'd walked in on him earlier. She couldn't put her daughter in such a volatile situation.

Unable to devise a better plan, Tessa called her neighbor. Mrs. Henry wouldn't ask questions. They often traded favors; they'd bring in each other's mail and water each other's plants, Tessa fed their cat when they traveled, and Mrs. Henry always offered to watch Ronnie if Tessa needed to run a quick errand without dragging the baby trappings with her. Tessa just began punching in her neighbor's phone number when she heard a car. She parted the mini blinds over the kitchen sink and peered out. Ken lumbered from the car.

Tessa let the blind snap shut and stepped back from the window. She hung up the phone and rested her head against the wall. A combination of relief and anxiety washed over her. She imagined this is what parents felt like when their teens stayed out past curfew and they had no idea where they were, anger quickly replacing worry when their son or daughter returned home safely.

She sat down heavily in a wooden kitchen chair facing the door.

Ken, head down, hands shoved deep in his pockets, entered the kitchen and leaned against the door frame. He averted his eyes and said nothing. Tessa didn't look up. Her fingers traced the plaid pattern on the tablecloth.

Finally, Ken spoke so softly that Tessa had to strain to hear him. "Is Ronnie sleeping?"

Tessa swallowed hard and didn't trust herself to speak. She nodded her head and concentrated on the tablecloth.

"Tess, I . . ." Ken ran his fingers through his hair and sighed heavily. He pulled out a chair next to his wife and sat down. "I'm sorry."

Tessa finally met his eyes. She took in the sight of him— pale, disheveled, bleary-eyed—with a fresh understanding that was anything but comforting. All those months agonizing, not knowing, and now there was no way to un-know the truth. She'd been chasing down questions she hadn't realized she didn't want answered. The puzzle, once assembled, was more confusing than it had been in scattered pieces.

"You're sorry." Tessa wanted to laugh but knew that if she did, it would be a maniacal, wholly inappropriate one she'd seen in movies from people who'd lost their minds. She held on to the table's edge. "Is that all you have to say?"

Ken took her hand in his. "I don't know what else to say." He looked out the window at the thin clouds in the late summer sky. "It's stupid, really, the way it started." He paused for such a long moment Tessa wasn't sure he was going to continue.

"And?"

Ken jumped slightly, as if he momentarily forgot he wasn't alone. He cleared his throat. "One night I was working late, and I was just so beat, you know? It's been a bitch getting the office open and the practice off the ground. I was working on a mailer to send out to try to attract patients. All of a sudden, I couldn't keep my eyes open. My eyelids felt like thousand-pound weights. I needed to sleep, but I had more work to do. I stretched out in the chair and closed my eyes. I only meant to take a twenty- or thirty-minute break."

Expressionless, Tessa silently waited for him to go on.

"Anyway, I fell hard. I slept like a rock. When I woke up, the sun was coming up. I couldn't believe the whole night had passed. I jumped up and drove home to shower before going back in."

Tessa furrowed her brow. "But were you using the gas? Is that why you slept so long and so soundly?"

Ken shook his head. "No, no, I just slept like that because I was exhausted." He leaned in close to Tessa's face and took both her hands in his. "But, babe, while I was asleep, I had the most vivid dream of my mom. She looked so good, you know, like she did before she got sick. Her cheeks had this sun-kissed glow, and she was outside pruning her garden."

Tessa sat up straighter. She pulled her hands back and nervously tucked a strand of hair behind her ear. "I don't understand. How did this dream lead to . . . to . . . ?"

Ken stood and walked to the sink. He took a glass from the cabinet and filled it with cold water. Tessa wanted to grab it from him and hurl it at the wall. She was crawling out of her skin. Ken drained the glass and turned back to her.

"I couldn't get the dream out of my mind for days. It was so . . . real. I wanted so badly to dream of her again. I wanted to see her healthy again." He turned to face Tessa. "But I couldn't get it back. Every time I went to sleep, I prayed I would dream of her, but I didn't." He paused and looked at the floor. "The next time I was at the office late at night, I remembered something a classmate in dental school had told me. He said he tried nitrous oxide once the night before an exam to relax. He said he'd had the wildest dreams while he was on it."

Tessa closed her eyes and pursed her lips as her husband's words registered. "So, you thought if you were on the gas, it might help you dream of your mom." She wondered if it sounded as irrational to Ken as it did to her now that he was hearing it out loud.

He stared at Tessa long and hard. "Yes. That's what I thought."

"Well? Did it work?"

Ken's shoulders sagged. "No. It didn't. I haven't dreamed of her since that first time." He became agitated and paced the floor. "It's so frustrating! I just wish I could . . ."

"Ken." Tessa stood and looked her husband in the eyes. "Listen to yourself. You're huffing nitrous oxide. Nitrous oxide is not something people use to help them sleep, like"— she paused and waved her hands in front of her—"herbal tea or Tylenol PM." Her voice was steady, commanding. "Nitrous oxide is a controlled substance used for dental procedures and surger—"

"Don't you think I know what the hell it's used for? God, I'm trying to tell you what I've been going through! I don't need a sermon right now." Ken walked out of the kitchen and down the hall to the bedroom.

Tessa followed him. Flashes of earlier that day, Ken hooked up to the gas, resurfaced in her mind. Flashes from over two decades ago—her biological mother's demons, her father's pleas, her own confused sadness—merged with those. *It's not your fault, Tess. She's sick.* She feared she was on the brink of something that, once started down the path, there would be no coming back from.

She walked into the bedroom and closed the door. "What you need is to listen to reason. I'm not trying to lecture you, but, for God's sake, do you know how you sound? You're acting

like this is perfectly normal behavior! You're smarter than that."
She sat on the edge of the floral comforter and tried a different
approach. Her expression softened, and she patted a spot next
to her. "Come here. Sit down."

Sadness overcame Tessa as she took in Ken's pale countenance, tousled hair, and rumpled clothing. Calmer now, he
shuffled over to the bed and plopped down next to her. She
grasped his hand and held it in her lap. She turned her body
and sat cross-legged so she faced him.

"Look, I understand you've been stressed getting the practice off the ground. And I get that you miss your mom and want
to dream of her. I miss her too. It's just . . . holing yourself up
in your office alone all night doing that gas is not healthy."

He said nothing, so Tessa continued carefully. "I think
you're depressed. Your mom missed your graduation, our
wedding, and now Ronnie is here as a daily reminder of the
grandmother who isn't around to spoil her." Ken blinked back
tears and Tessa put her arms around him. "But this is not the
answer. There are people who can help you, people who deal
specifically with grief counseling. I'll talk to a teacher I know
at the high school. She once mentioned someone she saw when
her dad—"

Ken jumped up and swung around to face Tessa. "I don't
need a shrink! I'm not crazy!" He clenched his fists and walked
over to the window. "Christ, I go through a rough spot for a
few months, and right away you assume I'm nuts. So I miss my
mom. Since when is that a crime?" His zero-to-sixty escalation
unsettled Tessa.

She stood up and, attempting to hide that she was rattled,
held her chin high. "No one said anything about being nuts.
But huffing nitrous oxide is reckless and downright dangerous." She measured her next words before speaking. "Ken, you
have to stop this. You lie to me. You're out all night. When
you finally crawl home in the morning, you're disoriented,

irrational, combative . . . That stuff is changing your entire demeanor. It's like you're not even the same person. This is not the answer to whatever is bothering you, and I know you know that."

Ken waved her off. He went to the oak dresser, pulled open the top drawer, and grabbed a striped polo shirt and jeans. "Thank you very much, Dr. Tessa. Are we done here? Send me a bill for your services. I'm going to take a shower." He stopped in the doorway, looked up at the ceiling, and turned around. "Look." He exhaled deeply. "I know things can't go on like this. Just . . . I need to figure things out in my own time."

Tessa turned away, her eyes burning. Outside, the sun began its descent behind the mountains. How Ken could think his behavior was acceptable, she had no idea. Tessa shuddered at Ken's rage and cruel tone. She realized with a start that, since the scene earlier that day, she was different. She was afraid of Ken.

She wished she could tell him that. She wished she could tell him that she was just trying to help. She heard the shower running in the next room, and a reality hit her hard: She may not know her husband at all. And if he thought she would eventually come around and accept what he was doing, he didn't know her either.

Chapter Eight

"Dr. C., I'm finished with Mrs. Peters's X-rays. Looks like a nerve thing."

Ken smiled at Brenda, his hygienist. She was around Ken's age and had long wild hair that at work she fastened behind her head with a large banana clip. Brenda and Tessa were high school classmates, and their families knew each other. Ken and Tessa occasionally crossed paths with Brenda and her husband, Hank, in social situations. Brenda had a reputation as a party girl, something Ken had asked Tessa about before hiring her. Though Tessa confirmed the rumors, she also knew Brenda's reputation as a quality hygienist. Brenda and Hank had a son one year older than Ronnie, so Ken and Tessa figured Brenda was settling down. So far they'd been right; she was dependable and had a positive rapport with patients. Brenda currently performed double duty as Ken's chairside assistant, but as business improved, he hoped to hire a new assistant soon.

"'Nerve thing'? Is that your technical diagnosis?" Ken sat in a swivel desk chair in his private office. Outside the window, yellow and red leaves floated from the trees, a common autumn sight in Pennsylvania. He took a swig of his coffee. "Be right there."

Ken was in a good mood. Business was picking up, and he wasn't as stressed as when he opened the office five months earlier. As he stood up and straightened his paisley tie, Tessa and Ronnie smiled at him from framed photos on his cherry credenza. He and Tessa were getting along better, but things were still tense. His wife had agreed to give him some time to right the ship, but her patience had limits. He glanced at the business cards of grief counselors she'd collected for him, and a twinge of guilt stabbed him. He'd told her he would check them out. She believed him when he said he wanted to quit abusing the gas.

He sometimes believed it himself.

Whistling, he walked into the exam room, where a fiftyish lady sat in the chair, hands folded on her abdomen. She was stylishly dressed in black pants, a cheetah-print blouse, and a tan shaker sweater. A paper bib fastened by a thin metal chain rested under her neck on her chest.

After greeting her warmly, Ken pulled on a pair of latex gloves, placed a paper mask over his nose and mouth, secured the stretchy strings behind his ears, and positioned an overhead light suspended from an arm attached to the ceiling over Mrs. Peters's head. "Let's see what we've got here. Open, please."

He probed around in her mouth for a few minutes and then motioned to Brenda, who handed him the X-ray film. Ken clipped it onto a screen that was lit from behind and studied the film. He turned off the bright overhead light and pulled up a stool next to his patient. "Okay, Mrs. Peters, here's the situation. You see this dark area here?" he asked, pointing to a spot on the X-ray and tracing a circular motion with his finger. "The nerve is infected right there at the gum line. That's what is causing your pain."

He gently pulled back her lip with a gloved hand. "You can even see some discoloration of the tooth without looking at the X-ray."

"Ugh." Mrs. Peters frowned. "So, what do you recommend?"

"Well, you'll need a root canal, but I don't think you have to see an endodontist. I can do the procedure here without involving a specialist." He leaned in closer to the X-ray. "Are you sensitive to heat and cold in that area?"

"Am I ever! I ate ice cream at my grandson's first birthday party on Saturday and almost jumped out of my skin! Let's schedule it as soon as possible. I need my ice cream! Not to mention my morning coffee!" Mrs. Peters tried to make light of the situation, but Ken could see she was suffering.

Grinning, he took down the film and switched off the light on the apparatus. "I hear you. There are some things we can't do without." He scribbled a note in the patient's chart. "Brenda, irrigate the infected area as gently as possible today. I don't want to aggravate it any more. It's angry enough."

"That makes two of us!" quipped Mrs. Peters. "So, what exactly is a root canal?"

"It's not as bad as it sounds. I wish people would stop with the 'I'd rather have a root canal' comment to describe the most unpleasant events." Ken laughed and tried to reassure her. "Basically, I need to clean out the infection in the interior of the tooth. Then I'll fill in and reseal the space inside that tooth where the nerve was. That will allow your body's natural healing process to restore the health of the surrounding tissue."

Mrs. Peters cringed. "Well, I'm beginning to understand that joke." She sighed. "Will the procedure at least fix the problem permanently?"

"Yes. The infected nerve is causing contaminates to leak out of the root tip and inflame the tissue around it. After the root canal, nothing will be able to leak back in or out of it. That's what the seal does." He pulled his gloves off with a snap and used the foot pedal to raise the lid on a round aluminum receptacle before dropping them inside.

"I'm nervous just thinking about it." She squeezed her eyes shut and shook her head. The autumn sunlight through the window caught the gray threaded through her otherwise dark chin-length bob. Tiny lines were visible next to her eyes when she opened them again. "Just make sure you dope me up. I mean it! Use any means necessary to knock me out. Numbing shots, laughing gas, conk me over the head with a frying pan . . . I don't care!" She chuckled.

Ken paused for a moment. *Laughing gas.* "Well, we'll see. I'm thinking you won't need the gas. Hopefully local anesthesia, a shot of lidocaine, will suffice."

Brenda, who was attaching a tip to the irrigation hose, shot her boss a puzzled look.

Ken ignored her. "Besides, I broke my frying pan over the last patient's head, so that's not an option." He smiled and winked at his patient. "Don't worry, I'll take good care of you." He finished making notes on her chart and stood up. "See Tracy at the desk on your way out. She'll set up the procedure for you as soon as possible."

"Okay, thanks, Dr. Cordelia."

A few minutes later, Brenda caught up with Ken in the lab. She placed a tray of instruments into an autoclave resembling a space-age toaster oven. She leaned on her elbows on the counter and looked at his blue eyes as he inspected a denture model. "You don't think she's going to need nitrous oxide sedation? We usually use it on root canal patients. And that tooth looks pretty nasty."

Ken feigned casual disinterest in her opinion. "Hmm? Oh, I don't know. I'll see how she is when she comes back. A lot of people don't like the gas. They say it makes them feel loopy." *And I don't want to waste all my stash.*

"Yeah, but she said—"

"I heard what she said." He turned toward the door.

Brenda said nothing as she refilled her tray with sterile, packaged instruments. As Ken left the room, she muttered, "Whatever you say. You're the boss."

The rest of the morning went quickly: three fillings, an extraction, and a few routine cleanings. One patient named Jeremy, an apprehensive six-year-old boy with blond wavy hair, refused to get into the chair. He finally relaxed when Ken allowed him to blow up a rubber glove. They knew they had him when Brenda drew a rudimentary depiction of a turkey on it, the thumb being the head and the fingers representing the feathers. Jeremy clutched the "turkey" and remained still for his exam.

"Nice work there, Picasso. You may have missed your calling," Ken teased after the boy and his mother left. He wanted to smooth things over from his earlier curtness.

Brenda snickered, happy to be back in Ken's good graces. "I'm just glad he has no cavities and doesn't have to come back soon. I don't think I can convert an inflated glove into Santa or a reindeer without art lessons."

The rest of the patients were good-natured, chatting animatedly about their upcoming Thanksgiving plans, everyone agreeing it was hard to believe that the Christmas holidays were just around the corner. Brenda and Tracy both had excellent people skills, and the environment in the office was fast-paced but pleasant.

Finally, just after noon, the last patient was checked out, the exam rooms were clean and ready for the next day, and the phones were switched over to the answering service.

Ken rounded the corner and stood next to the chest-high reception desk. Tracy stretched and yawned loudly. She was pretty in a natural way, with long strawberry-blonde hair that she wore in a braid and cheeks sprinkled with freckles.

"My work here is done," she announced. She took her

sweater off the back of her chair and grabbed the strap of her brown leather purse from under the reception desk. Despite being new to the dental business, she was thriving as the front desk receptionist. She was a quick study and took direction well. Scheduling and checking out patients was not difficult for her to learn, but dealing with insurance companies was challenging. Red tape led to patient responsibility for uncovered expenses, which was the most delicate aspect of Tracy's job. Ken had sent her to a few training seminars, and overall, the twenty-four-year-old was making great progress.

"Hang on, I'll walk out with you," Brenda called as she turned off the lights in the two exam rooms. She added to Ken, "I like only scheduling patients until noon on Wednesdays. Good call, Dr. C."

Ken shifted his weight from one foot to the other and shuffled some papers around on the counter. "Well, enjoy it while it lasts. Remember, I'm just doing it for now to try to tighten up the schedule. Having too much time between patients isn't cost effective. Hopefully, we'll be busy enough soon that we can fill up all the appointment slots and work full days Monday through Friday."

Brenda waved her hand and defended her statement. "Oh, we get it. We just like having the afternoon free. I'm sure you do too. More time with your family."

Ken dropped a folder onto the carpeted floor. "Of course I do. Why wouldn't I?" The words came out louder than he'd intended.

She raised her eyebrows as she shrugged into her jacket. "I didn't mean . . . Well, yes, okay then. See you tomorrow." She fished around in her purse for her keys.

"Bye, Dr. C." Tracy pulled the door closed behind them.

The girls gone, Ken dialed the number to his house. Tessa answered on the second ring.

"Hey, what are my two favorite girls up to?"

"Oh, hi, hon. We're just eating lunch. Rather, I'm stealing bites of my sandwich and trying to get Ronnie to eat peas. She's not a fan," laughed Tessa. "You should see your daughter. It looks more like she's bathing in green slime than eating lunch. Here, say hi to Daddy." Ken could hear Tessa stretching the phone cord to reach Ronnie in her high chair.

Her gurgling laughter made Ken feel like such a cad he almost hung up and drove home.

Almost.

"Okay, that was a mistake. Now the phone has been slimed too." Tessa sounded frazzled as she turned her attention back to her husband. "So, are you coming home for lunch? I know Wednesday is your late night with patients."

Ken's body tensed, and he was glad his wife could not see him. He hated this part. The lies.

"Uh, no, I can't today. We're actually working through lunch. We ordered pizza, but we'll be lucky if we have time to eat it. I'm sure it will be ice cold before we get to it."

"Oh, that stinks. But it's good that you're getting so busy. Maybe I'll grill steaks for a late dinner?"

Ken lowered his head and pinched the bridge of his nose. "Um, I probably won't be home until after eight. Our last patient isn't until seven." The fib caught on his tongue, leaving a sour taste in his mouth.

Tessa's silence irritated Ken. *Here we go.*

But then she seemed to rally. "All right, no worries." She sighed. "Maybe I'll run over and see my parents. I need to take that bouncy seat over there. The one I found at the yard sale? With Ronnie starting to crawl, Mom needs something to keep her contained when I'm subbing all day—"

Ken wanted to get off the phone. "Listen, Tess. I gotta go. Sorry."

"Oh, okay. Sorry. See you tonight."

Ken hesitated. "Tess."

"Yeah?"

"Nothing. I . . . I love you. I'll see you later."

Tessa hung up the phone. Ken stared at the receiver in his hand for a long moment before placing it back in the cradle.

I can stop.

I will stop.

He made sure all the doors were locked to the outer office and turned off the rest of the lights. The office was closed. His new plan was working. For now.

He wheeled the tank out of the closet, dragged it chairside, and lay down.

I can stop anytime I want. Just a few hours. If I don't stay out all night, I'm not harming my marriage or family.

He pulled a small alarm clock from a drawer and set it for 8 p.m. After turning it to the highest volume, he placed it directly next to his head.

I have this under control. I'll be home by eight thirty, just like I said. It wasn't a lie.

Finally, he opened a drawer and took out a few pieces of gauze. These he wrapped around the edges of the mask so it would not leave marks on his nose. He placed the mask over his nose and mouth and adjusted the knobs on the tank. The last image to cross his mind as he closed his eyes was a smiling woman pushing a swaddled baby in a stroller on a cool autumn day.

But the woman and baby were not Tessa and Veronica. They were Mary and Ken.

Chapter Nine

Tessa hung up the phone and forced a smile at her daughter's pea-smeared face. She watched Ronnie swirl what was left of the green goo on the high chair tray and fought the unease forming in her gut.

True, Ken seemed better in the weeks since she discovered him on the gas, but things were still not right. His moods were as erratic as ever. She never knew which Ken was going to walk through the door. Some nights he came home whistling, a bouquet of flowers in his arm for Tessa and a new teething toy for Ronnie. He'd scoop up his daughter, take his wife in his arms, and whirl around the room with them as if he had struck gold. Other nights, especially those when he worked late, he was sullen. He'd trudge in the door, avoid eye contact, mutter that it had been "one of those days," and head straight for the shower. Still other evenings he was quiet and distant.

Tessa chewed her lip and wondered what was in store for her tonight. Her nerves were shot from playing the "Which husband do I get tonight?" game. When he pulled into the driveway, she'd brace herself, wondering if it was going to be a pleasant night or if she and Ronnie would play in the nursery until the baby's bedtime to avoid a confrontation. She looked out the window at the front lawn that had been brittle with autumn frost early this morning. It was bright outside now, the leaves rich shades of crimson and gold, but in late October, nighttime came earlier and earlier, making everything a grayish-purple shadow of itself. It would be too dark to dodge Ken by taking Ronnie for a stroll around the neighborhood. Tonight, after seeing patients until eight o'clock, he would likely come home in a dour mood. He'd rarely stayed at the office all night since she found out about the nitrous oxide, only once or twice since that day. They'd fought after those nights, but Ken swore he was trying and begged her forgiveness and patience.

She hated this roller coaster. But she'd promised Ken some time to figure things out. She'd given him the names of a few grief counselors, one of whom was the woman who helped her teaching colleague through her father's unexpected death. Tessa knew Ken was trying to fix this. Or this was what she told herself. It was a slippery slope. The more vehement she was that Ken seek counseling, the more he opposed the idea. On his "good" days, sometimes he was the one who brought it up. When he did, Tessa seized the opportunity and gently tried to sway him into reaching the conclusion on his own. It was exhausting.

The worst part was how alone she felt. She couldn't talk to anyone about this. She had inexplicable shame about what Ken was doing, like it was her secret, not just his. She'd known people in college who smoked pot, some who did every day. She even knew people who occasionally used cocaine, but, harmful as that was, it was a social activity people did at parties to fit in. Ken's habit was darker and more detached than drinking or social drug use.

And, of course, Tessa was all too familiar with alcoholism.

She crossed the kitchen to the sink and ran warm water onto a soft dish cloth. She wiped Ronnie's face and hands as the baby tossed her head left and right. Ronnie screeched and stretched out her arms toward her mother, her nonverbal "hold me!" command. Tessa unlatched the high chair tray, lifted her daughter, and kissed the feathery hair on her head. With Ronnie on her hip, she put her plate and coffee mug in the sink. She gazed at the ceramic coffee mug and was transported to a day more than twenty years earlier.

No. This isn't the same as that. He's not addicted. He can stop.

One morning when Tessa was eight years old, she sat at the kitchen counter eating a "dippy egg" and an English muffin with grape jelly. Sal had hastily prepared her breakfast and told her to finish eating and wait for him outside to take her to school. Her two brothers had already eaten and were outside throwing a football around while they waited.

Tessa hadn't thought anything of Sal's claim that Caroline wasn't feeling well. Caroline often didn't feel well. Tessa suggested to her on more than one occasion that she take the fruity vitamins that Tessa took with her milk every morning. Tessa doted on her mother when she was sick in bed, bringing her tea and extra blankets. Usually Caroline just slept, and Tessa would return hours later to the dark room to find her mother's still figure, the tea and blankets untouched.

So, when Sal hurried upstairs to check on his wife, Tessa finished eating and carried her dishes to the sink. At the time, Sal owned a restaurant across town. Longing to work there one day, Tessa wanted to prove she could clean up the kitchen. As she set her plate and glass on the counter, an unfamiliar smell wafted up from the sink. It was strong and perfumy, and Tessa didn't recognize it. She wrinkled her nose and looked around. The only other item in the sink was her mother's mug, about a third filled with black coffee. She picked it up to rinse it, and the odor hit her square in the face. Furrowing her brow, she bent her head and inhaled deeply. The strong smell stung her eyes. Shrugging her shoulders, she poured the remaining liquid down the drain, rinsed her dishes, and put everything in the dishwasher. Then Tessa gathered her school supplies, put on her sneakers, and joined her brothers outside to wait for her dad.

Now Tessa stared into the distance and held her own coffee mug in her trembling hand. She recalled the exact moment when she realized what had been in her mother's coffee cup all those years ago. She was sixteen and at a party at Katie McMahon's in Yellow Tree Hill, about three miles from Tessa's house. Katie's parents were in New York for the weekend. Though her parents' liquor cabinet was well-stocked, Katie made it clear that guests should bring their own beverages. She swore her father measured the liquid level in each bottle. Before they drove away, Katie said he'd issued a stern warning, wagging his finger at his daughter, "Behave if you don't want to be grounded until you're twenty-five."

The party didn't get too out of control. Katie only invited about a dozen people, and everyone stayed overnight, something Katie wisely insisted on. It was just after ten when a few football players showed up hooting and hollering, "The captain is in the house!" They produced several two-liter bottles of Coke from their grocery store bags and three bottles of Captain Morgan Rum from a brown sack. They promptly went about mixing the rum and soda and pouring it into paper cups. Someone passed a cup to Tessa, and she raised it to her lips.

The smell almost knocked her over. She knew she'd never drunk this concoction before, but she was having a bizarre déjà vu experience that made her strangely uncomfortable.

Much later that night, Tessa, tipsy, lay in a sleeping bag on Katie's bedroom floor next to her friend Izzy. Tessa was in the middle of telling her she'd kissed Bruce Stanton on the back porch earlier, when she suddenly realized that rum was what she had smelled in her mother's morning coffee mug several years earlier.

By the night of Katie's party, Caroline was long gone.

Ronnie's fussing brought Tessa back from her reverie. Tessa prepared a bottle before the baby's afternoon nap. As she drank, Ronnie reached up and played with her mother's nose. Tessa held her daughter close. She'd worked so hard to repair the smoldering wound Caroline had left in the pit of her stomach. Now Ken's actions threatened to reignite the flame. She couldn't fight the feeling that the tighter she held on to the people she loved, the easier it seemed for them to let her go.

Chapter Ten

Tessa's dismayed expression stared back at her from the bathroom mirror. After cleansing and splashing water on her face, she dabbed her cheeks, forehead, and chin dry with her flowered hand towel and applied a nighttime moisturizer. She brushed her teeth and ran a comb through her hair. *Not that Ken would notice, even if I swung into the bedroom naked on a trapeze.* Shedding her clothes and throwing them in the wicker hamper, she grabbed her pink-and-white plaid pajamas from a hook on the back of the bathroom door.

Before going to her bedroom, Tessa checked on Ronnie. The baby slept peacefully on her belly, her thumb in her mouth and diapered bottom sticking up in the air. Tessa touched Ronnie's smooth cheek before pulling the nursery door closed.

Ken had come home around eight as promised, but his demeanor was frigid. He'd ignored Tessa, refused dinner, and gone straight to the bathroom. After showering, he'd retreated to the bedroom and didn't come out. That was three hours ago.

Tessa had gone about her usual evening routine of putting the house back into order. After cleaning up the kitchen, she picked up Ronnie's playthings and put them in the toy box. She folded the powder-blue chenille throw blanket and arranged the sofa pillows neatly, their structured order a striking contradiction to the disarray in her life.

The noise in her head thwarted her attempts to read or watch TV, so she gave up and decided to go to bed. She turned off all the lights and started down the hallway to the master bedroom. The door was closed; she paused and considered knocking but realized that would be outright bizarre. Reticently, she pushed the door open.

Ken was sitting up in bed, leafing through a magazine. He was wearing a Drexel School of Dentistry T-shirt, the beige sheet and floral comforter pulled up to the middle of his chest. The image of her husband in bed alone reading in his dental school T-shirt somehow made a lump form in Tessa's throat.

She looked at her feet. "Hi." She closed the door and took a step forward. "I didn't know you were still up. I didn't know what you . . ." She trailed off and shifted her weight from one foot to the other.

"Hi." Ken put down the magazine, and Tessa saw it was *Car and Driver*. The earlier coldness gone, his expression was soft, even loving. Or was she just imagining that?

She moved toward the bed. "What are you doing?" They both looked at the magazine and smiled at the obvious answer.

Ken tossed the magazine aside. "I was looking at SUVs." He tilted his head and studied her. "But I feel like doing something else." He extended his hand, which Tessa accepted as she sat down on the bed. They sat that way for a long moment, not looking at each other, so much hanging like fog in the air between them. Finally, Ken turned to her and tenderly brushed a strand of her hair back that had fallen over her left cheek. His blue eyes searched hers as he pulled his shirt over his head, then raised Tessa's arms to remove her pajama top. She reached for him, and he pulled her down next to him and removed her bottoms.

He kissed her softly and rubbed his hands on her breasts, down her stomach. Tessa hungrily returned his kisses and breathed in the scent of him. He smelled like mint and soap, a smell Tessa was always conscious of but at that moment felt drugged by. They shifted so he was on top of her. She arched her back. She needed to feel her husband's warm skin touching hers, needed to feel a comfort she wasn't sure existed anymore. Tessa lay underneath him and, overwhelmed with a range of desires—desire for Ken to be the man she married, desire to help him, desire to save her marriage and family, desire to save herself—a tear and then another escaped her eye and slid down into her ear.

Afterward, he held her tightly and kissed where the salt-water now ran freely down her face. "I know, Tess, I know, I know. It's going to be okay. I promise. It's all going to be okay."

She wept quietly.

He didn't know. And it wasn't all going to be okay.

Chapter Eleven

Business was typically slow at the Sunrise Diner after the winter holiday season, as if people had spent all their money, eaten all they could, and were just plain out of good cheer. Even the neighborhoods looked depressed. Deflated Santas and snowmen doubled over in half, their heads flopping drunkenly, hitting the ground with a thud every time a strong wind blew. Holiday lights, once carefully strung and held securely in place, hung loosely where they broke free from their clasps over windows and doors. Sal always said people went into hiding after Christmas when the credit card bills started rolling in. "It's a cruel irony. They stop going out to eat to help pay their bills, but that means less money for me to pay mine!"

Today Sal had a doctor's appointment and needed to leave the restaurant early, so Tessa offered to close up with the other employees. She was glad to get out of the house and have something to occupy her mind for a few hours. Subbing at the high school was slow also this time of the year; the teachers just had a week off for the holidays, so they didn't take off many days in January and February. That would change when the weather warmed and the kids turned more rambunctious.

Tessa had taken Ronnie to Val's and would pick her up after she closed the diner. She didn't have to rely on Ken, so she could relax for the afternoon. Her brother Joey was coming over tonight to help Ken take down and dispose of their Christmas tree. Being at the diner took Tessa's mind off whether Ken would keep his word and show up at home on time to meet his brother-in-law. And if he did show up, would his appearance arouse Joey's suspicion? More than once she'd caught her brother studying Ken's dilated pupils and the marks beside his nose, which were often red and sore. She never knew what she was in for. Sometimes he acted like his old self: pleasant, loving, and trustworthy. Other times he was sullen and combative—if he showed up at all. The roulette game wore Tessa out.

With just a few minutes left until closing time, Tessa, Linda, and Maggie—a new hire—were almost finished cleaning up. Maggie, who wore a different brightly colored headband in her short black hair every day and took orders with pens adorned with feathers and rubber cartoon character tips, shadowed Linda as the veteran server showed her the ropes.

Tessa methodically carried near-empty tureens of soup, chili, and gravy, their rich comforting aromas wafting from the pots to the kitchen. In the dining room, a group of three was finishing their lunch of tomato soup and grilled cheese sandwiches. A figure bundled in a bulky coat crossed the parking lot, the door chime sounded, and a woman entered. Linda and Maggie were in the middle of a conversation about Maggie's new boyfriend. "I know he's safe and dependable," Maggie sighed. "But girls don't like safe and dependable. They like bad-boy rule breakers." She stuffed some napkins into an empty dispenser.

"Is that a fact?" Linda looked skeptical as she unscrewed the lids on empty sugar containers. "Then how come there are so many married accountants?"

Tessa cleared her throat to get their attention. She nodded toward the woman and looked expectantly at the girls.

"Never fails," Linda lamented, out of earshot of the customer. "We're all but cleaned up, and someone straggles in five minutes before we close."

"You guys keep at it." Tessa grabbed a pad and pen. "I'll get her."

The woman sat in a booth facing the door and unfolded a newspaper. Her light brown hair was tucked up in a baseball cap, and she wore large sunglasses. She shrugged out of her heavy suede coat but left it around her shoulders. Taking a newspaper and red pen out of her purse, she inspected the table for a menu.

Tessa approached her. "Hi, what can I get you? We're about to close, but I can make you something simple."

Behind her glasses, the woman studied Tessa for a long moment. "Oh . . . sorry. I just . . . assumed you'd be open all day. How about a cup of coffee and whatever kind of pie or muffin you have today?" She folded the newspaper into neat sections so the classifieds were on top.

"Sure," Tessa responded. "We have coconut custard and apple pie, and I think there are a few blueberry muffins left."

"Coffee and coconut custard pie sounds great." The woman continued fussing with her paper but watched Tessa walk behind the counter.

Tessa returned a minute later with a steaming mug of coffee and a slice of pie piled high with whipped cream. The lady didn't look up. She held her head with one hand and circled ads for apartments with the other.

Tessa cocked her head and tried to get a better look at the woman's downturned face. "Are you new in town?"

"Oh, no. Well, kind of." The woman opened a creamer and emptied it into her coffee. Stirring it, she added, "I used to live around here, but I've been out of the area for a while. I'm thinking about moving back." She took a sip and searched the newspaper page.

Tessa lingered at the table for a moment. She pointed at a listing the woman had circled. "I know that apartment complex. It's nice. It's next to a park. My baby and I go to Mommy and

Me classes every other Wednesday at the library right across the street. Sometimes we walk in the park afterward."

"Look at you." The woman smiled shyly and studied the listing. "You run a restaurant and dabble in real estate too." She took a bite of the fluffy pie, and a bit of whipped cream stuck to her upper lip.

Tessa's face reddened, and she raised her hands, palms out, to correct the woman's assertion. "Oh, no, actually, I don't do either. This is my parents' place. I'm just helping out today."

"Your parents' place. Huh." The woman's eyes darted around behind her glasses. "Are they here?"

"No." Across the room, Linda made a circular *let's go* motion with her arm. The other customers had left, and the girls were finished preparing their stations for the next day. Tessa wiped her hands on her apron and turned back to the woman. "Well, I'll let you get back to it. Good luck."

Tessa walked behind the counter, and Linda handed her a stack of guest checks. "We finished cleaning, filling, and sweeping, your majesty. May my ugly step-sister and I be excused?" She genuflected dramatically.

Tessa missed the comradery with Sal's employees. Raising her eyebrows, she joined in the fun. "Did you sweep the chimney and mend all my party dresses?"

"Yes, fair queen. And I darned your darn stockings."

Tessa dismissed Linda with a snobby hand wave, and both women giggled. "Well, then you are excused." She glanced toward the woman in the booth. "I'm sorry. I kept you here later than necessary. I shouldn't have chatted her up like that. Go ahead and leave. I'll tally the checks while she finishes her pie and clean up after her."

"What is she, some kind of celeb? What's with the shades?" Linda studied the woman as she untied her apron.

"Well, she chose the sunniest booth in the place. She probably has spring fever like the rest of us."

"She's been eyeing you up. Maybe she doesn't like the pie. Or maybe she loves it and is trying to figure out the recipe so she can open a rival diner next door and force Sal out of business." Linda rubbed her hands together sinisterly.

"No." Tessa shook her head. "My guess is she thinks I need to mind my own business. She's looking at potential apartments, and I put in my two cents."

"Ha!" Linda winked. "If she wants to be where people mind their own business, she came to the wrong place." She shrugged into her wool coat and pulled on gloves with little faces at the end of each finger. She smiled at Tessa. "Bye, Tess. Always good to see you. Tell Sal we didn't break anything or start any fires while he was gone."

"He has the utmost confidence in his loyal staff!" Tessa followed the women to the back door and locked it behind them.

After Linda and Maggie left, Tessa went through the slips and counted and bagged the money in the register. She would put everything in the safe in Sal's office after the woman left and she locked the front door.

The customer looked up. Appearing to grasp that she was the only person left in the diner besides Tessa, she hurriedly glanced at her check, removed some bills from her purse, and laid them on the table. She patted her lips with a napkin and gathered up her newspaper. "Thanks. Sorry for holding you up. Keep the change." She headed for the door.

"No problem at all. Maybe we'll see you again."

Tessa looked anxiously at the wooden clock on her living room wall for the tenth time in an hour. She finished feeding Ronnie her bedtime bottle and gently patted her daughter's back. *I'm going to kill him.*

It was almost eight o'clock. Joey would be there any minute.

Every year after the holidays, Ken and Joey took down all the family Christmas trees and removed them from the houses. They all loved having huge fresh holiday trees decorated with thousands of twinkling lights and dozens of colorful ornaments—until it was time to take them down and get rid of them. Ken and Joey always did the honors. Sal Jr. was single and didn't bother decorating his one-bedroom apartment, a decision Joey applauded his older brother for every year at this time. Joey had a midsize Ford truck with an open bed in the back, so he was the designated transporter of all items too large for a regular car trunk. Last weekend they'd disposed of Joey's and their parents' trees, and Ken had asked Joey to stop over tonight to remove their ten-foot Fraser Fir.

He said he'd be home before eight.

Tessa's shoulders tensed as Joey's bright headlights swung into the dark driveway. Dampness spread under her arms and on the back of her neck. After laying Ronnie in her Pack-and-Play, she pulled open the front door and gave her brother a hug. Pasting on her best smile, she waved him inside.

"Hey, Sis. Freakin' freezing out there." Joey blew into his hands, fisted in front of his mouth. He pulled down his hood to reveal black hair, which he wore in a buzz cut. He goofily rubbed the top of his head and said in a feminine voice, "Ooh, that hood messes up my fancy hairdo!" He gestured toward the driveway and Ken's empty parking space. "Where's the good doctor?"

Tessa's gaze wandered nonchalantly out of the foyer. "Umm . . . He must be on his way. I just tried to call him and—"

Just then Ronnie, rolling around in her Pack-and-Play, squealed with delight at the sound of a visitor. Joey forgot his question and turned his attention to her. "Hey, Peanut! You're still up!" He pushed past Tessa and scooped up his niece, who laughed and clapped at her uncle. She grabbed his nose, and he feigned agony. "Owww!" Joey pretended to cry, which drove the seventh-month-old into hysterics. "Keepin' some late hours, huh, kid?" He glanced back at his sister. "Just like your dad."

Tessa chuckled nervously and panic gripped her. These were the most stressful times for her—when she and Ken were supposed to be somewhere together or, instances like tonight, when someone showed up at their house and Ken was conspicuously absent. She hated having to invent plausible explanations for his whereabouts. It killed her to lie to her family and friends.

But she had to, at least for now. She had to keep things together. Someone had to. She felt like an angry mob was pounding at her front door, and she was inside, leaning against it with all her might, throwing her shoulder against it again and again, desperate to keep them away from the secrets inside. They'd force the door open an inch or so, but she'd manage to slam it shut again before they could see anything damning.

Ken was livid when Tessa suggested they talk to her parents or anyone else about his problem. He even fumed when she referred to his nitrous oxide use as a problem. "It's not a *problem!*" he'd snarl. "A problem is when you can't stop. I *can* stop! I just need you to get off my back and let me figure things out!"

As Joey swung Ronnie through the air, Tessa felt the familiar weight pressing down on her, threatening to flatten her. She twirled a clump of her hair around her fingers and searched her brain. *Come on, think of something.*

A few weeks ago, when Val invited the family over for dinner, Ken hadn't come home from the office. Tessa finally left without him. She'd told her mother that Ken was Christmas shopping and he'd be there soon. When Val insisted on waiting for her son-in-law, Tessa knew she had to do something. Sal Jr. and Joey were already seated at the long dining room table. Tessa and Alyse, Joey's wife, were filling glasses with water and iced tea. Tessa excused herself to page her husband.

Fearing Ken wouldn't show up at all, Tessa, cursing under her breath, paged him with trembling hands. Val was consumed with finishing dinner, Gina and Tony noisily entertained Ronnie in her high chair, and Sal dozed in his recliner, waiting to be woken for dinner. Tessa slipped out of the room and walked downstairs to the den. Thinking fast, she picked up the cordless phone from a cherry end table, called Mariel, and told her that Sal and Val were having trouble with their phone service. Tessa hastily said they thought it was fixed, but they needed someone to call the house and see if the ringer was working. They both hung up, and Mariel called right back. Tessa thanked her and said it was working fine now, and they hung up again.

That is, Mariel hung up. Tessa continued talking, pretending that when the phone had rung, it was Ken responding to her page. "Hey, babe, dinner's ready. Where are you?" For good measure, she walked with the cordless phone back to the kitchen area. "Oh, really? That bad, huh?"

Val pulled a tray of lasagna out of the oven and looked quizzically at her daughter. "What?" she mouthed. She closed the oven door with her knee.

Tessa moved the mouthpiece under her chin and answered her mother. "He's stuck at the mall. He said the crowds and lines are fierce." Turning her attention back to the phone, she sighed into the dead air. "Well, okay, if you're sure. I'll ask Mom to fix a plate for you, and I'll bring it home. Okay, love you too. Bye." She walked back toward the den to return the phone to its cradle, calling over her shoulder, "He said we should go ahead and eat. He's not sure how long he will be. I can take a plate home to warm up later."

Val shook her head as she mixed the salad. "These damn holidays. I love them, but they take a toll on everyone."

Joey listened to this exchange and stole a look at his wife. Alyse gave him a *don't start anything* look and unfolded her napkin on her lap.

Tessa, not for the first time, marveled at how easy it was becoming to concoct these elaborate lies, like an actress in a bizarre live impromptu stage performance.

Now she watched Joey playing with Ronnie next to the dried-up Christmas tree and knew it was showtime again.

Chapter Twelve

Ken's mood matched the cold gray January day. Draining his fourth cup of coffee, he set the mug down hard on his desk. He rubbed angrily at a scratch on the cherry finish. Earlier that morning, he'd chastised Tracy for a billing error. The girl was near tears after his diatribe. His reaction had not fit the minor infraction, and he knew his irritability had caused it. He had a nagging cough that wasn't helping either. Rubbing his temples, he regained his composure before entering the exam room, where Brenda was finishing a routine cleaning.

"He's all yours, Dr. C. Everything looks good."

Ken wordlessly pulled on his gloves and fastened his mask. He pulled up the stool next to Evan, a quiet thirtyish man dressed in a burgundy button-down shirt and khaki pants. The patient, arms folded on his chest, addressed Ken with a nod and closed his eyes. Ken was glad for this. He wasn't in the mood for small talk.

"Open," Ken instructed. He pulled back the man's lips and cheeks with a retractor and inspected the inside of his mouth, gently probing each tooth. "Your teeth look good. I don't see any problems. You floss every day?"

Evan managed a garbled, "Yes."

"Good. I guess we'll see you in six months."

Satisfied, Ken sat back and started to remove his gloves. Another dry coughing spell seized him, and he turned away from Evan. His arm caught the tray of instruments that Brenda had swung over next to him. A few of the metal tools bounced from the tray and clanged noisily to the floor.

"What the—" Ken glared at Brenda, who scrambled to pick up the instruments. "Could you put the tray any closer to me?"

Evan's face reddened, and he shot Brenda a sympathetic look. Ken mumbled a hurried good-bye to his patient, stood up, and left the room.

As he retreated to his private office, he heard Brenda making a flustered apology.

"Don't worry about it," Evan reassured her. "Everyone has off days."

Several minutes later, Ken was reviewing charts when he heard a noise in the doorway. He looked up to find Brenda, fidgeting with a box of gloves in her hands.

"Err, sorry about that, Ken. But I always position the tray in the same place so you can reach the instruments easily —"

"Well, maybe you put this one a little too close to me." He threw a chart down on the desk. "Way to make me look like an amateur."

She bit her lip. "I don't think it was that big of a deal. Neither did Evan," she said softly.

"Well, I do! Try to be more careful." Dismissing her, Ken looked back at his paperwork. Brenda backed out of the doorway.

Ken looked toward the locked supply closet.

Calm down, boy. You just have to get through two more patients.

He closed his eyes. Tessa would be mad at him tonight, but, what the hell, she was always mad at him lately. They'd gotten through the holidays and Ronnie's first Christmas, but the atmosphere in their house was as frosty as the weather. The hectic activity of the holidays camouflaged Ken's disappearances a bit, but he couldn't rely on that any longer. Last week when he left Joey stranded with the Christmas tree, Tessa was furious. He'd slipped up that day. He'd forgotten to set the alarm. She'd stayed mad this time. Her eyes barely met his, and she only spoke to him in front of other people when she couldn't avoid it. Even when they were alone, if she absolutely had to talk to him, it was in a businesslike way that was, in its dispassion, worse than anger.

Even before the tree incident, Tessa had been pressing him harder than ever to seek professional help. She'd moved on from suggesting grief counseling to pushing substance abuse counseling. Substance abuse! She treated him like a common drug addict.

What happened to my supportive wife? I give her everything. I just bought her a diamond bracelet for Christmas. Can't I have this one thing?

He stifled a cough and walked into the exam room to greet his next patient.

Brenda and Tracy silently rode the elevator to the building's ground floor. They turned right down the corridor toward the exit to the parking lot. Brenda, the distance between her and her boss shifting her earlier submission to anger, spoke first.

"God! He can be such an asshole!" She swung her suede fringed purse over her shoulder and shoved her hands deep into her coat pockets. "I'm definitely opening a bottle of red tonight. Maybe two!" She was bothered on several fronts; on one hand she was pissed at how Ken reacted, and on another, she was pissed that she cared.

Tracy lowered her eyes. "It's so strange. It's like he has multiple personalities or something." She shivered as the winter wind blew the hair into her eyes. "You never know how he's going to act from day to day. Last week I botched an insurance claim so badly he was on the phone for thirty minutes trying to straighten it out. I cringed the entire time, dreading the reprimand I was sure was coming." Tracy shook her head as if to erase the painful memory. "But when he hung up the phone, he calmly explained what I did wrong and walked me through the process to fix it. Today I make a much smaller, much more easily fixable mistake, and he blows his stack!"

Brenda leaned against her dark green Toyota Camry and stared at the gray clouds overhead. On the highway next to them, cars sped by, heading to unknown destinations west of town. "I know! Did you hear him rip my head off today when *he* knocked those instruments on the floor?" Fuming, she kicked at some gravel. "And have you noticed how pale he looks?"

"Well, it is January in Pennsylvania," Tracy joked. "We don't exactly look like Bahama Mamas ourselves."

Brenda was shaking her head. "No, it's more than that. Like the color has permanently drained from his face. And his eyes. Sometimes he looks, I don't know, out of it. And he's got those sore marks on his nose. What's up with that?"

"Yeah, I know. I asked him about them, and he said they're from the goggles he wears when he makes molds in the lab. Oh. You know what? He's been coughing for several weeks too. Do you think it's possible that he has . . . that he's, you know, sick or something?" She clutched the collars of her coat together against the biting air. "What if it's something like that, and here we are bitching about him?"

Brenda was only half listening. She was thinking about Tessa, who rarely stopped by the office anymore. She used to bring Ronnie in to see Ken, or pick up lunch that they would eat together in the break room. Though she kept it to herself, Brenda thought Tessa was too much of a goody-goody for Ken. *Trouble in paradise?*

She looked at Tracy. "I don't know. I guess it's possible. But something tells me that's not it. There is definitely something going on, but I don't think that's it."

"What do you think it is?"

Overhead, a plane rumbled through the clouds, leaving a trail of gray exhaust behind it that would soon disappear, erasing any trace that it had been there at all. Brenda glanced up at the second-floor windows of Ken's office. She hit the remote to unlock her car. "I don't know. But I'm going to find out."

Chapter Thirteen

Ken cursed his stupidity. *How did I let this happen?*
The employee at the nitrous oxide supply company on the other end of the phone made a rapid clicking sound with his tongue that set Ken's teeth on edge. He could hear the guy using his computer mouse to scroll through the dental office's account.

"Hmm."

Ken tried to contain his frustration. "What? Can I get a delivery today or not?" He dropped into Tracy's chair at the reception desk. A framed photo of her Yorkshire terrier fell with a clang facedown onto the desk. He checked his watch. Almost one. He still had several hours before Tessa expected him home. As far as he could tell, she bought the story that Wednesday was his late night with patients. He made a mental note to remember to position the mask so that it didn't dig into the sides of his nose. That was a dead giveaway.

"Well, our records show you just had a delivery last week. You are only scheduled for once a month and—"

"I know when my last delivery was! I'm telling you I need more. I'm trying to run a business here." Ken coughed and covered his mouth with his hand. He willed himself to calm down. "Look, I'm sorry, um, what did you say your name is?"

"I didn't. It's Stan."

"I'm sorry, Stan." Ken turned on the charm. "It's just been very busy here. Lots of root canals and crowns. The gas calms my anxious patients."

"I understand. But our trucks are already out." He paused, and Ken could hear more scrolling, more clicking. "I can put you on the schedule for first thing tomorrow morning. What time do you—"

"That's not good enough!" Ken paced the carpeted floor. He looked wildly at his watch again. "I'll come down there and pick it up myself. How about that?"

Stan was quiet for a moment. "Uh, well, I guess that's okay if it's what you want to do. We're open until five. Bring your practitioner's card and another form of photo ID."

"Fine. I'll be there in twenty minutes."

Stan hung up the phone. He drummed his fingers on the gray laminated desktop. His chair creaked loudly, straining against his weight as he leaned back and linked his fingers behind his blond head of unkempt hair. He stared up at the fluorescent lights in the stained drop ceiling tiles, a collection of dead flies inside dotting the panel covers. Formulating a theory, he moved the mouse around on the counter and brought the computer screen to life again. He leaned in close to the screen, the fringes of a question nagging him. Pecking the keyboard, he reentered his username and password to gain access to customer records. Then he typed in *Kenneth Cordelia, D.M.D.* and chose the "last six months" option to view the dentist's account activity. He read over it three times, a smile spreading across his face, realization shaping a plan in his mind.

Relishing the moment, Stan leaned back again and folded his hands on his abdomen.

He opened the desk drawer and removed a round plastic pill bottle. He'd been careful lately to use the little jewels sparingly. They'd been hard to come by. Sensing that this was not going to be a problem much longer, he tilted the bottle and tapped it against his hand until a capsule fell out. He popped it into his mouth, threw his head back, and swallowed.

Just then Corky, a driver with shoulder-length wavy brown hair and a goatee, strode in from the warehouse. After pulling off his gloves with his teeth, he unzipped a letter-sized notebook and grabbed some papers from a pocket inside. He regarded Stan as he rolled a thick rubber band off a stack of signed invoices and tossed them into a metal bin labeled "Accounts Receivable."

"What's that shit-eating grin for?"

"Here." He lobbed the bottle at Corky. "Enjoy. I think I found us a new Candy Man."

Chapter Fourteen

"Are you watching this?"

Ken didn't look up. Slouched on the sofa, bleary-eyed and unfocused, he stared at the TV without blinking. Clad in a sweatshirt and faded jeans, he appeared more boyish to Tessa than his thirty-two years. "Huh?"

"Are you watching this? Do you mind if I change the channel?" Tessa barely looked at him. Though it was almost eleven o'clock, she was too keyed-up to go to bed. She picked up the remote control from the coffee table. As she brushed by Ken, he protectively cradled a rocks glass in his hands. The ice cubes clinked together as he raised it to his lips.

"No." He waved a hand in the air. "Go ahead. Put on whatever you want." Struggling to pull himself up to a sitting position, he drained his drink. He was only wearing one sock. He pointed to the glass. "I'm going to have another. You want anything?"

"You're going—" Tessa stopped herself and shook her head. "No, I don't want anything."

She watched Ken walk into the kitchen, listened as he unscrewed the cap on the whiskey bottle and refilled his glass, the liquid sloshing against the sides like the inside of a washing machine. Tessa sat motionless and waited for him to reenter the living room, a seemingly endless stretch of time in which her mind traveled over the miles and miles of terrain it took for them to arrive at this juncture. She pinched the bridge of her nose. *When did one or two glasses of wine turn into several? And then the whole bottle? And when did wine become a glass of whiskey? And then two? And then this?*

An image from an autumn afternoon many years ago took shape in her mind. Sal Jr. had called their father at the restaurant and told him Caroline wouldn't get out of bed. It was dinnertime, and they were hungry. Sal raced home with sandwiches for Tessa and her brothers. He climbed the stairs, unaware that Tessa had followed him. She'd sat outside the bedroom door, hugging her knees to her chest, picking up only a few muffled phrases from her dad: " . . . said you'd try . . . have three kids . . . do it for them?" He emerged from the room minutes later, face crumpled, startled when he saw his daughter. He'd put his arms around her, and Tessa could feel her heart thudding against his.

The ice cubes clinked again as Ken returned, unsteady on his feet. He sat down heavily on the love seat next to Tessa. She hugged a throw pillow close to her and looked straight ahead.

"Come on, babe. Have a drink with your husband." He nuzzled her cheek playfully, his whiskey-laced breath hot on her neck. He traced a finger down the silky sleeve of her pajamas. "You look nice in these." He put his arm around her shoulder, and a few drops splashed out of his glass onto her top.

She pushed him away. "Great. Now I can go to bed smelling like booze." Tessa heard the bitchy edge in her voice, but she didn't care. She brushed her hand over the wet spot. "That makes two of us."

"Don't be like that." Ken's eyes were half-closed, and his voice was thick. He took another sip and wiped his mouth on the back of his hand.

Tessa felt like she was at school about to lecture a student about making poor choices. On the TV, a commercial ad for a gym boasted that, for just $9.99 a month, it wasn't too late to look and feel great for the summer. Tessa idly wondered if she'd ever feel great again, no matter the season.

She didn't want to set Ken off, but she couldn't avoid it any longer. She exhaled deeply, knowing she was venturing into the briar patch. "Ken, I know you're trying to stop doing the gas and be home more. You want to get things under control on your own, without professional help, and I'm trying to see it your way and give you the space you need, I really am." She paused, stole a quick look at him, and smoothed her pajama top. Glancing at his whiskey glass, she continued, "But don't you think you've been drinking an awful lot lately?"

Ken's jaw tensed. His narrowed eyes, more focused now, drilled sharp holes into her.

She cleared her throat and turned to face him. "I've been reading some of the brochures I collected for you. I'm worried that you're trading one vice for—"

Ken, fully alert now, slammed the glass down on the coffee table and raked his fingers through his hair. "Oh, here we go. Wait, Mrs. Cordelia, shouldn't I be sitting in the principal's office for this? How many hours of detention do I get? Are you going to call my—" His slurred words trailed off, and Tessa closed her eyes, stung by her husband's cruelty. Stumbling to his feet, he grabbed the arm of the love seat to steady himself. "Christ, it never ends."

As he raised his voice, Tessa instinctively peeked toward the short hallway that led to Ronnie's bedroom.

Ken waved his arms wildly. "What? You think I'm going to wake up the baby with a drunken rant? Let's add that to my list of transactions . . . transgressions . . . whatever." His head lolled to one side. "Fuck it. I'm going out." He jammed his feet into his loafers by the love seat.

Alarmed, Tessa sat up abruptly. "Out? Out where? You can hardly walk, let alone drive!" She rose and followed him to the front door. She took his arm as he grabbed his trench coat from a hook on the wall. His arm brushed a framed photo of Ronnie hanging on the wall as he roughly pulled away from Tessa. It rocked back and forth on its nail like a pendulum on a grandfather clock, Ronnie's bright blue eyes and toothless grin swaying disconcertingly with the movement. He shrugged into the jacket and groped around in the pockets for his keys. Tessa moved between Ken and the door.

Ken glared at her. "Get outta my way. Now."

Shaking, she swallowed hard. "Ken, you're drunk. You can't drive. Where are you even going?"

He leaned against the wall. "Move."

"Don't go. Please." Her voice was barely audible. She felt small, childlike. *Don't leave me.*

But he reached past her and yanked open the front door. Tessa shivered as the cold night air blew through the thin material of her pajamas. She hugged herself tightly and stood rooted in the open doorway. She stayed that way as Ken got into his car and started the ignition. She stayed that way as he backed out of the driveway and drove down Orchard View Street and out of sight.

In the distance, she could make out the silhouette of a new condominium complex. She'd read in the newspaper that the modern buildings had eight floors containing six units each, making them the tallest residences in the surrounding area. People who worked in King of Prussia and even Philadelphia bought them, a more affordable option that allowed them to work in the city but live in the suburbs. From a few of the units near the top, dim lights shone, and Tessa imagined their occupants watching TV, paying bills, making love.

Staring at the high buildings, it occurred to her there were many ways to fall. You could climb to the roof in broad daylight and move dramatically to the edge, garnering attention from horrified onlookers below, before gracefully swan diving—back arched, arms in a perfect V—through the air. Or you could stumble onto the roof in the dark of night, unbeknownst to anyone, hurl yourself over the side, and plummet rapidly, turning clumsily end over end.

It really didn't matter.

The outcome when you hit the pavement below was the same.

The next morning was crisp and sunny; birds chirped in the trees, promising the approach of spring. Shortly after eight o'clock, Tessa had just finished feeding Ronnie and was changing her diaper. In the nursery, she worked methodically. She dressed her daughter in a denim jumper, a pink striped shirt, heavy ribbed tights, and a soft cloth headband. The baby squirmed and knocked over a powder bottle, its contents emitting a puff of a smoke-like cloud as it hit the floor. Tessa covered the baby's eyes and pulled them away quickly to distract her. "Peek-a-boo!" she shrieked, and Ronnie erupted into laughter. The game precluded Tessa from hearing the front door open.

Carrying her daughter in her arms, she approached the front of the house, where the diaper bag was already packed and sitting by the door. Ken was in the foyer on his hands and knees, still dressed in his sweatshirt, jeans, and trench coat from last night. Through puffy eyes, he glanced up at his wife briefly and then vomited onto the hardwood floor. Humming, Tessa chose a sweater from a hook and put it on. She picked up her sunglasses and keys from the table and dropped them into her pocket.

"Tess," groaned Ken. "Get me a bucket. I'm sick."

Tessa started softly singing a song she and Ronnie had heard on *Sesame Street* yesterday. "Who are the people in your neighborhood, in your neighborhood, in your neighbor-hood?" Forgetting the next lines, she began humming the tune. She walked to the fridge and took out an insulated bag containing two bottles and a snack for Ronnie. She picked up the diaper bag and slung it over her shoulder. She stepped over Ken's coat sleeve, which was splattered with vomit. "Ready, kiddo?" She rubbed noses with her daughter.

Another moan escaped Ken's lips. "Tess, please. I had too much of the gas. I need help."

Moving past him, she opened the front door. She squinted into the sunlight and stepped onto the front porch. In the beds lining the walk, coneflowers she'd planted last year showed signs of resurgence. She didn't look back at him as she spoke. "Finally. Something we agree on."

Chapter Fifteen

The early April air had a chilly bite, and Tessa was glad she'd put Ronnie's heavy yellow hooded cable-knit sweater over her jumper. She fastened the belt on the stroller and handed her daughter her favorite toy, a red plastic telephone with a springy spirally cord. Not that the nine-month-old knew what to do with it, but she seemed to enjoy the feel of it on her gums as she chewed it. Shoving her small purse in the pocket on the back of the stroller, Tessa started off on the walking path that wound through the park. Ronnie pointed to various objects around her and looked back expectantly at her mother.

"Tree. Bird. Bike." Tessa dutifully named each object Ronnie poked her chubby finger toward. They'd just left Mommy and Me class at the local library where they'd—well, Tessa had—glued pointy bunny ears and pipe cleaners to a paper plate to fashion an Easter bunny with whiskers. The activity made Tessa more stressed about the upcoming holiday. She, Val, and Val's mother took turns hosting family holiday gatherings. Easter was Tessa's turn, and the prospect of having company in her house of secrets tied her stomach in knots.

The wheels on the stroller locked up, and she jiggled the handle to set them straight. Ahead, a young woman pushed her toddler on a green swing shaped like an airplane. The delighted toddler's hair rushed forward and backward around her face with the whooshing of the swing. To the left, an older man sat by a sandbox as a little boy and girl filled buckets, patted the sand down with their small shovels, and flipped them over. "Great work!" The man clapped and smiled. Ronnie dropped her phone and screeched as it hit the ground. As Tessa stooped to pick it up, a twentysomething woman in jogging attire ran by, her blonde ponytail swinging behind her in time with her graceful strides.

Tessa handed Ronnie her toy and tried to push the earlier scene at home from her mind. The thought of Ken—doubled over, throwing up all over the floor and himself—rattled her to her core. She'd had to get away from him, but guilt gnawed at her gut.

What kind of person am I?

It wasn't that she didn't feel sorry for him in the way a person feels sorry for anyone who is physically sick. But that sorrow had gradually moved aside over the last several months, making room for something else: anger. She was sick of Ken and his empty promises. She was sick of lying for him. She'd taken on the shame of her husband's actions and been avoiding her family and friends. She'd put far more effort into seeking out counselors for Ken than he had.

Still, her heart was heavy as she turned right on the path that ran next to a residential community. It wasn't like her to abandon someone in need. She knew all too well what that felt like, how lasting the damage could be. Once a girl in her English class fainted before a test. Tessa didn't know her that well but was so concerned about her she'd asked for coverage to monitor the students taking the exam so she could sit in the nurse's office with the sick girl. And last year when Val had the worst stomach flu of her life, Tessa slept at their house on the sofa for two nights in case her mother needed her help.

This is different. Ken is doing this to himself.

She thought again of Sal. Had he felt this way about Caroline? Had he started out sympathetic and supportive? Had those feelings turned to disgust and anger when she refused help? The night she'd left it was raining, a chilly gray drizzle. When Tessa asked her father why she'd gone, tears had stung his eyes, and he looked much older than his thirty-seven years. He offered a strangled explanation that Caroline was sick, that it wasn't anyone's fault. Tessa had never seen her father so broken.

No, she couldn't tell Sal that his daughter was now living the same nightmare he had all those years ago. It would kill him.

Ronnie bounced up and down in her seat and pointed at a flock of birds. Tessa cupped her hand over her eyes and looked upward at the object of her daughter's interest. Over Ronnie's clapping and laughing, Tessa almost didn't hear the voice that had approached her from behind.

"Must be Wednesday."

Tessa, blinded from staring toward the sun, squinted and looked in the direction the voice came from. She blinked several times as a figure came into focus. "Um . . . Are you talking to me?"

"Yes, I said it must be Wednesday." A woman wearing jeans, sneakers, a burgundy windbreaker with the hood up, and large sunglasses gestured toward the nearby library. "I'm guessing today is a Mommy and Me day."

The voice was familiar, and Tessa slowly identified it as belonging to the woman she had served in the diner a few months ago. "Oh, yes, hi . . . how did you—"

"Sorry, I didn't mean to startle you." The woman crouched down next to Ronnie, who tried to grab her sunglasses. "You recommended this apartment complex." She waved her hand behind her. "You said it was near a park and sometimes you and your baby take walks here after Mommy and Me on Wednesdays." She stood up.

Tessa recalled the conversation. "Oh, right!" Ronnie began throwing herself back and forth in her stroller. Tessa picked her up and wished Gina were here to keep Ronnie occupied with her rhymes and silly faces. "Okay, okay, are you hungry?" She turned back toward the woman and laughed. "Sorry, she'll only tolerate being contained for so long. Then I need to bust her out of there or she'll try to jump ship." She looked around quickly. "I'm going to give her a bottle. She's getting better with sippy cups, but I don't want to subject people to that in public yet. It's not pretty. She wears more than she drinks." She balanced Ronnie on her hip and directed the stroller toward a wooden bench along the side of the walking path. "Do you want to join us?"

The woman paused. "Uh, sure, why not?" They settled on the bench, and Tessa nudged a Minnie Mouse bib under Ronnie's chin. Ronnie began drinking, and Tessa turned to the woman.

"So, you decided to move here?"

"Yes. You are a good real estate agent," she teased. "I looked at a few places, but this one was the nicest for the money." She looked around the park, which had become busier in the last hour. "But you were right. The park was the selling, well, in my case, renting point. I take walks every day unless it's raining." The woman adjusted her sunglasses; her fingernails were cut short and painted royal blue. She fixed her gaze on the baby. "She's beautiful. Looks like . . . almost a year old? What's her name?"

"Thanks. Yes, she's almost ten months. Her name is Veronica, but we usually call her Ronnie. Funny, I always said I'd never give my kids nicknames. My brothers have teased me my whole life making nicknames out of my name. Messa. Yes'suh. It used to drive me crazy, but now I'm used to it." The woman listened pensively. Tessa shook her head. "God, I'm rambling. I'm not myself today. Rough morning. Speaking of names, despite what my pesky brothers call me, my actual name is Tessa. It's nice to see you again."

"You too. I'm CeCe." The woman noticed a pair of trim young mothers jogging, pushing their babies in strollers as they ran. She relaxed and crossed her right knee over her left. She nodded toward the joggers. "You prefer the traditional method?"

Tessa regarded them and groaned. She knew she'd get back in shape faster if she exercised more, and these wonder-woman moms made her self-conscious. She pictured them doing crunches while their babies napped, hamstring stretches while they fed them. "Yes. I don't run. In fact, if you ever see me running, you should run too because it means a bear is chasing me."

CeCe laughed. "Well, don't sweat it. I think you look great." She picked at a blue nail, then bent over and plucked a dandelion from the grass. "You had a rough morning, huh? The little angel keeping you up at night?"

"What? Oh, no. Ronnie sleeps like a rock. I just . . . I don't know." To her embarrassment, Tessa's voice cracked, and she felt a tear threatening the corner of her eye. She hoped CeCe didn't notice. She stroked Ronnie's delicate cheek, rosy from the brisk air. "I have a lot on my mind."

The two women sat silently for a few minutes, watching the activity in the park. Tessa finally spoke. "So, how do you like it here so far? It's not exactly a bustling metropolis, but it has its charms. And if it's bustle you want, you can be in King of Prussia in thirty minutes and Philly in an hour."

"I'm okay with quiet. I've had enough hustle and bustle to last a lifetime. I lived in Vegas for the last several years. I'm ready for the boring routine most people complain about."

Tessa frowned and nodded. "I could do with a little boring myself."

CeCe regarded Tessa thoughtfully. "I hope I'm not overstepping, but don't be too hard on yourself if you're having trouble adjusting to motherhood. It's not an easy job."

Tessa wiped Ronnie's chin. *Neither is marriage.* "Do you have kids?"

CeCe didn't answer right away. She pulled her hood tighter around her face and dug the toe of her sneaker into the grass in front of her. "Yes. But they're grown." Her lips curled upward, and Tessa couldn't tell if the smile was a happy or sad one. "I don't see them as much as I'd like."

A silver minivan, the poster-vehicle of young moms, pulled up at the curb next to the apartment complex. Two mothers and four toddlers spilled out of it. The kids ran squealing and jumping toward the playground equipment. Ronnie's head jerked up at the noise. Tessa dabbed at the baby's chin again and held up the bottle. "All done. Listen, I need to get her home for a nap." *And I have no idea what awaits me there.*

CeCe stood up. "Sure, sure. Don't let me keep you. I saw you and recognized you from the diner, and I wanted to thank you for the apartment recommendation. Here, let me help you." She took the bottle and bib from Tessa and stuffed them in the diaper bag while Tessa put Ronnie back in the stroller.

"Thanks." Tessa turned to CeCe. "Hey, look for us again here. I mean, if you want to. I'm sure you have better things to do." Tessa blushed and pushed her hair out of her eyes, but CeCe shook her head and spoke immediately.

"I will definitely do that. Nice talking to you."

"Good. Me too. Mommy and Me is the second and fourth Wednesday of the month." Tessa felt lighter than she had in months. Chatting with someone new improved her mood. She'd been feeling so alone. The realization that so much of her life now was dealing with and covering up Ken's problem drenched her like a sudden downpour. CeCe didn't know Tessa or anything about her, so she didn't have to guard her words or pretend. She didn't have to lie. It was liberating.

Tessa flung the bag over her shoulder and released the brake on the stroller. "This little one is going to start walking soon. She's already pulling herself up and trying a step or two. Of course, she quickly stumbles and falls like a sloppy drunk, but I guess you have to start somewhere." She laughed and tied Ronnie's hood under her chin.

"True." CeCe turned toward the apartments, and Tessa swore she saw regret cross the woman's lined face. "You have to start somewhere."

The sun had risen, and the office complex had not yet woken up for the day ahead. Brenda pulled into the parking lot and was about to get out of her car at the office when she saw a man leaving the building, head down, one hand covering his mouth. She leaned forward and thought she must be mistaken.

It was Ken.

She glanced at her watch. *What is he doing here this early? And where is he going?*

Brenda was ninety minutes earlier than her usual start time. Hank's car was in the shop, and she'd had to drive him to work that morning. He started work at the consulting firm every morning at 7 a.m., and instead of dropping him off and heading back home, she opted to come in to the office early to work on her recall list and organize her patient charts.

She didn't think Ken saw her when he exited the building and headed to his car at the opposite end of the parking lot. Not that he'd looked around at all. His hair was disheveled, and he was dressed in jeans and his long trench coat. He looked as though he was in a hurry.

Unsettled, Brenda changed her mind about going into the office. Instead, she drove the short five miles to her house. Her son was already at daycare, so the house was quiet and empty. Sunlight streamed in the kitchen window, casting beams across the tile floor. She made a cup of coffee and sat at the table, tracing her finger up and down the smooth ceramic handle. *What is going on with Ken?*

In the last few months, she and Tracy had walked on eggshells around him. They never knew which personality would walk through the door: jovial, kind Ken or his surly and argumentative twin. On his bad days, he forgot to make notes in charts and stared blankly at them when they spoke to him. He looked terrible, as though he hardly got any sleep. One day last week, he'd dropped the drill on the floor as he stretched the hose toward a patient who needed a filling. The patient, a fifteen-year-old boy, didn't seem particularly bothered by it, but Brenda was taken aback. She'd been on high alert for clues to explain his bizarre behavior, but so far she'd come up empty.

The telephone rang and interrupted her thoughts. She looked at the clock. Just before eight. "Hello?"

"Hey, it's Tracy."

Brenda held her breath. "What's wrong?"

"Nothing, unless you consider having the day off wrong. Dr. C. just called me. He's sick and won't be in today."

Brenda wrapped the phone cord around her fingers. The phone suddenly felt heavy, too heavy to hold. "Sick? Sick how?"

"He said he has the flu. He asked me to call you. He wants one of us to go in and call today's patients and reschedule them."

Brenda considered telling Tracy about the scene she happened upon earlier but decided against it. No sense upsetting her coworker. Plus, she didn't want Ken to know she had seen him, and she wasn't sure Tracy wouldn't tell him. "Ummm . . . How did he sound?"

"He sounded like he has the flu." Tracy's voice was muffled, as though she was balancing the phone between her chin and shoulder, and Brenda could hear a coffee maker gurgling to life. "So, I'll go in and reschedule—"

"No." Brenda was careful to keep her voice at a normal pitch. "I'll do it. I'm dressed and ready to go. I wanted to work on some recalls anyway."

"Okay, if you insist. Luke DeCulva is our first appointment at nine, so make sure you get to him before he leaves the house. And don't stay in there all day. Enjoy the time off!" Tracy hung up.

Brenda stood with the phone in her hand for a minute. She felt disoriented.

She thought about how stressful it was to be around Ken lately. She'd once read an article about people who lived with confused and moody senior citizens. The article said that sometimes the people who lived with them became confused and moody also, and before they knew it, one thing had the strangest way of blurring into another.

Chapter Sixteen

Brenda hung up the phone at the reception desk and drew a red line through the final name on the list. All the day's patients rescheduled, she leaned back in her chair and considered what to do next. She felt like she was standing at the entrance of a hay maze and had to choose one of the unfamiliar paths. Ken had been here early this morning, so maybe there were clues as to what he was doing. Not used to being alone in the office, she wandered from room to room, taking in her surroundings, unsure what she was looking for.

In her exam room, she ran her hand over the clear plastic headrest on the chair. Below it, the floor's surface shone in the bright morning sunlight, stretching out the shadow of the chair so it appeared distorted and twice its size. Sterilized tools in sealed bags lined the laminated countertop. A stack of charts stood neatly in one corner of the counter next to "gift" bags containing a toothbrush, toothpaste, and dental floss Brenda gave patients at the end of their appointments.

Next she moved to the doorway of Ken's private office. She hesitated there and glanced over her shoulder at the shadow-drenched hallway. Tentatively, she entered the office and sat in the gray upholstered chair behind Ken's desk. She ran her fingers over the smooth cherry edge. A framed photo of Ken and Tessa, tanned and relaxed, on a Caribbean island stood under the desk lamp. In the picture, Ken is behind Tessa, looking over her left shoulder with his arms clasped around her torso. Tessa casually drapes her arms over his, her large diamond gleaming on her left hand. Staring at the photo, Brenda felt a pang of something she couldn't identify, like waking up with a large purple bruise on your leg and not remembering how it got there.

The other contents on the desktop were neat and organized: stacks of invoices near Ken's business checkbook and ledger, charts of recent patients in the center of the blotter, and junk mail consisting mostly of brochures and catalogs on the far side. Careful not to rearrange anything, Brenda thumbed through the items, but nothing offered any clues.

She turned and peered out the window at the traffic on Route 422 beyond the parking lot. An impatient truck horn sounded in the distance. The town was fully awake now, and vehicles rushed to offices, schools, and appointments. Mesmerized, Brenda stared at them and thought about Ken. His harried appearance and rushed exit combined with this tidy organized workspace suggested he had not been working at his desk this morning.

Gingerly, she pulled the handle on the center desk drawer. Narrow compartments in the front held pens, sticky notes, mints, and a tangle of paper clips. Behind them, notepads, prescription pads, and empty chart folders slid around as she yanked the drawer open wider. Finding nothing of interest, she closed that drawer and opened one to the right of it. Besides more brochures and catalogs, it contained only an array of business cards from dental supply companies, dental labs, and pharmaceutical salespeople held together loosely by a binder clip. The drawer caught on something as she closed it, causing a few of the cards to break free and scatter about the drawer. Hurriedly, Brenda gathered them, anxious to leave Ken's private space without any signs of intrusion. As she lined up the cards to clip them together, one escaped the pile and caught her eye: *Douglas Cramer, Ph.D. and Associates – Berks Counseling Services.*

Brenda examined the card. Dr. Cramer was not a patient of Ken's, nor was he a salesman. *Is Ken seeing a therapist? Are he and Tessa having marital problems?* She pushed this thought to the back of her mind for the moment. Suddenly, she just wanted to get out of there.

Brenda hit the light switch to darken the room as she left Ken's office and moved swiftly through the suite, turning off the rest of the lights. The only light in the office now came from outside, so the windowless interior hallways were dim. She was just about to grab her jacket and purse when a light under a door at the end of the hall caught her eye. It was the door to a closet seldom opened; in it, Ken stored rarely used items like holiday decorations, unwanted displays from salespeople, and oversized boxes.

That's odd, Brenda thought. Since the light switch was inside the closet, she crossed the hallway and grabbed the door-knob. It was locked. She searched her memory for the last time anyone on the staff opened that closet. When they put away the winter decorations? When they changed the counter display a few weeks ago? She was sure the light hadn't been on when they left last night, so had Ken been in there this morning? What could he have needed in there? And did it tie in with his hasty exit?

Brenda did not have a key to the closet, so she had no choice but to leave with the light on inside. Thoughts she couldn't make sense of but knew were somehow connected bounced around her head, like a murder mystery movie where every object and event was important to solving the murder, but the viewer had no idea why. It wasn't until the end that it all made sense: *Oh, that dime under the coffee table had the killer's prints on it* or *Oh, the dog barked at his owner because it wasn't really him; it was his long-lost identical twin.*

She closed and locked the outer office door. Lost in her reverie, the elevator's *ding!* startled her. The doors opened to reveal a custodian with his cleaning cart inside. Medium height and middle-aged, his slight paunch was visible under his navy-blue shirt and pants. He held on to the cart handle with a large, callused hand. He was normally the second-shift custodian, but lately Brenda had seen him in the building in the morning. She smiled and gave him a familiar nod.

"Hi, Chuck. How are you today?"

"Mornin', Miss Brenda. I'm good." He looked up at the lighted arrow above the door and hesitated before speaking again. "Better than your boss, I'll tell you that much."

Brenda swung around to face him. "What do you mean?"

Chuck looked sheepish. "Well, um, I saw him this morning. Actually, I heard him before I saw him." He studied the contents on his cart, seeming worried that he'd talked out of school. They arrived at the ground floor, but Brenda's glare told him neither one was getting off the elevator yet.

"You *heard* him? Heard him what?"

Chuck hit the button to keep the door closed on the elevator. He lowered his voice. "I get here real early lately; me and Jack have been taking turns coverin' Frank's shifts since he's been out with knee replacement surgery." Brenda nodded, remembering she'd known that. "Anyway, Frank said sometimes he washes some of the windows inside the suites early in the morning before the sun comes up. Says they don't get streaky that way." He chuckled and leaned on his cart. "I'll tell you, that guy is so fussy—"

"But what about Dr. C.?" Brenda asked impatiently.

"Right, so anyway, I went into his suite, and I heard a weird noise. It took me a minute, but then I recognized it. He was in the john throwing up something fierce. So, I ran to the bathroom door to see if he needed help, but—" Chuck paused and shoved his hands in his pockets.

"But *what*?" Brenda wanted to throttle him.

"He yanked his head out of the john and growled at me to get lost. I swear, I've never seen him like that. He's always so quiet and polite. I ain't ever had a problem with him, but, this morning, I'll tell you what, if looks could kill . . ." He let out a low whistle.

Her brow furrowing, Brenda struggled to process what Chuck was telling her and piece it together with what she had witnessed this morning.

Chuck released the locked door button and maneuvered his cart off the elevator. He scratched his head. "Aah, probably no big deal. My guess is he and the Mrs. had a fight and he came here and spent the night with a bottle of Jameson. Don't solve nothin', but seems like a good idea at the time. Don't I know it." Chuck whistled as he made his way down the corridor.

Outside, Brenda took comfort in the law and order of nature. In the grassy areas surrounding the building, small buds on maple trees were beginning to open for springtime pollination. She knew that eventually, lime-green leaves would appear, as they did every year in spring. It made sense. She could count on it.

An eighteen-wheeler roared over a bridge on Route 422; the vibration rattled through Brenda's body, starting in her feet and traveling up to her pounding head.

Her head still swimming, Brenda chirped open her car door with the remote. She slid into the driver's seat and rested her head on the steering wheel. She'd come here in hopes of figuring things out. Instead, she found more questions.

Chapter Seventeen

Ken paced the floor. He replayed the scene of Tessa leaving him on the floor this morning over and over as if on a continuous loop.

Though it was fuzzy, when he left last night, the wind shaking the trees in the darkness, the look in Tessa's eyes was different than other times. She looked detached, like she was somewhere else, imagining another world with blue skies, lush green grass, a different husband. This morning was even worse. On her way out the door, she'd hummed a ridiculous juvenile tune that made her sound maniacal. She'd left him there on the floor like a pile of dirty laundry. Everything about her lately was unsettling; one minute she was completely familiar and the next absolutely alien.

He'd been tossing Ronnie's rubber ball up in the air as he paced. Now he hurled it at the sofa. She wouldn't leave him. She was just flexing her muscles. She always made such a big deal out of nothing. All he wanted was this one thing. He'd built his world around her, given her everything. But it wasn't good enough, not for her.

But what if she did leave? She'd ruin everything. Everyone would know their personal business. She'd run to her family and friends, demonizing him when he worked so hard to make her happy. She'd exaggerate the situation, crying about how unbearable her life was. He could picture Val hugging her daughter, pushing Tessa's tear-soaked hair from her eyes. *How could he? You poor thing! Why didn't you come to us sooner?* Sal would say very little but shake his head in utter disappointment at the son-in-law he'd welcomed into his family. *He isn't who we thought he was,* he'd sadly tell his customers, who'd then look for another dentist. Tessa's family knew everyone in town. The life he'd worked so hard to build would unravel like a ball of yarn.

He couldn't let that happen.

Ken yanked open the door to the laundry area and grabbed a bucket from a shelf above the washer. He poured in some disinfectant, filled it with warm water, and hurried to the foyer. On his hands and knees, he scrubbed the floor until it shone. For good measure, he did the kitchen floor also. Satisfied, he peeled the yellow latex gloves from his hands. He dumped the foul-smelling water down the sink drain and wrung out the dripping rags. These he tossed into the washer with his raincoat.

It was ten thirty. He figured he had until lunchtime before Tessa and Ronnie arrived home. Ken knew Tess so well; this was just the type of crisp fall day that she would take Ronnie for a walk in the park after Mommy and Me. He moved methodically through the living room, straightening pillows, folding throw blankets, picking up colorful plastic stackable rings and wooden puzzle pieces that made a smiling clown face when assembled. Staring at the toys, his throat tightened. He could picture Tessa on the floor with Ronnie chewing the puzzle pieces instead of placing them where Tessa showed her. "No, silly, it's a puzzle, not a pizza!" she'd say, ruffling the baby's feathery hair.

Ken pulled open the sheers on the French doors and tied them in the middle. Something sparkly on the end table caught the sun's lemon-yellow rays. Frowning, he realized it was his whiskey glass, still there from last night. He picked it up, and the putrid smell made him gag. The few hours he'd slept after arriving home this morning had rejuvenated him a bit, but the odor of the whiskey turned his stomach. His mouth still felt gravelly, like the bottom of a birdcage. He carried the glass to the kitchen and was about to put it in the dishwasher when he changed his mind. Instead, he washed and dried the glass and put it high in a cabinet.

He raised the blinds in the kitchen. Clouds moved across the sky, turning it the color of stone in some spots. A rabbit hopped across the lawn, though, a sure sign that spring was near. He wiped all the countertops and put away the few clean dishes in the drainer. Then he put Ronnie's breakfast dishes and Tessa's coffee mug in the dishwasher. Inspecting the freezer's contents, he decided he'd have to go grocery shopping. Tonight's dinner had to be special. No frozen burgers or canned vegetables.

Ken grabbed his keys and rushed out the door to his car, ignoring the neighbor's yapping dog. He was on a mission. He wanted to be back before Tessa and Ronnie returned home. Glancing at his watch, he estimated he had about one hour to shop for a meal that would put him back in his wife's good graces and keep her from blowing the lid off his nice, neat world.

Tessa eased the car into the driveway next to Ken's and sighed. She'd half hoped he wouldn't be there. She thought about the times at school when she'd asked disruptive students to come in after dismissal to talk about their unruly behavior; sometimes they didn't show up, and Tessa was secretly relieved she could put off the unpleasant task. She wasn't so lucky with her husband today.

She opened the rear car door and reached in to Ronnie's outstretched arms. It was almost noon, and Tessa knew her daughter would soon proclaim loudly, needing no words, that it was lunchtime. Next door, Cheeku, the neighbor's fox-faced Pomeranian, yelped playfully and ran in circles inside the fence that separated him from Tessa and Ken's yard. Tessa lifted Ronnie out of her car seat, and the baby squealed and waved. Normally,

Tessa would carry her over to see Cheeku, but not today. Today, under a sky that had turned from unclouded and bright to gray and mournful, she shivered and headed for the house.

The wind picked up, blowing Tessa's dark hair harshly into her face and stinging her eyes. She wondered how it was that life happened this way. How she could be a happily married woman one minute, laughing with her husband in their sunny kitchen while their daughter pasted sticky Cheerios in her hair, and then, in what seemed like ten seconds, turn into a completely different woman who felt pressure in her chest, like a weight threatening to stop her breathing, at the prospect of entering her own house and facing that same husband.

The front door squeaked as she pushed it open, the way it always did when the weather was changing. She balanced Ronnie on her hip and her bag over the other shoulder. The scent of disinfectant struck Tessa as she tossed her keys onto the foyer table; it was everywhere, as if someone had run through the house squeezing lemons and sprinkling ammonia. The storm door, still slightly ajar, caught a chilly gust of wind and blew open fully. Sitting Ronnie on the floor, Tessa grabbed the door handle to pull it shut. When she turned around, Ken startled her, and her right hand flew to her chest when their eyes met. Ken bent and picked up Ronnie, who was pulling the contents from Tessa's bag and scattering them as far as she could throw them.

"Hey, easy there, little one. You're a one-woman destruction crew." Ken nuzzled his face against Ronnie's soft cheek and peeked bashfully at Tessa. "Hi."

"Hi." Tessa reclaimed her bearings. "Give her to me. I need to change her."

Ken reached for his daughter. "That's okay, I'll do it." He turned to walk toward the nursery, Ronnie still in his arms. "Did you guys eat lunch? I wasn't sure if you went for a walk or stopped for a bite."

Tessa's pleasant walk and chat with CeCe allowed her to shed her cloak of secrets for a brief time, but here she was, back in the very foyer where just hours earlier she'd stepped over the hungover body of her vomiting husband. Now the floor was spotless and lemon-fresh. *Like it never happened.*

She shrugged out of her jacket and went into the kitchen to fix Ronnie's lunch. "We went for a walk," she called down the hall.

Ken returned and buckled Ronnie into her high chair. The baby fussed and bounced up and down in her seat. "Ma-ma-ma-ma-ma!"

"Okay, okay. Here we go." Tessa pulled a chair next to her daughter. Ronnie opened her mouth like a baby bird at a spoonful of sweet potatoes.

Ken opened the fridge and rubbed his palms together rapidly. "Do you want a salad?" he asked cheerfully. "I went to Giant. We should eat something light for lunch because I plan to fix us a feast for dinner tonight."

Tessa stared blankly at Ken and was just about to open her mouth when the phone rang.

She handed the bowl and spoon to Ken and grabbed the receiver. "Hello?"

"Hey," Mariel said. "Did you hear? Billy Joel is coming to Philly again! Rob heard it on the radio this morning. Even though you've seen him, like, a billion times, I figured you'd want in."

Tessa turned her back on Ken and twirled her hair around her fingers. She closed her eyes and recalled her college days, when she'd blow all her spending money on Billy Joel tickets. If he played three consecutive nights in Philly or Harrisburg, she'd go all three nights. Once she'd even convinced Mariel and a few other friends to hop a train from Lancaster to New York to see him at Madison Square Garden. She'd called her parents from a phone booth outside the arena. "Guess where I am?"

she'd excitedly asked Val over the street noise, the city lights dull compared to the gleam in her eyes. "Oh, no! Don't tell me you're chasing Billy Joel up and down the east coast? What about your classes? Sal, she's at it again!" Val had called to Tessa's father. Tessa had shouted back, "I'm in New York! I'm finally going to see him at MSG! Don't worry, Mom, I'm fine! Only the good die young!" *Is it possible that was only nine short years ago?*

"No, I didn't hear, but I definitely want to go!"

"What? Billy didn't call you himself to tell you?" Mariel teased. Tessa could hear her rumpling a sheet of paper. "Okay, Rob said the concert is at The Spectrum on the second Saturday in June. With Ronnie's first birthday on the sixteenth, you'll have to make sure you don't plan her party that day. Too bad she's not old enough to go! I'm sure you'll have her at one of Billy's concerts before she turns five!"

"If I can hold out that long," Tessa amiably agreed. "So when do tickets go on sale?"

"May first. Now, the question is, do we take the guys or make it a girls' night and leave them home to watch the kids? Either is fine with me; plenty of time to get sitters if we need them."

Tessa looked over at Ken wiping food from Ronnie's pudgy face. His hair was combed, and he wore a pale blue polo shirt and jeans. He had showered and sobered up, but images of his cruelty the night before and his crumpled form this morning were seared into her mind, the pain of them raw and stinging.

The concert was almost two months away. Tessa rubbed her temples.

"Um, how about if we make it a girls' night?" Ken glanced toward her curiously. Tessa stood straight and cleared her throat. "The guys went with us the last three times. We're due." Her eyes were on Ken but looked right through him.

"Just as well," chuckled Mariel. "You're on pace to spend Ronnie's college fund on Billy Joel tickets. It will take you longer if Ken doesn't go with you to every show!"

After they hung up, Tessa opened the fridge and grabbed a strawberry yogurt. Ken eyed her guardedly. "What was that all about?"

Tessa tore the top off the yogurt carton and licked it. "Billy Joel's touring again. He's coming to Philly in June." She continued matter-of-factly, "Mariel and I are going." She filled Ronnie's sippy cup with milk. "Here you go, Peanut." She pulled playfully on her daughter's soft earlobe before walking to the living room and sinking down onto the sofa.

Ken was silent. He picked up Ronnie and followed Tessa into the other room. His eyes darkened and he spoke slowly, enunciating each word distinctly. "What do you mean, 'Mariel and I are going'? Rob and I aren't?"

At Ken's icy tone, Tessa's spoon stopped midway to her mouth. The pause was momentary, and she caught herself. Tessa casually tossed her hair over her shoulder, but her hand shook slightly. "We figured it would be fun if just us girls went this time. The four of us went the last few times." Looking directly at Ken, she added, "Besides, I hardly ever have time with Mariel alone to talk. Maybe we'll have dinner in Philly before the concert. I have a lot on my mind, and I'd like a few hours with my best friend. Is there something wrong with that?"

Ken fixed his gaze on Tessa for a long moment without speaking. Finally, a small smile spread across his face. He put Ronnie on the floor to finish her milk and sat on the love seat. Nonchalantly draping his arm over the back of it, he wrinkled his brow in an embellished quizzical look of almost mocking concern. "What's weighing so heavily on your mind that you need to talk to Mariel about?" He cocked his head and blinked several times as though he was honestly perplexed.

Tessa licked her dry lips. Her last bite of yogurt caught in her throat in a lump that felt the size of a bowling ball.

Ken didn't let her answer. "*You* have a lot on your mind? *Really?*" He emitted an incredulous laugh. "What? Not working unless it's convenient for you, going out to lunch, taking walks in the park whenever you want stresses you out?" He shook his head. "Everyone should have that kind of stress."

Ken's flippant tone unsettled Tessa, and she nervously played with the sofa's arm cover. He wasn't done. "You know, I bust my ass for you and Ronnie. Yeah, okay, I'm struggling lately with a few things, but you have no idea what real stress is. So, what, you're going to run to Mariel and tell her what a horrible husband I am and how your life is a living hell? You're going to wear your designer clothes with your new diamond bracelet dangling from your wrist and have a pity party for yourself? Jesus Christ! Do you think the way you act helps me?" He paused and let that sink in, let it fill her head, word by word. "The more you bitch, the worse you make things for us."

Ken stood and crossed the room to where Tessa sat, frozen. He kneeled in front of her. "You know, if you start airing our dirty laundry, it won't just affect you. What about my practice? I'm trying to build a reputation and a business so you and Ronnie and our future children can have a nice comfortable life. Do you want to take that away from all of us?"

What is he talking about? Ken was twisting everything. She didn't want to take anything away from her family; she wanted things to be the way they were before. She didn't want to feel afraid all the time, wondering if Ken would come home and what state he'd be in if he did, covering for him, lying to everyone she knew.

He wasn't making sense. The fact that Tessa only worked sporadically and took Ronnie for walks in the park didn't give Ken the right to drink too much and abuse nitrous oxide.

She was the one holding everything together, not tearing it apart. She opened her mouth to say as much, but Ken's words swirled around in her head.

She felt confused. *Was* she making things worse? Adding to Ken's stress instead of helping him? Her confusion dizzied her, crashed through her like a wave, slammed her shores, eroding her ability to make sense of things.

Tessa turned and looked into the eyes of the man she married. She thought about when Mary died, how broken Ken had been, how fragile, as if the lightest touch would shatter him into a million pieces. He'd wandered from room to room as if searching for the reason such an unthinkable thing could happen. Like he might open a closet door and inside would be a perfectly logical explanation why his mother died a painful death at age forty-seven.

She knew this was one of those moments where what she said next would determine the path of the rest of her life. She wondered if she'd look back on this moment and remember every detail. Would she remember that the wind shaking the trees outside the living room window made it seem more like early winter than early spring? That she'd banged her elbow on the refrigerator door when reaching in for her yogurt and wondered for the thousandth time why it was called the funny bone? That Ronnie made a "mmm, mmm, mmm" sound as she drained her sippy cup, oblivious to the precipice her parents stood on?

Ken raised his eyebrows slightly in a way that said, *I'll wait. I have all day.*

Tessa thought of the moment she first saw him. When his look was flirty and shy, not menacing and taunting. The way he'd walked her to her friend's car outside the bar, opened the passenger door for her, and, when she'd rolled down the window because he knew she wasn't ready to say good night to him, leaned with both arms on the window opening and gently played with her hair.

She realized that was the Ken people saw. The one who happily filled in at the Sunrise when Sal's dishwasher had appendicitis. The one who sang "Itsy Bitsy Spider" to Ronnie in restaurants so Tessa could eat her cheeseburger while it was hot. The one who stood back at parties and gazed at his wife with a look that said he'd love her forever.

They'd never even believe this Ken existed. She'd built her world around him and made everyone around her believe it was the smartest thing she'd ever done. They'd think she was crazy to leave him and separate Ronnie from her father. And where would she go? Home to her parents'? Into a small apartment just big enough for Ronnie and her? How would she afford to live?

If she squinted, could she still see the old Ken, in the shadows, beyond his angry stare? She still loved him, but it was not the same. It was thicker and weightier and much more complex than she would have ever imagined sitting on the balcony of their first apartment holding hands.

Ken was an addict.

And yet she was about to open her mouth and make being an addict okay. Being married to an addict made Tessa behave in a way that mystified her. She thrived on order and logic, but addiction turned her into someone who could step over her husband's vomiting body in the morning and that night sit on the couch next to him and ask if he wanted to watch the Phillies or a movie.

She knew then how she would respond.

Ken was good to her most of the time, wasn't he? She couldn't just walk out on him like Caroline walked out on her family. Didn't Tessa still carry the scars from her mother's desertion? Ken was trying to stop using the gas and not drink so much. What kind of person leaves her husband when he's battling a problem like that? Her stomach sank as she pictured the looks of everyone they knew if she left Ken. They'd shake their heads, incredulous. *What the hell does she want?* they'd ask, as if she and not Ken were responsible for the destruction of their family.

Tessa blinked, as if by doing so she could bring into focus a scene other than the one in front of her. "No, of course I don't want to destroy my family," she managed softly. She shook her head. "I . . . I don't know what I was thinking. Of course I won't say anything to Mariel. Or anyone."

Ken moved to sit beside her on the couch. He placed his hand on Tessa's shoulder, and it made her want to cry. "You have a lot of time on your hands, and your imagination runs away with you." He stroked her hair and pulled her close to him. "Don't worry, doll. I'll always be here for you. It will be all right. You're feeling overwhelmed, but I'll always be here for you."

Tessa was struck by the vast distance between what she felt and what she was able to say. "I worry sometimes that it's too much. That there's too much wrong in our marriage."

"Oh, Tess." Ken gave her a look of pity. "You'll find something wrong in every marriage if that's all you look for."

Chapter Eighteen

"Okay, boss, I think that's everything. I put the last of the instruments in the autoclave. I'll come in a few minutes early tomorrow and set up the exam rooms. Too beautiful outside to stay here later than necessary today!" Brenda paused in the doorway of Ken's office. "You coming? I'll walk out with you. Tracy left already."

Ken looked up from the pile on his desk. "Huh? Oh. I just want to go through this mail, and then I'll take off." The circles under Ken's eyes exacerbated his pallor.

"It looks more like you're moving it around, not opening it," Brenda joked. "Don't you have a little terror—I mean, little darling—waiting for her daddy to get home?"

"No, Tess and Ronnie are at the beach with her family. I'm heading down after work tomorrow night and spending the weekend with them." He looked so distracted Brenda felt sorry for him.

"Hey, you know what? Hank is taking our little guy to a baseball game tonight. It's so cute the way my husband thinks a three-year-old can understand the rules of the game." She continued without stopping to think. "Do you want to grab a drink? The patio at Mulligan's is open."

Brenda held eye contact with Ken until finally he pushed back his chair and stood. "Actually, that sounds good. I have a quick errand to run, and then I'll meet you there. Say, forty-five minutes?" He checked his watch as he turned off his desk lamp.

"Works for me. I'll run home and change out of these scrubs. See you there."

Ken pulled into the parking lot at Lux Air and cut the engine. He was relieved to see no other cars around. The less explaining he had to do, the better. He crossed the lot and pulled open the door.

"Can I help you?" From behind the counter, a stout woman with graying hair looked at Ken over her reading glasses.

Ken stammered, "Um, well, is Stan—"

"I got this one, Tammy." Stan emerged from a back room with a stack of papers in his hand. Ken, preferring to say as little as possible, let Stan drive the conversation. "As I said earlier when we spoke on the phone, Dr. Cordelia, I apologize about the mix-up with your order. I'm sorry you had to drive all the way down here to personally pick up your tanks."

Ken easily picked up on Stan's angle. His expression softened, and his blue eyes conveyed kindness and understanding. "It's okay, Stan. Things happen. People make mistakes."

Tammy watched the exchange with interest and shook her head. "Sounds like the work of one of the new hires. These young folks. Can't keep their heads in what they're doing for longer than ten minutes. Every morning when I come in, I spend at least half an hour cleaning up their mistakes." She adjusted her glasses, pushed up the sleeves of her pink cardigan, and scrolled through her computer screen. The phone rang, and she turned her attention to the call.

Ken waited for Stan to complete their business. He widened his eyes as if to say, *Come on, let's go. I want to get out of here.*

With Tammy busy helping the customer on the phone, Stan took advantage of the moment. "I have your order ready.

I'll help you carry the tanks to your car. And, again, please accept our apologies." He disappeared into the back room again and returned a moment later. "Here we go. Mind gettin' the door?"

Ken nodded a quick good-bye at Tammy and pushed the metal bar on the door. Stan maneuvered the wheeled canisters through the opening. As they crossed the parking lot, Ken couldn't hide his agitation. "Jesus Christ." He ran his fingers through his hair, causing it to stand up wildly.

"Hey, dude, don't look at me. You usually come an hour later after everyone is gone."

"Yeah, well, an hour later didn't work for me tonight. I have plans."

"Suit yourself. So, you have something for me?" Stan closed Ken's trunk after arranging the tanks inside.

Ken glanced back toward the door. He could see Tammy, her head cocked to balance the phone between her ear and her shoulder, still involved in her call. He handed Stan a folded script. "This is all I can do for now. I can't write you another prescription for thirty days. This stuff is regulated, you know. It would help if you'd come into the office complaining of pain. Give me a leg to stand on."

Stan leaned against Ken's trunk and pushed a stringy strand of blond hair out of his eyes. His complexion was ruddy, and he looked as if he'd spent a lot of time in the sun. His mouth twisted into a crooked smile. "Oh, I know all about regulations. Remember, I'm putting my ass on the line for you too. I have to fudge invoices and records to keep you feelin' good. You're not the only one here with something to lose."

Ken straightened his tie and grabbed the handle on his car door. "Somehow I think I'm taking a bigger risk than you are."

"Oh, really?" Stan asked. He pointed a finger whose nail was bitten down to the skin at Ken. "We're no different, you and me. I'm just more honest with myself."

After Ken drove away, Stan went back into the office. "He seems nice," Tammy offered. "Do you want me to prepare an invoice for him? What's the name of his practice?"

Stan fingered the piece of paper in his pocket. "No need. I took care of it earlier when he called. It's all good."

Mulligan's was a small sports bar only a few minutes from Ken's office. It attracted families for dinner on Tuesdays because a clown made balloon animals for the kids. Thursdays drew a big happy hour crowd as people began to look forward to the weekend. It also didn't hurt that they had ten different varieties of wings.

Brenda checked her lipstick in a small compact mirror and dropped it back into her purse. She'd changed into jeans and a light pink low-cut blouse. Leaning on the bar, she signaled to the bartender, a tall thin man with reddish spiky hair. "I'll have a glass of Merlot."

"Starting without me, huh?" Ken laughed and slid onto the barstool next to Brenda. "Was it that rough of a day?"

"Aren't they all?" Brenda joked. "Not that looking in people's mouths all day isn't glamorous work or anything." She flipped her hair over her shoulder and turned her body slightly to face Ken. "So, did you take care of your errand?"

Ken looked momentarily taken aback and then remembered he'd mentioned it to her. "Yeah, no big deal. Not enough hours in the day to get everything done."

"What can I get you?" the bartender asked him.

"I'll have what she's having."

"Good idea," Brenda offered. "You need something to mellow you out. You look so tense and serious." She picked up her wine as the bartender set down a glass and filled it for Ken. "To . . . let's see . . . almost the weekend. Friday Junior!"

Ken smiled and nodded as he clinked glasses with her. "Sure. That'll work. To Friday Junior."

They sipped their wine quietly for a moment. Brenda broke the silence. "So, how long has Tessa been at the beach?" "They left on Monday. Her whole family's down there." He traced the rim of his wine glass with his middle finger. They'd had a pretty good stretch for the last few months. He'd managed to keep his cravings at bay for the most part. The night Tessa mentioned unburdening on Mariel had been a wakeup call for Ken, though he didn't let her see that. He had to be more careful than ever. Tessa was weakening, and it wouldn't take much for her to crack. He drank too much at home when he couldn't get back to the office for his fix, but that didn't madden her as much as when he did the gas. He cleverly made use of every opportunity. Sometimes on Saturdays, Tessa went to Philly or New York with Mariel or friends from school; Val would keep Ronnie, and Ken had the day to himself.

They'd been spending more time together recently, and things were fairly calm. They went out with friends, and, laughing and talking over appetizers and drinks, it felt like old times. They had Tessa's family over for cookouts, Ken at the grill patiently showing Tony and Gina how to tell when the burgers were done just right. Some Saturday mornings they took Ronnie to the playground together and strolled hand in hand while the busy toddler ran from the slide to the swings and back again.

But he'd slipped up a few weeks ago. After Brenda and Tracy left, he locked up the office and stayed there all night on the gas. Tessa had been up most of the night and was waiting for him when he crept into the house just after 5 a.m. This time, though, she hadn't yelled or threatened to leave. She was crying softly, but her calmness shook Ken more than her usual anger. It was easier to handle her anger; they'd go around and around, and it always ended with him convincing her she didn't want to know what her life would be like if she left him, exposed his problem, and ruined his career.

Her sadness was another story. The look of utter disappointment in him. The way she wouldn't let her eyes meet his. The stony mornings where she went about getting Ronnie's day started and worked around him as if he were invisible.

He just didn't get her. It wasn't like she didn't know where he was when he stayed out all night. He didn't lie to her about where he was or what he was doing. He just didn't let her know ahead of time. Hell, sometimes he didn't know himself when he left the house in the morning that tonight would be the night. Why did they have to have the same fight over and over? He loved her. He just needed this *one* thing.

They were beginning to find some peace again when her family trip to the beach came up. Before she'd left, he asked her again to forgive him and start over. He swore yet again to try harder. He'd been making progress; couldn't she see her way to stand beside him a little while longer? She'd agreed, but she looked battle weary when she left. He promised they'd have a nice long weekend together when he arrived at the beach. He'd convinced her some time away from home and the office would be good for them.

"How is Tessa anyway?" Brenda's nonchalant question brought Ken back. "She hasn't stopped by the office lately with Ronnie."

Ken shifted in his seat. "No, she hasn't. I guess she sees enough of me at home." He shrugged his shoulders a little and took another sip.

Brenda turned so she faced him directly. She leaned on the bar, propped her head in her hand, and studied her boss.

An attractive brunette in her mid-thirties walked up to the bar to order a drink. She wore a tight cream and taupe wrap dress and strappy heels. The brunette smiled at Ken as she motioned to the bartender. Brenda took in Ken's deep-set blue eyes, dark hair, charcoal pleated pants, starched white shirt, and gray and blue striped tie.

"I think she likes what she sees," Brenda whispered to Ken. She playfully gestured toward the woman, who was on her way to a table with her martini.

Ken followed Brenda's gaze. "Who? Oh. Yeah, right. I doubt that."

"Seriously, she was checking you out. Tessa better hurry back," she teased. She crossed her legs and bounced her peep-toe pump up and down.

They talked for several minutes about dental patients and cases. Then Brenda put up her hand and shook her head. "Wait a minute! We're off the clock! I thought the idea here was to unwind and forget about work. What do you think? One more? It's still pretty early."

"Why not?" Ken waved the bartender over. "No one waiting at home for me."

Brenda steered her car out of Mulligan's parking lot. She turned left onto the highway and immediately hit a red light. "Damn," she said aloud.

She'd enjoyed the evening. It was nice to get Ken out of the office. He needed to unwind. Sometimes he came to work looking like he hadn't slept a wink all night, and he was often irritable and distracted. His comments tonight at the bar about Tessa were odd. She recalled the counselor's business card she'd found in his desk and the night Chuck said he'd spent at the office.

She looked at her reflection in the rearview mirror. Her cheeks were pink; she wasn't sure if it was the wine or the fact that she was thinking about how good-looking Ken was. Embarrassed that he might pull up next to her at the light, she again checked her mirror.

She did a double-take when she saw Ken's car exit the lot. Instead of turning left as she had, toward his house, he turned right. Toward the office.

The light turned green, and Brenda was forced to accelerate. She drove a few hundred feet and then pulled off the road at a gas station to think. *Was Ken going back to the office at this hour?*

She looked at the clock on her dashboard. Hank and Zach wouldn't be home from the baseball game yet. She'd left a note saying that she'd gone out with friends, so Hank wouldn't expect her home early.

Brenda sat in her car under the bright gas station sign for a few minutes. She didn't think she imagined that she and Ken connected on another level tonight. When he talked, she listened, really listened. She held eye contact with him when he told her his aspirations for the future of the practice. She'd nodded and touched his arm lightly, encouraging him. His shirt that had looked starched and crisp was in fact delicate and smooth to the touch.

Tonight Ken looked like a man who needed someone to pay attention to him, and she'd been glad to oblige. Hank didn't seem to care if she paid attention to him or not. He was content to fall asleep on the sofa every night, sometimes not exchanging any conversation with her beyond dinner.

She looked down the highway in the direction Ken had driven. Maybe she was way off. Maybe Ken didn't go back to the office. Maybe he went the opposite direction to go to the ATM or grab a coffee from Wawa.

Brenda felt flustered, as if someone had shaken her like a snow globe. Without fully comprehending why, she pulled out of the gas station and drove back in the direction she'd just come from. She felt drawn toward Ken; in her mind she saw an imaginary finger, curled and motioning her to follow.

By the time she pulled into the parking lot at the office, the night had grown dark.

But not so dark that she didn't see Ken's car parked way on the far end of the lot.

Chapter Nineteen

Brenda's car made a soft pinging sound as the engine cooled. She sat in the driver's seat looking up at the windows of the dental suite. Nothing, not even a shadow, moved in the darkness. *Is he going to sleep here? But why? Even if he and Tessa are arguing, she's at the beach. He has the house to himself.*

Brenda's stomach roiled. She and Ken had shared a few appetizers at Mulligan's, and now they weighted down her insides. She opened the car door and got out.

"Ronnie, you little rascal, come here and say hi to Daddy!" Tessa kept her tone light as her daughter raced away. "I'm telling you, Ken, she's hell on wheels even though it's way past her usual bedtime. We couldn't wait for her to walk, and now she won't stay still." She made her way into the hallway of the beach house to momentarily escape the noise of the living room. She also didn't want her family within earshot if the conversation took a negative turn. She'd become deft at removing herself from scrutiny and questioning; as much as it wore her out, she now did it instinctively. She noted the late hour but tried to sound casual. "So, how was your day? Are you just getting home?"

"Yeah, Scotty and I grabbed some dinner and a beer after work. I ran into him at the gas station this morning. His wife is out of town also," Ken lied.

"Oh, good. Mom and I made stuffed shells for dinner, and I was feeling guilty thinking about you eating all alone. Although, between the commotion and the cleanup, you probably got the better end of the bargain." Tessa felt like she was trying to handle a delicate glass object without breaking it. She wondered what Ken was up to, but she didn't want to sound suspicious or accusatory. Ken was trying to get better, and he'd made it clear that her constant badgering didn't help. He made her see that no one would be served by ending their marriage. She didn't want to be the one who brought their life crashing down; Ken reminded her regularly how selfish that would be, how Caroline had done that to her, how lasting the impact was. She willed herself not to ask too many questions. After all, she was enjoying herself at the beach while Ken was home working. That point would not be lost on him if she pushed his buttons.

She looked over her shoulder at her family and chattered on nervously. "I thought Joey was going to throw the remote through the TV screen tonight. The Phils were winning the whole game, and the pitcher gave up a home run in the ninth to tie it. They ended up losing in thirteen innings. Even my dad was yelling. We're lucky the people in the rental next door didn't call the police for disturbing the peace. Don't be surprised if Ronnie's first full sentence is 'Throw a freakin' strike, you bum!'" Her voice trailed off into the dead air space.

"Ken? Are you there?"

"Mmm, yeah. It's crazy the way they act so nuts over a stupid game."

Tessa almost opined that there were worse ways to spend an evening, but she restrained herself.

Ken yawned. "I'm going to hit the hay. I'll see you tomorrow. I'll try to get an early start to beat the weekend exodus to the shore."

"Okay. Love you."

"Love you too."

Tessa hung up the phone and closed her eyes. *Good. He's home safe and sound.*

Brenda used her master key to let herself into the building. The lobby was dark except for the soft illumination from the gold-plated wall sconces. Their light cast eerie shadows on the doors of the suites. There were no custodians in sight; the second-shift staff was no doubt in the break room, and the third shift would not begin for another hour. She approached the elevator but at the last minute changed her mind and took the stairs. Climbing to the second floor, her mouth felt dry from the wine.

Brenda hesitated for a moment and then let herself into Ken's suite. She silently closed the door behind her and leaned against it. Thoughts of what she was doing rang in her ears. It was almost ten at night. Ken was alone in the office. Hank wasn't expecting her home for a while. The thought dizzied her, but she knew what she was going to do. Before she lost her nerve, Brenda smoothed her hair, licked her lips, and called out softly.

"Ken?"

Her eyes adjusted slightly to the darkness. The suite was silent but for the usual nighttime pings and clinks from pipes and appliances.

"Ken? It's me."

She eyed Ken's private office door, expecting to see light emanating from under it or hear him shuffling papers behind it, but she detected no movement or sound from that direction. Instead, she heard a faint humming noise coming from the first exam room.

Again using her key, she opened that door.

It took her a few seconds to process the sight. A thousand thoughts rushed her brain, but the most striking one was the sudden clarity after months of questions. Images of Ken's disheveled appearance, pale countenance, and erratic moods flashed through her mind. All at once, she felt Ken's torment and bizarre behavior untwist themselves and settle gently in her mind and heart.

If Ken knew she was there, he did not acknowledge her. After silently watching him for a few minutes, Brenda quietly pulled a stool next to him, sat down, and took his hand.

Chapter Twenty

The late summer air was soft and warm, and time seemed to slow down, as if the lazy season never wanted to end. Ronnie, on the other hand, sped up more each day. Her first birthday now three months behind her, she took off in every direction as soon as her chubby feet hit the ground. Tessa chased the sweaty giggling toddler around the backyard under a sky so blue it looked like an artist's painting.

She redirected Ronnie away from a rose bush. Mariel and Alex had planned to come for a play date, but Mariel called this morning with the news that Alex had an ear infection. With Alex howling in the background, she'd been on her way out the door to the pediatrician. Tessa had barely seen Mariel since Ronnie's birthday party. They'd gone to the concert the week before that and talked and laughed about all the things best friends normally talked and laughed about. Tessa amazed herself; she could easily go on at length about the latest fashions, trends in education, child-rearing, and even politics, all the while not mentioning that her husband was an addict. She wanted to tell *someone. Anyone.* The secret bore down on her, threatening to crush her under its mammoth weight.

Sometimes she thought she might just blurt it out. While Mariel perused the menu, noting, "This place supposedly has the best calamari," Tessa pictured herself announcing, "Really?

Well, get this: Ken is addicted to nitrous oxide!" Ordering Ronnie's birthday cake on the phone, she had bizarre fantasies of telling the baker to make this cake extra special because if her husband didn't stop huffing nitrous oxide, it might be the only one of her daughter's birthdays they would celebrate as a family. She'd almost done it, countless times, but the reality of what that admission would set in motion stopped her. She wouldn't be able to unring that bell. As Ken constantly repeated, if she blew his cover instead of giving him time to fix things, she'd destroy their family with an unremovable stain. What if Ken came to his senses and stopped? Their family and friends would never be able to un-know what Tessa had told them, and Ken would never forgive her for that.

Lately she'd also been thinking about her father, wondering if he had felt the same way covering up Caroline's drinking all those years ago. Did he lie to his family, friends, and colleagues in the hope that one day his wife would wake up and seek help for her problem? Did he beg her, using all the tools in his arsenal to convince her? *Please, please, we have three children who need you. Aren't they worth it to you?* Did Caroline make Sal feel guilty, selfish if he talked about divorce? *Why can't you stand by me? What kind of man deserts a wife with a problem? Are you so perfect?*

Talking about addiction was even more taboo when Tessa and her brothers were growing up. How alone Sal must have felt. Tessa pictured him at work—in those days he owned and operated three restaurants—his body going through the motions of ordering inventory, managing staff, and overseeing the daily operation while his heart was breaking.

As Ronnie chased a butterfly, Tessa made a decision. Truthfully, she knew in the back of her mind when she got up this morning that she would do it. Operating on autopilot, she scooped up her daughter and took her in the house to change her diaper. She grabbed a cup of juice and a snack and stuck them in the diaper bag before belting Ronnie in her car seat.

She exited her neighborhood and took Route 422 toward Pennside, a small suburban community in the next town whose roads stretched like bony fingers downward from a wooded mountain. Driving through the business section of her town, she passed a McDonald's, a Wendy's, a video store, two pizza shops, and an auto repair shop with *May We Have the Next Dents?* on its sign. At a traffic light, she took a sharp right turn and headed down a steep hill. The car windows were down halfway, and in the rearview mirror, Tessa watched Ronnie's fine hair blowing straight back and her blue eyes blinking against the rushing wind. She turned left onto Carsonia Drive and drove for a few miles past modest brick houses with small front porches. Ronnie waved vigorously at a puppy chasing a small child around a tree-lined yard. At a red light, Tessa gazed at a small luncheonette named Jake's. Once upon a time she and her brothers rode their bikes there and sat at the counter drinking thick milkshakes through straws, sucking in their cheeks until it hurt. An ornate corner building that once housed a small movie theater was now occupied by insurance offices. Tessa narrowed her eyes and conjured up images from more than twenty years ago. Some were crystal clear; others were blurred as if viewed through a rain-splattered windowpane. Even though it was all a little different, somehow it was also still the same.

Thirty minutes after she left her house, they entered a neighborhood where white clapboard houses with black shutters stood side by side, like soldiers at attention, on a series of parallel streets on an incline. She knew before she got there that a red brick elementary school sat on a grassy hill just beyond the houses. Slowing down as she drove past the school, her mind's eye saw a small girl with swinging ponytails walking down the alley that led to the school grounds, her pink bookbag loaded with too many pencils, erasers, and folders slowing her down as her older brother tried to stay several steps ahead of her, and her younger brother galloped to keep up.

The playground was still there, though the equipment had been updated, but the wooden picnic tables were gone. Tessa wondered if teenagers still volunteered there as playground leaders on summer mornings, helping young children string colorful plastic beads onto yarn, wetting it between their lips so it would be easier to thread. The box-hockey structures were also gone, but she could hear Sal Jr. rapidly tapping his stick against the ground and his opponent's stick three times—*one, tap, two, tap, three*—before the ball dropped into the box.

Tessa turned the car into the alley toward the white houses. Her tires found the ruts in the dirt and gravel. In one of the houses now partially concealed by tall, thick maple trees, Vicki, her childhood babysitter, had lived. Tessa loved when Vicki babysat; she played Crazy Eights and Sorry! with Tessa and her brothers, gently calling out the boys when they cheated. Sometimes she'd bring cookie dough she'd made at home and let Tessa drop rounded spoonfuls onto the cookie sheet. While the cookies baked, Sal Jr. and Joey tried to stick their hands in the remaining batter, and Vicki would shoo them out of the kitchen so she and Tessa could carefully remove the golden-brown gooey spheres from the pan with a silver spatula. "My helper gets an extra cookie," she'd say.

Finally, Tessa found the street she was looking for and steered her car down the paved hill.

There it was. It seemed strange somehow that it was still there after all those years, looking much like she remembered. The cement porch steps where she played jacks and cat's cradle so many summer afternoons with her friend Susan now had a striped runner down the middle of them. The little strip of garden that ran along the front walk was dotted with purple and yellow pansies. The mailbox looked freshly painted, the rectangular 1 and 8 placed carefully and evenly side by side to display the house number. Oddly, it made Tessa feel good that the owner of the house tended to it.

Then, as she gazed at the outside of the house, the inside filled her mind like a roaring wave she couldn't stop or outrun. She saw the black wrought-iron railing, its question-mark-shaped spokes attached to the rail, leading upstairs to her bedroom, where she and her cousins cut and traded pictures from *Tiger Beat* magazines. They'd giggle and suck on sugary candy cigarettes that they held between their index and middle fingers, removing them in mock sophistication, blowing out the "smoky" powdered sugar. She saw the bathroom in the hall where Caroline put on makeup and perfume before she and Sal went out on Saturday nights, Tessa sitting on the pink ropey toilet seat cover contorting her own face as her mother applied her eye shadow and blush. Sometimes Caroline dusted Tessa's cheeks with blush or swiped a bit of lip gloss on her lips with her pinky before spraying her nearly black hair into place with Aqua-Net. Just down the hall was the room Tessa's brothers had shared, football pennants on the walls and navy-blue matching bedspreads on side-by-side twin beds.

She thought of the couch in the living room where Caroline sat at night to crochet, the light of the television screen reflected in her glasses. She'd call upstairs to Sal Jr. and Joey to stop fooling around and get ready for bed, winking at Tessa. *If only they behaved as well as you, my girl.* She saw the kitchen table, the round tray that held a wooden napkin holder, cut-glass salt and pepper shakers, a clear-glass butter dish with a domed lid. She could see Sal bustling around making breakfast, humming, holding the pan of scrambled eggs with a potholder as he scooped them onto each of their plates. Caroline held her steaming coffee mug with both hands, blowing on it while she laughed at how Sal fussed if the eggs weren't just right.

When did Sal stop humming and Caroline stop coming downstairs for breakfast? When did Caroline start spending so much time "sick" in bed?

Tessa looked again at the front steps, but this time saw her father sitting there, hunched over, patting the space next to him. She saw herself moving slowly to sit beside him, kicking stones with her canvas sneaker. Neither spoke, she because there were so many questions she didn't know which one to ask and he because such a veil of sadness covered his face that his lips couldn't form any words. Tessa couldn't truly empathize with her father then; somewhere in her mind she'd realized he'd lost his wife, but all she could feel was the vacuum created in her own life when Caroline left.

She couldn't empathize with him then, but she could now. She thought of Ken and felt the ache in her stomach that for her lately was just the pain of existing, a kind of visceral despair that came with coping with her situation. Sal must have felt that ache also. Tessa wondered how he'd kept it all together, left with raising three children whose mother had abandoned them. Sometimes, after Caroline left, she'd see her father's face full of sorrow and ask "What's wrong?" when what she really should have asked was "What's right?"

Tessa turned and looked at her daughter, who had fallen asleep, her hand clutching a round yellow Cheerio container. Her head was tilted at such an unnatural angle against the side of her car seat that Tessa wondered how she could sleep that way. She reached back and gently stroked Ronnie's soft leg and thought for the thousandth time that nothing in the world could ever make her leave her.

Then another scene took shape in her mind. Ronnie growing up catering to Ken because she sensed, no matter how Tessa hid it from her, that something with him wasn't quite right. Would she bring him tea and blankets when he was "sick" so he knew what a good girl she was? Would she keep her room immaculate, not because she was a neat freak but because she didn't want to give Ken any reason to leave and not come back?

Tessa remembered a clip from a documentary she'd seen in a sociology class in college. Researchers did a study on parent-child relationships using apes to demonstrate how children relate to their parents. The film explained that in one case, the adult ape was given very little exposure to the baby, largely ignoring it and rarely showing affection. In another case, the adult fawned over the baby, making sure it was well-fed and protecting it from danger.

At the time Tessa had thought the study was zany, but now she remembered what was so fascinating about it. The fussed-over baby ape learned quickly to be independent. It was almost as if its parent said, *Okay, you know I love you and I'll always be here for you. Now go out into the world and be your own person.* The case of the neglected ape was completely different. That one continually sought approval from its parent, trying harder and harder to get attention each time it was ignored or mistreated.

It was as if the baby ape blamed itself. As if it felt unlovable.

Tessa put the car in drive and started down the street. As she turned onto Carsonia Drive toward home, she knew she had to stay with Ken. But not for herself. She owed it to Ronnie. She couldn't bear the thought of Ronnie asking through teary eyes why they couldn't live together as a family. She wouldn't sentence her daughter to a life of thinking that the people she loved and depended on one day wouldn't be there anymore. And worse, that maybe it was somehow her fault.

Ken gave in to his cravings sometimes, but without Ronnie and her to come home to, who knew what would become of him? At least now, between binges, Ken was a good husband and father. Hadn't he surprised Tessa just a few weeks ago by getting a babysitter and making dinner reservations for the two of them at a new restaurant she wanted to try? Hadn't he taken Ronnie to the playground last Saturday so Tessa could get a pedicure?

Every marriage had problems. Some had awful, hopeless problems. Abject poverty. Children with cancer. Spouses killed in car accidents. Sal and Val didn't raise Tessa to run when things got tough.

Caroline had chosen to leave, and that decision crushed her husband and children. It had taken them years to pick up the pieces. Then Sal met Val, and things improved vastly, but Tessa might not be so lucky. Maybe Ronnie would have to grow up without a father.

No, leaving Ken would not be in anyone's best interest. If Tessa left Ken, he would spiral completely out of control and maybe disappear completely from their lives, as Caroline had. Tessa just needed to be patient. It wouldn't be easy, but she could do it. Ken would see how much he had to lose. He'd stop abusing nitrous oxide. He loved his wife and daughter. He'd do it for them.

She glanced in the rearview mirror. She was glad she went back to her old neighborhood, but she knew she'd never go again. For the last time, she saw the house, the garden, the porch steps, a broken father slouched over on them rubbing his daughter's back, assuring her it wasn't her fault her mother left. Only now she saw them fading from sight as if on a train speeding away. As she drove, the house shrank smaller and smaller, and then it disappeared.

Chapter Twenty-One

"You don't need to hire a contractor to break through your kitchen wall for your addition. Save your money. We'll bring Ronnie over—she'll hurl her toys through the wall for free." Everyone laughed as Ken put his arm around Tessa. "Don't believe those stories about little girls playing daintily with dolls and boys running around and wrestling each other to the floor. You should see Ronnie when her Uncle Tony and Aunt Gina get their hands on her. It's an all-out free for all."

Tessa and Ken sat with friends around a rectangular table on a paver patio. Across the lawn, half a dozen guests played bocce ball and bean bag toss, and others relaxed on folding chairs set up around the yard. After a feast of burgers, hot dogs, corn on the cob, potato salad, and deviled eggs, they picked at various desserts. Wine and beer flowed, and everyone soaked up as much of the mid-September late afternoon sun as they could, like a good friend come to visit who would have to leave too soon.

Patty, the hostess, took a bite of a fudge brownie and pushed her plate away from her. She was a dermatologist in Ken's building, and every year she and her husband, Sean, hosted an end-of-summer cookout for a few of the building tenants and their staffs. "Come on, Ken. Look at her." She gestured to a corner of the yard where their teenage daughter Allison did crafts with the younger children. She was demonstrating how to turn iced tea cartons into bird feeders. Just then a three-year-old boy dumped a plastic cup of green paint onto the lawn beside him while Ronnie and the other toddlers looked on. "She's the best-behaved kid over there. A perfect angel!"

Ronnie noticed the adults watching her and climbed down from the picnic table. She ambled up next to her parents and pointed at the green paint blob. "Uh oh, Mommy. Mess!" She stuck up her pudgy index finger and waved it back and forth. "No, no."

Everyone laughed as Tessa scooped her daughter onto her lap. "Yes, it is. Looks like painting time is over." She called out sympathetically to Allison. "You might do better with Ring-Around-the-Rosie, Ali. They might not listen any better, but at least you won't get hit by flying paint!"

Tracy, who had just lost her third bocce match, approached the table and plucked a chocolate chip cookie from a tray. "Paint dumping breaks one of your cardinal rules, doesn't it, Tessa? Thou shalt not make a mess!" She giggled and sank into a chair next to her boss's wife. "Seriously, though, I'm so jealous. Every time I've been to your house, it's spotless. And not just because you know someone's coming over either." She picked up a bite-sized cheesecake and peeled the mini foil wrapper from it. She nodded toward Brenda, who looked on with a bored expression. "Bren, remember that time we were out to lunch and Ken asked us to swing by his house to pick up the mail? I swear, nothing was out of place. I don't know how you do it with a toddler, Tessa. I don't even have kids, and it looks like a bomb went off at my place."

Tessa shrugged and waved her arm. "It's just how I am. I like law and order, I guess." She laughed at a memory. "My college roommates used to call me the house mother. I had a list of weekly chores for each of us. One of their moms said her daughter had never hung up an article of clothing until she lived with me." She laughed self-consciously and shook her head.

Brenda drained her beer bottle and set it loudly on the table. "Well, if house cleaning ever becomes an Olympic sport, we'll look to you to bring home the gold." She reached in the cooler for another beer as the others exchanged knowing glances. "I guess not working helps. My house would be clean too if I didn't have to go to work every day."

Tessa's face reddened. "Oh, sure, I mean, of course, that's true. I have a lot more free time than you girls do." She studied her hands folded in her lap.

Ken chimed in. "I don't think that would matter. Tessa likes a neat house, and if she worked every day, she'd stay up half the night putting the house back in order." He gave his wife another squeeze. "There are worse habits."

"Yeah, Sean." Patty teased her husband, who worked very part-time as a freelance writer and loved his stay-at-home dad duty. "I wish you'd catch a little of Tessa's neatness disease. Not that I don't love tripping over everyone's shoes and bags when I come home at night."

Sean heartily chimed in, waving his hand dramatically. "I prefer more of a lived-in look."

Brenda opened her beer and glowered at Hank, who'd joined the group and sat across from his wife. "I'm just saying, whatever you're into, if you don't have to work, you have a lot more time to do it." She took a long pull and turned her glare toward Ken and Tessa.

"You have to work, hon," Hank offered jovially while stuffing a brownie in his mouth. "I couldn't afford your bar tab."

Everyone chuckled, thankful that Hank had come to the rescue with his easy humor. Brenda had been drinking all day, and she'd moved from cheery to loud-mouthed. They were used to it, but her awkward display still cast a shadow over the casual gathering.

The sun had moved directly over the yard, and there wasn't a hint of a breeze. One of the toddlers waddled over to his mother, his hair plastered to his sweaty paint-stained face. "Water please, Mama."

"Oh, look at that. I think that's our cue," offered Michelle, Patty's receptionist and the mother of a two-year-old who was pulling up fistfuls of grass and tossing them into the air. "Patty, Sean, thanks for another great picnic. Can we help you with the clean up?"

Patty shook her head. "No, don't worry about it. We got it. I'm glad you all could make it. It makes saying good-bye to summer a little easier."

As the other guests gathered their children, bags, and empty dessert trays, Tessa helped Patty carry plates and glasses inside. She looked around the finished basement in which Sean had built a small second kitchen. Tessa helped cover leftovers and put them in the fridge next to the sink. "I love what you've done down here, Patty. It looks great and it's so nice for entertaining. We just started talking about upgrading to a bigger house. We love our place, but it's small. We're overrun by Ronnie's things. How can a kid who's not even two have so much stuff?"

"I know, right? It's amazing. We were in a starter home too, and the same thing happened to us. Our kids forced us into a bigger space. Ken's been practicing almost two years now, right? You should be able to make a move soon, no?"

Tessa ripped off a piece of aluminum foil and covered a plate of deviled eggs. Things had been going smoothly lately. Ken's practice was booming, and he'd been doing better controlling his problem than he had since the very first incident. It was as if he woke up one day and decided he no longer needed the gas. He had his drinking under control too. He drank in social situations, but his drunken episodes were rare. Tessa hadn't thought it was possible for him to beat it on his own without professional help, but now she was cautiously optimistic.

"Yes, I think some positive changes are in our very near future." Tessa glanced outside at the remainder of the party guests and saw Brenda standing in the doorway listening to the exchange. She threw a few bottles into a recycling receptacle before turning to walk away.

Half an hour later, Ken steered the car into their driveway. Ronnie had fallen asleep in her car seat, and Tessa leaned in to lift her out. Across the street, a man with stringy blond hair leaned against his parked car.

Ken saw him and turned to Tessa. "Go ahead and take Ronnie in. I'll get the rest of the stuff." The man watched them. He threw a cigarette on the street and ground it out with his dirty high-top sneaker.

"Who is that? Do you know him?"

"Yeah, he's a patient. He owes me money. He's harmless but a little strange. Go ahead in. I'll handle him."

Ronnie stirred in Tessa's arms. "What's he doing here?"

"I don't know." Ken was irritated now. "I'll get rid of him."

Ken walked toward Stan's car. He turned around to make sure Tessa and Ronnie were in the house before he spoke angrily. "What the fuck are you doing? Showing up at my house? What's wrong with you?"

"Chill, dude. Nothing that a little candy won't help. Where you been, man? You haven't been coming around much lately. I thought we had a . . . what do you call it? . . . gentlemen's agreement." He pointed back and forth to Ken and then himself. "I help you, you help me."

"Christ, are you nuts? You can't come to my house, you idiot!" Ken kept his voice low, but that only made him sound maniacal. "Look, I've, um, not needed as much product lately. I'm trying to cut back." He glanced toward the house.

"Oh, I get it, man. Gotta make sacrifices for the family." He thrust his chin toward Ken's house. "Wouldn't want that clean-cut little wife of yours kickin' your sorry ass to the curb. But here's the thing. I'm *not* trying to cut back. I don't have anyone at home tellin' me what I can and can't do. I have an itch, and you gotta help me scratch it." A strand of hair fell into his eyes as he lit another cigarette. He blew a long puff of smoke in Ken's direction. "You see my dilemma?"

"Are you fucking stupid? Do you think I just keep bottles of Oxy and Percocet around my house?"

"Let's ease up on the name calling, bro. Delightful as you are and all, I don't really like you much either, but as I said, you have something I need. And if you ever decide you're tired of being a good little boy again, I'll help you out too."

Ken knew Tessa would start to wonder what was taking him so long to come in the house. "All right, all right, asshole."

"Again with the name calling—"

"Shut up. Come by the office tomorrow before anyone gets there. Be there by seven thirty. But I've told you before, I can't get an unlimited supply of these things."

Stan was already getting back into his car. "Details, details. You bother me with details."

Tessa had watched the last of the exchange through the kitchen blinds. Ken's back was to her, so she couldn't gauge his reaction to the man. She was at the sink rinsing out Ronnie's sippy cups when Ken came in. She looked over her shoulder. "So what did he want?"

Ken coolly played it off. "He wanted to know if we need any maintenance or yard work done. He needs a crown and can't afford it, so he offered to barter. He doesn't have insurance." He dried a cup and put it in the cabinet.

"That's a shame."

"He's not a bad guy. I told him to stop in the office and we'll talk about options."

"I guess he got our address from the phone book?"

"Yeah. Maybe we should change to an unlisted number."

Later, when Tessa got into bed, Ken was already there flipping through the TV channels. She lay next to him and took his hand. "Nothing good on?" She leaned against him. "That was fun today. Oh, but what was up with Brenda? All that stuff about me being a clean freak and her not wanting to work? Hank seemed amused, but I think he was embarrassed."

"Oh, you know how she gets. She has a few beers and runs at the mouth. It's kind of her thing." Ken yawned.

"I guess. But she was really jazzed about it. It's weird, but lately I feel like she doesn't like me. I catch her looking at me like I'm an annoying bug she wants to flick off her arm. We always got along okay before. Maybe I'm imagining it. She sounds like she really resents working. Do you think she'll quit?"

"Nah, you heard Hank. He doesn't earn enough to keep her in Merlot and Heineken." He sat upright. "Hey, I almost forgot. I picked up that new John Grisham book you wanted. I was near the mall the other day at lunch. It's in your nightstand."

"Really? Thanks! Maybe I'll start it right now." She reached over to open the drawer, but Ken pulled her back.

He switched off the TV and rolled on top of her. "No, not right now. I have other plans for you."

Afterward, Tessa lay on her side. Ken was behind her, his arm draped over her, holding her close. "Ken?" she whispered. "I know you are trying. I don't want you to think I don't see it. I know it must be hard. But I'm here for you. If it gets too hard and you need me to help you, I'm here."

"Mmm, I know, doll." He nuzzled her neck.

"Isn't this so much better? We're so good together when it's like this." She sighed and closed her eyes. "I think we're going to be okay."

She said it as much to herself as to him.

Chapter Twenty-Two

Tessa read over the lesson plans on the teacher's desk twice and figured it should be an easy day. She preferred subbing for high school English teachers, but this week they'd needed her in the social studies department at the junior high. Only late September, it was unusual that they needed subs at all yet. Poor Barry Burkholder thought he'd pulled a muscle in his lower back, but it turned out he had appendicitis. He'd be out all week, and Tessa agreed to fill in. Barry prepared lesson plans for each day, and Tessa fell into a comfortable routine with his classes. It was Friday, the last day of the assignment, and she had to admit she would miss subbing for him. With a few exceptions, his students were polite and hardworking.

"Last day, huh?" The voice at the door belonged to Kelly Masterson, a friendly reading teacher whose room was just down the hall. "Bet you're going to miss us."

"Believe it or not, I was just thinking that. I didn't think I'd like it here at the junior high, but I do. There's an energy here that the high school doesn't have. I may put my name on the permanent sub list here."

"You call it energy, I call it craziness," Kelly joked. "You should, though. This is the best building in the district. We don't take ourselves too seriously." She lowered her voice and looked over her shoulder. "And rumor has it that some permanent positions may be opening up soon in the language arts department. Just FYI."

"Interesting. Thanks for the info." The bell sounded to release the students from their holding places in the cafeteria into the halls. They'd have ten minutes to go to their lockers and get to homeroom.

"Sure. Gotta get to my post. The hounds have been released!"

The first four periods flew by without incident. The kids worked on group presentations about ancient Greece. They'd been gathering information and planning the specifics of the presentations all week. The groups worked cooperatively, and Tessa was impressed with their work ethic and the depth of their research. Only one student, a spirited boy, annoyed his group to the point that they good-naturedly threatened to lock shields and drive a spear through his eye socket. Luckily, the class ended before the rebellion, and everyone escaped unscathed.

In the staff lounge, Tessa heated her lunch in the microwave. Kelly came in behind her. "You're brave. Looks like there's a science project growing in there."

Tessa wrinkled her nose. "Yeah, I noticed. I have a great cleaner at home. I'll bring it in next time I'm here." She opened the door and grasped the steaming container by its edges. Grabbing a seat next to Kelly at the round laminated table, she opened a water bottle and took a swig.

Kelly unwrapped a ham and cheese sandwich. "My kids are wound up today. Is it a full moon?"

"Hey, Tessa! I heard you were here all week, but I haven't had a chance to get up here at lunch to say hello! How are you?" A large man with a moustache and beard entered the room and hugged Tessa. He wore a plaid sweater vest with a long-sleeved collared shirt underneath and wrinkled khakis. "I thought you only did high school gigs. What brings you here?"

"Hey, Eric. I'm filling in for Barry. Today's my last day, but I think I may start subbing here regularly." Eric and his wife,

Becky, an assistant at a podiatrist's office, lived near Ken and Tessa. They had a daughter six months older than Ronnie, and they were patients of Ken's.

"She's been bitten by the junior high bug," Kelly said as she popped a mini pretzel into her mouth. "God help her!"

"It grows on you. Kind of like mold." Eric opened the microwave door. "Mmm . . . speaking of mold."

"Kelly's trying to entice me to come work here permanently. She has an excellent pitch: The kids drive you crazy, but you have the most fun staff in the district. She said you guys go out for happy hour one Friday a month. That's enough to convince me right there." Tessa took a bite of her Lean Cuisine stir-fry.

"Are you trying to say the kids drive us to drink, Kel?" Eric brought his pizza to the table and pulled out a chair. "And Ken can't complain. You get Ronnie duty when he goes out to Mulligan's with his hygienist, right?"

Tessa stopped chewing and twitched as though jabbed with a sharp object. "Mulligan's? What?"

Eric spoke through a mouthful of pizza. "Yeah, Mulligan's. Beck saw them there one night at the end of the summer. She was out with the girls and saw Ken and his hygienist—what's her name again?—at the bar."

What is he talking about? Not that it would be such a big deal for Ken to go out with his staff. He'd just never mentioned it.

"Brenda." Tessa's stomach churned, but she fought to remain nonchalant.

"Yeah, Brenda. That's it." He stuffed the crust into his mouth. "Now I remember. I was beside myself because the Phils blew a lead in the ninth inning and lost in thirteen. I was still fuming when Becky came home. She plopped down on the sofa next to me and yammered on and on about how nice it is that Ken gets along so well with his staff, but her coworkers at the podiatrist office are stiffs and don't ever do anything fun together."

Tessa pieced Eric's words together. He continued talking, but the buzzing in her head drowned out his voice. Ken and Brenda were at Mulligan's together? When? In slow motion, the night Eric was referring to came to her.

Yeah, Scotty and I grabbed some dinner and a beer after work. I ran into him at the gas station this morning. His wife is out of town also.

She'd tried so hard not to interrogate Ken about his night.

I thought Joey was going to throw the remote through the TV screen tonight. The Phils were winning the whole game, and the pitcher gave up a home run in the ninth to tie it. They ended up losing in thirteen innings.

Ken and Brenda went out after work while Tessa was at the beach, and Ken lied about it. Why would he lie about that? On its face there was nothing wrong with that. So why lie?

Tessa gathered her half-eaten lunch and water bottle. She felt heat creeping up her neck onto her face, wondered if the others could hear her heart pounding. She hoped they didn't see realization dawn on her, threatening to bury her like lava from an erupted volcano. "I, uh, better get back. The room is a mess from the last class, and I need to get it ready for the next one. See you guys."

"Bye, Tess. Hope we see you again soon."

Later that night after putting Ronnie to bed, Tessa opened a bottle of Cabernet and poured herself a generous glass. She lifted her glass in a mock toast. "To me, and the fucking mess that is my life. Cheers." She drank a big swallow and refilled her glass.

She'd fumbled through the rest of the day at school in a fog. She was grateful for the distraction. It forced her to slow down and gather her thoughts. It also kept her in check. At one point a nervous overachieving girl came to her upset because the glue she used on a sword she'd made for her presentation wouldn't hold. Tessa wanted to answer, "Well, I can top that.

I thought my husband was just a drug addict, but now it turns out he might be fucking his hygienist. Sucks, huh?" Instead she'd dutifully helped the distraught girl affix the sword pieces with thin wire.

Now, still somewhat numbed by today's revelation, she pulled a chair next to the window and sat cross-legged, watching the cars' headlights as they passed on the street beyond the driveway. She wondered idly about the lives of the cars' passengers. Though she couldn't see them from the house, she imagined their stories in her mind. A man heading home after a long week at work, anxious to get there in time to tuck his small children into bed. A family driving home from pizza and movie night, young children in the back seat repeatedly singing songs from the movie, their parents smiling at each other in the front seat. A single woman dressed in a new outfit on her way to the bar to meet friends and kick off the weekend.

Then her mind brought into focus another scene: Ken and Brenda at the bar at Mulligan's. Why wouldn't Ken tell her about it? Why lie and say he had dinner with Scotty?

Because Ken is a fucking liar, that's why. Lying was as natural as breathing to him. It was involuntary, like blinking. He told so many lies he even lied about things it would be just as easy to be truthful about.

Unless there *was* a reason. She remembered how uncomfortable she'd felt around Brenda lately, like the only person who wasn't in on a joke. And Brenda's drunken diatribe at Patty and Sean's picnic. At the time Tessa thought it was directed at Hank, but maybe it wasn't. *Well, if house cleaning ever becomes an Olympic sport, Tessa, we'll look to you to bring home the gold.*

She took a sip and laughed out loud at the irony. "A dentist fooling around with his hygienist. How original." Shaking her head, she had to admit it was pretty clever. She was so consumed with Ken's substance abuse issues she never gave it a thought that he might be getting a little on the side.

She would have to muster the energy to broach all of this with her husband, but not tonight. Tonight, it was clear by the late hour, Ken wouldn't be coming home. After a few months of relative peace, of hopefulness that maybe he had seen the light and slain his dragon without professional help, just like that it all started up again. A giant *Oh shit* after months of *Atta boys*. Only tonight Tessa added a whole new hell to the equation. Was Ken using nitrous oxide? Was he with Brenda? Both? As worn out as she was, she was almost glad she didn't have to deal with it tonight.

As another set of headlights made their way up the dark street in the distance, Tessa imagined that she was back at the bar where she and Ken met. She saw them in that smoky room, the backlit stage and pulsing music the backdrop to their mutual attraction. Then she imagined that someone had approached her that autumn night and warned her, "He will turn into an unfaithful substance abuser, and you will spend your marriage trapped in a web of codependency and lies." Draining her glass, she wondered whether it was good or bad that people didn't know their futures. True, it would save a lot of heartache, but it would also prevent them from enjoying the present.

Chapter Twenty-Three

Tessa clutched her bathrobe in front of her and stared into her full coffee cup. She raised it to her lips and winced. Though she hadn't taken one sip, it had gone cold. Her feet were tucked under her on the sofa, and she tried to summon the strength to make it to the kitchen to heat her coffee in the microwave.

"Okay, I'm off." Ken emerged from the bedroom, fastening his watch around his wrist. He looked at her curiously. "What's up? Aren't you supposed to sub at the junior high today?" His pupils were still dilated, and dark circles rimmed his eyes.

"Yeah, but I called in sick. I uh . . . I'm having a little trouble getting moving this morning."

She'd barely slept last night. She was still awake when Ken sauntered in just after 4 a.m. He didn't bother with apologies or explanations anymore. And she didn't have the strength to bring it up. How many times could they have the same go-around? She'd yell about how he was supposed to be trying, and he'd yell back about needing a break when he backslid.

A few weeks ago, after Eric told Tessa about Ken and Brenda at Mulligan's, just as Tessa figured he would, Ken coolly played off the whole thing and denied anything was going on. He claimed he actually had met Scotty for dinner that night and spotted Brenda alone at the bar as they were leaving, so he chatted with her for a few minutes before heading out. When she questioned Brenda's recent disdain with her, he said Tessa was paranoid and inventing new things to argue about. He'd refused to discuss it any further. Tessa wasn't sure she believed him, but she was too weary to argue.

She felt like she was losing her mind. She tiptoed around Ken as though *she* were the one with a problem. Instead of pushing back, she remained silent, afraid of what would happen if she removed the lid from her steaming bowl of secrets.

Through the sheers on the living room windows, Tessa watched the thin October light seep into the house. Outside, she knew the neighborhood was waking up to another commonplace day. People were on their way to work, school, or breakfast. They were going about their business, enjoying whatever was on their schedules today, untouched by addiction, unscathed by a spouse hellbent on destroying their lives. She envied them this, and at the same time she felt like a kindred spirit with those who were going through a situation like hers. For all she knew, the nice lady who pushed her grandson in the stroller past Tessa's house had a husband at home who began drinking bourbon every day at noon. Or the boy who bagged her groceries went home every night to a mother slumped on the sofa, numbed by painkillers. She'd never know. They were covering it up just as she was.

For Tessa, Ken's addiction was a tenacious and unwanted companion that threatened to upend every event. It waited in the wings always: holidays, birthdays, Tuesdays. At any moment it might emerge, barge into every crevice of their life.

And yet she knew she had no one but herself to blame for her predicament. This was the sentence she imposed on herself: Keep quiet, be supportive, don't rock the boat. Her silence was the only thing buying them time. If she let even a bucketful of water in the boat, it would submerge slowly, and then it would only be a matter of time before it sank completely.

In everyone's eyes, Ken was a model husband, father, and son-in-law. He brought flowers home for Tessa for no reason, pushed Ronnie around the neighborhood in her orange-and-yellow Little Tikes car, and mowed Sal and Val's lawn when their regular guy went on vacation. She'd be a damn fool to leave him. Or so everyone thought. All he asked of her was this one thing. One thing he'd convinced her she must never tell anyone about.

And now the stakes were even higher.

It was exhausting, all of it. The uncertainty of the future. Her marriage in constant peril. They'd have a calm period, and then, *BAM*; Ken would revert to his old ways.

She could get up. She had to. Tessa stretched her legs, tingling from lack of movement. She willed herself to crawl out of her burrow, rise to her feet, try for the thousandth time to make sense of her world. She felt capable of neither decision nor action.

Ken shrugged into his coat. "Come on, girl. Buck up. Drink some orange juice. You'll feel better." He whistled as he went out the front door, and it felt like needles piercing Tessa's brain.

The morning started off chilly, but the autumn sun quickly warmed Ken's car windows. He was still whistling when he entered his office building. Riding up in the elevator, he marveled at how energized he felt this morning, considering his activity the previous night. Hell, he shouldn't be surprised. It was just what he'd needed. Tessa just didn't understand. Occasionally he had to give in to the craving. He put it off and put it off until his mood was so sour he couldn't even stand himself. He was better, *they* were better, when he cleaned out the cobwebs from time to time.

As he hung up his coat in his private office, Brenda walked in briskly with a stack of charts. She took one look at him and stopped, hugging the charts to her chest.

"You okay?"

"Better than ever," he said, smiling contently.

"Good." She returned the smile and let her gaze linger on him a moment longer. She placed the charts on his desk and walked out into the hall. "I'll get you some coffee."

Chapter Twenty-Four

Tessa saw CeCe waving at her from across the park. The weather had turned, and though it was only the first week in November, the temperature was unseasonably cool. All along the park's perimeter, the leaves on the trees were rich oranges and reds. Soon Tessa would replace the light cotton blanket on her bed with a heavier quilted one and dress Ronnie in fleece footed pajamas because she kicked her soft blanket off during the night.

Tessa was glad she saw CeCe as soon as she got to the park. She wasn't planning to stay long; she wanted Ronnie to have a nice long nap this afternoon. Gina was a "mighty-mite" cheerleader and had a game at the local stadium under the lights tonight. She'd called Tessa excitedly this morning to tell her that her squad had learned a new pom-pom routine, and she couldn't wait for Tessa to see it. Tessa pulled her jacket tightly around her and made a mental note to bring Ronnie's hat and gloves to the game.

Ronnie was having no parts of the stroller, so Tessa let her walk. She held the toddler's little hand in her left and pushed the stroller onto the walking path with the right. Ronnie jumped up and down as she walked, causing the hood on her brown and pink floral jacket to slide down off her head. She counted benches along the edge of the path. "One! Two! Two! Two!"

Tessa laughed and shook her head. "No, silly, three comes next after two." Ronnie giggled and jumped over a crack in the macadam.

Tessa hadn't told anyone about CeCe. She liked the idea of having someone to talk to who wouldn't question why she was cool to Ken at family gatherings. She liked having a friend who wasn't half of a couple with whom Tessa and Ken went out to dinner, who might notice her pull away slightly when Ken draped his arm over her shoulder. She liked that she didn't have to grit her teeth and nod in phony agreement when fellow teachers or Sal's customers gushed about what a gentle and caring dentist Ken was. And she still felt like Brenda was judging her. She and Ronnie had gone out to lunch with Ken and his staff last week a day after Ken hadn't come home until 3 a.m. Tessa had been tired and edgy, and when Brenda and Ken told entertaining stories about patients, she swore she saw Brenda roll her eyes at Tessa's lack of amusement. Tessa hadn't brought up the Mulligan's incident or Ken and Brenda fooling around again. Ken had made her feel so silly about her irrational paranoia that she convinced herself she'd made something out of nothing.

With CeCe she didn't have to pretend.

It had been much warmer outside the last time Tessa saw CeCe. They'd met in the park several more times since that first day last April, though lately Tessa had skipped the park after Mommy and Me—if she went to Mommy and Me at all. Tessa missed their relaxed walks and chats. Once when it started to rain, they'd even gone to Dunkin' Donuts and talked over hot chocolate and warm croissants. Little by little, like a spool of thread, Tessa unraveled bits of her life, baring only what she wanted to talk about. CeCe did the same, and Tessa got the feeling the older woman was holding back more than she revealed, but who was she to judge? She was doing the same thing.

The funny thing was, recently Tessa thought about confiding in CeCe. CeCe didn't know Ken, wasn't around them in social situations, wouldn't forevermore examine them like specimens under a microscope. That was what most prevented Tessa from telling her family and friends about Ken's problem. Besides infuriating Ken, she knew she could never un-tell them. Like squirting too much toothpaste out of the tube, she wouldn't be able to push it back in. What if she told them all and then in a few months Ken got help and stopped? She couldn't very well just then say, "Okay, never mind. Forget I ever said anything. Nothing to see here."

For the rest of their lives, every time she and Ken had an argument or he was ten minutes late, they'd all look at each other in deafening silence: *I bet he's at it again.* Would they pity her or figure she deserved it for staying with him? She didn't know which was worse. Tessa didn't want to go through the rest of her life with her marriage as everyone's sociology project.

But CeCe was different. An uninvolved third party. It would be like talking to a counselor.

As CeCe walked toward them, zipping up her hoodie against the chilly breeze, Tessa tried to remember how many weeks it had been since they'd last seen each other. She didn't feel much like socializing these days. Sometimes it took all her energy to cover up for Ken, wondering if he would come home, tiptoeing around the minefield of his erratic moods, explaining his mysterious absences, and being both mother and father to Ronnie. Some days, if she wasn't subbing or helping Sal, she didn't even get out of her pajamas. Mariel pressed for Ronnie and her to come for playdates, but Tessa invented excuse after excuse not to go. She couldn't face Mariel; her best friend would know instantly something was very wrong and wouldn't rest until Tessa came clean. She'd turn Tessa upside down and shake her until all the secrets fell from her pockets.

Tessa was so tangled up in Ken's problem she wasn't sure she existed anymore without their secret. That was her reality; everything else seemed made up. When she filled in at Sal's and asked customers how they wanted their eggs, she felt like a character in a play. When she subbed in English classes and explained why linking verbs weakened persuasive essays, it was as if she were reading from a movie script. Going through the motions, pretending their lives were normal, Tessa felt as if she'd wandered into a dream. Everything around her felt hazy and half-true, as if at any moment it might all disappear in a puff of smoke.

Val suspected something was wrong. She didn't push, but sometimes she'd gently ask Tessa if there was anything she wanted to talk about. "I know my kids," she'd say. Tessa waved her off with phony explanations and platitudes. Last month they'd gone shopping together for Halloween costumes for Ronnie and Gina. Tessa had been on edge, and though she'd done her best to hide it, she came close to showing her hand. Gina had tried on a hideously gory monster mask and popped out from behind a display. "Arrrggghhh! Trick-or-treat!"

"Good God, Gina!" Val clutched her chest. "You don't want to give your classmates a heart attack, do you?"

"What do you think, Tess?" Gina peeled the mask off over her head, her hair a tangle of static electricity. "Do you like this one for my parade at school or should I be a Disney princess?" She picked up a wand and swirled it around in front of her as Ronnie tried to grab it. "Ronnie, you're my minion!"

Val laughed. "The stuff she picks up from those Disney movies."

Tessa turned to her little sister. "I like the monster one. It's more realistic. Nobody lives that fairytale princess life in those Disney movies, but lots of people have monstrous qualities under the surface." Gina twirled around with her wand and was no longer listening, but Val regarded her older daughter with raised eyebrows.

"Well, that's a cynical answer to give an eight-year-old, don't you think?"

"Maybe. I just don't want her growing up thinking some prince is going to come along and sweep her off her feet and whisk her off to his castle to live happily ever after. It's all bullshit."

"True. But how about we leave the deep lessons for another day and let the kids enjoy Halloween? It's more about getting free candy than choosing a life path." Val touched Tessa's arm. "Are you sure there's nothing on your mind?"

Tessa straightened up and looked around the shop. "Yeah, I'm sure. So, do you see anything for Ronnie?"

"Oh, look at this little ladybug costume. Wouldn't she look adorable with these antennae sprouting from her head?" Val busied herself tying the red hood on her granddaughter while Tessa scolded herself inwardly for her morose display.

She usually tried to avoid her parents during particularly dark times, but that only succeeded in setting off her mother's radar even more. Still, Tessa knew if she even ventured close to confiding in Val, the floodgates would open and there would be no turning back.

And sometimes it just plain looked to everyone as though Tessa was an ungrateful bitch. Last week they had Sunday dinner at Sal and Val's with the whole family. Ken hadn't come home the night before, and Tessa was sullen. Ken, however, having had his fix, was in good spirits. He was usually on his best behavior after a binge, like a child who does extra chores after being disciplined for finger painting on the living room wall. Tessa hadn't had much of an appetite, and Ken fussed over her, offering to get her more ice water and rushing to wipe Ronnie's spaghetti-smeared face and hands when she finished eating. He even casually threw out during dinner that he had been looking at new Jeeps for Tessa. He wanted one with a five-star safety rating; he only trusted the best and safest vehicle with his precious wife and daughter.

He'd shown his in-laws the brochure, and they admired the sleek design of the new models.

Later, as they filled the dishwasher, Val told Tessa she was one lucky girl. She looked sternly at her daughter when she just stared straight ahead and said nothing. Later, when they'd packed away the leftovers, Val had whispered, "Maybe you could go a little easy on him, huh? He's one of the good ones." Tessa had wanted to scream.

"Buhdie!" Ronnie's shriek returned Tessa to the present. A flock of birds flew overhead, and Ronnie eagerly pointed and twisted her little body so far around to watch them that she tripped over her feet and landed on her backside.

"Whoa, there!" Tessa brushed off the seat of Ronnie's overalls and helped her back on her feet.

CeCe wasn't involved in Tessa's life, but odds were she'd wonder where Tessa had been lately. She tied Ronnie's hood under her chin as the older woman approached, and readied herself for the inevitable questions.

"Hey, over here!" CeCe called out, brushing her hair out of her eyes. She was so happy to see Tessa and Ronnie that she broke into a trot. She'd glanced at her watch a minute ago and worried that Tessa would be a no-show again today. She'd come to enjoy her time with them. *Who are you kidding?* she thought as Tessa steered the stroller in her direction. *You look forward to it.*

"Long time, no see, you two! I was getting ready to send out a search party!" CeCe caught up to them and bent down to hand a small pumpkin to Ronnie. It had a turkey face painted on it, and Ronnie immediately held it up to Tessa and poked her chubby finger at the painted beak.

"That's the turkey's nose, sweetie. And where's yours?" Ronnie promptly tapped her own nose while CeCe clapped in admiration.

"Beautiful and smart too." CeCe lightly pinched her cheek before turning back to Tessa. "So, how have you been?"

"Oh, okay, I guess." Tessa studied the ground.

"Mmm-hmm. Well, listen, don't ever consider a career as a professional poker player. You'll lose your shirt on the first hand." CeCe fell into step next to Tessa and playfully nudged her with her elbow. Her nails were painted bright orange with a thin strip of yellow at the nail base and strip of white at the tips. She saw Tessa notice them.

"Silly, huh? A woman my age with a candy corn manicure." She shoved her hands in her pockets. "It's just something I do for fun."

"No, I like it. It's unique. Why be like everyone else, right?"

They chatted as they walked for a few minutes until they came to a swing set. Ronnie pulled on Tessa's jacket hem and then zoomed off in the direction of the swings. "Up, up, up, RoRo up!" she yelled. CeCe laughed at Ronnie's nickname for herself.

Lifting Ronnie into a bucket swing and fastening the seat belt, Tessa looked over her shoulder at CeCe. "How do you like your apartment by now?" Then she added, "Do you like living alone?"

CeCe sat on the swing next to Ronnie's and turned, twisting the chains, so she faced Tessa, who stood pushing the squealing toddler. She studied the serious look on the younger woman's face. "Oh, the apartment is fine." CeCe gazed into the distance. "And living alone . . . Sometimes it gets lonely. But I think I'm better being on my own."

"Really? Why do you say that? What is it about living alone that appeals to you?"

CeCe considered the question, and Tessa continued, retying her ponytail, which had come undone. "I mean, it must be peaceful, right? You don't have to worry about a husband's schedule or a roommate's sloppy habits. There's something to be said for that, isn't there?"

Tessa stopped pushing and let the momentum carry Ronnie. "You mentioned once that you have grown children you don't see very often. Have they come to visit yet?"

CeCe closed her eyes and lifted her feet, which caused her swing to spin in circles as the chains untangled. She opened her mouth as if to speak, but Tessa stopped her.

"Don't mind me. I'm being nosy and rude. You didn't come here to be interrogated."

"No, it's okay, Tessa. I'm happy to answer your questions. I'll let you know if I'd rather not. But first I have a question for you." She tilted her head and leaned forward. "Why the fascination with living alone?"

Chapter Twenty-Five

"Ma-ma-ma-ma!"

"Well, look who's up! Let's have some dinner and get ready for Aunt Gina's game!" Ronnie stood in her crib, clapping and waving her arms. "I think you'll be the next cheerleader in the bunch!" Tessa placed Ronnie on the changing table, applied a fresh diaper, and dressed her in a purple fleece matching top and pants. "You'll need your warm coat tonight, little one."

She felt better after her afternoon stroll and talk with CeCe. She'd let her guard down a bit and, without going into specifics, alluded to the fact that she was dealing with struggles in her marriage. The older woman didn't fish for information. She let Tessa say as much or, more accurately, as little as she wanted. She didn't offer any advice, but Tessa found it comforting just to talk freely without worrying about having to go into lengthy explanations. When Tessa said Ken spent an inordinate amount of time at his office after hours, CeCe let it go at that. Tessa liked being able to speak to someone who would not watch her every move or possibly catch her in a lie constructed to cover up for Ken. CeCe was impartial and uninvolved in their lives. Talking to her was harmless.

Tessa had just put pieces of shredded chicken and bits of steamed carrots into Ronnie's bowl when Ken came through the door.

"Hi, girls! What's up?" He washed his hands and sat down next to Ronnie, who eagerly offered him a fistful of her dinner. "Looks delicious, but I'll pass, sweetie."

Tessa methodically packed the diaper bag with snacks, drinks, and a knit blanket. Ken looked confused. "Are you going somewhere?"

"*We're* going to Gina's game, remember? The concession stand has pizza, burgers, and fries. I thought we'd just eat something there. The game starts at seven, so we'll be late if we try to eat before we go." She picked up a piece of chicken Ronnie had dropped on the floor. "You should change. And bring gloves. It's already getting dark, and it's going to be chilly tonight." She paused and looked at her husband, who was fidgeting with his keys.

"Um, I guess I forgot." He gave Tessa a beseeching look. "I'm not going to the game. I'm going back to the office."

Tessa froze. "Ken, no. Come on. I already told my parents we were coming."

"Well, tell them I had work to do."

Tessa shook her head. "No. Please. Don't do this tonight." She attempted to dial back her emotions. "Come to the game. Spend some time with us. Think about how good things are when you aren't using. The craving will pass. If you give in to it every time, you'll never beat this."

But Ken was already backing toward the door. They both looked at Ronnie, still in her high chair, and kept their voices level so as not to upset her.

Ken slumped his shoulders and bowed his head. "Tess, you have no idea how often I fight it. I don't give in to it every time. Not even close. I just . . . tonight . . . tonight I need to go to the office."

Tessa felt herself losing control, freefalling as if in a dream. Ken tried again. "I'm sorry, doll. I really am. Have fun at the game. You know where I'll be. Don't think about it. Just go to the game." He kissed the top of Ronnie's head, grabbed his coat, and headed toward the front door.

Unable to stop herself, Tessa ran after him. She caught up to him and took his arm. "Please, Ken. Come with us." He reached the car door and grabbed the handle. The evening sky was thick with swirling clouds. A car drove up the road, but between the darkness and the long driveway, they couldn't tell whether it was someone they knew or a total stranger. Oblivious to the scene, the driver continued past Ken and Tessa's driveway.

"Go back in the house, Tess. I mean it." Ken's voice was quiet and measured. He got behind the wheel and started the engine.

Tessa looked around wildly, as if she were looking for something to hurl at him. Not knowing how else to stop him, she hopped up on the trunk of the car. Ken looked in the rearview mirror and angrily threw open the car door. "What the hell are you doing? Are you crazy?"

"Maybe I am. Maybe I am, but I can't take it anymore."

"Tess, come on. Get off the car!"

"No! I won't! I don't want you to go!"

"Get off the car right now or I'll drive away with you on it." Malice laced his voice.

"No you won't. You won't do that." She was crying now. She shivered, and her nose was running into her mouth, but she didn't care. She'd stop him no matter what. If he just came with them, he'd enjoy the night with his family, and when they came home, she'd tell him—

Her thoughts were interrupted by the backward lurch of the car. She cried out as her neck jerked to the left and her legs swung out from under her. She hit the ground with a thud and rolled onto her right side. Her right arm and leg scraped the driveway, and a burning sensation gripped her. She lifted her head just in time to see Ken's car swing out of the driveway and speed off down the street.

Shaking and gasping for breath, Tessa lay on the ground for a minute with her eyes closed. Finally, she picked herself up and, wincing, trudged back up the walk and into the house. She reentered the kitchen, where Ronnie still sat in her high chair, babbling a song. Tessa leaned against the wall and sank down to the floor.

Upon seeing her, Ronnie began to fuss. "Out! Out! RoRo out!" Tessa picked herself up and went to her daughter. She hugged her tightly to her chest. She stood like that for a few minutes, rocking back and forth.

Ronnie touched Tessa's bruised arm. "Uh oh, booboo." She lowered her face to her mother's arm and made kissing noises.

Trembling less now, Tessa held Ronnie's hand and guided her to the bathroom. The toddler plopped down on the floor and emptied a bucket of bath toys. Tessa turned on the faucet and held a washcloth under it. When the water warmed, she wiped her face and dabbed her arm and leg. Her jeans were ripped, so she stripped them off and threw them on the floor. She picked pieces of gravel from her abrasions and then took out a tube of antibacterial ointment from the medicine cabinet. She ran a brush through her hair and put on a pair of fresh jeans.

As she bundled Ronnie into the car, Tessa noticed that, although she was covered by long sleeves and pants, the top of her right hand had a brush burn on it. On the drive to the game, she concocted plausible explanations to tell her parents. *Oh, that? I did it when I was putting Ronnie's outgrown clothes into the crawlspace.*

She'd come up with something. There were thousands of ways to bang up your hands just going through the motions of a typical day.

It was the bruises they couldn't see that threatened to break her.

The morning sun had barely risen over Neversink Mountain when Ken left the office and crossed the parking lot. He felt like shit. His head pounded and did his grogginess no favors. It was Saturday, so the parking lot was empty. There was no one to see the disheveled and disoriented figure plodding to his car after a night of huffing nitrous oxide. No one to ask him why he wasn't home with his wife and baby. No one to tell him he looked as shitty as he felt. No one to tell him he *was* as shitty as he felt.

He pulled out of the lot after looking left and right for other cars. Had he looked straight ahead at the upper parking lot of the office complex on the other side of the service road, he might have noticed the woman sitting behind the wheel of her Honda Civic, tapping her orange fingernails on the dashboard and watching him with interest.

The house was pitch black when Tessa returned after the game. Ronnie had fallen asleep in the car, her mouth sticky from dinosaur-shaped fruit snacks and her fist clutching a mini pom-pom from Gina. Thankfully, she didn't wake up when Tessa laid her on the changing table to put on her flannel sleeper. Tessa pulled Ronnie's bedroom door closed and dragged herself into the living room, where she fell exhausted onto the sofa.

She was still there the next morning at daybreak when Ken came home. She heard him come in but couldn't clear her head of the heaviness of deep sleep. Slumber would not release her, as if someone held her head under water. She felt the cushion move next to her as he sat down. He pulled a blanket from the back of the sofa and gently covered Tessa with it.

She blinked several times and managed to pry open her eyes. Tiredness permeated her body down to its core, weighing down her bones and draining every ounce of her energy. She had been this tired for over a year now, and she craved the merciful amnesia that came with sleep. The first five seconds of the day were her favorite, before her memory came alive, before she had to face it all over again.

Ken was staring at her. His face was blank. He didn't so much as blink. Her right arm hung off the side of the couch, revealing her bruises. She saw him studying them. "You know, Tess. It doesn't have to be like this every time."

She stared at him and said nothing.

"Why would you make me hurt you like that? Why do you have to act so crazy?"

Awake now, she pushed herself up into a sitting position. Ken ran his hand through his oily hair and exhaled loudly. "I'm not perfect. Far from it. I know that. But I'm a pretty damn good husband most of the time. Why can't you just be happy when things are going well and look the other way when I backslide? I'm sober most of the time. Do I have to be perfect?"

His words hung in the air between them. She considered his talent for this, saying things so bizarre that they almost swung back around to sensible. The room was silent except for the ticking clock on the end table. Whenever Gina slept over on the couch, she hid the clock because she said the ticking kept her awake. She'd make a game out of Tessa finding it in the morning. One time she'd hidden it in the dryer.

Tessa sat curled up in the corner of the sofa with her knees pulled up to her chest, her arms clasped around them. When she finally spoke, it was barely audible. "No, you don't have to be perfect. Your periods of sobriety are good, but they're not enough to make it all okay. They don't salvage the rest of it. They're like a week of warm weather in a cold rainy spring."

Ken sighed and rubbed his eye sockets with his thumb and middle finger. "We'll be okay. We'll figure it out. We have time."

Tessa looked directly at his face. "No, we don't, not really. I'm pregnant."

Chapter Twenty-Six

Joey reached in and turned on the last of the three showers in the four-bedroom two-story stone house. "Mmmm. Nice. Passes my test."

"Joey, you lunatic," Tessa hissed, looking over her shoulder for the real estate agent. In spite of herself, she had to laugh at her brother. "Knock it off. Why don't you just climb in and lather up while you're at it?"

He gave her a mockingly smug look and dried his hands on his jeans. "Not a bad idea. You know what they say, Tess. 'Location, location, water pressure.'"

"Yeah, they definitely don't say that." Tessa shook her head and sighed. This wasn't the house for them. True, there was no denying its charms. It was built around 1930 and had an expansive front porch that wrapped around the entire front and the right side. Bay windows adorned with stained glass flanked the front door. Its dark wood foyer and winding staircase had seen better days, but the realtor assured them that these could be stripped and refinished to perfection. In truth, Tessa found the dark interior and well-worn floors depressing. For someone, it would be a great renovation project. The outdated rugs could be pulled up and the heavy draperies at the windows removed. Painters could brighten up the rooms, and newer, fresher cabinets would update the kitchen and baths. It would be a great renovation project for someone, but not for them. They had enough going on. They'd told the realtor they were interested in new or recent construction, but she couldn't resist showing them what she referred to as this "sprawling charmer."

That had been two weeks ago, and Ken and Tessa had seen at least ten houses since then. They asked Joey to go with them to see older houses, since he was the handyman in the family. "No offense, Ken, but you're a white-collar guy. Gotta do more than kick the tires," he instructed them. "You need a genius like me who knows what he's looking for."

Today they were only scheduled to look at new properties, so Joey gave them permission to go without him. They'd just left the fourth house of the day, and Tessa was growing weary of comparing crown moldings and light fixtures. While these houses didn't need all the work that older houses required, the tradeoff was that they all tended to look the same.

"I want to show you one last property. But you have to keep an open mind. I've been doing this a long time, and I'm picking up a vibe." Elaine, the real estate agent, shot Ken a knowing smile. "Especially from you, Dr. Cordelia. I don't think you want a cookie-cutter house. I think you're ready for something more. Come on, you can follow me. It's just a few miles from here." Elaine was about fifty years old, her hair was cut in a sleek blonde bob, and she wore bright apricot lipstick that seemed too tropical for the January chill. She climbed behind the wheel of her white Volvo, waved and honked her horn, and steered out of the driveway of the last listing.

"What did you think of that one, babe?" Ken spoke freely away from Elaine. "I didn't like the kitchen or bathroom cabinets. They look cheap. But it did have lots of closet space, and I like the finished room in the basement. That would make a sweet toy room for Ronnie and her little brother or sister. Still, it's just so . . . I don't know . . . ordinary. I'm waiting for Elaine to wow us."

Tessa stared out the passenger car window without blinking.

"Tess? What do you think?"

What do I think? Tessa never knew what to think from one day to the next. Today she and Ken were house hunting, discussing wainscoting and granite versus laminate countertops, and tomorrow Ken might disappear, his untouched dinner coagulating on its plate long after Tessa went to bed.

She put her hand on her swelling abdomen and fantasized about throwing open the car door and running away, her chestnut hair and beige knit scarf blowing behind her as she soared to . . . where? She was inside an unbreakable soundproof glass box. She could see out, but no one could see in. Even if she pounded on the glass until her fists bled, no one could hear her. She was alone, untouchable.

Her conflicting emotions were a tumor on her lung, causing her breath to labor. Ken's addiction was an ulcer that burned deep in her stomach. But these agonies now took a back seat to the guilt she felt about bringing another baby into her hell. She turned it over in her mind again and again. How had she allowed this to happen? Had she really believed Ken had stopped using for good during one of his sober stretches, or was she naïve enough to think that another baby would make him realize how much he had to lose?

He promised it would. And she desperately wanted to believe him.

If possible, the situation had become even more complicated. Ken was ecstatic over her pregnancy. He doted on her, bathing Ronnie at night and reading "If You Give a Mouse a Cookie" umpteen times before bed, telling Tessa to put up her feet and relax. He did the grocery shopping and helped with the dishes. He searched endlessly for the perfect house for his growing family. Tessa was the envy of everyone they knew. Her body ached under the weight of their secrets. She felt strapped to her deserted island like a crazy person to an asylum bed.

"Tess?"

"Hmm? Yeah, it's nice, I guess."

They followed Elaine along the suburban streets, past lawns draped in last night's light snowfall. The neighborhoods were nice, more affluent than the one Ken and Tessa lived in now. Tessa imagined the manicured lawns under the snow, the curb appeal created by landscape designs in the spring and summer months. Ken drove up a windy tree-lined road and turned right onto a street that led up a steep hill. It appeared to be a kind of development, though it was composed of only the houses on that street. The houses, each one unique from the others, sat on wooded spacious lots. Elaine swung into an S-shaped driveway near the top of the road. It was on an incline and was lined by tall trees on either side. Finally, they arrived at a clearing on which stood a large two-story brick colonial house.

The house was finished on the outside, except for a few minor details, such as shutters and walkways. There was no landscaping, and it was unclear if there was a lawn under the light blanket of snow. The house was stately, perched at the top of the lot with about an acre of land cleared around it but otherwise surrounded by woods. It faced the road, and though the trees were bare now, it would be completely hidden in the full bloom of spring and summer.

"Wow," Ken managed as he stepped from the car. He leaned on the door for a minute, taking in the scene. Elaine, smiling, made her way toward the couple. "Okay." Ken was nodding. "I'm listening."

Tessa asked quizzically, "What is this place? Is it finished or still under construction?" She glanced back toward the road, but it was too far to see clearly from the house. "I didn't see a For Sale sign."

Elaine shuffled through some papers in a folder. "No, there isn't one. This place isn't on the market yet. It's an interesting story. The owners hired a custom builder—I'm sure you noticed all the homes up here are custom built—but ran into a snag."

"What kind of snag?" Ken shoved his hands deep in his coat pockets against the cold.

"It's a heck of a thing. The guy found out he's being transferred to Indiana. The house is all but completed. You'll see when we get inside. Just some finishing touches that the buyers will be able to choose. The owner's company bought the house and is getting ready to put it on the market. They'll finish it if necessary, but they'd rather sell it as is and let the buyer complete it."

Ken raised his eyebrows at Tessa and shrugged. "Might as well take a look, no?"

Elaine led them to a side door next to a two-car garage and entered a combination into the lockbox hanging from the doorknob. They entered the house via a mudroom that led to a spacious kitchen. It had cherry cabinets, recessed lighting, and a built-in desk, but the countertops and floors were not yet installed.

"You see?" Elaine waved her hand dramatically. You'd be free to add the final touches of your choice.

They proceeded through the generously sized rooms: a bright family room with a fireplace, a smaller room off that one that Elaine explained could be either a media room or an office, formal living and dining rooms in the front of the house on either side of a vaulted foyer. Upstairs, a long hallway separated three nice-sized bedrooms, a full bathroom, and a master suite with two walk-in closets and a luxurious bathroom with a whirlpool tub.

Tessa wandered along behind Ken and Elaine, who extoled all the possibilities of the house. She painted a picture of Ken and Tessa and their children celebrating holidays, entertaining friends, and enjoying all the space the house had to offer. As she talked, Tessa saw a light in Ken's eyes that showed he envisioned it too.

"There's a full basement that you could finish if you want to," Elaine said as they followed her back downstairs. "But, obviously, there's plenty of living space without it. The square footage without the basement is 3,400 square feet."

"So, let's talk numbers," Ken turned to Elaine. "We would buy the house as is and choose flooring, countertops, and paint colors to finish it?"

"Yeah, pretty much. Why don't you take another spin around? I'll call the listing agent and get more details. As I said, the place isn't even on the market yet." Elaine pulled out her flip phone and punched in some numbers. "These phones are great, aren't they? It's like having a mobile office."

"Yeah, we just bought them also," Ken agreed. "With the new baby on the way, I want Tessa to be able to reach me no matter where I am." Tessa raised her eyebrows at her husband as he led her to the foyer. *Wherever you are? If only.*

Ignoring her skeptical look, he spread out his arms in front of him. "What do you think, babe? Pretty awesome, huh?" He ran his hand over the walnut banister and then pulled her in close for a hug. "You know what? I can see us here. I really can. This is the kind of house you deserve. It's three times the size of our house."

He walked to the back of the house to the family room and gazed out the window. "Nice big yard for the kids to play in. Maybe we could even put in a pool someday." He turned to Tessa. "Do you love it?"

"It's beautiful. It really is. But aren't we getting ahead of ourselves? Shouldn't we talk numbers before we get our hopes up? I'm sure it's a fortune. I don't think overextending ourselves with a monster mortgage is wise—"

"Okay, guys," Elaine interrupted. "I have the full scoop. Do you have time to go back to my office and talk details?"

"Sure!" Ken took Tessa's hand as he followed Elaine out the side door.

Back in the car, Tessa tried again. "Ken, that house is gorgeous, and it's hard not to get excited thinking about living there. I know we need a bigger house, but I'm not sure taking on something like this is the best thing for us." She looked down at her lap.

"Hon, listen to me. I disagree. I think this is just what we need. A fresh start. Leave all the bad memories behind at the old house." He paused and let his words sink in. "I know I've been a shit. But I have a good feeling about this. This is something I can be proud of, something I can pour my energy into." He looked back at the property again before steering down the driveway. "Plenty there to keep me busy. I can do some of the painting and landscaping myself. And you love to decorate. Imagine being able to pick out *real* accent pieces instead of using Ronnie's toybox as an end table."

Tessa couldn't help but smile, but then furrowed her brow and studied her husband. "Ken, I just worry about the stress of taking on too much. We have a budget. What if buying and finishing this house is way out of our league? I feel like when you first opened your practice at the same time Ronnie was born, it might have driven you to—"

"No." Ken shook his head vigorously. "It won't be like that. I promise. I'm so pumped about this I feel like we already live there. C'mon, babe. Think about it. All our hard work paying off, a big, beautiful house to show for it."

The January sun glinting off the windshield paled in comparison to the gleam in Ken's eyes. Tessa weighed the situation. Maybe this would be a boost for Ken. The fruits of his labor. They could host cookouts and parties instead of always going to friends' houses who had more room. Maybe he'd be content staying home more with the kids and her in a house he was proud of. A house he and Tessa could truly make their own. She was toying with these thoughts when Ken interrupted her reverie.

"Call Alyse and Joey and ask if they can keep Ronnie a little bit longer. Let's go hear what Elaine has to say. Don't fret before there is something to fret about."

Tessa flipped open her phone. "Okay."

But they both knew she already was.

Chapter Twenty-Seven

"Don't lift that, hon. I'll get it for you." Val took the box of miscellaneous kitchen items from Tessa. "Which cabinet should I put baking stuff in?" She swiped a strand of hair out of her eyes and looked around. "Probably near the oven makes the most sense, right? Man, I wouldn't know how to act if I had a kitchen this size! I have so many things stacked on top of each other in my cabinets, Tony says they are boobytrapped. Poor kid knocks something over every time he gets out an ice cream bowl."

Tessa leaned on the counter. "Yeah, I don't think I even have enough stuff to fill them all. It'll be weird to have unused cabinets and closets." She removed pots and pans from a box on the counter. "Gina, here's another one!"

"Yay!" Gina ran into the kitchen with Ronnie in tow. "Oh, cool! That's a good one! C'mon, Ronnie. Your chariot awaits!" She picked up her niece and plopped her inside the box.

"Go, Dina, go!" squealed Ronnie. Gina took off pushing the box in front of her, skating across the cream tile kitchen floor.

"Be careful with her!" Val called. "You know she's a real person, right, not just a toy to play with!"

"She loves it," Tessa reassured her mother. "Besides, I don't think we could unpack the rest of these boxes without someone to entertain Ronnie. She'd undo all our good work. I should pay Gina a babysitting fee." She finished stacking pots and pans in a large cabinet under the kitchen's center island and turned to the next box. "This one says 'serving plates and bowls.' I guess I'll run these through the dishwasher before I put them away." As she loaded the dishwasher, Val gazed out the kitchen window.

"So, Ken said you guys are thinking about a pool? There's plenty of room out there. But you'll want to get an alarm on the back door like we have in case the little ones wander out there—"

"Mom, we're not putting in a pool. At least not anytime soon." She closed the door of the dishwasher and hit the "on" switch. "I think we've bitten off all we can chew here. A big house, hefty mortgage, another baby on the way. That should be quite enough stress for now."

Val strolled into the family room and ran her hand along the edge of the sofa. It had wide green and cream stripes. The sofa faced the fireplace, which was flanked by large overstuffed floral-patterned chairs in hues that complemented the sofa. A square French Country coffee table in soft ash separated the furniture, and there were matching sofa and end tables. At the room's six large windows, valances in the same fabric as the chairs pulled the look together while still letting the sunlight stream in. "I love how you decorated this room, Tess. I feel like I'm in Florida."

She glanced into the smaller room off the family room that Ken had decided they would use as a media room. Through the French doors was a chocolatey-brown leather sectional that faced a maple entertainment center and a sixty-inch TV. There was one window partially covered by a striped Roman shade. "And this is perfect décor for a TV room. I can just hear the boys screaming at the Phillies and Eagles in here. At least we can shut the door on them!" She turned back to Tessa and smiled. "How awesome to have all new furniture. Things are going well at the office, huh?"

"Yes, it's all great, and the monthly payments will be too. And don't forget, we need new bedroom furniture for Ronnie, since this little rascal will be inheriting the nursery furniture." She patted her belly. "I tried to tell Ken we don't need to furnish the whole house immediately, but you know him. He loves this house. He's all smiles when he talks about having people over. Hey, let's take a coffee break. I haven't had my one allotted safe-pregnancy cup yet today." She opened a few cabinets until she located the coffee mugs. "We've been here four days, and I still open every cabinet trying to remember where we put things." She began measuring spoonfuls of ground coffee into a paper filter while Val went to check on Gina and Ronnie. In a few minutes, Tessa placed a steaming mug in front of her mother. Val blew on it and thoughtfully chose her words.

"Hon, I'm sure Ken wouldn't buy all this new stuff if you guys couldn't afford it. Try to enjoy it instead of stressing over it." She paused a minute and studied her daughter.

"What?"

"I don't want to butt in, but—"

Tessa leaned against the granite counter and folded her arms. "But what?"

"I just feel like there's something bothering you that you don't want to talk about." She looked around and waved her arm. "I mean, here you are in this fabulous new house filled with gorgeous new furniture. Your husband has a successful dental practice. You have a healthy beautiful toddler and another baby on the way. Ken is a hands-on dad who clearly worships you and Ronnie." Her voice trailed off. "Look, I know no marriage is perfect. Lord knows. But sometimes I feel like you have some kind of baffling resentment against Ken. Like he can't win with you."

"Mom, I . . ." Tessa swallowed hard.

"I don't know what, but something is making you unhappy. I know my kids." Val spoke softly.

Tessa turned to the arched window over the kitchen sink. She closed her eyes and considered the scenario she'd turned over in her head a million times: She comes clean to Val, her parents are heartbroken, Ken is furious, all hell breaks loose. No, as much as the secrecy weighed down her frame, flowed through her veins, choked her like a deranged killer, she had to protect it.

Ken was trying. Again. Still. Again. He loved this house and his family and was more upbeat and optimistic about the future than he'd been in a long time. It was like this house gave him a renewed purpose. She couldn't risk blowing the lid off things now.

A long pause hung in the air between the two women.

"We're hungry!" Gina bounded into the kitchen with Ronnie on her heels and broke the silence. "Me and Ronnie want grilled cheeses and fries at Daddy's. Can we go to the Sunrise for lunch?"

Tessa exhaled and ran her hand over her hair. "Sounds good to me. Just let me pee—my new favorite pastime—and then we can go. Okay with you, Mom?" Tessa called over her shoulder on her way upstairs.

Val, unmoving, stared straight ahead. "Sure," she called back. Then she lowered her voice. "But when you're ready to talk, I'm ready to listen."

"Hi, Dad." Tessa kissed Sal on the cheek as Ronnie leaned in to hug her grandfather. Gina plopped down in a booth by the window and shrugged out of her coat.

Sal called to her. "What, no kiss or hug from you? You're getting too big for that?" Gina ran over and bear-hugged her father. "That's better! To what do I owe this pleasant surprise?" He turned to Tessa, who was coaxing Ronnie into a booster seat that Linda brought to the booth. "Where's your mother? I thought you girls were finishing unpacking your kitchen?"

"She'll be here in a minute. She ran home to pick up Tony. Gina and Ronnie are hungry for your famous grilled cheese and fries."

Sal shook his head. "What a thing to be famous for, huh? The skill to butter a few pieces of bread, throw some cheese on, and grill them. Doesn't exactly make me a gourmet cook, does it?" He playfully mispronounced the word as "gor-mett."

Tessa laughed. "Well, your fan club here thinks it does." She chatted amiably with Linda while they waited for Val and Tony. Gina pretended to be a maestro and instructed Ronnie to sing the ABCs, and Linda made a suitable fuss.

"Listen to those Rs." Linda chuckled. "Where did she get that accent, Tess? She sounds like she's from the Bronx!"

"Who's from the Bronx?" Tony slid into the booth next to Ronnie.

"Hey!" yelled Gina. "Get out! I'm sitting next to Ronnie. It's too scrunched with you on this side!" She shoved her brother, who stuck out his tongue at her.

"Settle down, you two." Val gave Linda an exasperated look. "These in-service days. I guess the teachers like the peace and quiet, but they're punishment for the parents."

"Trust me, Mom," Tessa interjected. "Teachers hate in-service days. Nothing but excruciatingly boring meetings. They're so brutal they'd rather the kids were there."

Maggie, who was just finishing her shift, waved to all of them. "Bye, Sal. See you tomorrow. My ride is here." She picked up a stack of boxes Sal had given her for her upcoming move to a new apartment.

"Okay, Mags. Hey, need a hand?" Sal started toward her.

"No, I got it. Thanks."

Sal looked out into the parking lot and saw Maggie's latest boyfriend sitting in his car. Apparently thinking it was taking her too long, he honked the horn. Maggie's face reddened as she hurried out the door with the boxes.

Val shook her head. "Did he actually just honk the horn? Would it kill him to come in and get her? Maybe help her with those boxes?"

Linda rolled her eyes. "Chivalry may not be dead, but it's unconscious and throwing up blood." She looked out the window. "Mags sure can pick 'em."

"Hey, Tess." Linda turned back to them and lightly hit her temple with the butt of her hand as if she'd just remembered something. "Someone was in here and said she knows you from subbing at the high school. Maybe it was the junior high. I can't remember. Blonde, shoulder-length hair, about yay high." She held her hand up at her own eye level. "She didn't give her name."

Puzzled, Tessa racked her brain for a teacher fitting Linda's simple description.

"Anyway, she said she recently started going to Ken, but she may have to find another dentist." The kids starting fidgeting, and Linda took out her pad and pen as she spoke.

Tessa stopped fishing in her bag for Ronnie's bib and froze. "Why? Was there a problem?" Linda had Val's attention also.

"No, no, she thought he was a great dentist. She even made appointments for her husband and kids. It's just, apparently, she needs some pretty extensive dental work, and now that Ken isn't offering nitrous oxide anymore, she's not sure she'll be able to stand just having local injections."

Val looked quizzically at Tessa. "Ken isn't giving patients the gas anymore?"

Tessa felt like the walls were closing in on her. Just hearing her mom mention the gas made her lightheaded. "Um, I'm not sure. He didn't say anything to me. I'll have to ask him about it."

Thankfully, the kids veered the discussion onto a different course. Gina put her arm around Ronnie. "Ronnie and me will have grilled cheese and fries. No pickles on the side!"

Linda wrote down the order. "Why no pickles?"

"Tony said they make you go blind!"

Val glared at Tony, but Tessa laughed, glad to take the focus off Ken and nitrous oxide. "I'll have a cheeseburger with lettuce and tomato. And extra pickles." She gently tugged Gina's ponytail. "You can lead me around if I go blind."

Linda finished taking their food and drink order and gave the slip to Sal. Before he began making the food, he gave each of the kids a scratch-off lottery ticket to keep them busy. Gina and Tony huddled over Ronnie to help her with hers. Val seized the opportunity. "So, what do you think about that whole gas thing? I wonder why Ken isn't offering it to his patients anymore? Is it expensive? I hope that doesn't hurt his practice. Maybe if people start going elsewhere, he'll reconsider."

"Yeah, maybe. I have no idea," Tessa lied.

"Tess, Ronnie won five dollars on her ticket! Woo hoo!" Tony exclaimed. "Ronnie, do you want the five bucks or five more tickets?"

"Tickets!" Ronnie clapped at her uncle's excitement.

"Yeah, take the tickets!" Gina yelled. "Maybe you'll win a hundred dollars this time!"

Val seemed to forget about the nitrous oxide again. "That's it, turn her into a gambler, you guys. Poor thing will be the only one at Gamblers Anonymous in a booster seat." She shook her head as Linda began delivering food to the table.

After they ate, Sal pulled a chair up to their table. "Honey, I'm going to order a ham next month for you for Easter. The guy said he'll deliver it here a few days before. I'll bring it up to the house when I get it. I bet you're looking forward to hosting at the new place."

"And I bet you're looking forward to watching the Phils on that big screen, huh?" Tessa nudged his side with her elbow. "Yeah, it will be nice to have more room. Thanks, Dad."

"Speaking of Easter," Val added, "I think Ronnie's old enough to paint eggs this year, don't you?"

"If you spread out plenty of newspaper. That sounds like it has the makings of a tie-dye nightmare." Ronnie started protesting being constrained in the booster seat. "I better get her home for a nap. I may take one myself."

They finished the last of the fries and said good-bye to Sal and Linda. As Tessa drove home, she thought about the awkwardness of Linda bringing up the nitrous oxide in front of her parents. Though she had done her best to act nonchalant, she wondered if her mother had picked up on the fact that her silence was a clearer explanation than any words could be.

Chapter Twenty-Eight

"One more cookie, Mommy. One more."

"Okay, but this is it, Miss Ronnie. Leave some room for dinner." Tessa put a chocolate chip cookie on the plate in front of her daughter and went back to chopping lettuce and tomatoes. "We're having tacos tonight. You love tacos, don't you?"

Ronnie shook her head up and down enthusiastically. "I yuv tacos!" She pulled off her bib and held up her hands, twisting them back and forth for Tessa to inspect. "I get down now." Tessa wiped her face and hands and lifted her out of the booster seat.

"Okay, now you play with these puzzles here while I finish up. Then it's naptime, and CeCe will be here later for dinner!"

Ronnie dumped out the wooden puzzle pieces all over the floor while Tessa finished prepping the taco fixings. She was glad CeCe accepted her invitation for dinner. She wanted to introduce her to Ken. Feeling bad about portraying an unfavorable picture of Ken during their walks in the park, she wanted to give Ken a chance to show his decent side.

CeCe had balked at first. The woman was such a loner, it took Tessa several tries to convince her. Tessa had wanted to invite her parents and siblings also, but CeCe said she hardly ever had dinner with anyone and she'd prefer a small group if she were to come at all. "I don't think I could handle meeting all those new people at once," she'd admitted.

When Tessa floated the idea to Ken, he was all in favor of it. He said he was intrigued by how they'd met, their age difference, and that, from what Tessa had told him about her, CeCe seemed different from any of his wife's other friends. He said he was also glad that Tessa was socializing instead of constantly fretting about his whereabouts.

He'd agreed with CeCe's assertion when Tessa told him about it. "Meeting your whole family at one time? You have to admit, that's a lot. You don't want to scare her away, do you?"

After Tessa put Ronnie down for her nap, she dug out her colorful chip-and-dip bowl and margarita glasses. She'd have a virgin drink, but she'd make margaritas for Ken and CeCe. As she sliced limes and filled a shallow bowl with coarse sea salt, she looked forward to the evening. CeCe had been an easy companion and a sounding board for Tessa, simultaneously arm's length and someone safe to vent to. Though she hadn't gone into specific details, it felt good to be able to talk, even in general terms.

Lately, though, Ken seemed more like his old self. His eyes had a clarity that Tessa hadn't seen in months. He was more present, not just physically but mentally as well. The new house perked him up and improved his mood. He loved all the space for entertaining and a few times already had invited friends for game night and happy hour.

Tessa checked the time and figured she had another hour before Ronnie woke up. She straightened up the house's main floor, picking up toys and books and putting them in the toy box. She fixed the throw pillows on the sofa and cleaned the fingerprints on the glass top of the coffee table. Then she went upstairs, stripped out of her sweats, and took a warm bath. Afterward, she dressed in a light maternity sweater and jeans. She styled her hair and even put on a little makeup. As she finished up, she heard Ronnie calling to her from her toddler bed. Tessa and Ken wanted her out of her crib before the new baby arrived, and though Ronnie was doing well with the transition, she still didn't get out of bed herself.

"I need a go pee pee!" she called. Potty training was also on the list of things to accomplish before the new baby, and Tessa found it surprisingly easy. Of course, it seemed they'd visited every public bathroom in town since they started, and about half of those visits had been false alarms.

"Okay, good girl." Tessa took Ronnie's hand and led her from her bedroom and into the bathroom.

Downstairs, Ronnie picked out five or six favorite books and brought them to Tessa. "This one first, Mommy." They passed the time reading until Tessa decided she better get dinner ready. She told CeCe to feel free to arrive around five, but Ken probably wouldn't be home until six.

"Okay, peanut, movie time. What'll it be?" she asked, holding up a few selections. "*Beauty and the Beast, The Lion King,* or *Muppet Classic Theater?*"

"Muppets!" Ronnie climbed up on the sofa and settled in.

"Muppets it is." Tessa popped in the movie and marveled for the thousandth time at women who said they absolutely never let their kids watch movies or TV. *How do they get anything done?*

She sautéed the ground beef and shredded chicken. Then she made Mexican rice and heated up a bowl of black beans. She had just set the table and was grabbing her homemade guacamole from the fridge when she heard the doorbell. She wiped her hands and headed for the front door.

"Hey, CeCe! Come on in!"

CeCe stepped into the shiny tiled foyer and let out a low whistle. "Wow. That's about all I can think to say. My entire apartment would fit into these few rooms."

Tessa laughed and looked at the empty formal living and dining room on either side of the foyer. "Come to the back of the house with me. There's actually furniture back there. I promise you won't have to stand all night."

CeCe held out a bouquet of flowers. "Here, these are for you. Thanks so much for inviting me. This is a nice change from my usual spaghetti-for-one-in-front-of-the-TV Monday dinner plans."

"Thanks! You didn't have to do that, but they're beautiful." Tessa led the older woman through the foyer to the family room and into the TV room. "Speaking of 'in front of the TV.' Ronnie, look who's here!"

Ronnie waved and pointed at the TV. "Da boy who cried woof!" On the screen, various Muppets were acting out the fairy tale.

"I brought you something," CeCe said. She handed the toddler a Peter Rabbit book with finger puppets. Ronnie thanked CeCe but after a minute turned her attention back to the show.

"Sorry," Tessa said. "But don't take it personally. She gets mesmerized."

"No worries. Looks like a good flick." She followed Tessa back through the family room and into the kitchen. Seriously, though, this place is beautiful. I can't believe you've only been here a little over a month. It's so put together." She looked around admiringly. Tall pewter candlesticks and picture frames in various sizes adorned the sofa table. In the center of the mantel, a large framed impressionist print leaned against the brick fireplace. A cozy chenille throw was draped over the arm of one of the overstuffed chairs. "You have nice taste in decorating. Everything complements everything else, but it's welcoming, not stuffy."

"Thank you. I like doing it. I often think if I had it to do over, I might have gone into interior decorating instead of teaching." Tessa half filled a vase with water, arranged the flowers, and put it in the center of the kitchen island.

"Well, it's not too late. You're young." CeCe glanced into the empty dining room.

"We did pick out a dining room set. Hopefully it will be here before Easter, since I'm hosting. It has a china cabinet, but I don't own china," she said, grinning. "Maybe I'll put the plastic dishes from Ronnie's Fisher-Price kitchen in it." She set out chips, salsa, and the guacamole. "How about a margarita? I, of course, will not be partaking, but I can live vicariously through you for the evening."

CeCe hesitated and then shook her head slowly. "No, that's okay. I'll just have whatever you're having."

"Really? You don't need to. I'm going to have a virgin margarita. All the taste without the tequila." She rubbed a wedge of lime along the rim of a glass.

"Sounds great to me."

"Okay, then, two virgin margaritas it is. Go ahead, have a seat and enjoy some snacks. Ken should be home by six." She filled two glasses and brought them to the table. "Just give me a sec to check on Ronnie, and then I'll join you."

CeCe sipped her drink. She examined the artwork and photos on the fridge. She recognized a few of Ronnie's creations from Mommy and Me: a tree trunk with finger-painted branches and leaves, a star fashioned from popsicle sticks, and a bunny with a cotton nose and tail. Around the toddler's artwork were photos: Ronnie on Santa's lap, the three of them in front of the new house, a large group of various family members at the beach.

"She's still fixated on her video. I hope we can drag her in here for dinner." Tessa sat down, picked a tortilla chip from the bowl, and scooped up some salsa. "So, what's new with you? It's been a few weeks since I've seen you."

CeCe waved her hand in front of her. "Oh, nothing special. Same old, same old. I prefer a quiet existence these days. I did join a book club, though." She smiled shyly. "That's about my speed. A bunch of middle-aged ladies discussing how a story's island setting contributes to the main character's isolated behavior."

"You're joking, but that sounds nice to me." Tessa sighed.

"I love to read. I'd probably enjoy that. But I'm guessing the clubs don't read *Goodnight Moon* or Disney books. They're the only ones I'm guaranteed time to read right now."

CeCe laughed. "No, but maybe we should. Some of the women don't finish our assigned books and then try to fake their way through the meeting. You can always tell, though. Then we mess with them and make up stuff that happens in the book to see if they'll go along with it. That's worth the price of admission right there."

Tessa chuckled at the image. "Maybe you need me there deducting homework points! 'Okay, Mrs. Bingaman, what's your excuse this time?'" She checked the wall clock. "Oh, it's getting late. You must be starving. I guess I better finish dinner."

"Can I help?"

"Sure. We're having tacos. Do you mind putting out the bowls of fixings while I heat the rice and beans?"

The two women worked together, putting the food out on the island taco-bar style.

"Well . . ." CeCe put her hands on her hips and admired the spread. "Doesn't this look great! Do you like to cook, Tessa?"

Tessa lowered the flame and stirred the rice. "Yes, but I come from a long line of cooks. My mom and grandmother are great cooks. And you know my dad owns a diner and does all the cooking there. Food is the center of our family. I guess it's an Italian thing. It's a miracle we don't all weigh three hundred pounds. Every issue, good or bad, is excruciatingly analyzed over mounds of food, usually of the Italian variety." She laughed and shook her head. "I swear, your hair could be on fire, and my mom and grandmother would ask, 'But did you eat? Come sit down, have some pasta!'" CeCe's face took on a faraway look, and Tessa wondered if she'd said something wrong. "Hey, you okay?"

CeCe waved her hand. "Yes, don't mind me. I was just thinking how nice it is that you have such a close-knit family."

"Oh, I'm sorry, I didn't mean to—"

Ronnie bounced into the kitchen, singing a song from her video. "I'm hungry. Where my taco?" She climbed up onto her booster seat and fastened her Velcro bib around her neck. CeCe's expression brightened, and she took a seat next to Ronnie.

Tessa picked up the phone and dialed the office. "Let me see if Ken left the office yet." After several rings, an after-hours recording informed her that the office had closed for the day and gave instructions for emergencies. "He must be on his way home. I'll feed Ronnie, and by then he should be home."

"Here, I'll fix the little lady's taco." CeCe turned to Ronnie. "What would you like in your taco, Miss?"

"Teese!" Ronnie announced, and CeCe looked at Tessa for help.

"She'll have just a little bit of meat and a lot of cheese. Her palate isn't exactly refined. I guess she figures, why waste room in the taco shell for boring healthy things like lettuce and tomatoes when you can just as easily fill it up with cheese?"

"Can't argue with that logic," CeCe answered, heaping shredded cheese into the shell.

"Let's get started too," Tessa decided. "I don't want everything to get cold. Go ahead and fix yourself a plate, and I'll refill our drinks." She picked up the phone again and dialed Ken's cell number. It went straight to voicemail. Frowning, she closed her eyes momentarily and leaned against the wall. A light sweat broke out on her forehead, and a familiar tingle crept into her fingertips.

CeCe filled her plate and sat down next to Ronnie. "All that's missing are the sombreros! Honestly, Tessa, this is awesome. Thanks again for inviting me."

Tessa tried to gather herself. She smoothed her hair and picked up a plate. "I'm glad you came."

They ate dinner without Ken, Ronnie providing entertainment for CeCe and a welcome distraction for Tessa. CeCe had seconds and was dipping a chip into her third helping of guacamole when she sat back and waved her napkin in front of her. "That's it. I can't eat another bite or I'll burst. Delicious dinner, Tessa. The best I've had in ages. Your homemade guac is out of this world!"

Tessa picked at her food and kept her eye on the door. She offered no explanation for Ken's absence. What could she say? Ken knew they were having a guest for dinner. Absently, she searched her inventory of usual excuses and explanations. A wave of fatigue overtook her. She felt like a college student during exam week. Finally, she pushed her plate away and stood up to clear the dishes. She stammered, "Just . . . just relax for a few minutes. I'll make coffee. I have churros and ice cream for dessert."

"I keem!" Ronnie clapped her cheesy hands.

"Wow, you made churros? Now I'm really impressed." CeCe's eyes were wide.

"No, I didn't make . . . I bought them at . . . I bought them . . ."

CeCe stood up and carried some plates to the counter. Tessa, blinking back tears, leaned against the sink. "Tessa." CeCe touched her elbow. "It's okay. Don't worry about it. I'm sure there's a reasonable explanation."

Tessa stared at the plates of congealed food in front of her. CeCe continued. "Listen, I'll rinse these and, what? Put them in the dishwasher?"

Tessa managed a nod.

"Okay. You serve the little one some ice cream before she stages an overthrow. It'll be fine." She gently took a plate from Tessa's hand and guided her toward the freezer. Tessa got out a tub of ice cream and put a small scoop into a bowl for Ronnie. CeCe called to her, "Nothing like a bowl of ice cream to chase a cheese-filled tortilla, huh, Ronnie?"

Ronnie giggled and waved her spoon in the air. Tessa robotically made a pot of decaf and brought two mugs to the table. She sat down gingerly, as though any sudden movement might cause her to shatter into a million pieces. Her chin resting in her hand, she sipped her coffee and watched CeCe play "Itsy Bitsy Spider" with Ronnie. Thoughts swirled around her head like tumbleweed in a dust storm. She knew she should offer her guest something in the way of an explanation, but no words came.

Finally, she cleaned up her daughter's face and hands and unbuckled her from her booster seat. Ronnie ran into the other room, found a few puzzles, and dumped them onto the floor. She came back and grabbed her mother's hand. "Come on, Mommy!" She pointed toward the pile. "Do puzzles!" Tessa's face took on a fractured expression, her earlier cheeriness flown away like a flock of birds. Ronnie hopped on one foot and tried to pull her mother from her chair, but CeCe came to the rescue.

"I got this." She plopped down beside Ronnie and, keeping one eye on Tessa, helped reassemble the wooden pieces into pictures: one into a clown holding a colorful balloon bouquet and another into Mickey and Minnie on a tug boat. After a while, Tessa called softly to Ronnie and told her to say good night to CeCe. As Tessa carried Ronnie upstairs, the toddler asked, "Where Daddy?" Tessa didn't respond.

When Tessa came back downstairs, CeCe had finished loading the dishwasher. She'd also covered the leftovers and put them in the fridge. Outside, night had fallen, and the light over the table created a reflection in the sliding patio door. Tessa's pursed lips emitted no sound. CeCe smiled and said, "I hope you don't mind, but I helped myself to a churro. I'm trying to decide if I have room for ice—"

"Ken is addicted to nitrous oxide."

CeCe closed her mouth and turned around slowly to face Tessa. She didn't speak for a long moment. The house's sounds were exacerbated by the women's silence. The freezer's automatic ice machine dropped a fresh batch with a *thud* into the plastic tray. The wind slapped against the window like someone who'd gone out for the newspaper and accidently locked the door behind her.

CeCe let out a long breath and sank into a chair. She pulled out the one next to her for Tessa. "Here. Sit."

Tessa obeyed but remained perched on the edge of the chair. Tessa looked much older than her thirty-one years. Her frown made deep lines around her eyes and mouth, and her shoulders slumped as though she was trying to fold herself inside out.

Tessa shivered and pulled her sweater sleeves down over her hands. The enjoyment of the evening drained from her, oozed from her pores, spilled down her limbs, pooled around her feet. As she'd done a hundred times before, she'd pulled herself back from Ken's last episode, cautiously, a bit at a time, the way you treat someone who has fainted. You lay the person flat on her back, shake her to try to revive her, give her juice to sip until she comes around fully. But now, here she was again, dizzy, nauseous, falling.

She was cloaked in Ken's secret, like a protective suit. Later, she'd try to analyze what had made her blurt it out to CeCe with the taco pan soaking in the kitchen sink and a vase of Gerbera daisies on the island. She'd conclude the more fascinating question was why it hadn't happened sooner.

"Tessa? Can I get you something? A glass of water?"

Tessa didn't look at CeCe. She stared straight ahead without blinking or moving. When she finally spoke, her voice sounded like it came from behind frosted glass, like there was a barrier between her and her own life.

"He's addicted to nitrous oxide. He huffs it for hours at a time, sometimes all night. It started right after Ronnie was born, right around the time he opened his practice. He began staying out all night, claiming he was swamped with paperwork. It sounded reasonable. But I'd call and he wouldn't answer the phone. Then he'd claim he was in the lab and couldn't hear it, or that he'd fallen asleep out in the waiting room.

"I believed him. I mean, at first I believed him. It kind of made sense. He was under a lot of stress. New practice. New baby. It kind of made sense back then, but when I think about it now, I was just kidding myself." She paused and closed her eyes.

Tessa laughed a little then, the kind of almost silent snicker that says, *Can you believe how stupid I am?* Still not making eye contact with CeCe, she cleared her throat and sat up straighter. "I guess I convinced myself he was telling the truth, because what was the alternative? The only logical one was that he was having an affair. At the time I thought that would be the worst-case scenario. There I was at home with a new baby, and what? My husband was out with a gorgeous woman who didn't have stretch marks and wasn't sleep deprived? I couldn't let my mind go there. I couldn't let myself imagine them laughing over a cocktail, him tucking a strand of her hair behind her ear, her whispering his name while they had hot steamy sex."

She shrugged. "Who would have thought he was doing laughing gas? I'd never even heard of such a thing. I mean, people get hooked on cocaine or heroin or booze. But nitrous oxide?"

Then she began to laugh, almost maniacally. "You know what's funny?" CeCe remained silent. "When he told me, I almost said, 'Are you sure that's what you've been up to? Are you sure you're not having an affair?' In a weird way, I almost wished he *was* having an affair." She held her head. "At least *that* I've heard of. But . . . this . . . I don't know what to do with this.

"It's been going on for almost two years. He's had sober periods here and there, and each time I thought it was over." Her chin sank to her chest, and she touched her belly. "He won't get help, says he doesn't need it. Says he can beat it on his own. Then other times he says he doesn't want to stop. It's the one thing he asks of me, and he doesn't understand why I can't let him have it. He says he gives me everything I want, and I can't give him this one thing. It's beyond twisted, like he's asking for one day a week to play golf or go out to a bar with friends.

"I don't know if the marriage can survive if he doesn't stop. Some days I think about Ronnie and the baby growing inside of me, and it breaks my heart because I just know I'm going to be a single mom." She turned to face CeCe.

"Who does that? Who throws away a wife and two children for laughing gas? I'm saying it out loud to you, but if someone told me her husband was doing that, I wouldn't believe her. Who does that?" She searched the older woman's face.

"People do all sorts of inexplicable things to ruin their lives," CeCe said quietly.

Tessa continued as if CeCe hadn't spoken. "I mean, seriously, nitrous oxide? Nitrous oxide. He's going to give up his family for nitrous oxide?"

"Have you told him you don't know if you can stay in the marriage if he doesn't quit?"

Tessa waved her hand. "Oh, yeah, but he gets furious and tells me how selfish I am. He says I'll ruin everything if I leave and people find out. It could cost him his license to practice dentistry, and it will be all my fault. He says I'll destroy our family and his career, and then what are we supposed to do?

"To everyone else, he looks like a model husband and father. I don't even know if anyone in our circle would believe me if I told them what he's really like." Tessa covered her face with her hands. "I feel like I'm losing my mind."

"Tessa, I don't know Ken or anything about your life together except what you've told me. But I'm wondering, what if it hadn't been me here tonight? What if it had been . . . I don't know . . . your parents? They'd see for themselves that he didn't come home. They'd have no choice but to believe you, right?"

"Oh, that's the best part. That's when the show really starts. I've gotten really good at acting. I should go straight to Hollywood." CeCe furrowed her brow.

"Let's see, I'd call the office and pretend Ken answered. Then I'd have a nice conversation with dead air in which I'd weave an intricate tale. I'd pretend Ken had an emergency patient or a denture he was working on in the lab that he promised an old lady would be ready in time for her grandson's school play this weekend. I'd use my best sympathetic voice and tell him we'd miss him at dinner, but I'll keep a plate warm for him. It's quite something. Meryl Streep's got nothing on me.

"And the most nauseating part is how my parents would feel badly for him and how hard he works. It makes me want to put my fist through a wall.

"And you know what? Why shouldn't they? It's my own fault. I'm the one who's painted that picture of him. I lie for him and make everyone think he's the greatest thing since sliced bread. Sometimes I hate myself more than I hate him." Her face red with shame, she lowered her eyes. "That's real nice, isn't it? Sometimes I hate my own husband. A man who clearly has a problem and needs his wife's support. I sit here in my beautiful home, working only when I feel like it, lunching, shopping, hosting friends for dinner, and he's out working to make it all possible. And the thanks he gets is an ungrateful wife who bitches at him for not being perfect. A wife who threatens to leave and take his daughter with her. A wife who threatens to ruin the dental practice he's worked so hard to build to make a nice life for his family." She was crying now, and her voice was strained with misery.

CeCe folded her arms across her chest. "Wow, that's all really convenient."

Tessa wiped her nose and looked at CeCe quizzically. "What is?"

"That description of you. Sounds like you're not the only one painting an imaginary picture of your spouse." She pursed her lips, and Tessa saw a momentary flash of something resembling anger in her eyes. "That selfish, ungrateful person he describes? That's not the person you are. Take it from someone who knows. He's looking for someone to blame. If you listen to that shit enough times, you start to believe it."

Chapter Twenty-Nine

Mariel fastened the bunny mobile onto the crib and tightened the screws on the plastic handle. "I can't believe that in just about eight weeks, there will be another little Cordelia in the world." Mariel and Alex were visiting for the day, and Ronnie and Alex were playing in Ronnie's room while Tessa and Mariel fixed up the nursery. Mariel pulled bumper pads from a bin and began tying them onto the crib's spindles. She wore jeans and a long sweatshirt with hand-painted flowers all over the front of it. Her long dark hair flowed just below her shoulders, a section on each side pulled back and fastened in the back with a barrette. She ran her hand over the wall and nodded her admiration.

"Okay, so this sponge-painting technique you did on the walls in here. Can I borrow the instructional video you used?" Tessa had sponged the walls above the chair rail in a mixture of pastel greens, blues, pinks, and yellows. She'd washed all the items from Ronnie's nursery to use for the new baby. Ronnie's bedroom at the new house was decorated in all things Minnie Mouse. The walls were covered in seafoam-green and raspberry-pink striped wallpaper topped with a border of hundreds of Minnies in her signature polka-dot dress and black heels. Matching tie-back curtains, a fluffy pink-and-white comforter, and several Disney stuffed animals completed the look. Ronnie loved it, but Tessa jokingly told Mariel it looked like Disney World threw up all over the room. "I'm going to try it at my house."

Tessa folded a onesie and added it to the pile in front of her. "Really? In which room? You're not redoing Alex's room already, are you? I imagine he'd want eighteen-wheelers painted on his walls. I get such a kick out of how he knows the correct name of any kind of truck!"

Mariel gave her a sly smile. "Nope. Guess again."

Tessa furrowed her brow. "Oh, your powder room? Yeah, good idea to start with a small project until you get the hang of it." Mariel laughed and shook her head. "This is why I stand by my claim that you may have been the neat one in college, but I was the smart one." She put her hand on her abdomen.

Tessa stood and arched her back. "Ooh, I'm stiff. What are you . . . Wait! Oh! Oh! Really? You're pregnant?"

"Ding, ding, ding! Tell her what she's won, Bob! A best friend for the newest addition to her family!"

Tessa grabbed Mariel and hugged her. "Oh, that's fabulous! I'm so happy for you guys! And for us!" She beamed. "When did you find out? When are you due?"

"I just found out for sure two weeks ago. I've been dying to tell you, but I wanted to do it in person. My due date is mid-October, if the doctor knows what she's talking about. I'm still convinced she blew it with Alex's due date. What baby born three weeks early weighs almost nine pounds? Anyway, I'm going to be ready by Labor Day, just in case. That should give me time to hide all Rob's belts and shoelaces." She arranged a bunny comforter over the foot of the crib as Tessa giggled.

"Yeah, Rob is a tough sell. He worries too much. He should just do what the rest of us do: hold his nose and dive straight into the madness. If everyone waited until the time was perfect to have kids, the population would die off."

"He sure doesn't take the news like Ken does. You could probably tell him you're pregnant with your tenth, and he'd be thrilled. You're lucky there."

But Rob comes home every night. Who's the lucky one? Tessa almost said aloud. Tessa thought for the thousandth time what Ken looked like to everyone who wasn't covering for him, what their home looked like to everyone who didn't live inside its secrets.

"Great news, really, Mare. Your mom must be over the moon!" Mariel's father had passed away when the girls were in college. Her mother and siblings still lived in southern New Jersey, and Mariel was close with them despite the distance.

"Actually, I haven't told them yet. They're all coming for Easter on Sunday, so I figured I'd make the announcement then."

The women checked on Ronnie and Alex and then finished in the nursery. They put into dresser drawers all Ronnie's gender-neutral infant clothes Tessa had dug out and washed: T-shirts, pajamas, onesies, bibs, and socks. Then they hung pastel green valances at the room's two windows. "You know," Tessa said, "I just read in an article that some social scientists believe gender is socially constructed, that we actually create social norms as we believe they should be after we learn the sex of our children." She shimmied the fabric onto the curtain rod and stood back, tongue pushed out the corner of her mouth, to inspect her work.

"Umm, whoosa, whatsa, what?"

"That children develop their preferences based on the kinds of interaction and environment we expose them to. You know, like we buy Ronnie dolls and dress her in pink, and you buy Alex trucks and dress him in blue. In other words, they don't come up with those preferences on their own; we create the idea of masculinity or femininity. One scientist called it . . . let's see . . . 'an emergent feature of social situations.'" She gathered the valances' hanging instructions and threw them in the trashcan. "What do you think? Do you buy it?"

Mariel stared at her friend. "Hmm. I guess we do that. I mean, I can't imagine putting a dress on Alex."

"That would be a hoot. Alex in a pink sundress and headband identifying truck names from his car seat as you drove down the highway." They chuckled at the image.

"So, I assume these sociologists say this social construction of gender is bad. It's just one more way parents screw up their kids?"

Tessa stood up. "I guess. But I wouldn't worry about it. If it weren't that, I'm sure we'd find other ways to screw them up."

Later, after a lunch of chicken tenders and mac-and-cheese for the kids and grilled chicken salads and stolen forkfuls of mac-and-cheese for the adults, Mariel and Alex left, and Tessa put Ronnie down for a nap. She was grateful that, at just under two years old, Ronnie didn't fight her on this. She needed the midday break this close to the end of her pregnancy. Curling up on the sofa in the family room, she took out her checklist for Easter on Sunday. Ken had offered to pick up all the paper products—decorative cups, dessert plates, and napkins—as what Tessa figured was part of a peace offering for missing dinner with CeCe last week. She was going over the food list when she heard a soft knock at the back door. Tessa's puzzled look turned to a pleasant smile when she saw CeCe through the glass panes on the door. She wore a pale blue windbreaker over a white long-sleeved polo shirt and faded blue jeans. Flushed from the March breeze, each cheek sported a pink dot in the center.

They hadn't seen each other since the taco dinner debacle. Tessa had wanted to contact CeCe but realized she didn't even have her phone number. She felt somewhat lighter, relieved of Ken's burdensome secret, but she felt bad about the way it had been revealed. "Hey, how are you? Come in." Tessa pulled the door open and stepped aside.

"Oh, well, maybe just for a minute." She followed Tessa into the kitchen. "Are you alone? I just wanted to see how you're doing."

Tessa smiled, touched by CeCe's concern. "I'm hanging in there. And I'm never alone. Hurricane Ronnie is sleeping." She touched her stomach. "And this one goes everywhere I go."

"Oh, yeah, true. I guess I was really asking if Ken is here." She looked around tentatively. "I figured during the day was the best time to catch you at home without him." She fished in a canvas bag flung over her shoulder and extracted a few papers and brochures.

Tessa took a deep breath. "He's at work. Listen, I know I was in pretty bad shape last time you saw me. When you came over for dinner. I'm really sorry. I feel bad about dumping all that on you." She winced. "You come over for tacos and guac, and instead get a super-sized helping of my screwed-up life."

CeCe shook her head vigorously and touched Tessa's arm. Her nails were painted pale pink, and the index fingernail was adorned with a polka-dotted Easter egg. "No, no, don't apologize. Really. Seems like you've had that bottled up for too long. I'm glad I was here to listen even if I wasn't any help."

"You did help. I've been keeping that secret for so long it's become like an appendage. I'm not sure why I unloaded like that. I've been thinking about it, and it's probably because you are one person I haven't built up a false image of Ken for. You're not directly involved in our day-to-day life, so it felt safe. I guess I feel like everyone else would judge us every second from that moment on or worry every time he was ten minutes late." Tessa sighed loudly and pinched the bridge of her nose. "It's a blessing and a curse to have a family like mine. I mean, don't get me wrong. I love them and would do anything for them and vice versa. But we are all so entangled with each other. I want to see this through and decide on my own time what to do, but it's tough because they *are* directly involved in our day-to-day life. If I come clean, it will affect all of them too."

CeCe nodded so slightly it was barely perceptible.

"I've thought about telling them a thousand times. Especially my mom. Of course, she'd be upset, but she's tough. She could take it. She'd know what to do. But my dad, he's a different story. This would kill him." She sat down at the kitchen island and put her head in her hands. "See, he went through this too. With my real mother. She was an alcoholic. She left us when I was about nine."

CeCe pulled out a stool and sat. From her seat she could see pink dogwood trees blooming in the yard near the edge of the driveway where she'd parked her car. They looked almost fake, like a watercolor painting.

Tessa continued, "My dad was broken. He covered for her for years and turned himself inside out begging her to get help. Then one day she just up and left. Left him with three kids to raise and a business to run. I couldn't comprehend his pain then, but I can now.

"He loves Ken like his own son. This would break his heart. And to know I'm going through the same thing he did? He'd be crushed." Tessa brushed a tear from the corner of her eye. "And my brothers, Joey and Sal Jr.? Forget it. They'd want to pummel Ken until they knocked some sense into him. Things would never be the same again." She turned to CeCe. "Do you see what I mean? If I tell them, we can never go back to before they knew. Even if by the grace of God Ken gets his shit together and stops using. It will always be there, a stain, unremovable." CeCe looked over Tessa's shoulder toward the dogwoods. There was movement in the driveway, approaching the door. The color drained from CeCe's face.

Tessa had been so engrossed in her explanation that she didn't hear the back door open.

"CeCe? Are you okay?" She turned toward the door to see what had mesmerized the older woman.

In the mudroom, Sal gripped the wall and almost dropped the seventeen-pound ham he cradled in his arms. He looked like he'd seen a ghost.

Really, he had.

"Caroline?" he managed in a strangled voice. "My God, Caroline. What the hell are you doing here?"

Chapter Thirty

Despite the fact that it was spring, Sal's skin was the color of frost. Tessa felt dizzy. She vacillated between thinking her dad might throw up all over the kitchen island and worrying that she would do it first.

After what she had been through with Ken, Tessa thought she was impossible to faze. In a peculiar way, after Sal's stunning revelation and CeCe's hasty exit amid a stammering flurry of apologies, it seemed Tessa was right. She didn't scream or get hysterical. All she'd managed to do the moment she learned the woman she'd befriended several months ago was in fact her biological mother was sink back into her chair and say, "Oh. Oh my God. Oh." She felt like a new student in a foreign-language class where everyone was fluent in the language, but she only knew a few basic phrases.

Maybe Sal was mistaken. It had been over twenty years since he'd seen Caroline. Maybe CeCe resembled Caroline, or what Sal believed she would look like decades after he'd last seen her. Her mind bizarrely flashed on an episode of *Law and Order* where they used facial recognition software to estimate what a child abducted at age six might look like years later.

Sal finally gathered himself enough to look his daughter in the eye. His face was crumpled like an essay with a red *F* scrawled at the top. He searched Tessa's eyes, and she watched her father piece together that Caroline had not revealed her true identity to her. He knew this because Tessa looked as though she might fall apart like an overbaked cake. One he couldn't keep together by smearing thick layers of icing over it.

Tessa shifted, and Sal realized he still hadn't said anything. He wanted to scream. He looked at his little girl and realized he'd wanted to scream for over twenty years. Not because Caroline had abandoned them. Not because she was a drunk who didn't love her family enough to seek help. Not because she looked to the bottom of a bottle for happiness when she had three children who were growing up without her.

He wanted to scream because the worst thing he could imagine all the years she was gone had materialized.

She was back.

"Jesus." Val hadn't been able to stop saying it. "Jesus." A bomb had dropped in the middle of their lives, the smoking crater choking and blinding them all. She and Sal had sat in their living room with Tessa, Joey, and Sal Jr. for hours the night Sal had discovered Caroline at Tessa's house. For several minutes at a time they'd all simultaneously fire off questions none of them had the answers to, like stones plopping into a lake and disappearing beneath the surface. Then they'd all sit silently, the shock of it swirling around their heads like leaves in an autumn wind. The atmosphere was funereal—ironic because in reality, someone had all but come back from the dead.

Tessa was grateful Sal had rallied from the initial shock. In the moments after the revelation, her dad's reaction had been even stronger than her own. He had been in a car accident once; a distracted driver ran a red light and T-boned him as he crossed the intersection. Sal told his family seeing Caroline in Tessa's kitchen was that kind of blindside. After a few days to absorb it, his mood about the whole thing had progressed to anger that Caroline had deceived Tessa into befriending her.

Now they gathered at Ken and Tessa's for Easter. Ken's two brothers, Jerry and Andy, were there also, and they were just learning of the week's events.

"Sorry, guys," Tessa said sheepishly. "How about some family drama with your ham?" Jerry wiped his mouth and waved off Tessa's apology. Ken felt guilty for admitting it, but he was glad there was something else to focus on at Easter dinner.

Alyse, Joey's wife, carried a gravy boat filled with steaming sauce to the dining room table. "You know, I've been thinking." She turned to her husband and brushed her blonde bangs from her eyes. "Joe, remember we had that string of hang-ups a few months ago? When we'd answer the phone, the person didn't say anything and then just hang up? Do you think it could have been her?" One of the many questions that perplexed all of them was why Caroline had only sought out Tessa, not her sons.

Tessa nodded at her sister-in-law. "It could have been her. Who knows? Remember, the first time I saw her was at the diner. She came in one afternoon right before closing. Dad wasn't there. He had a doctor appointment, and I was helping Linda and Maggie close." She handed Ken a knife to carve the ham. "You know, I keep wondering how she knew I was there but Dad wasn't. Had she been watching the place? That's a creepy thought."

Joey used a spatula to slide two cheesy manicotti onto his plate. As he sprinkled them with cheese, he said pointedly, "My guess is she scoped out your house first. You know, familiarized herself with your routine, your car, stuff like that. So she knew your car, saw it at the diner, took a chance you were there without any of us, and figured she'd try her luck with you. It wouldn't take her long to figure out which car parked at the diner is Dad's. It's parked in the first spot, and it's the only one that's there every single day. She saw your car and not Dad's, and bingo."

He licked a glob of sauce off his thumb. "Think about it, how could she get an audience with Jr. or me? She'd have to come to our work or our houses. You're the most accessible, Tess." He bit into a huge piece of Italian bread slathered with butter.

Sal Jr. chimed in. "Yeah, she buddied up to you and figured you'd pave the way for her to see the rest of us. You innocently mention you and Ronnie take walks in the park on a certain day of the week, and *bam*—she knows where to find you and takes her time becoming your friend." His face darkened with anger, and he shook his head fiercely. "A lot of goddamn nerve, thinking she can just show up here after twenty-two years and slide back in without missing a beat. Who the hell does she think she is?"

Jerry had been listening quietly but spoke up now. "Honestly, I see it a different way. Tess, I think she was nervous, you know, testing the waters, but then she saw how you are. After being around you once or twice, she probably sensed you were her best chance of reconnecting with her family."

Everyone looked at him. Tessa leaned on the table, chin in hands. "What do you mean, 'how I am'?"

"I don't know, it's just your nature. You come across as a fixer. A problem solver," Jerry went on. Ken sipped his wine and looked over his glass at his brother through narrowed eyes. "You always seem to know what to do in any situation. She probably sensed that."

"True story, Tess," Joey chimed in, taking a drink of his wine. "It's that 'oldest girl in an Italian family' thing. We figure you always have your shit together. You can reel the rest of us in. It's like, if you start losing it, we're all in trouble." He raised his glass to her and grinned impishly. "No pressure though, girl."

Tessa tilted her head. "Hmm. Interesting theories. But I don't *always* know how to fix things." Her gaze shifted then from them to Ken. "I wish I did."

Ken said nothing. To the rest of the group, Tessa's comment sounded innocuous, but it was as loaded as a double-barreled shotgun.

"I wonder if she's sober now," Val interjected. "Tess, any of the times you saw her, did it seem as though she'd been drinking?"

"No, but I usually saw her in the park in late morning. She seemed fine. I have no idea what she did the rest of the day, though. And the time she came for dinner? I told you, she had a virgin margarita. I just figured she was doing it in solidarity since I can't drink while I'm pregnant."

"Hmmph," Sal grunted. "As I remember, mornings were never off limits for her before."

"Really, Dad?" Sal Jr. shook his head. "Even in the morning?"

"It's just so convoluted," Val continued, wiping butter from Ronnie's face and hands. "Why pretend? Why didn't she just say who she was and ask if you wanted to see her, Tess?"

Sal cut into a juicy slice of ham. He shook his fork at his wife. "I know why. Because secrets and lies are her specialty."

Later, after everyone left, Tessa pulled open the desk drawer in the kitchen and took out the brochures and papers Caroline had left on the counter when she fled Tessa's house. She looked at the shiny cover of one of the brochures. *Al-Anon: A Fellowship Program for Family and Friends of Alcoholics.* On the cover, an attractive strawberry-blonde woman of about forty years old had her arm around a teenage boy with neatly combed hair the same color as his mother's. In the background stood a man with a haggard downward-turned face. There was another brochure for a place called The Village that offered support for addicts and their families. *You are not alone*, it promised. The facility boasted professional coaches who helped find the path that worked for each individual situation. Tessa skimmed the descriptions of their programs: some inpatient, some outpatient, and some a combination of the two.

She stared at her reflection in the kitchen window. Caroline had brought these materials to Tessa after learning about Ken's addiction. But had she also wanted Tessa to understand Caroline's own problems, the ones that caused her to leave all those years ago? She was still flipping through the papers when she heard Ken behind her.

"Okay, Ronnie's down. She insisted on keeping the basket of plastic eggs from the egg hunt in her bed with her. I didn't have it in me to fight her." He yawned loudly. "What do you have there?"

Tessa folded the papers and stuffed them into her shoulder bag that was hanging on a hook in the mudroom. "Oh, nothing. Just some information about the preschool program I'm going to enroll Ronnie in next year. You'd think she's applying to college with all the paperwork they make you sign." She arched her back and stretched her arms out in front of her, fingers interlocked.

Ken studied her. "Tess," he began. "It's been a hell of a few weeks for you."

"Yes, and not just because of the Caroline bombshell." She lowered her eyes.

"I know. Not just because of that." He ran his hands through his hair. "Tess."

Tessa held up her palms to stop him. This wasn't going to happen tonight. It was too much. She couldn't handle her addict husband trying to comfort her because her long-lost alcoholic biological mother had deceptively resurfaced after more than two decades.

It was too weird even for them.

Chapter Thirty-One

"See you guys tomorrow!" Tracy called out over her shoulder. She rummaged in her purse for her keys and sunglasses.

"Bye, Trace!" Brenda made sure she was gone and then walked into Ken's private office, where he was finishing notes on a chart. She placed a small round plastic pill bottle on his desk.

"Thanks," Ken said quietly. "I'll give him a call." He put the bottle in his desk drawer and picked up the phone.

"Sure. I'm going to finish cleaning my exam room."

Ken rubbed his neck and punched in Lux Air's number. When no one answered, he pulled out his Nokia, glad that one of the features was the ability to send short text messages. He entered Stan's mobile number and typed *GOT EM*. He absentmindedly thumbed through a stack of mail on his desk but couldn't focus. Giving up, he threw them in a pile and then walked down the hall to the break room. Brenda was already there with two glasses and a bottle of Chardonnay.

"Sit down, take a load off," she said as she filled the glasses. "I don't feel like going home yet. I'm not ready for the wine police and his disapproving looks." She stretched her legs out in front of her and shook her long hair out of its clip. "Bottoms up."

Ken sat down at the table across from her and loosened his paisley tie. She was a good friend and had become, what? A confidante? Brenda was fun, not uptight like Tessa. Months ago, after their night out at Mulligan's when she'd come back to the office and discovered him on the gas, she didn't flip out and lecture him about all the reasons he should stop. She understood. She knew sometimes people needed to unwind in their own way. She even let him call in prescriptions for Oxy in her name so he could continue mollifying that pain in the ass Stan into selling him extra tanks when he ran out. Brenda's husband was hypercritical about her drinking, so she knew what it was like to be hounded constantly when all she wanted was some time to wind down.

"Did you reach Stan?"

"No, but he'll turn up. He's like a bad penny."

The thing that amazed Tessa is that she didn't think of this before. Someone who wants to stop eating potato chips just doesn't keep them in the house, right? It was so simple she kicked herself for not coming up with it until now.

In the weeks since she'd discovered CeCe's true identity, she'd come to a few realizations. One: She was tired of being duped. And two: Ken was going to dupe her as long as she let him.

Tessa had to admit his demeanor was better right after they'd moved into the new house. He was less restless, more focused, more content. They entertained family and friends like old times, but now Ken beamed with pride at their spacious new surroundings instead of making apologies that they had to eat in shifts in their small kitchen. He immersed himself in projects like painting, landscape ideas, and picking out new furniture and décor. Tessa thought he truly seemed happy, and she was hopeful that the worst was behind them. Transitioning their little family to the new house felt like a revival of sorts. Ken and Tessa spent more time together than they had in almost two years, painting the nursery and wandering hand in hand up and down the aisles of Pottery Barn Kids and The Disney Store, choosing bedding and furniture for Ronnie's big girl room. At night, they read or watched TV, and Tessa slept soundly with Ken next to her, his arm slung over her growing abdomen. It was like his two-year itch had finally been scratched and peace was restored.

But then, as always, the demons returned, like a dry cough, quiet during the day, back with a vengeance at night to make sleep impossible.

With every backslide, Ken chastised himself and promised it was the last time or, more often lately, chastised Tessa about hounding him incessantly. No, things would never change if she left it up to him. Of that she was sure.

These thoughts were firmly planted in her mind as she bathed Ronnie. Ronnie covered her eyes and tilted back her head as Tessa poured cupfuls of water over her to rinse out the shampoo. "Gimmee towel, huwee, huwee!" the slippery wet toddler squealed, standing up and hanging on to her mother's arm.

Tessa dried off Ronnie and slipped her *Lion King* nightgown over her head. She went over the details of her plan as she combed out her daughter's shiny wet hair. With just about six weeks until the baby's due date, she had to grab the reins and get control of things. As she'd hoped, Caroline hadn't tried to contact her, and though Tessa was certain she would one day, she was glad that for now Ken was the only problem she needed to deal with. One sneaky, lying addict at a time was plenty.

Tessa still hadn't deciphered how she felt about Caroline returning and not telling her who she really was, but one thing Tessa knew was that it awakened something in her. For two years, she had felt like the punchline in a bad cocktail party joke. She had been vulnerable, helpless, kept in the dark, like a hostage tied up in a deserted warehouse by a deranged maniac. No more. She would be calling the shots now.

She felt energized by her new mindset. She felt like she could lift her car over her head, run fifty miles through pouring rain and ankle-deep mud. No longer would she exist in the shadow of Ken's problem as though they were characters in a blockbuster movie where he was the star and she was just a lowly extra roaming around in the background.

Joey and Jerry said it themselves. She was a fixer, a problem solver. She'd allowed Ken's problem to bury her for almost two years, afraid of angering him, afraid of how her family would view him, afraid of people finding out, afraid of damaging his career. She'd taken it on and allowed it to swallow her up, rule her life, as though she was the one with the problem. She recalled the many times, after Ken's all-night binges, *she'd* been the one curled up on the sofa, shades drawn, unable to get out of her pajamas while he showered, dressed, and went about his day. *Codependence*, the brochures Caroline dropped on her counter called it. Her entire existence had been organized around Ken's addiction. She'd blushed with shame reading the Al-Anon literature. It was like it was written about her.

That was all going to change. Ken would thank her for taking care of things. Maybe not initially, but eventually he would see that she had to do it because he wasn't capable of finding a solution himself. He was the weak one, not her. He was the one endangering their marriage, their family, his career, not her. And no matter what he said, he would never voluntarily go into rehab. She knew that now for certain.

As she helped Ronnie brush her teeth, Tessa cringed at a memory from a few weeks ago. She'd driven Ken to an inpatient facility about twenty miles north of their town. Ken's car was in the shop for inspection, and Tessa had picked him up after work. He'd been bingeing for a few days prior, and as Tessa drove, they argued for the umpteenth time about his promising for almost two years to get help. Tessa had read about the facility in one of the brochures Caroline left behind. It was famous; celebrities and athletes traveled from all over the country to conquer their demons there.

Ronnie had fallen asleep in her car seat, and on an impulse, Tessa steered the car in the direction of the treatment center. Ken calmly explained that this tactic would not work. He was not going in, and she could not make him. His look mocked her, exposed how he pitied her stupidity. Tessa drove silently while Ken hummed along to the songs on the radio. She wanted to bash in his skull.

Once at the facility, they sat in the car for over half an hour in the parking lot. Ken drummed his fingers on the dashboard and raised his eyebrows impishly at Tessa whenever she looked over at him. From their vantage point they could see the lobby and front desk. A huge framed poster hung above the desk. It showed a man standing ankle-deep in the ocean, arms raised as if he had just won a marathon. Bright sunlight glistened on the water in front of him, and dark shadows, presumably representing his past, fell flat behind him. A few people came and went, most likely the family and friends of patients hooked on substances that were destroying their lives. They hugged each other and huddled against the wind, nodding hopefully to each other that this time things would be different.

Eventually, it was close to Ronnie's bedtime, and Tessa had to pee. Without a word, she started the car and drove back home, tears silently slipping from her eyes and sliding down her cheeks. She'd gone to bed without speaking to Ken.

That plan hadn't worked because she hadn't taken the time to think it through. She'd acted on a whim. That plan left Ken an out, a choice. This time would be different.

She read *The Berenstain Bears Go to School* twice to Ronnie and tucked her into bed. Ken was coming in the door just as Tessa descended the stairs.

"Hey."

"Hey."

"She asleep yet?"

"I just put her down. She's probably still awake if you want to say good night." Ken passed her and started up the steps. "I'm going out for a while. I need to do a Wal-Mart run."

Ken turned to look at his wife. "Now?"

"Yeah, it will take less time if I don't have Ronnie with me. I won't be long."

She already had what she needed in her car, but she double-checked anyway. Satisfied, she zipped up the black nylon gym bag and placed it behind the driver's seat. She'd dropped by the office a few times recently to familiarize herself with the details she'd need to carry out her plan.

Only two vehicles, a gray Honda Civic and a beat-up white Chevy pickup truck, occupied the parking lot at Ken's office building. *Second-shift custodians*, thought Tessa. *No problem.* She slid out from behind the wheel, her large belly adding clumsiness to her movements.

Carrying the gym bag over her shoulder, she used her master key to enter the main lobby. She took the stairs to the second floor and came face-to-face with one of the custodians. A bandanna partially covered his red curly hair, and he wore glasses with large plastic frames. "Oh, evenin', Ma'am. What brings you here after hours?" He rested his forearms on his cart.

Tessa played it cool. She'd prepared for such an encounter. "Hi!" She clutched her bag tightly and shook her head. "That husband of mine. So forgetful. He was supposed to bring home some paperwork for me. I've been helping out with some of the clerical stuff in the office."

"Well, that's sure nice of you, but looks like you're going to have your hands full with other things pretty soon." He gestured toward the bump in Tessa's abdomen.

"Yes, true." She laughed. "I've forgotten what my feet look like."

"Least you have an excuse." He rubbed his own stomach.

"Mine's the result of too much pizza and beer!" Tessa smiled and started down the hall toward Ken's suite. "Hey, you need me to unlock the door for you?"

"No, thanks. I got it." She dangled her key chain in front of her, and the custodian pressed the elevator button.

"Okay, then, have yourself a nice night."

Tessa let herself into the reception area and flipped on the light. Her hair was tied back in a ponytail, and she was dressed head to toe in black like a cat burglar. She wondered absently if that had been intentional.

She plopped the bag on the floor in front of the storage closet. On one of her recent visits, when none of the staff was looking, she'd tried her office keys on the closet, and none of them worked, so she'd have to remove the knob. She zipped open the bag and riffled through the contents until she found the correct screwdriver. After easily removing the knob, she pulled open the door and turned on the light.

The nitrous oxide system sat right inside the door. Tessa took a step backward, as if it might lunge at her, an unwelcome intruder. For a long moment, she stared at it, the tool of Ken's destruction. It housed his drug of choice. For some it was a bottle, for others a needle, but this was the apparatus that transported Ken from his life as a responsible husband, father, and professional to one somewhere out in the stratosphere where none of those things mattered to him. A noise out in the main corridor jolted her from her reverie.

She reached into the bag and withdrew the papers she'd printed from the internet. Flipping through them, she found the one with diagrams and labels. Biting her lip, she used her index finger to trace a diagram of the system that matched Ken's. She'd done her homework and knew what she was looking for. Working methodically and carefully, Tessa loosened the flow control valve on the main panel. She unscrewed it, and when it came off, she dropped it in the gym bag and replaced the washer that had held it on. Satisfied that the change was undetectable to average inspection, she moved on to the next task, even though removing that valve was probably enough to prohibit the system from working. She retrieved a needle from the bag and held it between her lips. After consulting the diagram again, she examined the tubes attached to the machine. She found the inlet hose, the one that allowed the gas to flow to the patient's—or in this case, Ken's—nose from the flowmeter. With the needle, she poked a series of tiny holes all along the length of the hose.

She'd thought about ripping apart the apparatus, smashing the glass panel, removing every valve, and shredding the hoses with a knife, but that was too violent, too vengeful. That would infuriate Ken. This way was gentler, but every bit as effective.

It's just your nature. You come across as a fixer. A problem solver.

She sat back on her haunches and examined her work. Using her forearm, she brushed some stray hair off her face. That should do it.

As Tessa returned the tools to her bag, she thought about the next time Ken entered this closet with the intention of a long night of inhaling nitrous oxide. She visualized him dragging the tanks into the exam room, placing the mask over his face. He'd settle in, as he had hundreds of times before, only this time it would be different. With an integral valve missing, the system wouldn't cooperate; gas wouldn't flow through the hole-ridden hose, wouldn't lift him from the chair into blissful blankness. And then what? What would he do?

It wasn't as if it was alcohol and he could simply go to the next bar if one wouldn't serve him. He wasn't using the gas on his patients, so he couldn't exactly bring in someone to repair it. That would make his staff ask questions. He'd bought the system, but Tessa didn't know if he'd purchased the insurance. That was the one wild card. However, it would be clear the damage was the fault of the operator, not a manufacturer defect, so they'd be less likely to repair it at their cost. She'd researched the price of a new system. No way Ken would plunk down that kind of money again. And if he did, she'd be back with her black bag.

Ken would figure out that Tessa was behind the sabotage, but it would be too late. No more gas. No choice but to finally make good on his promises. He'd thank her for doing what he'd been unable to do. He'd see how much better their life was without that damn gas. He'd put it all behind him. He'd wish she'd done it sooner.

Problem solved.

Chapter Thirty-Two

The doctor told Tessa—reminded her, really, since this was not her first baby—that in the last month of pregnancy it wasn't uncommon to have cramping, leaking fluids, and all sorts of unpleasantries, none of which necessarily signaled a woman was in labor. She tried to remember the weeks before Ronnie was born, but they were all a blur now. Noting her flushed face in the mirror, she turned on the cold water. Perspiration gathered in the folds of her neck, and she gulped a cup of water. She was refilling the cup when she felt wetness between her legs. She looked down just in time to see a trickle of blood make its way down her inner thigh.

"What the hell?" Tessa asked aloud, though she was alone in the master bathroom. Her words bounced off the high vaulted ceiling, sounded loud against the cricket hum of the still June night. It was warm already for June, and the window was open.

She grabbed a towel, awkwardly clutched it between her thighs as she walked to the bedroom, and grabbed the phone. Dialing Ken's office number, she tried to remember if the doctor had said anything about bleeding. She returned to the bathroom as the phone rang unanswered. It was almost eight thirty. She had just put Ronnie to bed, and Ken was not yet home. The tile felt cool under her feet, and Tessa considered lying down on it.

It had been about three weeks since her nighttime visit to the office. Ken had come home each night during that time period, so Tessa assumed he was still unaware of what she'd done. She was ready to face the music when he figured it out. He'd be puzzled at first, but he'd quickly realize it was her who'd put an end to it. She was ready, eager even, for that day. He'd thank her, she was sure of it.

Their baby was due soon, and he'd want a fresh start as much as she did.

She sat down on the edge of the tub and dialed his cell phone number. It went straight to voicemail. Tessa blotted her damp forehead with a washcloth and dialed her doctor's number. She tried to remain calm and told the answering service operator the reason for her call. They hung up, and her doctor called back within three minutes.

"Good evening, Tessa. What's going on?"

"Hi, Dr. Leighton." She relaxed at the sound of her doctor's voice. Constance Leighton was a tiny woman, not even five feet tall, with short black hair cut in a smart asymmetrical style, parted low and tucked behind her ear on one side. "It's probably nothing, but I thought I should call." Tessa relayed her symptoms to the doctor.

"Yes, you did the right thing. So, to be clear, we're talking bleeding that soaks your underwear, not simply spotting."

Tessa looked at the towel, which now had a grapefruit-sized blood stain on it.

"Yes, I'm bleeding."

"Any pain? Cramping?"

"No, not really."

Dr. Leighton asked Tessa a few more questions, including whether she had a fever. Tessa took her temperature with a digital thermometer and reported that she did not. "Okay. I want you to lie down and elevate your feet. Keep the towel under your bottom. If you are still bleeding in an hour, or if you start bleeding heavier before the hour is up, I want your husband to bring you to the hospital." Tessa winced and rubbed her temples at the mention of Ken.

"What could this mean?"

"It might be nothing, so don't worry needlessly. But if you are still bleeding in an hour, I want to check you."

"Why?"

"Well, the bleeding might mean the placenta separated from the wall of your uterus. But let's not get ahead of ourselves. It's a good sign that you don't have any pain." Tessa could hear activity in the background. She pictured Dr. Leighton standing at the nurses' station outside the delivery room, the doors swinging open as a mother-to-be was wheeled in after laboring for hours, her husband running beside the bed, clutching her sweaty hand, professing his love for her.

The doctor continued in a light, optimistic tone. "Listen, relax and get that handsome husband of yours to put some pillows under your feet. I'll call you in an hour to check on you. Unless, as I said, the bleeding gets worse. Then come in and I'll take a look."

Tessa cleaned herself up, changed into pajamas, and pulled an old towel from the linen closet. She spread it out on her bed and lay on top of it. As she situated two bulky pillows under her feet, she considered what to do if she needed to go to the hospital. She could drive herself, but she'd need to call Val or a neighbor to stay with Ronnie. Though they hadn't lived in the neighborhood very long, Tessa had become friendly with Laurie from across the street. She was an English professor at a local college, and her husband owned an area car dealership. Their son Ian was Ronnie's age, and the two women found they had much in common and bonded quickly.

Closing her eyes, she concentrated on breathing evenly to stay calm. Laurie would ask fewer questions. Tessa could say Ken was away at a continuing-education seminar. She could say aliens abducted him and were holding him hostage on the mother ship. She could say she had no earthly idea where her husband was or what he was doing.

Even as she dialed the office again and listened to endless unanswered ringing, she asked herself why she thought he might be there. He couldn't use the gas. She'd seen to that. So where was he?

Tessa didn't realize she'd dozed off until the phone woke her up. Disoriented, she grabbed for it on the bed next to her. "Ken?"

"Hi, Tessa. It's Dr. Leighton. How are you doing? Has the bleeding stopped?"

Tessa scrambled to her feet and headed into the bathroom. She checked her panties and pajamas. They were soaked with blood, and she gasped. "No, I'm still bleeding. What should I do?"

"Come to the hospital. I need to check you."

Tessa rubbed her neck, sore from the angle at which she'd fallen asleep. "I, um, I have to get someone to stay with Ronnie." *And I have no idea where my husband is.* "Are you sure it can't wait until morning?"

"No, you need to come in. Bring Ronnie with you if you have to. Go to the front entrance, and they'll get you a wheelchair and bring you up to maternity."

"Okay, I'll see you in a bit."

Tessa looked at the clock. 9:30 p.m. Deciding she had very few options, she called Joey and Alyse. She briefly explained what was going on and told them Ken was at a CE seminar overnight. They said they'd be there in fifteen minutes. Joey would stay with Ronnie, and Alyse would drive Tessa to the hospital. She changed into jeans and a long-sleeved cotton top, checked on Ronnie, and went downstairs.

Then she sat in a chair next to an open window in the family room to wait for Joey and Alyse. She listened to the night sounds outside. Cupping the screen with the side of her hand and peering out, she saw the cold light of fireflies dancing in the air just off the deck. Their intermittent glow teased her, now lit, now dark, as if they were trying to speak to her in code. Tessa envied them though, because they weren't trying to speak at all. They had nothing to say, no secrets to keep and none to reveal.

Three hours later, the two women arrived back at Tessa's house from the hospital. The doctor had given her a thorough exam and didn't find anything wrong. The bleeding subsided and then eventually stopped altogether, so Dr. Leighton allowed her to go home. She warned her patient to take it easy and call her immediately if it started again. She even mentioned the possibility of bedrest for Tessa's last few weeks, but Tessa assured her that wouldn't be necessary.

"Tessa, I hope I'm not overstepping, but you seem very distracted. Everything okay?"

Oh yes, everything's great, she wanted to say. *My husband is an addict and I thought I'd gotten rid of his drug of choice, but he never came home tonight. It's okay, though, he's probably just cozied up somewhere with his hygienist. She's a drunk, so she doesn't hassle him about his little problem. Glass houses and throwing stones and all that. Do you have the Real Estate section of the newspaper lying around? I'm probably going to end up a single mom and need a place to live. Oh, and my brother no doubt knows my story tonight about Ken's whereabouts is a bunch of shit, so I may have to face an interrogation when I get home. Then I have to hope he doesn't tell my parents Ken was MIA while I bled all over the bathroom floor and give them both a heart attack. Other than that, though . . .*

"Yes, everything's fine," Tessa answered.

Tessa and Alyse chatted on the way home, and Alyse asked if she wanted to call Ken with an update. "I'll call him when I get home," Tessa lied. Tessa was glad she'd spent the last few hours with her sister-in-law and not her brother. She might crack if Joey pressed her. He often looked like he knew something was up, but so far he hadn't mentioned it. It was more in his raised eyebrows and his deafening silence anytime Ken wasn't where he was supposed to be. Hours earlier, when she'd called them, there had been a long pregnant pause on the other end when she'd said Ken was at a seminar.

She'd kept their secret for so long she couldn't come clean this close to the birth. And Ronnie's second birthday was in a week. This was not a good time to untie the strings that had held her together for so long. If she tugged at one end, even lightly, it would be impossible to stop it all from unraveling.

Besides, she really didn't know what Ken was up to tonight. With no gas at the office, it was anyone's guess.

Chapter Thirty-Three

Sam Dinatelli was an oral surgeon whose office occupied most of the second floor next to Ken's suite. He'd been in practice for almost thirty years, and he and his family had lived in the township since he was a resident. He and his wife had known Sal and Val for years, and all their kids went through school together. Dr. Dinatelli's son and Tessa were close friends throughout high school. Dr. Dinatelli loved Tessa and often chided Ken that he'd always hoped she'd one day be his daughter-in-law. After Ken graduated from dental school, as a favor to Sal, the older doctor took Ken under his wing and helped him secure a residency in one of the city hospitals nearby. He'd also been instrumental in Ken finding office space in the building. Admiring Ken's intelligence and drive, Sam Dinatelli had grown genuinely fond of him.

"Good morning, Tessa. It's Sam Dinatelli calling." Tessa had just finished getting Ronnie ready for a playdate at Laurie's when Dr. Dinatelli called the house. Ken hadn't come home the night before, and Tessa was fatigued both from her ordeal and her husband's disappearance. She was glad when Laurie called earlier and asked if Ronnie could spend the morning playing with Ian. After Joey and Alyse left, she'd barely slept all night, tossing and turning, getting up multiple times to see if the imaginary noises she heard were Ken coming in the door.

"Dr. Dinatelli. Hi. How are you?" Tessa furrowed her brow.

"I'm well. Listen, do you think you can come down here to the office? Ken is here with me." He spoke softly and sounded to Tessa like he would rather walk barefoot over broken glass than say why he was calling. "Tessa? Are you there?"

Tessa was frozen in place and hadn't answered him. "Y-yes. I'm here." She checked her watch. Twenty minutes until she could take Ronnie across the street to Laurie's. "I'll be there in a half an hour."

"Good, good. We'll be here. We've both cleared our schedules for the morning."

"Dr. Dinatelli, is Ken okay?"

"I think he will be."

Tessa drove to the office in a fog. Why was Ken with Dr. Dinatelli? She steered her Jeep into the office complex parking lot. Beyond the complex, on the highway, a long, loud horn sounded from an eighteen-wheeler. The morning was warm and sticky. It was shaping up to be another hot, humid day.

The main door to Dr. Dinatelli's office was closed and locked, so Tessa knocked softly. She was holding her breath when he opened the door. The doctor was average height, had dark wavy hair that was beginning to gray at the temples, and wore round wire-framed glasses. He hugged Tessa and led her back to his private office. His huge cherry desk sat in the middle of the room. Thick leather-bound books and photos of his wife, children, and grandchildren adorned a tall bookshelf behind it. The walls were covered with creamy striped wallpaper, and a huge potted plant stood in one corner.

Ken sat in a high-back burgundy leather chair meant for patient consultations. His face was pasty white, his pupils dilated, as though he'd seen something terrifying. But Tessa took one look at him and guessed it was Sam Dinatelli, not Ken, who'd seen something that scared him.

Tessa stared at the indentations on either side of Ken's nose. He did not look at her.

"Tessa, sit down," Dr. Dinatelli said, and she did, mostly to keep from keeling over.

"This is your fault. I don't know how you could be so stupid." Ken, agitated and tired, paced the kitchen floor. He still wore his rumpled clothes from yesterday. His hair stuck up wildly like a mad scientist from running his hands through it. "So you thought dismantling my fucking nitrous system would make me quit? Jesus. Now look what you did. Nice work."

Tessa felt foolish. She sat in a kitchen chair, her hands resting on her belly. One strap of her cotton sundress fell off her shoulder, but she didn't bother to fix it. She closed her eyes and recalled Dr. Dinatelli's pained expression as he'd described the panicked call he'd received from Suzanne, his office manager, that morning as he was driving to work. He arrived at his office a few minutes later to find Suzanne visibly shaken, sitting in the reception room. She'd nodded toward the first exam room, and Sam approached Ken gingerly. He'd touched Ken's shoulder and gently removed the mask from the younger dentist's face.

When Tessa arrived at the office, he'd relayed the morning's events to her. "Last week we ran out of nitrous," he'd said, shaking his head. "That never happens. I thought there must be a leak in the lines." He'd given Tessa a sympathetic look. "This morning, when we caught him in the act, Ken admitted he'd come in several times the last few weeks and used the gas when I was in my satellite office across town. He said those times he'd only stayed an hour or so, but last night he'd fallen into a deeper sleep. He was still here when Suzanne got here."

Tessa hadn't seen Suzanne this morning—Dr. Dinatelli had canceled his morning and sent her home—but she pictured how traumatized the poor woman must have been to find Ken on the gas. Shivering, she recalled the first time she'd found him that way, almost two years ago.

Now Ken pounded his fist on the counter, and Tessa jumped and scrambled to explain. "I-I guess I was desperate. The last few months have been crazy. First, the new house, then CeCe turns out to be Caroline, and a baby on the way. I just felt like I had to do something." She stood and faced her husband. "You always say you could take the gas or leave it. You say you're not addicted. You keep telling me one day you'll just decide to quit and that will be that." Tessa had been calm but was angry now. "Ken, it's enough. It's time. *You* are the one who sold me on the idea of this house with all that fresh start and leave-our-troubles-behind-us bullshit. I just wanted to put an end to it once and for all." Miserable, she slumped back into the chair. "In case you haven't noticed, this baby is coming real soon."

"Why do you think I didn't flip out on you when I discovered what you'd done? I'm not an animal. I'm not going to scream at my wife who's eight months pregnant."

"That's lovely of you, thanks. Well, here's a question. How about if your wife who's almost nine months pregnant starts bleeding and needs to go to the hospital? Would you be there for her?" Sarcasm dripped from her. "You know, since you're not an animal."

Ken looked confused. "What the hell are you talking about?"

"That's right. Let me fill you in on what you missed last night." Exasperated, she briefly recounted the events of the last twelve hours. "Maybe you are an animal."

Ken exhaled loudly and held his head. "Jesus Christ. See? This is what I'm talking about. If you hadn't fucked with my machine, I would have been in my own office, and you would have been able to get to me in an emergency!"

Tessa pulled back, stunned, as if someone had slapped her. She replayed Ken's last words in her mind, just to see if she had missed something that would stop him from sounding unhinged. But no. There wasn't anything. He sounded nuts. "*That's* what you got from what I just told you? *That's* your take on all this?"

He stared at her hard enough to bore holes through her. Finally, he blinked, and his tone softened. "I know what you were trying to do, but it doesn't work that way. It has to be on *my* terms. It has to be when *I'm* ready."

"Well, I guess you better be ready now. You heard what Dr. Dinatelli said."

Ken's anger returned. "Yes, thank you very much. I heard him. What a fucking mess you've gotten me into." He picked up Ronnie's small rubber ball from the island and threw it across the room.

Sam had told Ken and Tessa that he would not contact the police nor the dental board if Ken checked himself into a rehab program. Ken immediately balked, but the older doctor had put up his hand to stop his protests.

"Ken, you have a problem. Think about it. You've been abusing nitrous oxide for the better part of two years." Tessa had filled in some of the gaps that Ken wasn't willing to share. "When you couldn't do it in your own office, instead of quitting, you broke into my office and stole mine." He'd let that sink in before he continued. "Look, you can make this right. You can stop this. I know your baby is due soon. But you can do inpatient treatment for a few weeks and then switch to outpatient therapy as long as you need it. Ken, I've known Tessa and her family for years. I'm doing this for them because I know they'd do the same for my son. I like you and will do what I can to support you, but you have to do this." Then he look pointedly at both of them. "If you don't, I'll make the appropriate calls."

"Sam, please. Can't we talk about this? What will happen if you press charges? I'll lose my license and who knows what else." Ken gestured toward Tessa, who was crying silently. "You said it yourself, we're about to have a baby. Can't you let us get through that, and then I'll deal with it?"

"No. I'm sorry, but I can't do that. I can't, with a clean conscience, keep quiet while you continue to abuse a controlled substance. I'll also have to notify the dental board. You're a smart man. Have you thought about how dangerous it is to treat patients while you're impaired?"

"I don't treat patients while I'm impaired. If I'm doing it all night, I cancel patients for the day." Dr. Dinatelli looked help-lessly at Tessa as if to ask, *Does he really think that makes it okay?*

Tessa was keenly aware of the shock of objectivity this moment brought about. Here was someone seeing Ken as an addict. Someone who hadn't vowed to love, honor, and respect him all the days of her life. She felt excuses forming in her head and almost voiced them. *I know he sounds like a wacko, but he's a good person deep down. I know he sounds crazy and irresponsible, but he loves us. It's just . . . he lost his mother so young, and that's how it all started.*

Ken's voice took on a frantic edge. "Please, Sam, let's talk about this some more. Let Tessa and I come up with a plan and get back to you. I swear. I'll stop. I mean it."

Dr. Dinatelli asked Ken to step out into the reception area so he could speak with Tessa alone. He closed the door of his private office and sat next to her.

She barely met the older man's eyes. "I guess you think I'm an idiot for thinking taking apart that damn machine would be all it took to make him stop. I just . . . I just didn't know what else to do. I figured if he couldn't get it, then he would stop. I never in a million years imagined he'd resort to breaking into your office. My God." She covered her face with her hands. "He's sicker than I thought."

"Tessa, I'm so sorry. Of course I don't think you're an idiot. You're going through hell. People go to extreme measures when someone they love is a substance abuser and won't admit it."

He handed her a tissue. "Who else knows about this? Do your parents know?"

Tessa blew her nose and shook her head. She thought about Caroline but kept it to herself. "No, no one knows. I've been hanging on to the hope that he'll stop and no one will ever have to know. He keeps saying he will. He keeps telling me if I just give him time, he'll stop." She twisted the tissue between her fingers and realized how ridiculous she sounded. "He says it would be selfish of me to tell anyone. That he's so good to me and would never leave me if I were going through something like this. That I'd ruin his professional reputation and humiliate him personally. That I'd never be able to support myself and Ronnie—and now the new baby—if I leave and he loses his license when his secret comes out."

Dr. Dinatelli looked heartbroken. "He's sold you quite a bill of goods, hasn't he? He's wrong. That's the addiction talking. No matter what happens, *none* of this is your responsibility. This is all him." He took off his glasses and rubbed the lenses with a soft cloth from his desk. He walked to the window and gazed out at the blistering sun blazing in a cloudless sky. After a seemingly endless moment, he turned to face her. "Okay. I won't say or do anything until after the baby is born and you guys are settled in."

Tessa looked at him gratefully.

"But under one condition," he went on. "He doesn't do the gas again. I need you to promise me you will tell me if he gets his system repaired and starts using it. And if he breaks in here, all bets are off. I go to the police and the dental board." He paused and took both Tessa's hands in his. "Tessa, I really think you should tell your parents. This is too much for you to shoulder alone. What if you had gone into labor last night while Ken was here in a stupor?"

Tessa thought about the bleeding and wanted to tell him his concern wasn't that far off the mark. Still, the thought of coming clean now, with the new baby due in a few weeks, was more than she thought she could handle. Her parents would be beside themselves. Especially Sal.

"You need a support system. If nothing else, I'm glad I know now. At least you can come to me if you need to. Here." He tore a paper from a notepad on his desk and wrote his mobile number on it. "Call me anytime. And if you want, I'll even go with you when you tell your parents."

Tessa thanked Dr. Dinatelli, and together they'd walked to the reception room, where Ken was waiting. The doctor held the door for them. "Go home and talk. Come up with a plan and get back to me. But, Ken, no more. You've got to stop this." He'd looked at the giant bump straining the fabric of Tessa's sundress. "You have a lot of reasons to do this."

Ken hadn't spoken to her on the drive home.

Now Tessa walked to the refrigerator and took out a pitcher of water. She poured herself a glass and said, "We can't go on much longer like this. You still think you don't have a problem? You *broke into* another doctor's office and *stole* his nitrous oxide."

"Yeah, and whose fault is that?"

"You have to get help. If you don't, I'm going to—"

"You're going to what? Leave right before the baby is born? Really? Maybe you can make the announcement when Ronnie blows out her birthday candles next week. That will be a great way to ruin two happy events for everyone." He stormed toward the stairs. "I'm going to take a shower. Then we'll talk, like we told Sam we would. We'll come up with a plan." As he walked upstairs, he called to her, "Don't say you're going to leave me. You don't mean it. I would never leave you, no matter what you did. For better or worse, right?"

"There's more than one way to leave me," Tessa answered, aware that he most likely didn't hear her.

Chapter Thirty-Four

Tessa was watching *Seinfeld*, the one where Kramer recreates *The Merv Griffin Show* in his apartment, when she felt the first death grip on her abdomen. She finished the episode—alternately wincing through contractions and cracking up at Elaine's plot to arm a coworker with noisy Tic-Tacs to prevent him from sidling up next to her—before she positioned her troops. Val stayed with Ronnie, and Ken drove Tessa to the hospital. Val wanted to be present for her second grandchild's birth, so Ken called her early the next morning when it was getting close, and Val dropped off Ronnie at Joey and Alyse's with a tote bag filled with bribe toys and snacks and the promise of a new sibling for her by lunchtime.

Tessa was in a wing of the hospital called Beginnings Maternity Center where mothers labored, delivered, and recovered in one private room. Newborns bunked with their mothers instead of taking their place on Baby Row in the nursery—that is, unless the little angel was a screamer and Mom wanted a good night's sleep, in which case this homey idea lost some of its appeal. Women who came in with no complications could choose this option, a new one since Tessa had delivered Ronnie. Laboring mothers were permitted to have anyone they wanted present in the room while they labored, and Tessa swore the woman in the next room had brought an army of extended family, a buffet spread, and possibly a DJ. Tessa opted to labor with just Ken in the room and invite Val in when the big moment was near, though it was hard not to be entertained by the party-like atmosphere next door.

Julia Valerie Cordelia came into the world much as her sister Veronica had—howling at the top of her lungs after twelve hours of excruciating start-and-stop labor for Tessa. At seven and a half pounds, she was more filled out than Ronnie had been at birth, and her hair was just as dark but much better behaved.

"My last one came out looking like Don King," quipped Tessa when the nurses commented on Julia's feathery wisps of hair. She held her daughter close, taking in her new-baby scent.

Julia was now several hours old, and the maternity floor was awash with activity. Busy nurses hurried in and out of rooms. Others pushed swaddled newborns in wheeled bassinets up and down the halls to the rooms of their waiting family members. The sun burned through the faded shade on the window in Tessa's room, and she closed her eyes against its harsh glare. She tried to ignore the cramping in her belly and focused instead on Julia, who lay with her in the hospital bed. She'd been cradling Julia, trying to give her her first bottle, when she discovered her arms felt like rubber and seemed to have forgotten how to function. Not trusting herself, she laid the swaddled newborn next to her.

A cheerful nurse entered the room and frowned when she took in Tessa's pallor. Her name was Ginny, and she had red hair that she wore in a messy bun on top of her head. Her scrubs were a teddy bear print, and a bright pink octopus clung to her stethoscope with the help of Velcro. She moved Julia to her bassinet and plopped down on the edge of Tessa's bed.

"Girl, you don't look so good."

Tessa opened one eye and sighed. "Do I look like I just forced a baby out of my exhausted body?"

"Yeah, yeah, but, I don't know, you don't look right. You came in with a nice tan, but right now your face is the color of Elmer's glue. I want to take your vitals again." She looked around. "Where is everyone? I saw your mom, husband, and other daughter out in the hall a while ago. Big sister seems thrilled with the new addition. She proudly announced that her baby sister's name is *Jew-ia Vow-a-wee*. Kid sounds like she's from Brooklyn, not Berks County." She laughed and unclipped the blood pressure cuff from its cradle on the wall next to the bed and wrapped it around Tessa's arm. Then she positioned the stethoscope arms in her ears.

"Mom chased them out," Tessa told Ginny as she squeezed the round rubber attachment and looked at the numbers. "She said the same thing. I don't look good. She ordered everyone out of the room so I could rest."

The air rushed out of the pressure cuffs, and Ginny pulled the stethoscope handles from her ears. "Don't argue with an Italian mama, right?" she joked. "I knew I liked her."

"Hey, when can I take a shower?" Tessa touched her sweaty, matted hair.

Ginny chuckled. "The grunge look is all the rage right now. What, you don't like it? I can help you—" She pulled back the sheet covering Tessa. "Oh! Now that's not what we want to see." Tessa glanced down toward her legs, and her eyes flew open at the sea of red on her bedsheets. She felt lightheaded and had trouble focusing.

"What's going on?" Tessa's voice came out in short puffs.

"You're still bleeding. I mean, some is normal, but it should be slowing down by now. Let's see, you gave birth"— she paused and checked Tessa's chart—"seven hours ago. Hmm. Okay, well, let's change these sheets."

Ginny gently helped Tessa roll from side to side so she could strip the bloodied sheets and replace them with fresh ones. She placed a fresh pad under Tessa's bottom. Then she took her temperature and frowned at the numbers. "You have a fever. I want you to rest while I contact your doctor. Okay, girl?"

Tessa was already dozing off, her arm dangling lazily off the side of the bed like an untied shoelace, as Ginny dimmed the lights. She pulled the door closed behind her and went to find Dr. Leighton.

An hour later, an intern from another obstetric practice entered the room with Ginny on his heels and woke Tessa. The intern cleared his throat as he turned up the lights and consulted Tessa's chart. "Hello, Mrs. Cordelia." He folded his arms in front of him and tilted his head. He wore a purple shirt and pink tie under his white coat. Tessa thought he looked to be about thirteen years old. "Congrats on the new baby. I'm Dr. Jewell. Dr. Leighton is tied up in delivery, so I'm going to check you. Your nurse said you are weak and have a fever. She also mentioned some blood loss." He looked at Tessa as though he wanted verification of these facts, and Ginny glared at him like she might take a swing at him. "Let me take a look."

Ginny pulled the sheet back and stifled a gasp. Trying to shield her face from Tessa, she turned to Dr. Jewell with wide eyes and raised eyebrows. The bed was soaked in blood again. He ignored Ginny's anxious look. "How are you feeling?" He pressed on Tessa's abdomen, and she groaned.

"Um, I don't know. Very tired. I can't stay awake. Also some cramping."

"Cramping?" Dr. Teenager studied her chart.

"Yes, almost feels like I'm still in labor." Tessa tried to sit up. "Ginny, may I have some water?"

"Sure, coming right up." Ginny poured water from a plastic pitcher and helped Tessa with a few sips. Then she turned to Dr. Jewell and kept her voice level so as not to alarm Tessa. "See what I mean about the blood? Let's get Dr. Leighton in here to check her."

"Get her temp again, please." Dr. Jewell made a few notations on Tessa's chart and returned it to its holder. Ginny placed a thermometer under Tessa's tongue and waited for it to beep.

"She still has a fever. One hundred and one degrees." Ginny put her hands on her hips. "And the blood? We should let Dr. Leighton know, right?" She began the task of replacing Tessa's sheets again.

"Well, some bleeding is normal, as you know." He ignored Ginny's steely look.

Tessa licked her cracked lips and spoke up. "I mean, this isn't my first baby, so I know what feels normal. I just feel like . . . like . . . I don't know how to describe it any better than that I still feel like I'm in labor."

"Well, luckily, that isn't possible, huh?" He patted the bed, "Try to sleep. We'll check you again in an hour." Dr. Jewell turned and left the room.

Ginny gave Tessa more water and hissed, "Yes, come back in an hour after your junior high soccer tryout." Tessa smiled as Ginny fluffed her pillow and placed the call button in her patient's hand. "You rest and call me if you need anything. I'm going to track down Leighton on my own."

An hour later another fresh-faced intern entered the room, followed again by an exasperated Ginny. The bed again was blood-soaked, and Ginny did her best to calmly explain to the young doctor that though he was only seeing the blood this one time, Tessa had been bleeding profusely for several hours. Tessa did her best to listen to the exchange, but a buzzing in her ears made her feel dizzy.

When the intern, Dr. Something-or-other, offered the same advice as the last—that Tessa rest and be checked again in an hour—Ginny shook her head and exhaled loudly. As the young doctor replaced Tessa's chart and headed out the door, she leaned in close and whispered in Tessa's ear. "You know what they call the student who graduates last in his medical school class?"

"What?"

"Doctor."

Tessa managed a strained laugh before closing her eyes and drifting off again.

The next time she woke up, Mariel was sitting in a chair holding Julia. She gently stroked the infant's soft chin and addressed her friend. "Nice work, Tess. Another beauty. I passed a few bald babies in the nursery on my way in. They're not happy. Yours got all the hair!" She stood and approached the bed. "Nice digs here too!" Mariel looked around at the wallpaper border and cushioned rocking chair in the corner. "It's like 'Maternity: Beverly Hills Style.' I think I heard some new dads in the hall discussing student-teacher ratios at the local private preschool."

"Very funny. Yeah, it's a new section of the hospital." Tessa struggled to sit up and failed.

"But, full disclosure, you look rough. Everything okay? Your nurse let me in but told me to let you sleep, so I figured I'd spend some quality time with my new buddy here." Mariel turned Julia so Tessa could see her.

Tessa licked her lips and tried again to push herself up to a sitting position. "I don't know. I feel banged up. My stomach is cramping like I'm still in labor, and I can't stay awake."

"What does your doctor say?"

Tessa waved her hand toward the hallway. "It's like Grand Central around here. She hasn't been in since the birth. My nurse Ginny is on the warpath about it. God help the next resident who dares to come in here. There's gonna be a throw down, and my money's on Ginny."

Just then Ginny bustled into the room. She took one look at Mariel's concerned expression and pulled back the sheet to feel Tessa's abdomen.

"Oh my God!" Mariel took in the bloody sheets, and her hand flew to her mouth.

Ginny grabbed the phone and punched in some numbers. "This is Ginny. I'm in room 112 in Beginnings. Page Dr. Constance Leighton immediately! Do not send me a resident! My patient is going to bleed to death!"

Tessa thought she heard Ginny saying something about bleeding to death, but the nurse's voice sounded muffled, as if she were under water. She vaguely saw Mariel's horrified face as she drifted in and out of consciousness. Ginny grabbed Julia from Mariel and put her back in her bassinet.

"What . . . what are they going to . . . are they going to—" Mariel backed away from the bed and gripped the rails of the chair.

The door burst open, and Dr. Leighton rushed in and grabbed a pair of rubber gloves from a box affixed to the wall. "Get her pressure!" she called to someone Tessa couldn't see. "Everyone out of here!"

Ginny led Mariel, who by now was crying, from the room.

"Tessa, can you hear me?"

Tessa floated above the chaos, a bird on a perch, a deity observing from beyond, and wondered why no one heard her shouting that it was time. The baby was coming. *Why are all these people running around in circles? It's time.*

"Tessa, I'm sorry, but this isn't going to feel good," Dr. Leighton was saying. She reached her hand up inside Tessa, and it felt as if she were being torn clear in half. Somehow, she found the strength to back up, trying to escape from Dr. Leighton's grip, but the bed was up against the wall, so she was cornered. She screamed and batted away the doctor's hands, but in a flash, two residents were there to hold down her hands and feet. One large blood clot the size of Julia's perfect head fell out of Tessa onto the already blood-soaked bed. It was followed by several smaller ones, like kindergartners tumbling down a grassy hill at recess.

"Call upstairs! Tell them to get an OR ready!" Dr. Leighton commanded loudly.

Through the whooshing in her head, Tessa was aware of nurses scrambling to unlock the brakes on the bed. She passed out momentarily and awoke to see the pale yellow walls of the corridor rushing past her as though she were in a speeding car. Time sped up and slowed down like it couldn't decide what to do. Next to her, Tessa thought she heard children laughing, but when she reached for them, they ran away from her, looking over their shoulders as they teased, *You can't catch me.* Then time seemed to pass painfully slowly, like when her childhood dentist, Dr. Kaplan, held up his drill and promised, *Just to the count of three . . . Ooooone, twooooo, threeeee . . .* and Tessa was sure he was drilling straight into her skull.

She came to and saw Dr. Leighton at the head of the bed, running as she pushed it. "My husband," Tessa thought she screamed, but she was barely whispering. "Call Ken."

"No time. I'll have someone call him, but I can't wait for consent. We've got to stop your bleeding." Dr. Leighton broke off from the rest to scrub for the procedure.

It was cold in the OR, despite the fluorescent lighting that mimicked bright sunshine, and Tessa shivered and sweated at the same time. She struggled to keep her eyes open even as a nurse covered her nose and mouth with a mask and told her to breathe normally and count backward from one hundred. People in scrubs and masks rushed around, placing instruments on trays and connecting tubes from machines to Tessa. *This is it. The baby is coming.* The laughing children were back, along with Kaplan and his whirring drill. *Oooooone, twooooo, threeeeee.*

Dr. Leighton appeared as if from out of nowhere and looked down at her patient. She wore a light green surgical cap, mask, and gown, and she leaned in close to Tessa and spoke directly into her ear in hushed tones. Tessa thought the doctor said everything would be okay, but she couldn't be sure, and then there was only darkness.

Chapter Thirty-Five

Tessa woke up, and the lights overhead stung her eyes. She squeezed them shut against their garish glare.

"Mommy, Mommy, wake up! Yook at my ponytail! Deena did it faw me!" Ronnie thrust her head at Tessa and shook it.

"Easy there, Ronnie. Let Mommy wake up slowly."

As Tessa's vision came into focus, she saw Ken and Sal standing next to her bed. Ken smiled gently and rubbed Tessa's arm. "Welcome back."

Tessa reached out to Ronnie and held her hand. "Where am I? What happened?"

Sal leaned in close to his oldest daughter. Her face was deathly pale, and her lips were dry and cracked. "I'll tell you what happened. You're not having any more babies. That's what happened." He folded his arms in front of him as though this proclamation had been written into indisputable law.

Ronnie laid her head on Tessa's arm as Ken filled in the gaps. "You're in the recovery room. You were hemorrhaging. Apparently, a piece of the placenta tore off and was left inside of you when you delivered Julia. That's why you felt like you were still in labor—basically, you were. Your body was having contractions, trying to deliver the rest of the placenta."

Tessa closed her eyes again and searched her memory. "But Dr. Leighton held it up after the delivery, remember? She said it was intact."

"I know." Ken nodded. "She thought it was. She said it was a small piece that broke off cleanly, so she didn't detect it. But it was enough to cause you to hemorrhage. Good thing she got to you when she did."

Tessa became serious. "Did she . . . Dr. Leighton . . . What did she do to get the bleeding to stop?"

"No hysterectomy. She was able to scrape out the placental tissue by doing a D&C. She'll explain everything to you when she sees you." He stroked Tessa's hair. "Boy, you owe your nurse a steak dinner and a martini. She made some noise about all the interns they kept sending in to check you. I heard she told one of them to come back after his high school dance." He and Sal both laughed.

Sal said, "I could use someone feisty like her at the restaurant. I wonder if she works here on weekends?"

"Where's Mom?" Tessa looked around. "I'm surprised she's not here."

"We called her. She was beside herself." Sal looked up at the ceiling as if recalling the conversation. "Imagine it. She shooed everyone out of your room so you could get some rest. She figured you'd get some sleep and be good as new. Tony had a baseball game this afternoon, and she and Gina went. I told her I was coming over and would let her know if you were up for her to bring them over after the game. I had no idea what had happened until I got here."

"Apparently it all happened quickly after Dr. Leighton got to you," Ken added. "You were already in the OR when they called me. I couldn't believe what they were telling me."

"Tess." Ken's face took on a sympathetic look. "You need to call Mariel. She was pretty shaken up. I called her after the procedure, before you woke up, and told her you are okay, but she's anxious to hear from you. She was in your room when it all went down. She was a mess."

"Poor thing. I'll call her when I get back to my room."
Tessa closed her eyes. "I feel weak."

"Mommy, I want to see Jew-ia! Whe-uh is she?" Ronnie
pulled on Tessa's bed sheet.

Ken picked up Ronnie. "She's downstairs in the nursery.
We're going down now." He turned back to Tessa. "They'll
take you back down to your room now that you're awake. We'll
meet you there."

"Good," Tessa said. "I'm exhausted. I can't wait to go home
and sleep in my own bed. When am I getting out of here?"

"Depends how you do over the next twenty-four hours.
You lost a lot of blood."

"Oh my God. Thank God you're okay." Mariel was practically
crying. "Tess, it was awful. I never saw anything like it. And
it happened so fast. I wasn't there more than twenty minutes
when your nurse started yelling that you were going to bleed
to death if they didn't find your doctor! They made me go out
in the hall, but when I came back in to get my purse after they
took you to the OR, there was blood everywhere—on the floor,
on the wall behind your bed. It looked like a crime scene."

Tessa lay propped up in her bed with her eyes closed as
she listened to Mariel describe what happened. "I'm sorry you
had to go through that."

"Don't be sorry for me! You're the one who was bleeding
all over the place while a string of twelve-year-olds kept telling
you they'd be back in an hour!"

Tessa smiled through closed eyes. "Now you sound like
Ginny. By the way, as soon as I got back to my room, she
handed me the phone and made me call you."

Mariel managed a small laugh. "She's awesome. I was so
upset, she sat with me and tried to convince me you'd be all
right. Finally, I realized she must have actual patients to take
care of. She said it could be hours before you woke up. I had to

get home to relieve my sitter, but I waited until Ken got there so you wouldn't be alone. I made Ken and Ginny swear like fifty times that someone would call me as soon as they knew anything. At that point, I wasn't sure what they were even going to do to stop all that bleeding."

"Yeah, luckily I only needed a D&C and not a hysterectomy. But my primary doctor—Dr. Sal—gave me strict orders not to have any more babies."

"That sounds like him." Mariel chuckled.

Ginny came into the room and sat on the edge of Tessa's bed. "I have to go, Mariel. The only person around here who seems to know what she's doing just walked in."

"Tell Ginny I said hi and thanks again. I'll see you soon. Hopefully with less drama next time!"

After they hung up, Ginny took Tessa's hand. "How you feelin'?"

"Like a truck hit me. A big one."

Ginny had a quilted bag flung over her shoulder and keys in her hand. "I'm heading home, but I'll be back tomorrow morning. Try to get some rest."

"Thank you, Ginny. For everything." Tessa narrowed her eyes and studied the wall clock. "I know I'm a little out of it, but haven't you been here an awfully long time today?"

Ginny shrugged. "Well, maybe I hung around a bit after my shift ended. Paperwork and stuff. You know how it is." She stood up to leave.

Tessa's eyes drifted shut again. "Yeah," she whispered. "I do."

"Tessa, can you hear me?"

She came to slowly, gradually bringing the scene into focus. It was fuzzy, like a snapshot taken by a moving photographer, but Tessa could make out Ginny perched next to her holding smelling salts in one hand and Tessa's shoulder in the other. Val, looking panicked, stood at the foot of the bed holding Julia.

Sounds of babies crying and nurses bustling up and down the hall indicated the maternity ward was open for business this morning. Tessa had slept like the dead all night, not moving until Ginny came in to wake her.

"What on earth? This happened last night when the nurses tried to get her to the shower. Thank goodness there were two of them there to catch her. Now she passed out just trying to sit up! What's going on?" Val laid Julia in her bassinet and placed her hands firmly on her hips in what Tessa and her siblings dubbed Val's *I want answers* stance.

"She lost a lot of blood. We did some blood tests after her D&C. Dr. Leighton is doing rounds on this hall now, so she should be in to talk to Tessa in a few minutes."

As if on cue, the door swung open, and Dr. Leighton appeared. She nodded to Val and peeked into Julia's bassinet before turning to Tessa. Under her white coat, she wore a light linen skirt and pale blue blouse. "Hi there, Tessa. How are you feeling? You've had a rough road." She hoisted her tiny five-foot frame onto the edge of Tessa's bed.

"I feel like a truck hit me. And then backed up and ran over me again."

"I'm sure." Dr. Leighton pressed gently on Tessa's abdomen. "So, the bleeding was caused by a miniscule—but big enough to wreak havoc—piece of your placenta that tore off during the delivery. That happens sometimes; a piece so small breaks off so cleanly that we don't detect it. I didn't have to do a hysterectomy, so future pregnancies shouldn't be a problem. You'll have some scar tissue, but you'll be able to get pregnant again."

"Right now I'd settle for being able to sit up without losing consciousness."

"Yes, well, your blood tests show that your hemoglobin levels dropped drastically from the blood loss. The normal level for women is around twelve grams per deciliter."

"And what is mine?"

"Four."

"Four?" Val exclaimed.

"Yes," Dr. Leighton continued calmly. "And you're anemic. You have thalassemia—the trait, not the disease. Were you aware of that?"

"No, what does that mean?"

"Well, the disease can be quite serious, but the trait usually doesn't cause problems. Some people constantly feel tired or listless; some have poor appetites. It depends which beta proteins are lacking. It's just good to know you carry it. It would be more of a concern if Ken had it too in terms of the risks of passing it on to your children." She sat up straighter and grew more serious. "Now, back to the important stuff. You lost a lot of blood. So much that you can barely sit up without passing out. We've got to get your hemoglobin up. Honestly, Tessa, it's not safe for you to hold Julia if you are standing up—that's if you are even able to stand up on your own. I don't even want you holding her when you are sitting down unless someone is sitting with you."

Tessa's head was spinning. "So, what's the plan?"

"You need to have a blood transfusion." Dr. Leighton paused and let that sink in. "Obviously, we can't use your blood. We can test your family members to see if any of them are viable donors, but that process will take days. My advice is to use blood from our hospital blood bank. All our donor blood is tested and screened. There's virtually no risk, and we could do it right away." The doctor shook her head. "Tessa, I can't even think about releasing you from the hospital with a hemoglobin level of four. We've got to get your count up."

Tessa turned toward Val. "What do you think, Mom?"

Val folded her arms and addressed the doctor. "You're sure the blood from the blood bank is safe?"

Dr. Leighton tucked a strand of dark hair behind her ear. "As sure as we can be. It went through the same testing and screening process we'd use if Tessa chose her donors. But we could do it today." She leaned in and took Tessa's hand. "You'll feel much better after the transfusion."

"How long would it take for my hemoglobin to go up on its own?"

"At your levels, it could take months."

Tessa hesitated a moment and then sighed. "Okay, let's do it."

Within ninety minutes, Ginny wheeled in the necessary equipment and got to work. She tested lines, adjusted knobs, and inserted an IV line in Tessa's arm. "Okay, try to relax and even sleep if you can. I'm going to sit here with you for the first fifteen or twenty minutes to make sure you aren't having any allergic reactions to the blood. Then I'll check on you intermittently until the transfusion is complete." She pulled Tessa's sheet up and smoothed it. "You need anything?"

"Yes." Tessa was already on her way to dozing. "I need a shower."

"First things first. Let's get you strong enough to stand up and walk without keeling over. And the dried blood on your gown? It's a good look. Gives you street cred."

"Yeah, that's me. Straight-up gangsta. So if you don't help me into the shower after this transfusion ordeal, you're in trouble. I'm street, so look both ways before you cross me." Tessa attempted a rapper gesture but looked more like she was having a stroke.

Ginny burst out laughing. "You might possibly be the least threatening-looking person I've ever seen." She made a few notes on Tessa's chart. "Now, relax, okay?"

But Tessa was already asleep.

"Six? My hemoglobin only went up to six after the transfusion?" Dismayed, Tessa exhaled loudly. The transfusion had taken about three hours, and Dr. Leighton was back to give her the update.

Ken addressed Dr. Leighton. "So, now what?"

Dr. Leighton finished scribbling on Tessa's chart. "My office manager just got off the phone with your insurance company. I want you to have another transfusion tomorrow. Then I'm going to keep you and Julia here another few days and send you home with a nurse from a home health care agency."

"A nurse at home with me?" Tessa furrowed her brow.

"Yes, we're in the process of making the arrangements. She'll be in your home from eight a.m. until six p.m. every day. Your insurance will pay for ten-hour shifts for thirty days. By then you should be back to full strength. Tessa, I can't emphasize enough—it is not safe for you to hold Julia while you are standing, and you definitely can't walk with her until we are sure you can do so without passing out."

"I'm a little confused. So, am I the nurse's patient or is Julia?"

Dr. Leighton smiled. "Actually, both of you. At first, you'll pretty much stay in bed. She'll help you when you need to get up and bring Julia to you for feedings or whenever you just want to hold her. She'll stand by when you shower and dress in case you decide it would be fun to pass out again. As you get stronger, the nurse will back off and let you do more on your own. She'll take your vitals every morning, and we'll have her draw blood every week to monitor your hemoglobin. It will go up. It would go up on its own eventually, but as I said, it could take months.

"I know you have family and friends to help with Ronnie, and you'll definitely need them too, but I can't release you without home health care. The risk is too great that you will either fall and hurt yourself or the baby." Tessa was looking out the window, and the doctor gave her a minute to process what she just heard. "What questions do you have for me? I gave you a lot of information at once."

"So, the nurse will help me all day and leave at six at night." Images formed in Tessa's mind.

"Yes, and then"—the doctor gestured to Ken—"that's when Nurse Ken will take over." She smiled at her joke.

"So, for middle-of-the-night feedings—" Tessa looked directly into Ken's eyes.

"Yep, I have night duty. I'll either give Julia her bottle or I'll bring her to you if you'd rather feed her."

"And you understand this, right? Every night for thirty days?" *Thirty days straight of coming home when you're supposed to.*

If Dr. Leighton perceived the heaviness in the air between Tessa and Ken, she didn't let on. She turned to leave and called over her shoulder, "You have nothing to worry about, Tessa. I can tell he's one of the good ones."

The motor of a riding mower outside Caroline's apartment window revved. Just as she'd done every day for the last two weeks, she flipped through the newspaper until she found what she was looking for. There it was, in the second section, the "Daily Docket." Caroline folded the page in half and read the announcement three times: In Reading Hospital, a daughter to Kenneth and Tessa Cordelia, Exeter.

She stared expressionless at it for several moments before taking another sip from her mug.

Chapter Thirty-Six

"You know, I'm beginning to think you like it down there on the floor."

Tessa scrunched up her nose and turned away from the smelling salts in Ken's hand. She'd just fainted, Ken grabbing her under both arms and guiding her gently to the floor.

"It's such a weird feeling. All of a sudden I feel the walls closing in, and then everything goes black."

"I saw that one coming," Ken said, sitting down next to her. "All the color drained from your face. Before you went down, your head lolled around like a boxer who'd just taken a right hook to the chin."

Tessa and Julia had come home from the hospital five days ago. Having spent a week in the maternity ward, Tessa was glad to be home. She was almost surprised to find everything the same—the same shoes tossed in a pile in the mudroom, the same stack of magazines she'd left on the coffee table, the same bath toys collected in a mesh bag hanging on a hook in Ronnie's bathroom. It felt like a lifetime ago since she'd last been there.

Rochelle, their home health care nurse, was working out well. She was helpful and pleasant, and Ronnie had also taken to her. Rochelle spoke in a sing-song voice that made everything, even baby bodily functions, sound like a fun game. "Ooh, good job, Juuu-li-a, that's a big spit-up! Such a biii-g mess from such a liii-ttle girl!" Ronnie liked her immediately, probably because Rochelle usually arrived with pocketsful of treats for her: one day an array of small rubber animals, the next day a game of jacks in a tiny blue velvet pouch with a gold drawstring. Today, Rochelle left at six after bathing Julia and putting a tray of Val's baked ziti in the oven. It was now ten o'clock, Ronnie and Julia were both asleep, and Ken was helping Tessa upstairs to get ready for bed when she'd fainted on the landing.

"This is getting old."

"I know you're frustrated, but Dr. Leighton explained that this might happen for a while. Remember, even after the second transfusion, your red count only went up to seven." Ken stood up. "Ready to try this again?"

Ken stood nearby while Tessa washed her face, brushed her teeth, and changed into her pajamas. When she emerged from the bathroom, he was taking a half-dozen ornamental pillows off the bed and piling them up in the corner. He shook his head. "I know I don't arrange these the way you do. Why do you put all these pillows on the bed when we're not allowed to use them? They sit on the floor all night and have to be repositioned on the bed every morning. What's the point?"

Tessa ran a brush through her hair. "I don't know. I guess I just like the way they look." She shrugged. "If I'm ever mysteriously murdered, the detectives who search the house for clues will comment on how nice and orderly they look. Order is good."

Ken laughed. "If you say so. I'll make sure they include photos of the carefully arranged pillows in their report."

After he had Tessa settled in bed, Ken changed into gym shorts and a Led Zeppelin T-shirt and switched on the TV. Tessa picked up her book but was restless and read the same page three times before tossing it back onto the nightstand. Then she spoke the four words that sent men all over the world running for the hills.

"We need to talk."

"Uh oh. Is this about me letting Ronnie choose her own outfits? I promise, only real clothes from now on." He put his right hand in the air. "Nothing from the dress-up box."

"No." Tessa laughed. "Although I have to admit the pink tutu and bright yellow tube top was an original. Good thing you were only taking her to my parents'. I'm not sure the grocery store is ready for that kind of edginess." She paused and grew serious again. "I think we should talk about the promise we made to Dr. Dinatelli."

"Oh, good. I thought it was going to be something unpleasant." He grinned and playfully jabbed Tessa with his elbow.

Ken's expression transformed at the serious look on his wife's face. "Oh, come on, Tess. We've been through such an ordeal. You just came home from the hospital a few days ago. Concentrate on getting your strength back. That's the most important thing." He picked up the remote and began channel surfing.

"I know, but he was serious about what he said. If you don't start some kind of treatment, he's going to the dental board and maybe the police."

Ken yawned. "You don't know that. He's probably forgotten about the whole thing by now."

Tessa turned her body so she was facing him. "No, Ken, he hasn't. The only one who thinks this isn't a big deal is you. And you promised. You said you'd get help after the baby was born and we were home and settled."

Ken sighed. "I know, I know. But I feel really good. I haven't even thought about the gas since before Julia was born." He waved his arm. "Why dredge it all up?"

"Because I've seen this movie before. You go a few weeks or even a few months without doing the gas, without even thinking about it, and you say you're cured."

Ken turned off the TV and threw the remote onto the bed. He looked down at his hands, folded in his lap. He wore the expression of a fourteen-year-old being lectured by his father for the umpteenth time to remember that Tuesday night is trash night.

He played with a loose string on their cream-colored cotton blanket. "Tess, I know you think that if I enter treatment, I'll automatically be"—he curled both index and middle fingers and pumped them up and down into air quotes—"cured." Tessa stared at him without blinking. "But I disagree. I question—as do many experts—whether traditional rehabilitation is effective. There are tiers of addiction, you know?" He raised his hand as though reaching for something on a high shelf. "It's not black and white, like you're either pregnant or you're not. It doesn't work like that. Believe it or not, I really have read the literature you've given me about therapists and treatment centers. And I've done some research on my own. Lots of studies suggest that less serious cases of addiction—" He dropped his hand down about two feet.

"Like yours?" Tessa asked, eyebrows raised.

Ken pursed his lips and looked at her as though she were an uncooperative child he was struggling not to lose his patience with. "Yes, like mine. With less serious cases, self-recovery is more likely. I'll grant you that more severe cases probably warrant treatment—"

"You mean"—Tessa gazed upward and tapped her index finger against her lips as though trying to recall the exact details of something extremely important—"like if someone breaks into an oral surgeon's office to steal nitrous oxide when his own machine is disabled?"

Ken groaned and shook his head. "We've been over that. I never would have had to do that if you hadn't messed with mine." Now he looked directly at her. "You know, that stressed me out. Knowing I didn't have access to the gas? It made me think about it constantly." He turned sideways and propped himself up on his arm with his fist under his cheek. "Look, I don't know. Maybe it's a safety net or something." Tessa was about to interject, but Ken hurriedly continued. "Like, Tracy buys these bags of mini chocolate bars and keeps them in the break room at the office. She loves chocolate, but she hardly ever touches them. She says she just likes knowing they are there. Makes sense, right?"

Tessa opened her mouth to say a mini Snickers is hardly the same as a controlled substance but changed her mind.

"So that plan, dismantling my nitrous system? It backfired on you."

"On me, huh. It backfired on me?"

"You know what I mean. Listen, you need to understand that everyone is different. I get that you are someone who benefits from talking things through with other people. You spend hours on the phone with your mom and Mariel. That helps you. But I'm not you. You see things one way; I see them another. I respect your beliefs about what is best for you. For some reason, though, you just can't seem to do that for me."

"For some reason." Tessa repeated phrases from Ken's speech to keep from losing it.

"Yeah. I'm not like you. I don't need to pour my heart out to strangers and tell them how many days it's been since I used the gas so they can all congratulate me. Rehab isn't one size fits all. And it's not a magic cure."

"A magic cure."

"I do things on my own. I don't need help from anyone."

"So . . ." Tessa touched Ken's arm. She searched every part of her husband's face. "Let me ask you the question I've asked you a hundred times before: What makes you think you can do it on your own? You haven't been able to in the last two years. I don't understand."

"I know you don't. You don't need to. You just need to believe me."

Ken stood in the kitchen holding the phone, listening to it ring on the other end. He was glad to escape the conversation with

Tessa about rehab. He'd already lied to Sam Dinatelli and said he'd joined an outpatient support group. The oral surgeon had cornered him just last week when they'd arrived at the office at the same time. Now Ken just had to hope Sam didn't contact Tessa to see if his story checked out. Exasperated, he exhaled loudly and began to pace. *Jesus, the way everyone is nipping at my heels, is it any wonder I need a release once in a while?* Finally, the ringing ceased, and a gruff voice on the other end said, "Yeah."

"Stan, it's me." Ken knew Tessa would not venture down the stairs yet on her own, but he cast a paranoid glance over his shoulder anyway. "Did you get the parts in yet?"

"Be here tomorrow. You want I should come by the office, or will you pick them up?"

"I'll pick them up." Ken closed his eyes and sighed with relief. *Maybe it's a safety net.*

"Super. And you got a little something for me?"

"Yes," Ken said and hung up.

Chapter Thirty-Seven

Balmy rain enveloped Caroline as she got out of her car, and large raindrops plopped onto the parking lot as she moved toward the office building. Humidity still hung in the air, but the brutal heat of summer waned as the days strode deeper into September. Caroline yanked open the door to the main lobby and studied the building directory just inside. *Kenneth Cordelia, D.M.D. – Suite 201.* Her sneakers squeaked on the tile floor and left a pattern of wet footprints that led to the elevator. She shook the hood of her windbreaker until it fell off her head, and listened to the hum of the elevator ascending. It wasn't yet 8 a.m., and she hoped she'd timed her visit to catch Ken before his patients began to arrive.

In Ken's reception area, a balding man with an egg-shaped head seated in one of the chairs glanced disinterestedly in her direction and then just as quickly shoved his nose back into the morning paper. He wore a tan suit, and a scuffed leather briefcase sat on the floor near his cordovan shoes. Caroline was taking in the office's muted colors when a cheery voice startled her.

"Good morning! May I help you?" Behind the reception desk, Tracy wiggled the mouse on her computer and began scrolling.

"Oh," Caroline fumbled. "I don't have an appointment. I . . ." She looked around cautiously. "Is Dr. Cordelia here yet?"

she asked, though she knew the answer, having seen his sleek silver car in the parking lot. "I just need a minute of his time." Tracy scrunched up her face in a *Hmmm, what is this about?* expression and studied the computer screen.

"You'd like a minute with me?" Caroline spun around to see Ken at the door to his private office. He wore light gray pants with perfect creases, a burgundy dress shirt, and a pink-and-gray-checked tie. He leaned casually against the door frame and cradled a steaming mug with both hands, his blue eyes twinkling with what Caroline perceived as mild amusement.

"You're good," Tracy told her boss. "First one isn't for another fifteen minutes." She widened her eyes and nodded surreptitiously toward Mr. Egghead in the reception room before contorting her lips to mouth silently, "Salesman." She lowered her head, lips pursed and eyebrows raised in the universal look reserved for salespeople and IRS auditors.

Ken smiled at Caroline and waved his arm, palm turned upward like a game show host, toward his office. "After you."

Inside the office, Caroline suddenly felt self-conscious in her faded jeans and *Nike* T-shirt. She smoothed her hair, frizzy and unkempt from the rain and her hood, and stuck out her hand. "I just want to talk for a few minutes. I'm—"

"I know who you are, Caroline." Ken tilted his head, clearly enjoying having the upper hand. "Or do you prefer CeCe?" Caroline shoved her hands in her pockets and rocked back and forth on her heels. Then Ken's expression softened, and he pulled out a leather chair for her. "Relax. It's okay. I'm actually surprised you didn't show up here sooner."

Caroline sat on the edge of the chair as Ken walked behind the desk to his own chair. Outside the window, the sky was dark, and thunder began to rumble. "Look, I'm not even really sure why I came."

Ken's chair creaked as he leaned forward. "You mean you're not here to ask me to plead your case to Tessa?"

Caroline exhaled loudly and shook her head. "No. That is most definitely not why I'm here."

Shrugging, Ken scratched his head, and Caroline grew tired of his smugness. She sat up straight and raised her chin. "I'm actually here to talk about you." Ken's amusement turned to puzzlement, and he leaned back in his chair. Caroline cleared her throat and went for broke. "We missed you at taco night."

Ken's smile returned. He rested his elbows on the desk and steepled his fingers. "Ah, yes, taco night. That was right before all hell broke loose." He picked up the bottom half of his tie and flicked it a few times. "Gotta admit, made for interesting chatter over Easter dinner. You caused quite a stir—"

"I know about the gas."

Ken tried unsuccessfully to hide his shock. A flush crept from under his collar up to the stern line of his jaw. Caroline felt like she was in a movie where the wealthy CEO, finally busted for his white-collar crimes, grabs the phone and barks, "Get me security!" She glanced toward the door, half expecting a couple of three-hundred-pound dudes with shaved heads to burst in, grab her under the arms, and toss her out on her behind.

Even though her heart was racing, Caroline attempted to look collected. Now that she had his full attention, she let the revelation hover in the air like a dense fog for a few seconds.

Ken tried to appear unruffled. "Oh, so, what? You want to talk to me addict to addict? An it-takes-one-to-know-one kind of thing?" He flicked his index finger back and forth several times from himself to Caroline.

Caroline picked at her cuticle. "Yes, kind of like that, I guess."

"Look, I don't know what Tessa told you—and she shouldn't have told you anything about our personal life—but she has a tendency to exaggerate. You know, blow things out of proportion."

"Is that right?" Caroline cocked her head to one side. "So, how would you describe your problem?"

Ken shrugged as if he couldn't see what all the fuss was about. "I wouldn't even call it a problem. It's more of a . . . let's see . . ." He tapped his steepled fingers together and looked upward, as if the correct answer was printed on the ceiling tiles. " . . . Bad habit," he concluded. "Lots of people have them." Then he leaned back in his chair. "But you know all about bad habits, don't you?"

Caroline looked directly into Ken's eyes. "No, I know about addiction. I know that you can tell yourself it's just a 'bad habit' only for so long. Until it starts to destroy the people around you. The people you love most. The ones you vowed to be there for, no matter what." Her voice cracked slightly as she struggled to keep her composure. "Then it's a problem."

"Listen, I assume you're a staunch AA member, and you're doing your fellow soldiers proud with this inspirational speech, but I'm not like—"

"*Those* people?" Her red-rimmed eyes shot bullets at him. "Is that what you were going to say?"

"Actually, yes. That is what I was going to say. I'm not like those people sleeping under bridges, reeking of vomit and piss, drinking cough medicine or whatever to get high."

"So you're not like the people whose substance abuse turns them into selfish habitual liars, shrouds them in secrecy, causes them to miss important family events, ruins their marriages—"

They both turned toward the noise outside the office door. Tracy opened it and stuck her head inside. "Sorry to interrupt, Dr. C., but your first one is here and in the chair. Root canal. He's a few minutes early, but we don't want to give him time to lose his nerve and bolt." She gave Caroline an apologetic look and nodded toward Ken. "One of my most important duties around here is keeping this guy on schedule." She disappeared back out to her desk, and Ken stood, signifying that the meeting was over.

"Ken, it's not too late." Caroline rushed to make her point. "You can fix this. Take it from someone who knows. You don't want to wake up one day and find yourself all alone."

Ken was on his way to the door when he turned around to face Caroline again. "But you didn't just wake up one day and find yourself all alone. *You* left. Why would you do such a thing?"

"Why?" Caroline pulled up her hood and slung her purse over her shoulder. "Because as I said, addicts who refuse to get help are selfish people. The way I was back then, the mess I had made of everything?"

She turned toward the door. "Leaving my family was the least selfish thing I've ever done."

Chapter Thirty-Eight

"Go, Mommy! Dis is on-y faw kids. No mommies!" Ronnie pushed on Tessa's legs, guiding her toward the classroom door. Around the door frame were twelve cardboard signs, each one bearing a month of the year and a related picture.

"Okay, okay." Tessa almost ran smack into "January" and its parade of ice skaters. She turned to Miss Kisselmeyer, Ronnie's preschool teacher. The young woman wore jeans rolled up to just above her ankles, a short-sleeved peach cotton top, and canvas Keds. Her chestnut hair, held off her face by a colorful stretchy headband, fell just below her shoulders. "Should my feelings be hurt?"

Miss Kisselmeyer laughed. "No, take it as a good sign. She's fine without you for two and a half hours. Some of the kids in these pre-three classes wail for the first hour after their parents leave." They sought out Ronnie, who was arranging large colorful foam alphabet pieces on the floor with a little boy in overalls who had a face full of freckles and a head of red curls.

"My husband and I weren't sure about this. But, with the new baby, we thought it would be good for her to socialize with other children her age." Ronnie and her curly-haired friend moved on to the bean bag toss.

"It's been over a month and she's doing great. And it's only twice a week for a few hours. Trust me, it's a good thing.

It will get her acclimated for more regular hours next year." Miss Kisselmeyer looked at the watch on her slim wrist. "Really, don't hang around. The two and a half hours go faster than you think, don't they?" She gave Tessa a warm smile before wandering over to a pint-sized girl whose shoelace had come untied.

Tessa waved to Ronnie, picked up Julia's car seat, and headed out to the parking lot. The preschool was in a church basement at the bottom of the steep hill that led to Ken and Tessa's street. The early October morning sun finally felt soothing instead of blistering. The sun still shone brightly some afternoons, but the mornings and evenings were cool and comfortable. Next to Tessa's Jeep, a young mother sat behind the steering wheel of her parked car. The window was rolled down, and she was sipping coffee from a Dunkin' Donuts cup with her eyes closed.

She opened her eyes at the sound of Tessa opening the back door of her car and buckling in Julia's seat. Tessa gave her a quizzical look. She raised her cup as if toasting a wedding couple. "Just enjoying the peace and quiet."

Tessa gave her a knowing smile and drove off, leaving the woman to enjoy her coffee under the shade of large trees that lined the parking lot. She contemplated heading to the Sunrise to have breakfast and visit with Sal. It had been two months since Rochelle left, and, little by little, Tessa had gotten her strength back and returned to her old self. She was driving down the twists and turns of Shelbourne Road toward the business section of the highway and Sal's diner when she abruptly got another thought. With Julia cooing in the back seat, she drove past the Sunrise to the park.

"This is where you and I will go to Mommy and Me when you're a little older." Julia, oblivious, continued to gurgle. Tessa steered into a parking space and cut the engine. Leaning her arm against the car door, she absentmindedly twirled a lock of her hair around her finger and stared at the walking path around the playground beyond. Finally, she opened the door and stepped out.

After positioning Julia in the stroller, she unlocked the brake and maneuvered it over the curb and onto the path. An elderly man walking a dog tipped his tweed newsboy cap at Tessa and pulled the leash tight so the curious animal could not reach the stroller. Two young mothers on a bench fed their babies bottles and chatted loudly about their sleep deprivation.

"Three hours of sleep last night and only two the night before," one said as she propped her infant over her shoulder and thumped him lightly on the back.

"Tell me about it," the other one agreed. "I hear that's how they break people at Gitmo. Lock 'em in a room with a colicky newborn."

Tessa smiled at the universally uniting language of new parents. She often found herself in conversations in elevators or grocery store lines with exhausted baby-toting complete strangers based on their shared experiences. "Have you tried putting the car seat next to the running dishwasher? Sometimes the repetitious whirring sound lulls them to sleep" or "Don't insist on silence after she falls asleep at night. They need to get used to sleeping through noise." She said a silent prayer of thanks that Julia, like Ronnie before her, slept pretty well as far as baby sleep patterns went. Tessa had enough to keep her up at night.

She peered into the stroller at Julia, who had dozed off. As she stopped to tuck a light blanket around her, Tessa heard footsteps approach behind her. She looked up and cupped her hand over her eyes against the sunlight as a figure slowly took shape.

"Well," Caroline managed. "Hello." She looked into the stroller at Julia, her biological granddaughter, and a lone tear threatened the corner of her eye.

Tessa stood there for a moment trying to process the situation. She'd known this encounter would happen eventually, but she'd pushed the thought far to the back of her mind, out of reach, like an old clothing item shoved to the back of the closet behind favorite pieces. Focusing on the damage and betrayal by her husband at least kept her from focusing on the damage and betrayal by Caroline. But here they were, face-to-face, and she had no choice but to address her. Blood pulsed through Tessa's eardrums. She heard cars slowing at the speed bumps in the parking lot and then speeding up again. She thought about the walks and chats she'd shared with Caroline, a woman she'd thought was just a harmless, friendly acquaintance. She tried to square that thought with the startling revelation that the whole time Caroline was pretending to be a harmless, friendly acquaintance, she was in fact Tessa's biological mother.

"Well," Tessa mirrored. She glanced around, looking for an escape route.

"Don't go," Caroline said, seemingly sensing Tessa's inclination to flee. "Even though I deserve it. Give me a minute." Caroline stuffed her hands in her jeans pockets and pursed her lips. "I'm sorry. I know that doesn't even begin to cover what I did, but for the record, I am sorry." She appraised Tessa over the tops of her sunglasses, as if trying to gauge her reaction. Tessa was rooted to her spot, gripping the stroller handle. "What I mean is, I'm sorry for deceiving you. For not coming clean about who I am. I wanted to, I meant to, so many times, but then we'd get to talking, and I felt like we were almost becoming friends. I guess I didn't want to ruin that." Caroline shook her head, as though she knew how pathetic she sounded. "That part I'm not sorry about. Getting to know you. I'm sure you'll never speak to me again, but at least I got to have you in my life for a brief time."

Tessa's eyes flew open wide at Caroline's last statement, and her faculties returned fully. "Got to have me in your life for a brief time?" She snorted. "If I've heard the story correctly, *you* left *us*. Not the other way around."

"I know, I know. It's just . . . I was . . . You were better off. If you can believe that. You were better off without me." Caroline trailed off. She seemed to realize there was no way to close the chasm of the last twenty-some years—certainly not standing here in the park. She stared at her sneakers.

Frowning, Tessa thought about this claim. Sal would agree with Caroline. He constantly told Tessa and her brothers when they were old enough to hear it, "If she can't stop drinking and be a good mother, let her stay where she is. We don't need that in our lives." She closed her eyes. Would she feel the same way about Ken one day? Was there a point where all bets were off? One of the Al-Anon brochures she'd read said that an addict should be treated like any other person with an illness. They needed treatment for their disease. *But what if the addicts don't want treatment? Are you better off without them?*

Tessa moved out of the way of a pair of joggers, their long hair flying like kite tails behind them. Julia began fussing in her sleep, and Tessa gently pushed the stroller back and forth in a rocking motion. "Come on," she sighed. "Let's walk."

They strolled in silence for about five minutes. Tessa stole a sideways glance at Caroline. She looked subdued, like a candidate who'd been reluctant to concede an election but now had no choice but to place a congratulatory call to her opponent. Caroline appeared tired, not just the typical signs of middle age but fatigued from her experiences. Part of Tessa knew that Caroline deserved pity more than anger, but she hadn't evolved to that point of graciousness yet.

For the first time since discovering Caroline's true identity, Tessa compared her to Val and was struck by the infinite number of differences between the two women. Sure, Caroline was several years older than Val, but their differences transcended age. Val, with her shiny hair and near-perfect complexion, exuded an air of contentment and happiness about her life with her topsy-turvy clan that she sported like a favorite pair of well-worn jeans. She made no apologies for the nontraditional family she and Sal created, and dismissed people who tactlessly asked questions like "What *is* the age difference between you and your husband?" or "Isn't it *weird* to have a daughter in grade school and a granddaughter in preschool?" She embraced the chaos of having kids of varying ages and jokingly referred to Sal as "Blake Carrington without the millions."

In contrast, whatever life Caroline had carved out for herself after she'd left her family didn't seem to fit well, like a too-tight dress constantly riding up and needing to be tugged into place. Tessa had thought it just part of her reserved personality, but Caroline's tentativeness and penchant for running every word she said through a filter of Tessa's expectations made perfect sense now.

They rounded the corner by the huge aluminum swing set, and Caroline finally spoke, her voice small and defeated, like she had nothing else to lose. "I'm not making excuses for leaving, but I really did you all a favor." She shook her head as if to dispel her memory of the person she was all those years ago. "I was a terrible wife, a terrible mother. I put your dad through hell. He never knew what each day had in store for us. He covered for me"—she paused and treaded lightly—"just like you do for Ken." Tessa opened her mouth to object, but closed it again and said nothing, so Caroline continued. "He lied to everyone we knew, always running in circles, inventing stories explaining why I wasn't where I was supposed to be or why he had to leave work to come home and take care of you kids. He did a good job of covering up what I was really like—I did an even better job of slowly wearing away who he really was until his whole life was about my drinking problem."

Caroline's face was red, and Tessa couldn't tell if she was embarrassed or angry at herself in light of this soul-bearing, but she wasn't finished. "It was sick, really. It got so that people felt sorry for *me*. They could tell your dad was fed up with me, but for the life of them, they didn't know why. He managed a few restaurants back then, and his employees thought he was too tough on me, cold to me much of the time, either snapping at me or giving me the silent treatment. And I was sweet as pie whenever I was around them, so of course, they blamed Sal for any hostility." Caroline paused and shook her head ever so slightly, as if even she couldn't believe what she had been like when Tessa was a child.

A picture of Ken formed in Tessa's mind, the man everyone else saw. The husband who jumped at her every need, opened every door, and pulled out every chair for her. Who pooh-poohed every compliment with a casual "Nothing is too good for my Tessa." The doting father and dutiful son-in-law who had the admiration of all their friends.

They'd all think Tessa had lost her mind if she told them what was really going on. They'd cast glances behind her back and whisper that she must be making it up. Sal had felt that way too. Now that Tessa was smack in the middle of living her own sham, she was certain of that.

"It got so bad he couldn't leave you kids with me anymore. I was disgusted with myself, and then I drank more so I could forget how disgusted I was with myself." They stopped walking and sat on a bench near a large tree to get out of the sun. "One morning it all came to a head. I drove home hammered out of my mind after drinking all night." Caroline nodded at Tessa's shocked expression. "That's right, I *drove*. Drunk as a skunk. I thank God every day I didn't hurt anyone. I completely missed the driveway and parked the car on the front lawn. That was the straw that broke the camel's back. Sal called my parents and told them everything. Of course, they'd suspected things weren't right, but they had no idea I was a drunk, because your dad hid it from them. They came over and tried a—what do they call it now?—intervention."

Tessa was listening intently to this account of Caroline

and her father's secret-filled marriage that sounded so much like her own. "I'm guessing that didn't work."

"No. Oh, I lied through my teeth and said everything they wanted to hear, mostly to get them off my back. I had to sneak around even more to drink because the three of them started monitoring my every move after that. I deserved it, but I still couldn't stand it. We got into a horrible cycle: I'd get drunk, they'd threaten taking you and your brothers away if I didn't go to rehab, and I'd drink some more. That went on for several months, until I did my disappearing act."

Tessa thought about her biological grandparents. They'd both died in their early seventies, right before Tessa started college. She'd seen them intermittently after Caroline left, but they were merely shells of their former selves, heartbroken by the destructive path taken by their only child.

Caroline stared out beyond the trees that were starting to drop their leaves. "My biggest regret, bar none, of my entire life, is leaving you and your brothers without a mother. Even though I knew somewhere deep down in my heart it was what was best for you, I still feel guilty about that."

At this, Tessa pushed her sunglasses up on top of her head and looked skyward as thoughts of Val filled her head. She thought about how, as a teenager, she often drove Val crazy. She'd slam her bedroom door, making the framed photos hanging on the hallway wall swing back and forth, if she didn't get her way. Every weekend she'd expect Val to drive the carpool home from movies or the skating rink because the other parents were older and preferred the early driving shift. And Val had happily agreed, rolling down the windows and singing along to the songs on the radio with Tessa and her friends.

Once, when Tessa was about thirteen, she'd locked herself in her bedroom for three days—aside from going to school— because Sal wouldn't let her go to a Billy Joel concert with a teenage driver. Sal had stood his ground, but Val finally came up with the solution that she would take Tessa and a friend. Tessa had often been bratty and dramatic, complaining in front of a closet full of clothes that she had nothing to wear, throwing top after top on the floor while Val helped her put together outfits for dances and parties.

She grasped now that, though Val was by no means perfect, Tessa never felt she had to behave in a certain way to get her to stay. Val had stepped into the role of mother with both feet and never looked back. No matter how many times Tessa slammed her bedroom door or Joey got detention or Sal Jr. stayed out past his curfew, they never once feared Val would throw up her hands and say to Sal, "That's it. I'm out." Now that Tessa was a mother herself, she understood the magnitude of that. She smiled and let the October sun warm her face. Tonight on the phone she would remind Val of her "sit-in" to protest Sal not letting her drive to the concert with friends. Val would laugh and say, "You were something, Miss Tess. I worried you might never come out of that room!"

Every night when they hung up the phone, Val left Tessa with, "Okay, hon, let's see what tomorrow brings." Tessa realized the power in those words now: There would always be a tomorrow as far as Val was concerned. Whatever it brought, they'd face it as a family.

A flock of birds flew overhead, on their way to a warmer climate. They'd be back again next spring, right on schedule, building nests under Tessa's deck, Ronnie standing on her tiptoes, hoping to see the fuzzy heads of the newborns. Tessa envied them the luxury of knowing exactly where they'd be a full year from now.

"Well," Tessa finally said, standing up and pointing the stroller back toward the parking lot. "Let me put your mind at ease on that one. No need to feel sorry for us. We didn't grow up without a mother."

Caroline flinched and gave Tessa an *I guess I deserved that one* look. "I'm sure you know I reached out to your brothers. They aren't interested in reconciling."

Tessa nodded. "Yes, they mentioned that." She recalled Joey and Sal Jr.'s colorful reenactment of their clipped conversations with Caroline. "Thanks, but no thanks," Joey had said while Sal had just shaken his head in disbelief that she thought they'd welcome her back after all these years. Joey had said Caroline sounded like she'd been drinking when she called him, but he couldn't swear to it.

Caroline didn't tell Tessa she'd also visited Ken. He could tell her himself if he wanted to. She zipped up her jacket and fished her apartment key from her pocket. "Listen, Tessa, you don't have to worry about bumping into me around town or anything. I'm moving back to Vegas. I leave next week."

Tessa thought about the last year, Caroline pretending to be a stranger, insinuating herself into Tessa's life under false pretenses, getting her to loosen the drawstring on her bag of painful secrets. She finally spoke. "Well. I guess that's probably for the best."

Caroline touched Julia's cheek. Then she leaned in and gave Tessa a light hug. She pulled away quickly, but not quickly enough that Tessa did not detect the sour smell of day-old liquor on her breath.

Yes, she thought, pushing Julia along the paved path, leaving Caroline standing behind her. *It's definitely for the best.*

Chapter Thirty-Nine

Tessa finished wrapping the pile of toys she'd stashed in her bedroom closet. She peeled sticky tags from their paper backing, pressed them onto the gifts, and wrote "To Ronnie, from Santa" in penmanship she hoped did not resemble her own. At two and a half years old, Ronnie's precociousness already amused her family. Tessa could picture the toddler suspiciously inspecting the gifts under the tree on Christmas morning and announcing that Mommy and Santa had the same handwriting.

She shoved the wrapping paper behind some shoeboxes and put the presents high on a shelf. Not satisfied that Detective Ronnie wouldn't spot them, she covered them with a blanket. Closing the closet door, she glanced at the clock. 9:38 p.m. Padding down the carpeted hallway, she checked on the girls before descending the stairs.

The only brightness on the main floor came from the single light above the kitchen sink and the white lights strung around the nine-foot Christmas tree in the family room. Barefoot, Tessa wandered into the kitchen and opened a bottle of Cabernet. She filled a glass halfway, took a sip, and poured a little more. Ken's uneaten dinner sat on the counter. Sighing, Tessa picked it up and scraped the food into the trash bin. She tossed the empty plate into the sink.

Curled up on a chair next to the fireplace, Tessa tucked her legs beneath her. Her hair was piled messily on top of her head with a clip, and she twisted a strand around her finger. She wore red-and-green leggings and an oversized sweatshirt that made her look as small as she felt. Outside, the chilly December air was still, and snow flurries danced so lightly none of them appeared to reach the ground.

She sipped her wine and closed her eyes, wondering how much longer she could put on a performance of marital harmony. Looking out the window at the snowflakes, she visualized assembling everyone they knew and telling them the truth about Ken's addiction and their sham of a life. But even though she wasn't sure she could pretend anymore, she was equally unsure if she could face the ensuing fallout.

And what about her part in the whole thing? What would she say when they asked her *that* question? What would she answer when asked why she'd made them all think Ken was a hero, a prince, a knight in shining armor? Why she'd made them love him as much as she did?

She drained her glass and dug into her well of excuses: I didn't want to risk ruining his career . . . He promised he'd get help . . . Ronnie's birthday was coming up . . . Sal wouldn't be able to handle it . . . He promised he'd get help . . . I didn't want to ruin the holidays . . . I was pregnant . . . He promised he'd get help . . . Julia was just born . . . He promised he'd get help. Tessa felt like a child pressing her nose against a window, watching her life instead of living it.

The room was silent except for the ticking clock on the mantel. 10:06. She knew Ken had repaired the nitrous oxide system she'd disabled. He'd told her that. Weirdly, she took his honesty about it as a good sign. He said he needed to know it was there. He wanted to stop, really he did, but he felt better knowing it was there. And they both knew what had happened when he didn't have access to it in his own office.

Tessa's eye caught the Christmas tree lights reflected on a photo on the mantel of Ken with the girls. In it, Ken cradled Julia in one arm while he lifted Ronnie's chin with the other to kiss the tip of her nose. It was one of many little crumbs Tessa clung to. The way Ken doted on their children, securely fastening Ronnie's pink helmet onto her head before teaching her to ride her tricycle. Walking the floors with Julia long after midnight on the rare nights she couldn't settle herself into sleep. Gently coaxing Tessa onto the sofa while he cleaned up the dinner dishes. But these sprinkled gestures were obliterated, washed away, by nights like tonight.

Tessa was so used to containing her emotions, reshaping them to make them presentable to the world, that she didn't know if she could handle coming clean. She'd been carrying a bucket full of lies and deception for so long, little drops sloshing out occasionally making indiscernible puddles around her feet. Would tipping the whole thing over cause floodwaters that would never recede?

She tried to envision the scale of upper hand shifting slightly in her favor if she confided in her family. She'd lost count of how many times Val had asked her what was wrong, why she seemed so miserable, why she rejected Ken's loving gestures and actions. On Tessa's last birthday, Ken had given her a diamond tennis bracelet. Val and Alyse had gushed over it, but Tessa was indifferent, shrugging and pulling her sleeve down to cover it. The confusion in Val's eyes, her disapproval at her daughter's ingratitude, was almost too much for Tessa to bear. She sensed Joey wanted to press her about Ken's behavior hundreds of times, but he held back, probably because Alyse cautioned him against sticking their noses where they didn't belong. She suspected even Mariel knew something was going on. When she thought they were jovially engaging in typical husband complaints, Tessa detected her friend picking up on her too-real caustic remarks, the stern set of her jaw and steely expression.

Would their initial shock be followed by moments of clarity and dot-connecting that would leave them shaking their heads for days afterward, one light bulb after another switching on until they had no choice but to believe her despite Ken's protests? Tessa's shoulders tensed. Topping the list of reasons Tessa had remained quiet was fear of Ken's reaction. Constantly weaved through her own pain was her dread of Ken's wrath if she outed him. It was like a weight she carried around her neck. No matter how many times they argued about Ken's problem, it inevitably came back to his questioning how she could be so selfish. She'd go into the ring, boxing gloves on, poised to land a right hook to his chin, and he'd end up delivering the knockout punch: She'd destroy all their lives if she opened her mouth. She'd be no better than Caroline, imploding everyone's world.

Ken was more persuasive than Winston Churchill when he made his case against Tessa revealing their secrets. Their families would try to strong-arm him into getting professional help that, according to him, wouldn't work. Then, no matter how careful he was and how the facilities and counselors swore to protect his identity, patients would find out and leave the practice. That might even lead to Ken losing his license, and then they'd be unable to pay their bills and likely lose the house. Their friends would rally around them at first, but eventually they'd stop calling, stop inviting Ken and Tessa to gatherings, stop knowing what to say. They'd be miserable, their lives in ruin, everything they worked for demolished. Ken would be humiliated publicly and privately, and it would all be Tessa's fault.

Tessa pulled her knees to her chest under her sweatshirt and wrapped her arms around them. She thought about marriage, how at first it stretches out ahead, like an exciting journey embarked on by two people in love. And the milestones— twenty-five, maybe even fifty years—joy-filled personal stories celebrated by children and grandchildren. It struck Tessa then that most of marriage is the routine middle part—paying the electric bill, calling the repairperson, taking the kids to the park, deciding between Chinese and Italian for dinner—and that was what she wanted most. The parts everyone else seemed to find boring. The parts it seemed Ken just couldn't be satisfied with.

She stood and crossed the room to head upstairs just as the automatic timer switched off the lights on the tree. On the sofa, color coordinated decorative pillows were lined up in perfect order. Tessa swiped at them, knocking them like bowling pins to the floor. She knew Ken wouldn't be home tonight. She also knew she'd somehow get through the holidays. Cruise control, autopilot . . . they'd become her defaults, the mechanisms that got her from point A to point B.

Tessa headed for the stairs but stopped midway and turned around. She picked up the scattered pillows and arranged them uniformly on the sofa.

Chapter Forty

FOUR MONTHS LATER

"Mommy, Cokey is scaad in my backpack. Huh eyes can't see 'cause it's too daak when I zippah it." Ronnie pulled her favorite doll from the bag Tessa had packed to send to Val's. Tessa looked up from stuffing Julia's diaper bag and smiled.

"Okay, hon. Lay Cokey on top of the bag so she won't be afraid." Tessa stood and looked at the clock. She had to finish getting the girls' things together so she could pack her own suitcase. On Christmas morning, she'd been confused at first when she'd unwrapped a gift from Ken with a label that read *Happy 5th Anniversary!* since their anniversary wasn't until late April. Inside the package was a brochure for Cape Cod and two plane tickets. Ken had beamed at his wife as he watched her furrowed-brow confusion turn to clarity about the long weekend for two he'd planned without her knowledge. "It will be so good for us, doll. Three nights, four days away from all our stresses."

At first, she'd protested, reminding Ken about the almost-three-year-old and almost-one-year-old they'd need to make arrangements for while they strolled the cobblestone streets or took a sailing tour of the Cape. Ken had stopped her midsentence, putting up his palm and shaking his head. "Nope, don't worry, I've taken care of everything. Val and Alyse are happy to share childcare duties for a few days. It's all set."

But Tessa remained conflicted. And not just because she didn't want to sentence her mom or sister-in-law to four days of Julia flinging Cheerios around their kitchens or Ronnie carpeting their living rooms with Cokey's clothes and accessories. Just last week Tessa had stepped on Cokey's sunglasses and had to bite her tongue to stifle a string of expletives when the pointy handles dug into the bottom of her foot. Val and Alyse could handle that part of her messy life.

It was the messier part that was a problem: She wasn't sure she even wanted to spend four days away with Ken. He showed no signs of giving up the gas. If anything, he seemed to have gotten worse. Sometimes he could go a few weeks without it, but when he did give in to the cravings, he binged hard. Several times, Tessa had had to run interference, placing frantic early morning calls to Tracy, lying that Ken had come down with this or that illness and would she mind canceling the day's patients? A few times he'd put on the mask after the last patient on Friday and not come home until late Saturday night.

Tessa became increasingly reluctant to make plans with friends on weekends because she never knew when a binge was coming. After the holidays, Tessa had asked for a compromise: She made Ken promise he'd tell her if he was planning to use the gas so she wasn't left scrambling to rearrange plans at the last minute. He'd kept that promise exactly twice, but eventually it fell by the wayside, in a heap with all his other broken ones.

Amid Ken's pleas that this was just what they needed and not knowing how she'd explain—without sounding insane—to her family that she didn't want to get away for an anniversary trip, she'd finally relented. Val and Alyse were happy to have the girls, and even Joey thought it sounded like fun. "Don't worry, Tess," he'd teased. "I'll have everything under control. Jewels and I can have a bottle together. I just hope I don't mix up the beer and the milk!" And Sal joked, "I'll oversee everything and make sure your mother does everything right," a comment that drew an eyeroll from Val and a reminder to her husband that he had never so much as changed a diaper or picked up a toy at home. "True," he'd answered with a wink. "I'm definitely more of a foreman when it comes to raising kids."

The phone rang and interrupted Tessa's thoughts. "Are you getting excited?" Alyse asked. "I'm looking forward to it. Maybe it will inspire your brother that it's time for us to start a family."

"Either that or he'll make an appointment for a vasectomy." Alyse chuckled. "I doubt it. He gets such a kick out of Ronnie. I just hope she doesn't pick up any of his off-color language. I apologize ahead of time!" Both women laughed and then went over for the tenth time when the girls would be at their house and when they'd be at Sal and Val's.

Tessa cradled the phone under her chin and searched her kitchen table for the schedule she'd made up and copied for her mom and sister-in-law. "Hang on," she said, moving the newspaper to find the paper she was looking for. The newspaper fell to the floor, its sections coming undone and scattering in a pile at her feet. As Tessa gathered the pages, an obituary caught her eye. The photo of a young man looked vaguely familiar, but Tessa couldn't place him. She studied his thin angular face and longish light hair. *Where have I seen him?*

"—and I told Gina we'd take the girls to the pond to feed the ducks if the weather is nice on Saturday," Alyse said, bringing Tessa back to the present.

"Yes, Gina already told Ronnie that, and she's been trying to teach Julia to quack all week," Tessa said, smiling. "Make sure you take video of that."

"Okay, safe travels, and have a great time. I'll pick up the girls from your mom's tomorrow after lunch, just as the schedule says!"

Tessa hung up just in time to see Ronnie plop a long blonde wig from the dress-up box on Julia's head. She positioned it cock-eyed, and the baby squealed as the strands of hair covered her chubby face. "Yook, Mommy," Ronnie proudly proclaimed. "Rapunzuh!"

"Rapunzel looks more like Cousin It." Tessa laughed. She fixed the wig and went back to stuffing the bag, the young man's obituary forgotten.

"What is it?" Ken growled as Tracy knocked on his office door a third time. The last two patients had canceled their appointments, and since they'd finished earlier than on a usual Thursday, she'd decided to get a jump on some clerical work that had piled up.

Tracy clenched her teeth. "Sorry to bother you, but I have a question about a charge on a patient's chart." Ken glared at her without speaking, so she continued before she lost her nerve. "I'm going over the billing for this week. Patricia House-man's chart says I'm supposed to bill the insurance company for two crowns, but didn't she only get one?"

Ken stood up slowly and looked at Tracy through narrowed eyes. He had loosened his tie and pulled his shirt out from his pants. "What are you implying?"

"I . . . I'm not implying anything. I'm just checking with you before I enter this, so I don't make a mistake I have to correct later."

"If the chart says to submit for two crowns, submit for two crowns. I coded everything for you. All you have to do is submit the claim."

"Right. Okay. Just checking." She started backing out of the room, anxious to get away from Ken and his foul mood. "So—"

"So, what?" Ken pinched the bridge of his nose and exhaled loudly. "Is there something else?"

"I just wanted to ask you if there is anything besides billing you'd like me to do tomorrow when you're not here. I don't want to bother you after you and Tessa leave for your long weekend away." The corners of her lips raised into a tentative smile. She refrained from commenting that Ken looked like he needed a few days off.

At the mention of his anniversary trip, Ken blinked several times, as though he'd forgotten all about it. "No, just work on billing and collecting some money. That's fine. Thanks." He looked down at some papers on his desk. "Close the door on your way out."

Before returning to her work, Tracy stopped in the break room to make a cup of tea. Brenda was there at the table working on patient charts, a steaming mug of coffee and a cream-filled donut next to her. While she heated the water for her tea in the microwave, Tracy poked around in the box of donuts she'd brought in this morning and raised her eyebrows at Brenda. "You're smart, hiding out back here," she said, selecting a chocolate-frosted cruller.

Brenda closed the folder she was working on. "What do you mean?"

Tracy took a bite and nodded toward Ken's office. "The boss. He's a bear today. This trip will do him good."

Brenda rolled her eyes. "Yes, I'm sure the lovebirds will have a great time." She grabbed the next folder.

The *ding!* of the microwave broke the uncomfortable silence. *A few days away from each other will do us all good,* Tracy thought, returning to her desk.

As she bobbed the tea bag up and down in her cup, she heard the muffled sound of Ken on the phone behind his closed door. She sat down at her computer and clicked on the next patient invoice.

In his office, Ken ran an impatient hand through his hair. *Where the fuck is that asshole?*

He grabbed the phone and punched in Stan's cell number for the fifth time in two days. It went straight to voicemail, just as it had the first four times. He threw the phone onto his desk, and it bounced off a pile of mail and landed on the floor. "Shit," he muttered, picking up his office phone. He tried not to make a habit of calling Stan during Lux Air's regular business hours, but he was getting desperate. Hopefully, it was close enough to the end of the day that Stan would be the only one there.

"Lux Air, Tammy speaking. May I help you?" Ken recognized the older woman's voice, though she sounded glum, not chipper like when he'd seen her several months ago.

He cleared his throat. "Yes, hello, I'm trying to reach Stan. He always handles my account. Is he working today?"

Tammy hesitated before answering in a strained voice. "Oh, I . . . Stan isn't . . . Maybe I can help you."

Ken closed his eyes and struggled to remain calm. "I believe we met one other time when I botched up my delivery day and had to drive down there to pick up a few tanks. It's just that, I misplaced my paperwork, and I think I may have done it again." He turned on the charm. "I don't want to bother you since it was my mistake. Stan is always so good about keeping track of things for me. That's why I always deal directly with him."

He thought he heard a small sound, like a whimper.

"Tammy? Are you there?"

Tammy sniffled. "Yes, I'm here. I remember you." She paused, and Ken heard her blow her nose. "Oh, you haven't heard. It's terrible, just terrible."

A chill crept up Ken's spine. "What? What's terrible?"

Tammy stifled a sob. "Stan. He's dead. He overdosed on pills three days ago."

Chapter Forty-One

Tessa awakened, the morning sun streaming through the bedroom blinds, and reached next to her. As expected, her hand touched not her husband but the cool smooth sheet, Ken's pillow plump and undisturbed.

She'd slept surprisingly well. After taking Ronnie and Julia to Val's, she'd come back home to concentrate on last-minute details for the trip, and when at eleven o'clock Ken still wasn't home, she made a decision. In a dreamlike state, like she had been sitting on a dock, her feet dangling over the edge, it came to her. She drifted off to sleep just as the clock on the nightstand flipped from 11:59 to midnight with a gentle click, and she felt no fear. She recognized at last her part in their private hell, and she knew what she had to do.

Stretching and blinking against the bright sunlight, she felt lighter than she had in over two years, resolve lifting her from the bed and moving her legs in the direction of the master bathroom. It was as if she were floating as she showered, dressed, and finished packing her suitcase, stretching the elastic straps over her neatly folded clothes in a perfect X and closing it with a decisive thud.

She went downstairs to wait for the car. Unused to silence in the house—no *Sesame Street* on the TV, no Ronnie entertaining Julia with her made-up rhymes—she sipped coffee, the cream forming random clouds on its surface as it cooled.

Perched on the edge of a stool at the kitchen island, her suitcase and carry-on bag at her feet, she glanced at her watch. Five minutes until the car would arrive to take Ken and her to the Philadelphia airport. Upstairs, outside his closet door, Ken's own suitcase stood empty, its wheels all pointed in different directions as if they couldn't agree on a destination. His unzipped toiletry bag sat agape on the vanity next to his sink.

The whir of a car's engine in the driveway caught her attention, and she rose, feeling an invisible force releasing in her, guiding her toward the door. She grasped the doorknob and faltered for a moment, as if without it to steady her, she might teeter and then collapse. Looking back one last time at the empty kitchen, empty house, empty marriage behind her, she handed her bag to the driver.

Later that evening, alone at her table, sipping a signature cocktail on the deck of Baxter's Boathouse, Tessa could almost pretend that nothing was wrong. She adjusted her sunglasses and looked out at the peaceful waters of Hyannis Harbor. A boat pulled up to the dock, and a group of eight laughing, sun-kissed revelers stepped off and made their way inside the restaurant. A tall dark-haired man lightly held his wife's elbow and kissed her cheek as he guided her toward the bar with the rest of the party. The man wore a teal-blue sweater. It suited his frame, and Tessa wondered idly if his wife had picked it out. She looked away, suddenly feeling intrusive at her window into their intimacy.

Hours earlier, in her driveway, she'd smiled sweetly at the driver who'd arrived to take her to the airport and told him his notes must be wrong—he was transporting one passenger, not two. She chatted with him as they drove, the distance between Ken and her growing larger with every passing minute, and marveled at how easy it was for her to lie through her teeth.

"My husband is at a conference in Boston. He'll rent a car and meet me in Cape Cod tonight just in time for dinner." She'd relaxed, leaning against the headrest, and studied the driver's friendly eyes in the rearview mirror as she sprinkled small truths throughout her tale. "It's our anniversary. We've so been looking forward to this trip."

Her sureness had grown, puffing up around her like smoke the farther she traveled from her house, the car seat next to her empty except for her own bag. It grew as they sped toward the airport, past the knitted branches of the trees along Route 422, weaving in and out of rush hour traffic on I-76. Self-confidence filled her lungs with each inhale as she passed through airport security, boarded the plane, ascended through milky clouds on her way to celebrate her wedding anniversary alone.

By the time she landed in Boston and hopped on a Cape Air small craft to Hyannis, an otherworldly calm had settled inside her. And when she arrived in the hotel room Ken had reserved months earlier, fondling the wall for the light switch and dropping her suitcase on the floor with a thump, she felt her phone vibrating impatiently in her purse. Ignoring the call from Ken's number, she called Val to check on Ronnie and Julia, who were having too much fun to miss their parents, one on her scheduled romantic getaway, the other in his private darkness with his irresistible mistress. She knew Ken, desperate to conceal his worst blunder yet, would not call Val or Alyse or anyone other than her and risk exposing the truth.

"Would you like another cocktail or are you ready to order dinner?" A tanned, blonde-haired server wearing the standard uniform—polo shirt, khakis, and Baxter's visor—picked up Tessa's empty glass.

Tessa's flip phone buzzed again and shimmied like an upside-down turtle on the table. She ignored it and smiled at the server. "Both. I'll have the seafood bisque and another drink. The Harbor Sunset."

"Excellent. Be right back with that."

The peach-colored sunset was just beginning to spread beyond the harbor, where a lighthouse bobbed on the water. Tessa's phone buzzed again. This time she flipped it open to see Ken's message. *Call me. Now.*

She closed the phone, stunned at Ken's audacity to make demands on her after planning a romantic anniversary trip to New England and then huffing nitrous oxide instead of showing up for it.

The server arrived with her soup and drink, and Tessa dropped the phone into her bag so she wouldn't hear its constant buzzing.

She didn't answer when Ken called as she strolled along the cobblestone street that led back to the hotel room.

She didn't answer when he called six more times as she relaxed on the balcony of the hotel room, stretched out on a lounger, a light blanket thrown around her shoulders.

She didn't answer as she drifted off a few hours later in the king-size bed, surrounded by so many pillows it was like hiding in a cave.

"Fuck!" Ken threw the flip phone across the room. He held his head in both hands and massaged his temples. His fingertips tingled, and he rubbed them together. He was wound so tight he felt like thousands of ants were marching up his body, starting at his toes and making their way up his legs, his arms, his torso. The tingling licked at his shoulders, his face, his scalp, and he feared he would crawl out of his skin. "Fuck!"

He paced the bedroom floor, cursing silently. *Answer the fucking phone!*

Earlier, when he'd arrived home exactly three hours after the car was scheduled to pick them up for the airport, he'd expected to find Tessa crazed and ready for battle. He'd braced himself for it. Amid her tirade, he'd call the airline, car service, and hotel and make new arrangements. He'd fix it while she ranted, threw things, sobbed. He had been ready.

But this? He had not been ready for this.

As hard as it was for him to fathom, it appeared she went on the trip—or somewhere—without him. He moved from room to room like a ghost, fingertips pushing open each door, the emptiness of the house making the silence heavier, like the muffled whispers of mourners at a funeral.

In their bedroom, a thick, dense silence pressed down on Ken like a hand holding his head under water. With his index finger, he touched Tessa's pillow, tracing the indentation of her head still visible on it. He stumbled into the bathroom and eyed her vanity, the colorful bottles of perfumes and lotions grouped together on a mirrored tray. A few, though he couldn't say which ones, were missing, a thin layer of dust surrounding the circular shapes where they'd stood before she'd packed her travel bag.

Finally, he'd sunk into the leather sectional in the media room, his head buzzing with what to do next. The news about Stan overdosing had thrown him for a loop. He didn't know him well outside his mutually beneficial arrangement. They had an uncomplicated relationship, and Ken had wanted to keep it that way.

He raked his fingers through his hair. His gaze was fixed on the blank TV screen, but his mind filled with the many narcotics scripts he'd written for Stan. *It's not my fault. He was a fucking junkie. He would have gotten them somewhere.*

He hadn't planned on doing the gas last night. He'd just needed a few hours to escape the stress about Stan. He'd kept the craving at bay until he got the news. Then it found him, pounced on him, and ripped away his restraint. It consumed him, filling his veins, his bones, his mind, weighing on him so heavily he was sure it would suffocate him if he didn't give in to it.

Afterward, his mind whirled, and he couldn't come up with his last conscious thought before covering his face with the mask. He had every intention of being home in time for the ride to the airport. He'd used the last of his stash and risen from his fog only after the empty tanks hissed to a stop, oxygen the only thing flowing through the hoses up his nose. Flinging himself from the chair and tearing the mask and hoses away from his face, he looked around wildly and realized the night had been replaced by the thin light of a new day. By then, it was too late.

He felt like a caged animal. Tessa wasn't answering her phone or his messages. He couldn't call her family. He didn't even know for sure where she was. Would she have gone to Cape Cod alone or fled elsewhere, somewhere he did not know to look?

A dull chill crept over him. For the first time in a long time, maybe ever, he had no idea what his wife's next move would be.

Chapter Forty-Two

Though the late-April temperatures in New England were too chilly for beach-going, they were perfect for historical sightseeing, something Ken and Tessa both enjoyed. Ken had said that was one reason he chose Cape Cod for their anniversary trip, a thought Tessa remembered as she toured a shipwreck museum in Nantucket. The stories of the shipwrecks and rescues captivated her, and the irony of her museum choice was not lost on her as the guide regaled her group with colorful tales.

From there she took a walking tour, enthralled with the history and hidden secrets of the island. After resting on a bench outside a cedar-shingled bakery with a coffee and a fried dough pastry dusted with confectioners' sugar, she called Alyse to check on the girls. She'd spoken to Val the day before, and neither woman showed any signs of knowing Tessa was alone. Ronnie dominated the calls with excited stories of excursions to minigolf and the "ice queem" shop, so it was easy for Tessa to camouflage the truth.

She pulled her sweater tight around her against the spring breeze and headed to the ferry that would take her back to Hyannis. On the ferry, the incongruities of life struck her: The Cape was a perfect romantic getaway choice, but she was spending her anniversary there alone. Her hair whipping around her face, she finally allowed herself to admit—and she had to, no matter how she tried to deny it—that coming on this trip alone changed her marriage. *Ken did this*, she reminded herself, holding firmly on to the rail and looking out over the water, which glistened like diamonds under the sun's light.

She was amazed at the clarity of her thoughts, three hundred miles from home. Here, she felt like a spectator, looking at another woman's life, so sure what the woman should do. *Come on, really? How long are you going to buy his line of bullshit?* The obviousness of it all as viewed by an outsider looking in made her cheeks flush.

Ken's addiction stained their marriage, left muddy fingerprints on everything around them. Tessa turned so the wind blew her hair away from her face and heard herself lying to everyone they knew about Ken's whereabouts and behavior. She saw the scuff on the mudroom wall where he hit it with his briefcase trying to sneak in, wobbly and dazed, early one morning, and the worn spot in the carpet next to the arched window on the landing where she'd lain, dialing his number over and over, so many nights waiting for him to come home. She struggled to give words to the awareness that everything from now on would be different. All she could think about was how everything had gone so wrong.

She'd spent her life being afraid that the people she loved would leave her. Caroline had done that to her. Because of Caroline, she realized now, her relationship with Ken felt fragile to Tessa, like it could topple and shatter if she wasn't careful. So each time Ken told her how she would be responsible for ruining their lives, how selfish it would be for her to expose his secret or, worse yet, leave him because of it, she believed him.

She thought about how Caroline's abandonment all those years ago had damaged her, shaped her. It made her crave the harmonious order snatched from a child's world when a parent disappears. It made her obsessed with following rules, coloring inside the lines. It made her keep her house spotless; for

Christ's sake, she color coded the hangers in her laundry room. Caroline's desertion made Tessa turn herself inside out trying to please everyone so they wouldn't leave. She'd been afraid for so long she'd forgotten what it was like not to be.

People didn't stay in your life just because they gave birth to you or married you. They left if they felt they were driven to it, felt they deserved it. If her own mother could do it, was any relationship a sure thing? She'd hung on, made excuse after excuse, told herself she couldn't destroy her family like Caroline had destroyed hers. She'd lived in fear of causing the irreparable damage Ken warned her she'd rain down on all of them. She'd promised she would keep her mouth shut, and she'd kept that promise, even when it choked her, suffocated her, made her lose herself.

The ferry docked at the pier near her hotel just as Tessa made a set of new promises, this time to herself. She would tell Ken: Enough. She wouldn't lie for him anymore. She wouldn't put up with his substance abuse. She'd stand by him only if he sought help. She'd tell their families exactly what was going on. She wasn't a monster threatening to leave her husband who had a problem. He had to do his part. She would no longer be the only person invested in Ken's sobriety. And she would no longer bear the burden alone.

It was clear to her here, six hours from her house, what she had to do. She couldn't save Ken. She had to save herself and her daughters. When she returned home, she'd speak her promises aloud to Ken to make them real. As she stepped off the ferry onto the dock, the water slapping against the boat, a crew member reached for her hand. She stumbled at first, but his fingers lightly gripped her forearm. "You're okay, I won't let you fall," he assured her, and she believed him.

After the driver unloaded her luggage and dropped her off in her driveway, she stood at the back door to her house, unable to think straight for a moment. It was just after noon; bright sunshine bathed the yard in lemony light, and birds chirped in the tall trees that lined their property. Tessa sucked in her breath and forced herself to open the door. Her eyes struggled to adjust. The kitchen shades were drawn, and the house seemed silent, but she wasn't sure if it really was or if her pounding heart drowned out any sounds.

"Welcome home."

She started, not having seen Ken standing at the far side of the kitchen. Dropping her bags in the mudroom and shrugging out of her jacket, she felt his gaze linger on her, and her mouth felt dry. "Um . . . hi," she managed.

Barefoot, he wore a long-sleeved black T-shirt and faded jeans, his thumbs hooked casually in his belt loops. His eyes were rimmed in red, as though he hadn't slept. Tessa felt simultaneously twenty feet and millions of miles away from him.

She walked into the kitchen and sat down, and he sat next to her. Usually she could tell exactly what he was thinking, say the words he was about to say before he did, but now she couldn't read his face, had no idea what was going on in his head.

He tilted his head and studied her. "You went without me." He sounded more resigned than angry.

Their eyes met and locked, his serious, hers sad. Tessa struggled to find her footing, remember the promises she'd made to herself on the ferry. She looked away to steady herself and mustered up the confidence she'd felt in the days away from his manipulation. Finally, she cleared her throat and faced him again.

"You look like you're about to say something I don't want to hear." He managed a small smile and gently stroked her arm.

Tessa sat up straight in her chair. "I've made some decisions. The time away helped me do that." She looked down at her hands, as though searching for a script with her next line. "I can't do it anymore."

"Tess—"

"No." She put up her palm. "No. I mean it. I can't. You need help. If the last few days didn't prove that to you, I don't know what will. You missed our *anniversary trip*. Do you know how messed up that is? You were doing the gas and missed our anniversary trip." She leaned in so her face was inches from his, as if that would help her words sink in. "You get help, or I'm leaving. I don't want to, but I can't do this anymore. And one more thing." She watched him, her eyes steady, waiting for a reaction, but he was silent and still. "I'm going to tell our families what's going on."

Ken found his voice. "Tessa, you don't want to do that. You're upset—so am I—but you don't want to do that." The familiar darkness returned to his face, the expression he'd get every time she brought up telling someone about the gas. She saw it flash, and then saw him trying to control it, to convince her to listen to him. "I've been thinking too. I know I fucked up royally this time—"

"No. Don't do that. There's no 'this time.' It's always here. You're fine for a while, but it never lasts." She was talking faster now. She didn't want to risk being taken in again.

"Okay, okay. I've been thinking about counseling. Maybe you're right about that." They locked gazes, and Tessa heard his next words before he spoke them: *But you can't tell anyone. This has to be between us. Do I have to remind you what your life will be like if you leave?* The moment swelled between them, and she braced herself. "But I need you to promise me you'll keep quiet a little longer. Let me try counseling without everyone knowing. Please."

She looked for the anger again but saw only sadness on her husband's face. She closed her eyes and fought off the notion that she was betraying him. Here she was again, on the edge of the cliff, her head spinning, the last three years rushing through her head. Then another picture took shape: celebrating their anniversary alone in Cape Cod. She pulled herself back from the ledge.

"Sorry." She stood and crossed the room on shaky legs. "I can't promise that. I need support. I can't carry this around anymore. It's time to live in reality." She picked up her bags and headed for the stairs. "I'm going to my parents' for the kids. You can come with me or not."

As she climbed the stairs, she heard a sharp crack as Ken hurled something at the wall.

Chapter Forty-Three

"Hey, hon, welcome home! How was it? Ronnie's dying to know if you saw any whales." Val shuffled the phone's mouthpiece, and Tessa heard her daughter's excited voice in the background.

"Is that Mommy? Yemmee talk, yemmee talk!"

Tessa sat on her bed, the phone in her hand, and her heart broke. She knew things would be forever changed after what she was about to tell her family. She wanted to capture and save her mom's cheery tone, her daughter's view of a world with two happy parents, like a photograph showing signs of weathering over time but whose depiction remains constant.

She heard a scuffle as Val handed the phone to Ronnie. "Mommy! Wait till you see! Dina painted my nails pink! Did you bring Jew-ia and me any pwesents?"

The phone dropped with a thud, and Val came back on the line. "Short attention span, that one." She chuckled. "She's in perpetual motion. So, do you want to pick up the kids or should I bring them to you?"

Tessa almost faltered but then felt a guiding hand at her back. She remembered the promises she made to herself on the ferry and let them propel her forward. "I'll pick them up. And, Mom . . ." Since the first time she saw Ken doing the gas almost three years ago, she'd wrestled with the question: How do you tell the people you love and want to protect an awful truth? She thought about all the times she lied for Ken, the pounding in her head, the sinking feeling in her stomach. She couldn't let her heart slow, her resolve trickle away. She inhaled deeply. "You know how you always say you think something is bothering me?"

"Yes?" The background noise grew quieter, as though Val was walking away from the kids so she could concentrate on Tessa's words.

"And when I'm ready to talk, you're ready to listen?"

There was silence on the other end. Val was nodding, though Tessa couldn't see her.

"Well, I'm ready to talk."

"Are you a newcomer?"

"Yes."

"What is your first name?"

"Tessa."

"Hi, Tessa."

The group was composed of about fifteen people seated in a circle around a table. Tessa looked around the church basement and was struck by how similar the setting was to those she'd seen in movies. The participants were mostly women, many clutching books and journals, some whose eyes were forlorn and lost, others who looked grateful to be among people going through the same thing they were.

The woman who'd questioned Tessa seemed to be the leader. She said, "This is an open Nar-Anon meeting. Anyone is free to share, but no one is obligated to. Remember that anything or anyone you see or hear today stays right here in this room. We've all come here because we want and need help. We're here because of the effects of someone else's addiction, but we know that our own thinking has to change before we can make a successful approach to life." Several people nodded and smiled. One young girl sat rigidly, arms folded across her chest, anger darkening her eyes and turning her lips inward. Another twentysomething girl with purple hair, multiple piercings, and arms and legs covered with tattoos ignored everyone and concentrated on her knitting. The leader continued, "Does anyone have clerical information to share?"

While one of the two men in the group offered information about new meetings, changed meeting places, and additional resources, Tessa replayed the scene in her mind where she told her family the truth about Ken's substance abuse. She'd gathered them all in her parents' living room, Sal reclining in his chair, Val tossing aside a magazine she'd been leafing through, Joey surfing the channels for the Phillies game. It killed her to watch their calm faces change as she announced, slowly at first, that she and Ken had been living a lie. Their startled expressions inverted, like a waterfall halting and reversing its direction, when she told them he was addicted to nitrous oxide. Once she started, though, it was like an avalanche. She released everything she'd had bottled up for three years, blurting out stories and incidents, some in logical order, others spilling out randomly like ocean waves crashing onto the beach. She paced the room, alternately crying and getting angry, dabbing her eyes with a tissue one minute and ripping it to shreds the next. When she finished, she collapsed into a chair, sweaty and exhausted.

The color had drained from her parents' faces as she spoke. Val looked like the key to a great mystery had been unlocked, and she nodded as clarity dawned on her, question after question answered, blank after blank filled in. Tessa's brothers and sister-in-law had mixed reactions: Joey's anger soundless but palpable at what his sister endured alone, Alyse's quiet sadness causing her to choke back tears, Sal Jr.'s amazed proclamation of "Holy shit!"

But it was Sal's reaction that reminded Tessa why she'd kept quiet for so long. His ordinarily cheery face and twinkling smile crumpled in pain as though she were removing his teeth one by one with pliers. He'd held his forehead, shoulders sagging, eyes clenched shut, and when a single tear rolled down his cheek, Tessa almost regretted coming clean.

It was Val who put her arms around Tessa and told her it would be alright. She didn't chastise Tessa for waiting so long to tell them or accuse her of enabling Ken. She looked around at her family and told them—not asked them—that they would face this together. She reminded them that Ken was their family too, and they would all stick together through Ken's recovery. And there in that room, away from Ken's manipulative narrative and the tangled web of the last three years, Tessa believed things might be okay. She told her family that after the anniversary trip debacle, Ken had finally promised to get help, and she would also attend meetings for family members of addicts. Val and Joey both offered to go with her, but she said that, at least initially, she needed to do it alone. She had some work to do on herself.

The man finished his announcements, and the leader opened up the meeting for sharing. No one spoke at first, and then a slight woman in her mid-sixties said, "I'm Elaine."

"Hi, Elaine," the group responded.

"I'm happy to be here this morning." She took a deep breath. "I'm here because my son-in-law is an addict, and my daughter enables him. I'm now in the sad position of trying to figure out how to talk realistically to my grandchildren without alienating my daughter. They're starting to ask questions about their father's behavior." She looked around at the others. "I'm trying to work the steps of this program and grasp that I am only responsible for myself and my attitudes. That's how I can move the emphasis from my son-in-law and place it on my own life, and that will be the most beneficial to my grandchildren. Thanks for listening."

"Thanks for sharing, Elaine."

After another brief moment of silence, "I'm Lisa."

"Hi, Lisa."

Lisa and a few others shared their common experiences and expressed a desire to heal by focusing on themselves rather than the substance abuser. Tessa listened intently but did not speak. Like them, she'd lost her own self-worth in her attempts to manage Ken's problem. She nodded along as they spoke about the myriad of emotions they experienced living with a substance abuser: obsession, anxiety, anger, denial, guilt.

With only a few minutes left in the meeting, a pale fortyish woman with wild shoulder-length wavy hair said quietly, "I'm Stephanie."

"Hi, Stephanie."

"I'm having a rough time. I've gone to either Al-Anon or Nar-Anon meetings every day this week." Stephanie held a journal in one hand and a balled-up tissue in the other. Dark rings underlined her red-rimmed eyes. "I'm sad because I feel like I'm losing the friends my husband and I hang out with. I find myself not making plans with them because I know if we all get together, my husband will get drunk. I'll end up leaving him asleep in the car or trying to drag him into the house at the end of the night." She looked around miserably. "The toughest part is how resentful I feel because his alcoholism is making *me* lose friends. I miss them, and it pisses me off." Her eyes filled with tears, and she studied the tissue in her hand. Sitting up straighter, she continued, "So, I've made a decision. I'm going to make plans with these couples because *I* want to see them. If my husband can't control his drinking, that's on him. I'm going to work on changing my attitude and remembering the three Cs: I didn't *cause* it, I can't *cure* it, and I can't *control* his problem."

It wasn't until a woman next to her handed her a box of tissues that Tessa felt the tears rolling down her own face.

After the meeting, some of the group members introduced themselves to Tessa and said they hoped she'd come back. Their nonjudgmental support bathed her in warmth. As she drove out of the parking lot, gravel crunching under her tires, she thought about Ken at his own counseling session and hoped he'd find therapy as helpful as she had.

The exam room spun as Ken hastily grabbed everything he needed and assembled it next to the exam chair. It didn't take nearly as long as it used to. Since Stan's death, he'd had to go back to the normal process of having the gas delivered on a regular schedule instead of picking it up himself and hiding it in a supply closet. Brenda knew the real story, but he'd simply told Tracy that patients had been asking for it, so he'd decided to offer it again. The hard part was making sure he kept enough for them.

He worked methodically. He had to hurry if he was going to get a few hours in before Tessa expected him home. Now that she'd told her whole fucking family their personal business, they were on constant high alert. He felt like a bug under a microscope. If he was ten minutes late, Tessa would be on the phone crying to Val.

To their credit, he thought as he adjusted the valves, her parents had been supportive when Tessa told them. They talked to him privately after Tessa spilled the beans and told him they loved him and would do whatever they could to help. Val had been stoic, assuring him that it was good that they knew and they were happy he'd decided to get help. Sal was another story; he'd said little, and his face creased like he wanted to cry. Tessa must have laid it on thick. It seemed the way she'd made it sound, Ken was no different than Caroline, and Sal couldn't bear to watch his daughter living the same hell as he had. Afterward, Sal had hugged Ken and told him, his voice cracking, that he was like a son to him and he knew Ken would do the right thing for Tessa and the girls.

Joey wasn't as warm and fuzzy. He'd slapped Ken on the back and commended him for finally addressing his problem, but his eyes reflected all the times Ken had gone missing, all the times his sister had to lie for him. Alyse mostly stuck to supporting Tessa, making polite small talk with Ken but clearly unnerved by the situation. Sal Jr. chose to stay out of it, and Gina and Tony were too young to comprehend it. The family was careful not to discuss it in front of them, quickly clearing their throats and changing the subject when they entered a room.

Ken's one victory was that Tessa agreed not to tell his stepfather or siblings—yet. At Ken's urging, she'd acquiesced that he wanted to tell them in his own time, after he'd completed recovery.

Recovery. Like the counseling session he was supposed to be in right now.

He'd fabricate a story about that later, about how helpful it was, how glad he was that she convinced him to go.

Fuck that. He had everything he needed right here.

The hoses seem to sigh in relief as the gas began to flow. Ken stretched out on the chair and closed his eyes. He covered his nose and mouth with the mask and let his body inhabit the space where guilt and accountability melted away.

Chapter Forty-Four

Everything looked different to Tessa now. She was the same person as before she told her family—and now Mariel—about Ken, but where she felt isolated before, now she felt exposed. Instead of covering up every misstep of Ken's, now she had to explain them. If possible, she was even more on edge. If she were honest with herself, she'd admit that what set her most on edge was that she didn't believe Ken was following through with his treatment. He'd convinced her that he should start with outpatient sessions instead of going into a thirty-day inpatient program, claiming he couldn't close the office that long. She'd fought him at first, but then realized it was much more than he'd ever agreed to before. When he came home from a session, he often went straight upstairs to shower or lie down, rarely saying a word to Tessa about it.

Ken was angry that she'd told her family and her best friend about the gas. He took every opportunity to get his jabs in. When they arrived at Sal and Val's for Sunday dinner, he announced caustically, "Look, the bad boy is being good today. His mommy doesn't have to send him to his room!" And when Mariel and Rob came over for a cookout, he placed the sizzling burgers on a plate, casting an acerbic glance at Tessa before commenting, "These look perfect, just the way Tessa likes them. And we know Tessa needs everything the way she wants it." He tried to sound lighthearted, as if he was joking, but everyone shifted uncomfortably, eyes downcast, at his remarks.

Mariel had been shocked. Tessa almost felt more sorry for her friend than herself at Mariel's reaction. "What . . . what . . . he's been doing what?" She cried and apologized for crying instead of being strong for Tessa and then cried some more. She had so many questions she didn't know where to begin. "We have to . . . we have to do something, right? He has to stop this! Oh, my God." Not having known or been able to tell something was drastically wrong in her best friend's life made her miserable.

"It's my fault," Tessa told her. "I hid it from everyone."

Then there were times—albeit rare—when Ken seemed relieved that the secret was out. These were the times that made Tessa think her husband was honestly glad he was getting help and they could repair the pieces of their broken relationship. At night, they'd lie together on the couch watching a movie, their legs intertwined, his face buried in her hair. On weekends, they'd play together with the girls, Ken clear-eyed and in good spirits, and he'd stop suddenly and give Tessa a look so tender, a look she read as *I can't believe what an idiot I was. I have everything I want right here.*

Since attending Nar-Anon meetings, Tessa cringed with the realization that, until now, everything in her life had become secondary to dealing with Ken's problem. It had dictated her actions, her thoughts, her mood. It had filled her up so completely she had no energy to work at the school or the diner. Taking care of the girls was the only thing she had the time or motivation to do other than managing Ken. Just like Sal had been consumed with managing Caroline all those years ago.

It amazed her now that for three years she thought managing Ken would work. On the days he came home on time, sober, whistling, she'd viewed it as a personal victory. She'd grasp it and hold tight with both hands, sure the nightmare was over and everything would be wonderful from that point on. She'd dream about the future, plan their next gathering, research possible career opportunities for herself in education. She'd make mental notes about what *she'd* done that had worked this time—loved him enough, hated him enough, yelled loud enough, ignored him long enough, cried hard enough.

For three years, every time Ken had a sober stretch, Tessa was pacified. She'd told herself they simply had gone through a few rough patches, some growing pains, but they'd ridden the wave and come out on the other side.

She'd thought she could fix him. After all, she had to. He couldn't fix himself.

Summer came and went. With Ken finally in recovery, Tessa immersed herself in being a positive part of the process but shifting her focus from Ken to herself. She discovered that hers was the only behavior she had any control over. She read numerous books on addiction and kept in mind the mood swings and sometimes erratic behavior addicts went through in the process of getting clean. When Ken was moody or agitated, she gave him his space. Ken's addiction no longer dictated whether *she* had a good or a bad day.

She continued going to meetings, occasionally sharing with Ken her thoughts—never others' specific stories—about what she was learning that might help them move forward together. She'd try to get Ken to open up about his counseling sessions, but he always changed the subject. She didn't expect him to tell her everything he discussed with his therapist; she just wanted assurance that he felt it was helping. Once at dinner she suggested they go together, and Ken jumped up so abruptly he almost knocked over his chair. "Jesus, I'm doing what you want! Can't you leave me alone? Why do you think you should be part of my treatment? Not everything is about you!"

Wounded, Tessa was silent for a long moment before she stood to clear the dishes and asked softly, "Doing what *I* want? Don't *you* want to fix this and save our marriage, our family?" She felt her heart beat in the silent space left between them where Ken's answer should be. As she rinsed the dishes in the sink, she spotted a flock of birds flying far above the treetops beyond their back yard. She pushed down the envy she felt at their freedom to fly wherever they chose, far from the places they didn't want to be.

In September, Ronnie started going to preschool three days a week. She loved the interaction with other kids and complained on the days she didn't go. In particular, she became fast friends with a little girl named Michaela, and the two had already had a few playdates at each other's houses.

One evening when Ronnie was at Michaela's, Tessa and Julia wandered up and down the aisles at the grocery store killing time before picking her up. Ken was at counseling, and she hoped he'd get home before her and have a chance to unwind. Anything could fuel an argument between Ken and Tessa these days. Sometimes she'd ask a question too soon after he came home from work. Other times he'd accuse her of moping in front of her parents and arousing their suspicions. Once he caught her talking to Mariel about him on the phone and didn't speak to her the rest of the night. At times she swore they had a blowup if she just looked at him wrong.

Throwing a pack of chicken legs into her grocery cart, she steered down the cleaning products aisle. Julia began to fuss, and Tessa handed her a container of dry cereal. She sighed and looked at her watch. Still a half hour before she was due to pick up Ronnie. The family asked her to stay for dinner, and Tessa noted that Ronnie had gone out to dinner more in recent weeks than she and Ken had. Ken was so often in a bad mood these days she didn't know what they'd talk about if they did have a night out. Lately, the weather was the only safe topic.

She'd considered visiting her parents, but since telling them about Ken, she found it harder to fake cheerfulness when things were tense at home. Val would know Tessa was not herself, and Tessa didn't think she could keep from bursting into tears if her mom questioned her. Then she'd go home, her eyes red and puffy, and Ken would be furious, picturing his wife and mother-in-law sitting around the kitchen table, sleeves rolled up, trying to figure out what the hell to do about him. Though she didn't entirely believe it herself, Tessa assured Sal and Val that Ken was following through with his treatment. It was easier that way.

They passed the in-store bakery, and Julia, spotting a row of donuts with icing and sprinkles, bounced up and down in her seat. "You definitely have a sweet tooth, little one," Tessa laughed. Tessa had eaten dinner earlier with Julia, and Ken had told Tessa to keep a plate for him that he'd eat after counseling. Looking at the freshly baked cupcakes, donuts, and muffins, she suddenly had an idea.

"What can I get you?" A man in a frosting-smeared apron and a baker's hat leaned on the counter with both arms.

"I'd like an assortment of cupcakes and muffins. A dozen. You pick 'em—your most popular ones. And make sure they're fresh; they won't get eaten until tomorrow morning." Julia squealed, and she added, "Oh, and a mini cupcake for my mini cupcake here."

"Coming right up." The man handed Tessa a small cupcake in waxed paper. Then he arranged the other pastries neatly in a box and taped the sides. He handed the box to Tessa, who smiled widely, happy with her plan.

"Thank you. Have a nice night!" Feeling lighter now, she eased into the shortest checkout line. She paid for her groceries, loaded Julia and her bags in the car, and headed to Ken's office to drop off the pastries for his staff and him to enjoy the next morning. *I need to do things like this more often*, she thought. *It's the little things that count.*

At the intersection before Ken's office complex, Tessa turned to look at Julia in her car seat. "We'll just take the treats up to Daddy's office, and then we'll go pick up Ronnie." At the mention of her sister's name, Julia giggled and kicked her feet.

Tessa pulled into a space in the parking lot and dug through her purse for her key to Ken's office. Finding it, she grabbed the box of donuts and muffins from the seat next to her and stepped from the car. When she walked around to the other side of the car to get Julia, something across the parking lot caught her eye.

A minute later, she sped toward the exit, the box of pastries still on the ground where she'd dropped them after seeing Ken's car parked in a far corner of the lot.

Chapter Forty-Five

They hadn't spoken in three days.

Since the night Tessa saw Ken's car at the office when he was supposed to be at counseling, she'd been strangely calm. She didn't even pick a fight with him when he came home an hour later pretending he needed a shower to relax after a particularly grueling session. She almost felt renewed, like the first day keeping food down after a terrible stomach flu.

The rest of the week, when Ken came in at night, she'd busied herself with the girls, feeding Julia, playing games with Ronnie, displaying her disdain with Ken more by working around him as though he were invisible than by out-and-out combat with him.

In her weaker moments, her mind tried to go to the early years of their relationship, and she had to consciously drag it back to the present. The get-to-know-you first dates, Ken smiling, his chin propped up by his hand, his eyes never leaving her face as she talked. Doing dishes together in their first apartment, he playfully throwing bubbles at her, she swatting him with the dish towel. Bringing Ronnie home from the hospital, laying her between them in their bed and gazing at her for hours. Those times were worlds away now.

One October afternoon she drove along winding back roads, pointing out to Julia scarecrows, cornstalks, pumpkins, and other fall decorations adorning the houses and farms along the way. About halfway between Reading and Allentown, she pulled into the parking lot of a restaurant where she and Julia were having lunch with Mariel and her baby daughter, Jessica. With Ronnie and Alex both at school, they'd be able to talk freely. Tessa turned off the ignition and tried to decide if that was good or bad.

A hostess led them to a booth in the back. The restaurant was a renovated foundry and still had the original brick walls and exposed wooden beams. After settling the babies, Tessa and Mariel studied the menu. Tessa ordered a turkey club and a cup of soup, and Mariel decided on a Cobb salad. The server, a young girl with bleached spiky hair dressed in black pants and a black T-shirt, gathered up their menus, and Mariel's face dissolved into full-on concern as she looked at her friend. She shook her head. "I'd ask how you're doing, but the look on your face says it all."

Tessa managed a small shrug and picked at a loose thread on a seam in the booth.

"I don't even know what to say. Does he think the counseling is helping, at least?" They paused as the server set two Diet Cokes and straws on the table. Julia swatted at a soda, and Tessa grabbed it just in time to avert a disaster.

"Hmmph. Well, let's see." Tessa drummed her fingertips on her cheek in mock deep thought. "I'm no expert, but I'm pretty sure that for therapy to work, you actually have to go, not lie to your wife and hole yourself up in your office doing the gas."

Mariel's eyes flew open. "Please tell me you're kidding."

"I wish I were." The server brought Tessa's soup, and the two women turned their attention to Julia and Jessica until she walked away again.

"Ma-ma-ma-ma!" Julia spotted a pack of saltine crackers and stretched to reach them. Tessa tore open the packet and handed one to her.

"He's . . . I don't know . . . He's such an asshole," Tessa spat.

A blush crept across Mariel's face, and she looked down at the table.

"What?" Tessa asked, blowing on her soup. "You're taking his side?"

"Tess." Mariel shook her head slowly. "You know I'm on your side, always, no matter what. It's just . . ." Her voice trailed off.

Tessa put down her spoon and looked pointedly at her best friend. "It's just what?"

Mariel stuck Jessica's pacifier in her mouth and leaned in, her elbows on the table. "It's just that, you've had three years to get to this place in your mind about Ken. I'm still trying to process it. I'm still trying to reconcile—and I believe you, honestly, I do—that the guy you're describing now is the same guy I've known and loved since college."

Tessa nodded miserably, her shoulders sagging. "That's what my parents said."

"I mean, I'm thinking of the Ken I know. The guy who, in college, took you out to dinner instead of frat parties. The guy who drove a floor fan fifty miles to Millersville—even though he had a bio test the next day—because you were bitching about how hot it was in our dorm room. The guy who wouldn't let you do dishes right after you got a manicure—which, by the way, Rob still talks about—because he didn't want your polish to chip. The guy who plays round after round of Guess Who! with Ronnie and Alex so we can sit on the deck with a glass of wine and chat." She put her head in her hands. "You see my dilemma? You've been making your way slowly from *that guy* to *asshole* over the last three years. But, me? I've been hit over the head with it."

Tessa pushed her soup away. "I know, I know, it's a lot to take in."

"Look, I get it, I do. I'm so pissed off at him I could spit. Seriously, I feel like throttling some sense into him. I just feel like I went to bed one night believing a circle is round and woke up the next morning to find it's really square."

The rest of their food arrived, and they busied themselves trying to placate the babies long enough to eat. Tessa tore off a few bites of turkey and cheese and put them on the tray of Julia's high chair, and Jessica began dozing off.

"You know, it wasn't just him," Mariel added as she poured dressing over her salad. "It was you too. You both seemed like everything was perfect all the time. And you made it look easy."

Tessa bit into her sandwich and tilted her head to one side. "What do you mean?"

"What do I mean? C'mon. You're probably the most together person I know." Tessa's brow furrowed questioningly, and Mariel continued, cutting her salad into bite-size pieces. "Your house always looks perfect, never so much as a fork in the knife compartment of your silverware tray. You have a toddler and a baby who have matching headbands and socks for every outfit. Their dollhouse is more organized than my actual house." Now they were both laughing, and Tessa balled up her napkin and threw it across the table at Mariel. "Oh!" Mariel waved her fork triumphantly. "And you always remember to switch out your shoulder bag for a small clutch to go out for the evening." She gave a satisfied nod and crossed her arms. "That's what I mean. Zero signs of chaos in your world."

Mariel sighed, and her expression transformed from comical to serious. "A shrink might say you were trying to create order amidst bedlam."

Tessa thought about how Ken's addiction had resurrected the effects of Caroline's addiction and abandonment. "That shrink would be correct."

Julia threw the remains of her crackers onto the floor and clapped gleefully at her cleverness. As Tessa wiped her baby's face and hands, she leaned back against the booth and sighed. "So, class, what have we learned today?"

"That when something seems too good to be true," Mariel said, picking up Jessica, "it probably is."

Chapter Forty-Six

It felt good to laugh.

The last speaker delivered a comical anecdote about the retiree and returned to her seat amid roaring applause. Tessa turned to the other teachers at her table. "I'm sure it's going to seem weird at school without Irene around, huh?" Irene Davis had been assistant principal at the high school for the past twenty-one years. Now she was trading that in so she could travel, spend time with family—all the reasons people can't wait to retire. Irene was well-liked by everyone, and her sense of humor often landed her in comical situations, many of which were recounted tonight. The entire staff who'd worked in the building during her tenure was invited to her retirement dinner.

"You know it," said Kelly Masterson, her eyes tearing from laughing. "The end of an era." Servers began clearing cake plates and coffee cups from the tables. The crowd, taking the hint, began to disperse, several people approaching Irene to wish her well and tell her they were jealous.

Tessa sighed. She knew she'd have to go home soon, but she wasn't looking forward to it. She'd made up her mind, but going through with it was another thing altogether.

Pulling into the garage, her stomach sank like she was on the vertical drop of a rollercoaster. The reality that her life was likely to be forever changed weighed like a stone in her gut. She sat behind the wheel and tried to gather her thoughts. She was so focused that she didn't hear the door between the mudroom and the garage open. She jumped when Ken tapped on the window.

"Hey, I was just getting ready to drive the trash down to the curb." He opened his trunk and threw a few bags in.

Driven by sheer adrenaline, Tessa got out of the car and stood in front of Ken, planting both feet firmly on the ground. "No. Not yet. I want to talk to you first."

"It'll just take two min—"

"No. I mean it. Come inside." Feigning confidence she didn't feel, she walked inside and was relieved when Ken followed her. The house was silent. Both girls were asleep, and the kitchen was spotless. She went into the family room, where all the toys were picked up and the pillows were arranged neatly on the sofa. She wasn't surprised. After Ken's binge last night, she suspected he'd try to score some points with her today.

"Sit down." Tessa sat on the edge of the sofa and indicated the spot next to her. Ken obliged, trying to hide his face, which wore the sheepish smile of a teenager who knows he's about to get the car keys taken away for a week.

He rubbed his thighs briskly. "What's up?"

Tessa steeled herself and began. "Things haven't gotten any better. If anything, I'd say they're worse." Her eyes bore directly into his. "You refuse to get help. You—"

"What? I am going to—"

Tessa put up her palm. "Stop. You don't go to therapy. You say you're going, but you're really at the office doing the gas."

"Okay, last night I screwed up, but I've been going to my sessions." He held his hands out palms up. "I swear."

"Really? How about the Thursday night sessions?" She was shaking now. "How are they going?"

Ken's look challenged her. "What about the Thursday night sessions?" Tessa knew he was irritable from doing the gas last night. Normally, she wouldn't press him, but tonight wasn't a normal night.

Tessa's chin dropped to her chest. She was overcome with exhaustion. She felt like she hadn't slept in years. "You need inpatient treatment."

Ken started to protest, but she didn't let him speak. "This is it. You have until the end of the week to check yourself into a program or I want you to leave. I don't want to hear any bullshit about how our insurance doesn't cover it or you can't afford to close the office for a month."

Rage flashed in his eyes, but he controlled it. He looked at her as if she were a child, a very daft child. "But, babe, those things are true. They're not bullshit." He tried to take her hand, but she pulled away.

"I don't want to hear it!"

"Tessa." Ken's lips twisted into a menacing arc. "And exactly how are you going to support yourself if I leave? You think you can keep up this lifestyle?" He waved his arm around. "I won't give you anything. I'll fight you in court for years if I have to."

Tessa froze. He'd never said anything like that before. *Don't listen to him. Stay the course.* She stared straight into his eyes and fought the temptation to test him on his knowledge of Pennsylvania divorce law. "I don't care. I don't care what you do. A big house and new cars aren't worth living a lie anymore." She clasped her hands together to keep them from shaking.

Ken stood up, and she instinctively shrank into the sofa cushions. He studied her for a long moment. "You're tired. I'm tired. I'll drive the trash down, and then we'll get ready for bed and talk some more. We'll figure something out." He stroked her cheek, and a chill ran up her spine. "Stop this foolish talk, though. You know I'm not going anywhere." He went out to the garage, and Tessa heard him start the car.

She put her hand over her mouth to stifle a sob. On shaky legs, she dragged herself up the stairs and checked on the girls.

While she changed into pajamas and brushed her teeth, she renewed her resolve not to back down this time. She went over her speech in her head again, vowing to ignore his threats, so she'd be ready when he came upstairs.

It wasn't until several minutes later that she realized he'd driven away and hadn't come back.

Chapter Forty-Seven

THE NEXT MORNING

She hears the car pull up the driveway, the only noise in the silent early hour. She looks at the clock. 4:23 a.m. She may have dozed periodically through the night—she isn't sure. She hears the door to the mudroom open. He wouldn't come in through the garage; the door makes too much noise, and his only chance of avoiding a confrontation is if she is asleep.

But she's not sleeping. She goes into the bathroom and splashes cold water on her face, readies herself. He hears her and comes upstairs. He knows she heard him come in. He looks at her sheepishly. She is strangely tranquil. She is not crying.

She looks at him, this man, this stranger, her husband. He doesn't speak. She takes a breath. She speaks quietly. "This is it. Check yourself into rehab today, or I want you out of here. If you won't go, I'm leaving and taking the kids with me."

She is not prepared for his reaction. Sometimes she can predict it. He often waves her off and says he needs to sleep. But this morning he is ready for battle. His eyes darken. "What are you talking about?"

She is still calm, controlled, sure. "You know what I'm talking about. No more pretending you don't need help. No more chances. You get help today, or it's over."

He takes her by surprise. "You fucking bitch!" His anger seems misplaced in the quiet house. He lunges at her and grabs her by the throat. She gasps and tries to push him away, but physically she is no match for him. He half whispers, half snarls, "Only a selfish bitch would take two little girls away from their father."

He still has her by the throat and pushes her down onto the bed. She realizes then that he is still disoriented from the gas. She tries to get away. She backs up toward the headboard, but he doesn't let go. "Please," she begs. "Let go." His look is crazed, out of control. His pupils are enlarged, animal-like. His glare is somehow menacing and unfocused at the same time.

He almost seems to come to his senses. He gives her head a final thump against the headboard before letting go. He begins pacing around the room, muttering to himself, running his hands through his hair. "Why are you doing this? Why?"

With eight feet between them, she regains her composure. "I've tried. You know I have. It's been three years. Three years. *I don't know if you won't stop or can't stop. The lies, the secrets, the shame. You can choose it for yourself, but you can't choose it for me or our children anymore . . . I just want—"*

At the mention of the children, he snaps again. "You bitch! I won't let you do this!" He looks around wildly, grabs the nearest object, a ceramic lamp. He throws it at the wall next to her. It just misses her and shatters to the floor.

She knows she has to get away from him. She worries the girls will wake up and witness this scene. She runs from the room, but he chases her. She flies down the stairs, trying to put some distance between this madman and her sleeping children. At the bottom of the stairs, in the foyer, he picks up a small glass vase. He throws it in the direction she is running, and it too shatters against the wall. She knows she must talk him down, tell him what he wants to hear. She marvels again that the children remain in their bedrooms, asleep. Maybe she can still shield them.

"I'm sorry," she begins, her voice softening. "It's just that I've been up all night and I'm exhausted. You must be exhausted too." Now he's sitting in a chair, holding his head. He is receptive to her changing attitude.

"Yeah," he says, but his eyes are closed. "Yeah. I need to sleep. We can talk later."

"Th . . . that's a good idea. Wh . . . why don't you go up to bed? I'll call the office later and have them reschedule your appointments."

He doesn't answer. He is on his way up the stairs.

She is shaking. She climbs the stairs and checks on the girls. Miraculously, they are both sleeping soundly. She makes her way back downstairs and begins cleaning up the broken glass from the vase. She is wide awake. She picks up the bigger pieces with her hands and gets a dustpan and broom for the smaller ones. She works methodically, with purpose. Then she goes back upstairs to the bedroom. He is asleep under the blanket on their bed. She begins cleaning up the pieces of the broken lamp. She does not worry that he will awaken. She knows he will sleep for hours. She takes the remains of the lamp downstairs and puts them in a trash bag with the shattered vase. She carries the bag out to the garage and places it in the trash barrel. Nice and neat, like it never happened.

She is exhausted. She has been exhausted for years. She goes back up to the bedroom, takes the cordless phone from its cradle, and goes into the master bathroom. She looks into the mirror and sees a stranger. She leans in, looks closer. The woman looks familiar. She knows the woman, but something is covering her face. She squints, turns to the side. Then it comes to her. The face in the mirror is shrouded with someone else's burden. It is heavy, uncomfortable. It doesn't fit.

She punches some numbers into the phone. Her mother answers on the first ring. "I'm leaving. Today."

Epilogue

The days fell into a calm, if not yet comfortable, rhythm. While Ronnie was at school, Tessa and Julia took walks or ran errands. The three of them ate dinner together in their tiny kitchen and sang songs at bath time, Ronnie making crazy designs out of Julia's soapy hair. At night, after putting the girls to bed, Tessa curled up alone in her bed to read or stare out the large windows where she'd draped soft seafoam-green sheers over bronze curtain rods. She watched the stars twinkling in the sky and listened to the street traffic, something she never heard at the other house. On weekends when the girls weren't with Ken, she and Val drove them to parks or playgrounds, Tessa watching Ronnie and Julia's every move, hoping they knew how much they were loved and that, despite it all, things were going to be all right. She had managed to bring enough familiarity so the girls did not feel completely displaced: favorite stuffed toys, outfits, hair ribbons.

Mariel and Rob helped her plant flowers along the front walk, bright pansies and vinca, their low stems spreading quickly and creating colorful and simple, but welcoming, groundcover. Joey came over weekly to mow her small patch of lawn, the exact size and shape of the rest of the townhouses on the block. From the other house, she brought the girls' bedroom furniture and enough living room and kitchen pieces for the three of them. A friend of Val's gave Tessa a spare bedroom suite. She had no desire to sleep in the bed she'd shared with Ken, not that the rich, oversized cherry pieces would fit in her current space anyway.

She'd shown up on Sal and Val's doorstep with her kids four months ago, the same day Ken had attacked her. Her parents did everything they could to make things as normal as possible for the girls, stunned and heartbroken at Ken's refusal to repair the damage he'd done. For Tessa, the months went by in a blur of arguments with Ken, meetings with lawyers, scanning the classified ads for a house to rent while they negotiated the terms of their divorce. Tessa pleaded with Ken to leave their house so the girls would not have to be uprooted while they hashed things out, but he'd refused. He said *she* was the one who left, *she* was the one who destroyed their family, so she was getting what she deserved. He'd promised to make her life hell if she left and exposed him; she just hadn't believed him. She knew now that it was one thing he'd been truthful about.

He hired a lawyer who convinced him that Tessa was not entitled to any marital distribution, and, he boasted, when it was all said and done—despite the obvious fact that dentists far out-earn teachers—*Tessa* would owe *him* money, not the other way around. Ken ate it up, wrote check after check to his lawyer, whose nickname, Tessa learned, was "The Milkman"; and the nightmare Ken promised her ensued, the lawyers appearing to be the only ones with a prayer of benefitting.

Val saw the "For Rent" sign in front of the townhouse one evening while driving Gina to cheerleading practice. She'd gone with Tessa to see it and followed her daughter through the small rooms, comforting her when they'd stood in the tiny room that would be Julia's, knowing Tessa was envisioning the girls' spacious bedrooms and playroom at their other house. "It's okay, hon. They'll get used to it, and so will you. It's time you three started over in a place of your own." Though Tessa knew her mom was right, starting over in theory was far different from doing it in practice. When Ronnie asked why Daddy lived at the big house alone now, Tessa hugged her and fumbled through an explanation suitable for a child so young. She didn't know how to explain it to Ronnie when she wasn't at all sure how she'd gotten to this point herself.

Under different circumstances, the day she moved into the townhouse would have felt almost like a party. Her parents, siblings, and Mariel and Rob all showed up to help position furniture, unpack boxes, and hang pictures. Tessa was adamant about making it look like a home. She didn't know how long they'd be there, but she didn't want the girls feeling like they were living in transition. Mariel and Rob were the last to leave, and Tessa clung to her friend, crying and whispering in her ear, "What if I can't do this alone?"

"Who said anything about you doing it alone? You're doing it without Ken, not alone. There's a big difference."

Tessa stood at the door watching them leave, turning her head so Ronnie wouldn't see her choking back sobs. She put the girls to bed and gave them exactly one hour—fifteen minutes longer than the forty-five minutes it took to drive to Macungie—before she called Mariel. Mariel answered on the second ring with a chuckle. "What took you so long?" They talked and cried and laughed and were crying some more when Tessa realized the sun was just beginning to come up over the mountains she could see from her bedroom window. "See?" Mariel yawned long and loud. "You made it through the first night."

"Yeah, but what am I going to do tonight?" Tessa sniffled.

"I'll be here. I'll make sure I take a nap this afternoon."

One Saturday when Ken had the girls, Tessa drove two hours to the beach in New Jersey. The breeze off the ocean was chilly, and she walked on the beach for hours, the sand cool under the soles of her feet. She walked past the ride pier on the boardwalk and the Ferris wheel she and Ken had ridden together. She watched it going around, the way it had when they'd sat holding hands inside a car, the way it had for years before they rode in it, the way it would continue to do long after their marriage ended.

Tessa still went to Nar-Anon meetings. She mostly listened, only speaking once or twice, and eventually began to believe that, even though her life didn't go as planned, it was rich with blessings. The people at the meetings gave her the kind of comfort that can only come from those with shared experiences. She was grateful for the support; though she'd left one battlefield, she knew more combat was to come. Anyone who didn't believe there was another side to Ken now had a front-row seat to his vindictive cruelty.

She steeled herself against this thought as she turned off the light in the small living room and climbed the stairs. After checking on the girls, both asleep, hopefully deep in pleasant dreams, she walked down the hallway, the floor creaking under her feet, and settled into her own bed. As she closed her eyes, she reminded herself it's okay not to know exactly where you're going as long as you're sure what you're leaving behind.

Acknowledgments

A giant thank-you to Brooke Warner, Samantha Strom, Crystal Patriarche, Tabitha Bailey, Grace Fell, and everyone at SparkPress and BookSparks. Your talent, vision, and expertise got this debut author's book into readers' hands.

Thank you to my daughters, Rachael and Jaclyn, for believing your mom could do this. I learn as much from you as you've learned from me. Anything good I do in this life, I do for the two of you.

Much love and thanks to my husband, Jeff, for your undying love and support. You also make a mean pot of coffee.

Thanks to my big zany family who urged me to stop talking about this book and write it already. Even when you didn't say it out loud, I heard you.

Special thanks to my dad, Sam Padovani, for teaching me everything there is to know about diner culture. The only thing bigger than your pancakes is your heart.

A Week of Warm Weather is a novel about addiction, codependency, and family secrets, but the origin of Tessa's trauma is her biological mother's abandonment. Being abandoned by a parent profoundly affects the development, experiences, and relationships of children—young and grown. If those grown children are lucky, as I was, a window opens when a door closes. Thanks, Mom, for pulling me through that window and never looking back.

Thank you to my dear friend Ann Lemon. I appreciate everything you shared with me about addiction and Al-Anon. You've made the transformation from grief and loss to awareness and positive change an art form. Literally.

Thanks to my wonderful group of friends. Your support, early reading, suggestions, and feedback were beyond helpful. No matter how much time goes by in between, I cherish the times I spend with you.

And thanks to "Mo" Way. Every time I saw you, you told me you believed I would publish this book. I hope you find a big fluffy cloud up there to curl up on and read it.

About the Author

Lee Bukowski lives with her husband in Reading, Pennsylvania. When she's not teaching or writing, she loves reading and traveling, especially visiting her grown daughters in Boston and Fort Lauderdale. She's also a self-proclaimed Billy Joel superfan with a live concert count of forty-two shows. *A Week of Warm Weather* is her debut novel.

Author photo © Don Carrick at Studio 413 Photography

SELECTED TITLES FROM SPARKPRESS

SparkPress is an independent boutique publisher delivering high-quality, entertaining, and engaging content that enhances readers' lives, with a special focus on female-driven work. www.gosparkpress.com

Attachments: A Novel, Jeff Arch, $16.95, 9781684630813. What happens when the mistakes we make in the past don't stay in the past? When no amount of running from the things we've done can keep them from catching up to us? When everything depends on what we do next?

Absolution: A Novel, Regina Buttner, $16.95, 978-1-68463-061-5. A guilt-ridden young wife and mother struggles to keep a long-ago sexual assault and pregnancy a secret from her ambitious husband whose career aspirations depend upon her silence and unswerving loyalty to him.

Sarah's War, Eugenia Lovett West. $16.95, 978-1-943006-92-2. Sarah, a parson's young daughter and dedicated patriot, is sent to live with a rich Loyalist aunt in Philadelphia, where she is plunged into a world of intrigue and spies, her beauty attracts men, and she learns that love comes in many shapes and sizes.

Elly in Bloom: A Novel, Colleen Oakes. $15, 978-1-940716-09-1. Elly Jordan has carved out a sweet life for herself as a boutique florist in St. Louis. Not bad for a woman who left her life two years earlier when she found her husband entwined with a redheaded artist. Just when she feels she is finally moving on from her past, she discovers a wedding contract, one that could change her financial future, is more than she bargained for.

Tracing the Bones: A Novel, Elise A. Miller. $17, 978-1-940716-48-0. When 41-year-old Eve Myer—a woman trapped in an unhappy marriage and plagued by chronic back pain—begins healing sessions with her new neighbor Billy, she's increasingly drawn to him, despite the mysterious circumstances surrounding his wife and child's recent deaths.

9 781684 631377